THE TYRANT'S HEIR

ALSO BY KATE M. COLBY

The Desertera Series

THE TYRANT'S HEIR

DESERTERA BOOK THREE

KATE M. COLBY

BOXTHORN
PRESS

Published by Boxthorn Press

Spring Hill, KS

ISBN-10: 0-9967825-5-9

ISBN-13: 978-0-9967825-5-5

Library of Congress Control Number: 2017911402

Cover design by Damonza.com

Editing by Red Adept Editing

 Created with Vellum

1

———

*K*ing Lionel Willem Monashe straightened his back and strode through the double doors into the palace's grand ballroom. As he entered, the crowd of noblemen and -women parted to allow him passage. With each step Lionel took toward the center of the room, a new wave of nobles bowed or curtsied in greeting. Their postures appeared respectful, but from the edges of his vision, Lionel saw the narrowed eyes and wrinkled noses emerge as the people rose. Contrary to his advisers' assurances, the nobles had not warmed up to Lionel in the nine months he had reigned.

As he reached the center of the room, Lionel stepped onto the raised platform that held the three royal thrones. He resisted the natural urge to sit on the shortest throne, the one designated for the king's heir and Lionel's former seat as prince. Instead, he eased himself onto the center throne, the tallest of the three.

Ignoring how the nobles' gazes lingered on the empty seat at his right, Lionel straightened his top hat, the physical symbol of his position as king. At his valet's insistence, Lionel had allowed the hatter to redesign his top hat in a more traditional style, with a jeweled crown around the base and metal cogs near the top. While Lionel had to admit he fancied the new design, he didn't appreciate the added weight.

A cool palm squeezed Lionel's left hand, and he turned to look at the queen dowager. Because Lionel had not yet married, Zedara Ollessen, his father's final bride and Lionel's close confidant, retained the ceremonial duties of queen. Her blond hair shone gold under the ballroom's skylight—which allowed in sunshine from the *Queen Hildegard*'s deck—and her dark-blue eyes glittered with encouragement. Lionel couldn't help but return her gleaming smile, and a flurry of whispers rustled through the crowd. From the corner of his eye, Lionel could see a few nobles nodding in approval and others allowing their lips to curl into smirks.

Lionel understood why the nobles wished he and Zedara would marry. On the surface, Zedara acted as the perfect queen—elegant, obedient, and gracious to all. She was the confident and law-abiding monarch that Lionel had never been, exactly the kind of woman who could tame the playboy prince and reform the radical king. If only the nobles knew that Zedara had given her heart away a long time ago to a woman already burned on the funeral pyre. And more importantly, if only they would accept that Lionel's heart belonged to Aya Cogsmith.

The bishop stepped out from next to the thrones, and the crowd fell silent. In his typical grandiose fashion, the bishop stretched out his arms, letting the crisp white sleeves of his robes drape like wings. In one hand, he clutched the ceremonial golden goblet, filled to the brim with holy salt water. The other hand remained empty, but as sunlight ricocheted off his many jeweled rings, it looked as if the bishop held light itself in his palm.

"Today is a blessed day." The bishop's voice boomed over the crowd, and Lionel winced at the volume. "For today, we welcome a new life into our ranks. Lord and Lady Meeran, Count and Countess of the Hull, please bring forward your son."

The couple moved to stand before the thrones. Lady Meeran cradled the infant against her chest. Despite her corset and careful makeup, her body appeared soft and swollen, and shadows hung under her eyes. Still, the countess beamed with motherly joy, and the count's equally radiant smile revealed his own pride. Warmth spread through Lionel's chest, and he hoped that one day he and Aya would get to experience the love and satisfaction of bringing an heir into the world.

With his short stature, the bishop stood level with the baby, nestled in its mother's arms. Despite the happy occasion, the bishop's face remained stoic and smooth, as if it had been worn down by years of ritual. He reached up with his free hand and placed it on the infant's brow. "I pray to Her Holy Highness, the Benevolent Queen, as Her humblest of servants. Please send forth Your blessings upon this ceremony and Your grace to this child."

Lionel squeezed Zedara's hand tighter, embarrassed by the sweat that laced his palm. Over his life as prince, he had sat through dozens of naming ceremonies, but he could not remember the words his father had spoken. For all his faults, King Archon had always conducted himself with perfect pomp during ceremonies. He had thrived on the adoration and authority, which was why Lionel never paid attention—he couldn't stand watching his father gloat over the nobles. But in that moment, Lionel wished he would have studied his father's actions. How foolish he had been to dream of King Archon's death, to help orchestrate his father's execution, and not give a single thought to his own ascension to king.

Zedara inched closer to Lionel. "Are you all right?"

Lionel barely heard her whisper. He gave an almost imperceptible shake of his head as his eyes scanned the crowd. The nobles remained focused on the bishop, who was reciting a prayer for the infant. Lionel dared a response. "I don't remember my lines."

Zedara nodded and leaned away.

"Now, the new parents shall make their vows to the child." The bishop turned to Lord Meeran, who wrapped an arm around his wife and baby. "Do you swear to the Benevolent Queen that you will raise this child in Her name? That you will teach him the responsibilities and honors of his noble title?

That you will protect him from physical, emotional, and spiritual harm for as long as you both draw breath?"

Lord Meeran held his composure, but his voice cracked with emotion. "I swear all this to the Benevolent Queen."

Lionel's chest tightened, and he gripped the arm of his chair. King Archon would have made those same vows when Lionel was born. Though his father had been cruel to his subjects and had abused the adultery law, using it to trap several wives in the crime and execute them to make room for his next infatuation, he had never harmed Lionel. As a monarch, Lionel had done right by his people and brought a tyrant to justice. As a son, Lionel had betrayed his father.

The bishop faced Lady Meeran. "Do you swear to the Benevolent Queen that you will teach this child to practice fidelity in his every action? That you will give yourself to his care, providing for his every physical, emotional, and spiritual need? That you will never forsake him nor deny him your love as a mother?"

Lady Meeran grinned. "I swear all this to the Benevolent Queen."

Tears pricked Lionel's eyes as he imagined his own mother standing before the court to take the vow of motherhood. He wanted to believe that she loved him as much as the countess adored her son, but ever since King Archon's trial, Lionel had begun to doubt. For his entire life, Lionel had thought King Archon had murdered his mother. But if King Archon had been honest, Queen Lisandra had leapt from the deck of the ship because she had been unhappy with her marriage. But what about her relationship with Lionel? Would she—could she—have broken her vows of motherhood that easily? *Did I mean so little to her?*

Lionel shook his head. He still didn't know whether King Archon's words had been the truth or a desperate attempt to save himself from the executioner's ax. Either way, it didn't matter anymore. There was nothing Lionel could have done to help his mother, nor could he discern the truth of his father's words.

With the parental vows completed, the bishop dipped his fingers in the goblet and traced the holy salt water along the infant's forehead. "On behalf of the Benevolent Queen, I welcome you into Her divine kingdom. May you be a loyal son, a faithful lover, and a true friend to all."

A loyal son. Lionel swallowed. So he had forsaken his vows as well.

"The Benevolent Queen smiles upon this child." The bishop turned to Lionel. "Now, our terrestrial monarch will welcome him to Desertera."

All eyes fell on Lionel, and he rose on shaky legs. To his—and the crowd's—surprise, Zedara stood with him. Though the queen dowager never moved her lips, Lionel could hear the ceremonial words whispered through them. It was all he could do not to laugh with relief.

"I, King Lionel Willem Monashe, welcome this child on behalf of the people of Desertera." He smiled, a pause that allowed Zedara to finish whispering the next instruction. "Lord and Lady Meeran, have you chosen a name for your son?"

"We have, Your Majesty." Lord Meeran nudged the countess, and she passed the baby to Lionel. "Arthuro Thomas."

Lionel shifted Arthuro to his right arm, and the awkward movement made the infant wail. The bishop raised the goblet toward Lionel, and he hurriedly dipped his fingers in the salt water. While he sprinkled the drops on Arthuro's forehead, Zedara whispered the final ceremonial lines, but Lionel couldn't hear them over the baby's cries.

With a flushed face, Lionel looked up at the crowd. He stalled for a moment by rocking Arthuro, but when Zedara didn't repeat the words, he knew he had to improvise. "In the name of the Benevolent Queen and by the power She has bestowed upon me, I pronounce this child Mr. Arthuro Thomas Meeran, Viscount of the Hull, and accord him all the rightful honors and duties of his station."

The crowd showed no disapproval nor did the bishop and Arthuro's parents. Lionel looked at Zedara, and she grinned. After a long exhalation of relief, Lionel passed the wailing infant back to the countess. She scooped Arthuro up in her arms, and he quieted within seconds.

In the renewed silence, the nobles stared at Lionel. A jolt of fear coursed through him. *What am I supposed to do now?*

Zedara looped her arm through his and whispered, "Goodbye."

Of course. Lionel felt his eyes widen with remembrance, and he hoped he didn't look as dumb as he felt. "On behalf of Desertera, I would like to congratulate Lord and Lady Meeran on their son and say a final welcome to the young viscount. Bishop, thank you for a moving ceremony. I believe this draws the morning to a conclusion."

The crowd bowed to Lionel, and he felt a weight lift from his chest. His first naming ceremony as king had gone well—thanks to Zedara—and hopefully, it had earned him a fraction more of the nobles' respect.

As the people took turns congratulating the new parents and filing out of the ballroom, Lionel patted the queen dowager's arm. "Thank you, Zedara. I don't know what I would have done without you."

"Been a charming fool, as usual." Zedara softened the jab with a coy smile. "Though, you'd do well to start reading up on your duties in the royal library. I won't be around to save you forever."

A sense of dread crept up Lionel's spine. He glanced at the dwindling crowd, but only a few nobles dared to stare at him and Zedara, far out of earshot. "I know you're right, but I can't bring myself to go in that dusty old room. Besides, I've had more important problems to address—the details of Mr. Rutt's death, Rykart Farmer causing a religious and economic mess in Bowtown—"

"And your *friendly* meetings with a certain craftswoman?"

Lionel frowned. "Please tell me the whole kingdom doesn't hate the idea."

"From what I can gather, the feelings are still mixed. Half think that Aya's an unfinished conquest. The other half recognizes that you're serious, but I don't believe they're ready to accept a commoner as their queen." Zedara swept a strand of hair behind her ear. "The first half will catch up quickly enough. It's obvious you've started your official courtship. I'm relieved you've had the sense to remember a chaperone... even if he is just for show."

"Of course I did. Besides, when Aya and I first started courting, things were a bit awkward. Having Theo there helped take some of the pressure off." Lionel shook his head. "But anyway, from the looks you and I received this morning, I think all the nobles have forgotten about Aya."

"They haven't forgotten; they merely hope that you will. And who can blame them? Even married to a monster, I made a fabulous queen." Zedara winked. "I'll see you at the council meeting this evening."

Lionel bowed. "Ah, yes, unfortunately. Have a nice afternoon, Zedara."

After a quick greeting to the new parents, the queen dowager departed. Before Lionel could feel too alone, Eldric stepped up from the base of the platform and filled the empty place at his side. The valet had served King Archon, but after the king's execution, he had come to Lionel to confess his hatred for his former master. Like Zedara, Eldric had allied himself with Lord Varick in the plot to execute King Archon. He had faked an illness so that Aya could have a private encounter with the king. While Eldric claimed that he despised Lord Varick and would never aid him again, Lionel still worried that Eldric's loyalty could be swayed. So far, however, he had proved a capable adviser.

"You did well today." The valet smiled, the lines around his eyes crinkling. "I know it isn't what you want to hear, but you would have made your parents proud."

"Um, thank you." Lionel lifted his top hat to run his fingers through his thick brown hair. "Is it time for my next appointment?"

Eldric's grin turned sly. "You mean you haven't checked?"

Lionel narrowed his eyes and pulled his pocket watch from his vest. It sat smooth and heavy in his palm, ticking away the seconds in perfect rhythm. Though it didn't need wound yet, he turned the bronze crown to ensure the watch would run for the rest of the day. Then he flipped it over to the backside, which Aya had fitted with a custom plate from the glassblower. Watching the cogs and gears spin and sway comforted Lionel. He considered them a glimpse into Aya's sharp mind and the magic of her craft.

With a tender smile, Lionel remembered the day Aya had given him the pocket watch. It was a few weeks after Mr. Augustus Rutt's funeral, on their third official date. Aya had placed the watch in Lionel's hand, kissed him, and whispered, "I've had enough time for myself. I'm ready to give my time to *us* now." Despite all the gifts and heirlooms Lionel had been given as prince and king, he treasured the pocket watch above all other possessions—except maybe Penelope, his childhood mechanical bird.

As Eldric cleared his throat, Lionel shivered from his reverie. He tucked the pocket watch back into his vest. "There's still plenty of time. I should pay my respects to the new parents before we go."

Eldric nodded, and Lionel stepped down from the throne platform. The happy couple stood conversing with the bishop, as the rest of the nobles had dispersed.

"Count, Countess." Lionel inclined his head. "Though I've already congratulated you on behalf of the kingdom, please allow me to give my personal congratulations on the birth of your son."

"Thank you, Your Majesty." The count reached out a finger, and the infant grabbed it in his fist. "I hope you'll know the joy of fatherhood one day."

Lionel chose not to comment on his obvious lack of an heir and instead smoothed back the baby's wispy hair. "He has your lovely green eyes, Lady Meeran."

The countess blushed. "Thank you, Your Majesty. I think he has his father's strong chin, as well."

"A perfect combination." Lionel placed his hands behind his back. "You're a lucky man, Lord Meeran."

The count straightened with pride. "You are kind to say so, Your Majesty. I believe you'll find yourself equally lucky one day, when you're ready to settle down."

A coldness seeped through Lionel's veins, and his body stiffened. Was the count implying that Lionel's relationship with Aya was moving too slowly or that Aya was just another lustful dalliance? Lionel thought better of asking whether the count had sowed all his wild oats at the Rudder—it was no secret he'd been a regular customer of the brothel for years.

Instead, Lionel replied, "As a matter of fact, Lord Meeran, I think my bachelor days are nearly over."

Lord Meeran clapped Lionel on the shoulder. "Congratulations, Your Majesty. I think I speak for all of Desertera when I say that we are anxious to have a proper queen again."

Lionel raised an eyebrow, unsure whether the count meant Aya or Zedara. "As am I."

The countess snuggled the baby closer to her chest. "I hate to ask in this context, Your Majesty, but is there any update on the investigation into Lord Varick? He's a close family friend, and we were disappointed he couldn't join us today."

Lionel sighed. "I'm sorry about that." Lady Meeran hadn't been the first noble to ask about Lord Varick, and Lionel knew she wouldn't be the last. "With any luck, I'll have an update for the kingdom soon." *And finally expose him for the monster he is.*

The countess inclined her head. "Thank you, Your Majesty."

Shaking off the dour topic, Lionel turned with a tight-lipped smile to the bishop, who had remained quiet during the exchange. "A wonderful ceremony, Bishop, as always."

The short man bowed. "I'm glad you enjoyed it, Your Majesty. With all the recent changes to the kingdom, I think it's important that we respect our most sacred traditions."

"So do I." Lionel bit his tongue. Like most of the nobles, the bishop had not approved of Lionel's abolishing of the adultery law. He still believed that anyone who violated the Benevolent Queen's desire for fidelity should be executed. *Easy for a lifelong bachelor to say.*

Eldric walked over and bowed to the group. As he rose, he straightened his broad shoulders and exuded the polite authority so distinctive of elder gentlemen. "Excuse me, Your Majesty, Count and Countess, Bishop, but the king has another engagement."

"That's right." Lionel hoped he didn't look too relieved to escape the awkward conversation. "Congratulations again, and have a pleasant rest of your day."

The trio said their goodbyes, and Lionel hurried away with Eldric at his side. Once they had left the ballroom and emerged into the empty corridor, Lionel let out a long breath. "Thank you. I don't know how many more thinly veiled innuendos I could have handled."

"It's my job." Eldric waved his hand as if dismissing the thought. "Not to overstep, Your Majesty, but you know that you don't *have* to tolerate such language. You have every right to call out the nobles when they don't speak frankly or respectfully."

Lionel's brow furrowed. "You mean that's what my father used to do."

"I didn't say that." Eldric wrinkled his nose, and his bushy white mustache wriggled. "Though you shouldn't be resistant to everything your father did. While he might not have been well liked, he was certainly well respected."

Lionel sneered. "Fear isn't respect."

"Perhaps not, Your Majesty." Eldric shrugged. "But right now, you have neither."

Lionel sensed the challenge in Eldric's voice, and he knew the valet wanted him to lash back, to exert his authority, to stand up for himself at the expense of another's dignity. While the words bubbled up in Lionel's throat, he couldn't force them out. As painful as Eldric's statement had been, it was true. And no matter what happened during his time as king, Lionel would never punish someone for speaking the truth.

2

The metal stairwell creaked as Lionel and Eldric walked down to the dungeon. With only a lantern to light the way, they took careful, measured steps. Shadows danced along the walls behind the spiral railing, and Lionel's mind wandered to all the people who had been led down into the darkness to await their trials or executions. He remembered how Aya had trembled at returning to the dungeon with him and Dellwyn to question Rykart Farmer, and his hands balled into fists.

"Is everything all right, Your Majesty?" Eldric's voice echoed in the tight space.

"Of course." Lionel heard the hollowness of his words. "I must admit, though, I am nervous about what the investigation has uncovered. It's been weeks since the last update, and the nobles grow angrier with me every day."

"I think you're overexaggerating."

"Maybe." Lionel sighed. "Regardless, I'm relieved to finally see the scene of the crime for myself. I know the council expects a full report."

"They'll have to accept whatever you give them." Eldric's brow creased, and he held the lantern farther in front of him. "Watch your step, Your Majesty."

Lionel ran his hand along the wall, his fingers skipping over the rivets. "What a wretched place to die."

Eldric didn't comment. A few moments later, they reached the bottom of the stairs. Lionel tugged his jacket straight then knocked on the dungeon door. With a groan, the wheel spun, as if on its own, and the door wrenched open.

Captain Laurel Theophilus met Lionel with a grave face, and the king's heart sank. "Welcome, Your Majesty."

"Thank you, Theo." Lionel stepped into the dungeon's narrow hallway, Eldric in tow.

One of Lionel's proudest actions as king had been to make Theo, his closest friend, captain of the royal guard. When Augustus Rutt had been found dead minutes before his murder trial, Lionel knew Theo was the only person he could trust to run the investigation. Judging from his friend's downcast gray eyes, the mission continued to disappoint.

Theo led them past several doors before stopping at the cell that Augustus Rutt had occupied during his alleged suicide. At the sight of the dried blood, Lionel's hand flew to his nose by instinct. The smell of death no longer lingered, but the vicious red stain turned the king's stomach.

"Nasty, isn't it?" Theo wrinkled his nose. "Other than what's been necessary for the investigation, I've kept the scene intact, as you asked."

Lionel nodded, unsure whether he could speak without his voice cracking. Even though he had witnessed several executions—including his father's—the sight of blood still unnerved him. Somehow, this cell seemed more gruesome than a beheading. Here, a man might have taken his own life or had it ripped from him in darkness and secret. At least with an execution, a man had the dignity of knowing when, why, and by whose hand his death came.

"Very good. I'm glad you've decided to share your findings. The nobles are getting restless." Lionel glanced down the corridor, left then right. A guard stood sentry at either end. "Can your men be trusted?"

Theo smirked. "These two can. To be honest, I'm not sure

about certain members of the royal guard, but I'm working on that issue as well."

"That's reassuring," Lionel replied with a smirk of his own. His grin widened as Theo chuckled at the double meaning in the king's words. "Would you walk me through what you've uncovered?"

"Yes, Your Majesty." Theo took a deep breath. "As you know, the investigation started right after Mr. Rutt's death, with the examination of his body by Dr. Engel. She declared that the cause of death was blood loss. While she also found defensive wounds, she said they could have happened during the fight with Madam Dellwyn Rutt. However, she did admit that a few looked too fresh to be from that incident."

Lionel raised his eyebrows. "So, it's possible that Mr. Rutt had an altercation while incarcerated?"

"Possible, yes." Theo frowned. "He might have been roughed up by one of the guards on duty, or he could have self-harmed in a different way before taking his life. It's difficult to say."

"I assume you talked to the guards about it?"

Theo sighed. "They denied any mistreatment, but we both know that doesn't mean anything."

Lionel shuddered, remembering again Aya's fear of the dungeon. He pushed the thought from his mind. "And the rest of the investigation?"

"A lot of runaround." Theo's jaw clenched. "We spent the first few weeks combing the dungeon, as well as the Rudder and the corridors between the two, for any clues. But honestly, most of my time has been spent chasing down people to interview—every palace guard, every Rudder worker, every client Mr. Rutt served, any merchant who ever sold anything to him. It's been a slow process."

"I see." Just thinking about all the loose ends made Lionel's head hurt. He couldn't fathom Theo's frustration. "Well, why don't you show me the layout of the potential crime scene?"

"Of course, Your Majesty." Theo pointed to the end of the corridor, where one of his trusted guards stood before a plain wooden chair. "At any time, there is only one guard stationed in the dungeon. The cells are secure, and no one has ever attempted to break a prisoner out." Theo gestured to the other end of the hallway, and his leather armor creaked. "The door to the outside is always locked from the inside, so no one can enter without the guard on duty letting them in."

"So if Mr. Rutt's death were a murder, either the guard that was on duty is the killer, or he allowed the killer entrance." Lionel shook his head. "I'm assuming this guard maintained his innocence during questioning?"

"Indeed." Theo rubbed the back of his neck, ruffling his sandy-blond hair in the process. "He admitted to falling asleep on duty, but he said that he didn't kill Mr. Rutt and he didn't see anyone else during his shift."

Lionel's brow furrowed. "And you trust him?"

Theo shrugged. "I'm not sure. He seemed nervous when I interviewed him, but in retrospect, I think he feared that he'd be punished for falling asleep. I can't do that, though. Everyone stationed down here has done the same once or twice."

Lionel nodded.

"For now, let's assume the guard is telling the truth and Mr. Rutt did commit suicide." Theo stepped into the cell, ducking to avoid hitting his head on the doorframe. He rapped his knuckles on the wall. "As you can see, the dungeon cells are made entirely of metal. The only windows are the barred ones at the top and bottom of the door. The layout tells us that Mr. Rutt could not have left the cell to retrieve the weapon, but someone might have passed it to him through the bars. It also explains how the guards did not notice Mr. Rutt's death sooner. If you'll close the door..."

Eldric shut the door, and Lionel peered through the top window.

Theo had moved to crouch in the corner, his features obscured by darkness. "As you can see, from the guards' vantage point, it might have looked like Mr. Rutt had fallen asleep."

Lionel stepped back to allow Eldric room to reopen the door. "Is that where his body was found?"

"Yes. He was propped up in the back corner here." Theo held out his arms, palms up. "His forearms had been slashed from wrist to elbow and rested at his sides. You can see how the blood flowed in two separate streams until they merged near his legs."

Lionel couldn't tear his eyes away from the stains, which marred the floor in the shape of a wide letter V. "And the weapon?"

"Found next to Mr. Rutt's right hand, as if it had fallen from his fingers." Theo pulled a white shard from his pocket and held it up for Lionel to inspect. "I talked to the potter, and she confirmed it's porcelain, probably a piece from a plate or teacup. Maybe one got broken in the scuffle when he was detained, or maybe he had carried it in his pocket as a sort of trinket. Your guess is as good as mine."

Lionel frowned. "The potter didn't make the set from which the shard came?"

Theo shook his head.

"Hmm." Lionel squinted at the shard. Dried blood caked the surface at two of the most jagged points. An intricate purple swirl curled along the top, and Lionel imagined it encircling a plate or teacup to form a ring of amethyst smoke. While he'd only been to the Rudder once, a long time ago, Lionel didn't think the brothel would have a tea set expensive or fancy enough to produce a porcelain shard. Then again, Mr. Rutt *had* seemed to appreciate the finer things. "Did you ask Dellwyn about it?"

"Yes, we inquired with Madam Rutt. She says that she didn't find any matching dishware in Mr. Rutt's former office or residence." Theo tucked the shard back in his pocket. "Granted, that doesn't rule out the theory that it's something Mr. Rutt found or carried as a memento."

"True." Lionel appraised the barred windows on the door. The shard would have fit through them without trouble. "And you're certain no one could have given it to him?"

"No…" Theo let out a long sigh. "But given the guard's statement and the lack of other evidence, I have to assume that Mr. Rutt had the shard on his person when he entered the dungeon."

Lionel gestured for Theo to come closer so that he could whisper, and Eldric took a large, tactful step backward. "I *know* Lord Varick did this. That man is evil incarnate, and killing Mr. Rutt was the only way he could have escaped conviction in the conspiracy to murder Madam Huxley and control the Rudder by proxy."

"I believe you, Lionel, but he did it too well. We searched his estate from top to bottom for the tea set that could have produced this shard, an item of clothing stained with blood, anything to connect him to the crime. We didn't find a damn thing." Theo stood taller than the king, but the weary slump of his shoulders almost put him at eye level with Lionel. "Short of torturing Lord Varick or the guard on duty to coerce a confession, there's nothing I can do. And I don't think either of us has the stomach for that."

Lionel shook his head.

"Besides, maybe the guard is innocent." Theo's fingers traced his goatee in thought. "Lord Varick's involvement might have been indirect. Maybe he made Mr. Rutt swear he would die before betraying their plan, or perhaps Lord Varick subtly planted the idea of suicide in Mr. Rutt's mind for weeks before the opportunity arose. At this point, I don't think we'll ever know."

"Are there any other leads you can chase? Any path you can look down again?" Lionel winced as he realized his questions sounded like pleas. "Given how quiet you've kept the investigation—at my request, I know—the nobles, and the council especially, are breathing down my neck for an answer. If you declare an official ruling of suicide, I have to let Lord Varick off house arrest early."

Theo pursed his lips. "Couldn't you keep him detained until his involvement in the Rudder's ownership is determined? There's not much evidence there either, but searching through the palace banker's records will take time. I could delay that investigation for another month, minimum."

"I don't think the nobles would stand for that. They accept Lord Varick's house arrest because he might be a danger to others." Lionel sighed. "None of them will care about his financial meddling, not when they all have used their purses to gain power and influence themselves."

Lines creased between Theo's eyebrows. "How much do you trust Madam Rutt?"

"Dellwyn?" Lionel arched an eyebrow. "Completely."

Theo nodded. "Then I'll drag out this investigation on account of her word. Since she insists that Mr. Rutt had no way to access such fine dishware, I can continue researching where he might have gotten it." Theo's lips twisted into a smirk. "And besides, I'm sure in that long list of interviewees, I can find *someone* to question again."

"Thank you, Theo." Lionel reached out to shake his friend's hand. "I know this puts us both in a difficult position, but I can't allow Lord Varick to go free."

"I understand, Your Majesty." Theo stepped back and cleared his throat. In his normal, authoritative tone, he announced, "Unfortunately, I'm not yet ready to declare an official cause of death."

Eldric had the decency to raise his eyebrows in surprise, as if he had not been eavesdropping from only a few feet away. Not that Lionel minded—he would have told the valet the details of the conversation later, anyway. From either side of the corridor, Theo's guards inclined their heads in acceptance of the captain's decision.

Lionel straightened his top hat, uncomfortable with the obvious ruse. "I appreciate your careful attention to this investigation. If there is anything I, or anyone in the kingdom, can do to assist you, please let me know."

"I will, Your Majesty." Theo bowed to Lionel, and the king bit his tongue. When Lionel had been prince and Theo a regular palace guard, Theo had never bowed to him. No one had minded that they shirked protocol in the name of friendship. But now that Lionel had risen to king, the friends had to act by the expected social conventions, no matter how awkward it made Lionel feel.

"When can—I mean, I'll expect your next report in two weeks." Lionel widened his eyes in silent apology, but Theo didn't appear fazed. It seemed a reasonable amount of time—short enough that the nobles would tolerate it but long enough that Theo might still uncover something.

The captain bowed again. "I'll have it ready, Your Majesty."

"Thank you. I'll leave you to it." Lionel inclined his head in a cordial goodbye then turned to leave the dungeon.

Eldric matched him step for step, but the valet remained silent until they emerged into the stairwell and shut the door firmly behind them. "If I may ask, Your Majesty, what do you make of Captain Laurel's findings?"

"What findings?" Lionel smiled in a vain attempt to lighten the mood. "I appreciated learning the exact layout of the crime scene, and we do have the weapon—that's a good clue."

Eldric rubbed his bulbous nose. "I hope the council will share your optimism."

"Clearly, you do not." Lionel turned to ascend the spiral staircase, and Eldric rushed to light the way with the lantern. "You know how Lord Varick operates as well as I do. His craft is manipulation, and it leaves little evidence. But he'll mess up eventually, and when he does, Theo will catch him."

Eldric's eyes flitted up and down the stairwell. "Do you think Lord Varick killed Mr. Rutt himself?"

"No, I don't." Lionel rubbed his chin, wincing as the stubble pricked his fingers. *I'll have to shave before I see Aya again.* Before Lionel's thoughts could drift further, he replied, "Consider Lord Varick's last schemes. He sent his daughter, Isadona, to marry King Archon then Aya, as his ward, to seduce the king. And finally, he manipulated Augustus, as his business partner, into killing Madam Huxley. Lord Varick never does anything himself."

The lantern shook in Eldric's hand, and light rioted

through the dark space. "Who do you think his newest accomplice is, then?"

"It's not worth guessing." Lionel stopped to catch his breath. The rest of the staircase loomed above him, and as he stared up through its coils, he grew dizzy. He closed his eyes and pinched the bridge of his nose, waiting for the world to stop spinning. With a sigh, he said, "Let's not talk about it anymore today, Eldric. We still have a long way to go."

3

*A*s the sun dipped below the horizon, Lionel raced to the courtroom. Reluctant to attend the council meeting, he had dawdled too long at dinner, cutting his meat into tiny pieces and chewing each morsel several times. When he reached the courtroom's double doors, his face burned hot, and sweat trickled down his back. He doubted he looked the image of a dignified king, and the curious gaze of the guard on duty confirmed as much.

After dabbing his face and neck with his pocket square, Lionel tugged his jacket a final time. He motioned for the guard to open the doors then strolled into the courtroom with his head held high. His shoes clacked as he crossed the floor, the sound echoing back from the tiered benches that encircled the room. Though Lionel had presided over several meetings there, the courtroom still made his stomach uneasy. In every silent moment, the memory of King Archon's trial washed over Lionel, and his father's final pleas beat against his mind like sand in a desert storm.

When he reached the round table, Lionel clutched the back of his chair as if he could squeeze the painful remembrances away. The council members stood to welcome the king, each offering a small bow or curtsy.

"Please be seated." Lionel sank into his chair, his body

growing heavy with the weight of the problems he knew were about to be thrust upon him. "All right, let's begin with this week's reports. Your Highness, would you like to speak first?"

Zedara, seated in her usual spot at Lionel's left, folded her hands atop the table. The worn, scratched wood appeared dark under her pale skin. "You'll be relieved to hear that I don't have any complaints to share. In fact, the nobles seem in good spirits after this morning's naming ceremony."

Lionel withheld a pleased smile. "The best kind of news. Thank you, Zedara." He turned to Lord Stanton Collingwood, the Duke of the Bow, who sat at Zedara's left. "Anything to add, Uncle?"

"Nothing from my jurisdiction, Your Majesty." Lord Collingwood traced the small anchor that adorned his bronze cuff link. Dellwyn had given the pair to him after she had taken ownership of the Rudder and they had agreed to be exclusive to one another. "However, Madam Rutt would like to request an extra guard for the Rudder's entrance. She's caught a few adolescents sneaking in for a peek lately."

"Very well. I'll send an order to Captain Laurel tomorrow morning." Lionel dared a smirk. *Maybe this council meeting won't be too difficult after all.*

He turned to the final noble, Lord Collingwood's son-in-law of seven months and Duke of the Stacks, Lord Frederick Greyson. The young duke had taken Lord Varick's place on the council as the Starboardshire representative, at least for as long as Lord Varick remained under house arrest. Though some of the nobles, including the king himself, had worried about electing another of Lionel's relatives to the council, Lady Greyson had used her every social advantage to dissuade them and secure the vote for her husband.

At first, even Lionel had been hesitant to trust Lord Greyson. After all, Lionel figured that anyone who would marry the former Miss Madeleine Collingwood, his gossip-mongering cousin, had to be deranged. However, thus far, the duke had proved to be a fair and honest man, and he always took Lionel's side in council meetings. Lionel hoped that his cousin would mature under her new husband's influence.

"And Lord Greyson, how are things in Starboardshire?"

The duke fanned his face with his handkerchief, and Lionel noticed that his tanned skin appeared pale and held a thin sheen of sweat. "Everything seems in order, Your Majesty."

Lionel raised an eyebrow. "Even in relation to Bowtown?"

"Well, no… but there hasn't been much change since my last update." Lord Greyson attempted a chuckle, but it erupted into a wet cough. His dark eyes watered. "Pardon me, Your Majesty. I think Mrs. Farmer will be better able to enlighten us."

"So the nobles remain concerned that the religious sect will become a greater distraction for their farmers?"

Lord Greyson nodded through another cough. This one sounded more like a stomach heave.

Lionel frowned. "Are you okay, Frederick? Do you need to leave?"

"No, no." The duke made a show of straightening in his seat and slicking back his long black hair. "I'm fine. Just had a tickle in my throat."

"If you insist…" Before turning to the next representative, Lionel allowed Lord Greyson the opportunity for another polite refusal. When the duke held up his hands to indicate the fit had passed, Lionel moved on. "Mr. Wellman, anything from Sternville?"

Despite being the poorest of Desertera's villages, Sternville offered the fewest complaints. At every meeting, Lionel wondered whether the residents were too busy to participate in government, too jaded to believe the council could help them, or too reluctant to approach their representative, Mr. Jack Wellman. Lionel guessed all of the above.

"Not lookin' good, Yer Majesty." Mr. Wellman rubbed his eye, leaving a smudge on his face.

Lionel sighed. *Of course, I couldn't be that lucky.* "Care to elaborate?"

Mr. Wellman shrugged. His shoulders were thin but

muscular from years spent cranking water buckets up and down the wells. "With them farmers charging more for crops, we're havin' to pay more for our food. If it weren't for the laws you put in place to let us trade and give the young'uns jobs, I don't know how some people'd afford it. Some still don't."

Lionel frowned. "I'm sorry to hear the Bowtown situation is affecting your village, Mr. Wellman, but I'm glad that my policies have eased some of the burden."

While he'd never thought much about Sternville before meeting Aya and Dellwyn, the village had become a particular concern of Lionel's after learning how his lover and her friend had lived for the past decade. During his short reign, Lionel had tried to strengthen Desertera's economy from the bottom up. By abolishing a few ancient trade prohibitions and providing tax breaks for merchants and skilled laborers who took on apprentices, he'd been able to help free up goods for bartering and create new educational and career paths for people. It wasn't a lot, but it was more than any previous monarch had done.

"How about Portside, Miss Baker?" Lionel asked.

Miss Heidi Baker pushed a strand of hair back into the white scarf that covered her head. No matter when the council met, she always came clothed in her baking attire. "About the same, Your Majesty. Overall, trade between merchants in Portside and between merchants and other villages has picked up. However, we're already seeing price increases on crops and animal products from Bowtown." She shot an accusatory glance at Mrs. Farmer, who sat two chairs down.

"I can't say I'm surprised." Lionel's brow furrowed. "Other than raising prices, has the situation in Bowtown affected anything else in Portside?"

"As you'd expect, we food merchants have had to increase our prices to make ends meet." Miss Baker shifted in her chair, and it groaned under her broad frame. "It's created a lot of tension between the farmers and us, and between us and the people. Theft has risen in response, as well. I had a whole basket of rolls stolen while I turned my back to check on the oven. And that was just today."

Lionel's jaw clenched. If the people had already begun to steal, it might not be long until they resorted to vandalism or rioting. "Thank you for the report, Miss Baker." He turned to Lord Collingwood. "Uncle, you're the landlord of Miss Baker's shop, correct?"

Lord Collingwood stiffened. "Yes."

"Perhaps the two of you could work out an arrangement to ease the financial strain on the shop. Take the value of the stolen goods out of this month's rent, for example." At Lord Collingwood's pursed lips, Lionel added, "Just until we've gotten the situation with the farmers under control."

"Of course." Lord Collingwood put on a gracious smile, and Lionel hoped his own attempts at a charming grin didn't look so fake.

Miss Baker put a hand over her heart. "Thank you, Your Majesty, Lord Collingwood. I promise I will make up every coin once the economy has been put right."

"We're sure you will, Miss Baker." Lionel moved on to the next representative. "Mr. Chef, has the palace experienced any negative effects from Bowtown's price increases?"

"A bit, Your Majesty." Mr. Stefan Chef twirled the end of his thin mustache. "However, we're still managing fine."

"Good." Lionel gave a slight smile, relieved that the palace chef had the tact to answer without financial specifics. "Are there any reports or complaints from the rest of the palace staff?"

"Not this week." Mr. Chef winked. "But I'll try to make it up to you during our next meeting."

"How kind of you." Lionel shook his head at the chef's jest and turned to the next council member. "If you don't mind, Mrs. Farmer, I think we should save your report for last."

The woman's callused hands trembled as she slipped them into her lap. "As you wish, Your Majesty."

"Thank you." Lionel turned to the bishop, who sat

frowning on his right. "Bishop, anything to add from the spiritual sphere?"

Even seated, the top of the bishop's head only came up to Lionel's shoulder. However, he held it high with his nose pointed up at the king. "The queen dowager's earlier report was correct, Your Majesty—this morning's naming ceremony was a success. I believe I owe you *both* thanks for that." He shot Zedara a disapproving glare, probably for sabotaging his chance to make a fool out of the king.

Lionel put on his trademark smile, tugging one corner of his mouth up higher than the other. "Yes, I'm equally pleased that my former stepmother and I make such a good team."

Zedara shoved Lionel playfully, earning another scowl from the bishop.

The short man cleared his throat. "Afterward, you visited the dungeon, correct?"

"That's right." Lionel swallowed, all joking forgotten. With the concern about Bowtown, he had hoped to avoid this conversation until next week. Apparently, he wasn't going to be so fortunate.

Lionel cleared his throat. "This afternoon, I spoke with Captain Laurel Theophilus about the investigation into Mr. Augustus Rutt's death. The guards have spent the past few months reviewing the crime scene and related locations, as well as interviewing anyone who had dealings with Mr. Rutt during his regular life or his arrest. While they have a detailed layout of the crime scene and the weapon, if you will, Captain Laurel has decided that he does not have sufficient evidence to rule out murder at this point."

The bishop grunted. "And why not? It seems there's little evidence to suggest foul play."

Lionel tried to keep his face smooth and impassive. "That's only because you are on the outside of the investigation. The captain has more leads to follow, several of which are suspicious."

The bishop crossed his arms. "To clarify, Your Majesty, you intend to let Lord Varick—a member of this council and an upstanding nobleman—rot in his estate for six more months, based on leads you refuse to disclose."

Lord Greyson leapt to his feet. The action launched him into another coughing fit, but he won the council's attention. After a deep breath, he said, "If His Majesty says that the investigation must continue, then it must. Who are you to question his authority?"

"An *impartial* member of this council." The bishop gazed at each representative in turn, challenging them to stand by him. "We've all been brought here to advise the king and question his decisions."

"Not with such blatant disrespect." Lord Greyson shook his head, and Lionel noticed that he had one palm pressed over his abdomen. Normally, Lionel didn't mind allowing Lord Greyson to stand up for him—the duke made for a good example in how to respect royalty—but he was far too ill to argue with the bishop.

"That'll be enough, thank you. Please sit, Lord Greyson." Lionel clenched his jaw. "Bishop, I understand your skepticism. However, this investigation is out of your—and the entire council's—jurisdiction until Captain Laurel has finished. He's promised to give another report in two weeks, and until then, I won't say any more on the matter."

The bishop huffed again. "Very well. I'll convey your message to the concerned subjects who attend my prayer meetings. We'll continue imploring the Benevolent Queen to clear Lord Varick's name sooner rather than later."

"A sensible plan." Without giving the bishop the opportunity to raise any more concerns, Lionel turned back to the Bowtown representative. "Mrs. Farmer, you have the floor."

Mrs. Eveline Farmer sat rigid, her gray-streaked hair swept back into a simple ponytail. "Rykart Farmer remains camped out at the edge of Bowtown, beyond the crop fields. While he seems content to stay there and not interfere with the happenings of the village itself, more people go to hear his message every day, and a handful have decided to leave their farms and join his cause."

"How curious. You'd think they would be grateful to have land to work." Lord Collingwood's hazel eyes narrowed, and Lionel wondered how long it would take for his matching eyes to grow such deep creases. "They're damning themselves. The landowners won't hesitate to replace anyone who abandons his farm with a grateful young farmer or Sternville resident. I know I won't."

"I'd take that job," Mr. Wellman mumbled.

"Many other farmers have warned the deserters, but they do what they feel is right." Mrs. Farmer lowered her gaze to the table. "At this point, I suspect the price increases are their fault. With some farmers giving up the trade to join Rykart, the others foresee a shortage of goods and an opportunity for profit."

"Lucky us," Mr. Chef muttered.

Miss Baker tugged on her apron. "Ungrateful is right."

Lionel held up a hand to silence any more interruptions. "How many farmers have abandoned their plots so far?"

Mrs. Farmer counted them off on her bony fingers. "Seven or eight. Not too many."

"Do you know who owns their land?"

Mrs. Farmer shook her head. "Some, yes. I can ask about the others."

"Please do and report your findings to Lord Collingwood." Lionel turned back to his uncle. "The nobles who own these farms might not have realized that they've been abandoned yet. Can you work with them and Mrs. Farmer to get the farmers to return?"

Lord Collingwood's brow furrowed. "And if they won't?"

Lionel sighed. "Then do as you said a moment ago. Find young farmers who want to leave their fathers' shadows or residents from Sternville who want to better their stations."

Lord Collingwood bowed his head. "Consider it done, Your Majesty."

"If I may interject, Your Majesty..." The bishop waited for Lionel to nod permission before continuing. "As the spiritual leader of Desertera, the aspect of Mrs. Farmer's report that concerns me the most is this farmer's supposed 'cause.' What is his goal in all of this?"

Mrs. Farmer pursed her lips. "Rykart believes that the kingdom is not living up to the Benevolent Queen's standards. He thinks that She speaks to him personally and delivers orders for him to carry out. Right now, he's been told to wait in his commune on the outskirts of Bowtown and gather supporters. I suspect his protests will start again soon."

"What does he believe we're doing wrong?" Lionel had thought that Rykart approved of the abolishment of the adultery law and, by extension, Lionel as king.

"I don't know." Mrs. Farmer rubbed her temples. "Rykart speaks in riddles, and even then, he doesn't speak much. He says his followers must trust in Her word, and if they are true and faithful, She will bring the salvation rains and return the world to its former glory."

"Blasphemy!" The bishop hit his fist against the table, and Mrs. Farmer flinched. "The Benevolent Queen speaks to no one, but if She did, it would be to *me*. She has forsaken all Her children because we are unworthy. The only way to regain Her approval and bring the rains is to stay true to the traditional faith."

Out of the corner of his eye, Lionel saw Zedara tense.

A vein bulged in the bishop's forehead as he continued. "The farmer is the product of careless religious governance, for which I, as the rightful spiritual leader of Desertera, must take the blame. I never should have allowed the repeal of the adultery law, Your Majesty. It's caused the people to believe that our divine laws are equally flexible, that our sacred traditions are meaningless. But really, they are the only route to salvation."

Before Lionel could defend his decision, Zedara let out a loud scoff. "What are these oh-so-sacred traditions?" The queen dowager's cheeks flushed, and her petite frame shook with irritation. "That we stay faithful in arranged, loveless marriages? That we attend pompous ceremonies? That the poor pay taxes to us, which we then pay to you? That we pray privately—nightly, as you suggest—for forgiveness?"

Lionel could sense the anger brewing on either side of him, and he put his hand on Zedara's shoulder. "Take a breath, Your Highness."

"No! The bishop needs to hear this, Lionel." She brushed his hand away, and Lionel felt his own face burn with embarrassment. "I know, as we all do, that Rykart is wrong, mad even. But can't you see the attraction of his brand of faith? He encourages people to get involved, to be active participants in their salvation. What do you do, Bishop? Pop by whenever Lionel issues a new commandment and remind them to pay up and pray."

The bishop rose, shoving his seat over in the process. "You insolent—"

"That's enough!" Lionel jumped up to separate the two, using the full force of his height to tower over the short man. "Bishop, you've already insulted me today. You'd do well not to disrespect Her Highness." Lionel wheeled around to face Zedara. "And you, Queen Dowager, know better than to frame your arguments in such an accusatory tone."

Zedara lowered her eyes to the floor but kept her mouth set in a rigid line. Lionel sighed and shook his head. *Could this council be any more of a mockery?*

"Forgive me, Your Majesty." The bishop held his hands together behind his back. "I should never have spoken—"

Before the bishop could finish his apology, Lord Greyson stood and smacked his palms against the table. Lionel opened his mouth to chastise him then shut it as he realized what was happening. The duke's back arched, and his stomach trembled as wet, guttural coughs escaped his throat. They grew deeper and more violent, then without further warning, Lord Greyson vomited across the table.

The council members, Lionel included, jumped back from the spew. Lord Collingwood rose and patted his son-in-law's back, only to be thanked by another rush of vomit. A rotten, acidic stench filled the air, causing the representatives closest to

Lord Greyson to gag. Lionel pulled his pocket square from his jacket and handed it to Zedara, who covered her nose and turned away from the mess.

Lord Greyson emitted a third spew, this one a mere trickle of foam and the loudest cough yet. Lionel moved to stand on the duke's other side and helped Lord Collingwood ease him back into his chair.

"Here." Miss Baker passed her headscarf to Lord Greyson, and he wiped his mouth with the fabric. It came away pink.

Lionel's eyes widened, and he braved a look at the table. Most of the substance was chunky and brown, the remnants of a meat-and-bread dinner, no doubt. However, the liquid nearest the duke was crimson, mixed with a thick pinkish foam. *Haven't I seen enough blood today?*

While Lord Greyson finished cleaning himself up, the council members stood in silence. It took a moment for Lionel to realize they were staring at him, waiting for a command.

Lionel cleared his throat. "This council meeting is over. You're all dismissed." No one moved. "Zedara, on your way out, would you ask the guard on duty to send Dr. Engel to Lord Greyson's estate? And fetch a maid?"

"Of course, Your Majesty." The queen dowager scurried away, probably grateful to escape the smell. After another awkward moment, the rest of the representatives, save for Lord Collingwood, followed her out of the courtroom. Only Mr. Chef and Mrs. Farmer had the courtesy to mutter "get well" and "feel better" as they left.

After the other members had gone, Lionel crouched beside the duke. "Do you think you can walk, Frederick?"

Lord Greyson nodded, his complexion even paler than before. "Please forgive me, Your Majesty. I don't know why I've fallen ill."

Lionel shook his head. "You never have to apologize for being sick. I only wish you would have taken my offer to leave sooner."

Lord Collingwood clapped the duke on the shoulder. "I'm

sure you just ate a bad piece of meat with dinner, or maybe you've caught a stomach sickness. I've heard it's going around."

"But… the blood…" Lord Greyson's voice cracked, and his eyes widened in alarm. "What if there's something wrong with me?"

"It's nothing to worry about." Lord Collingwood shrugged. "You must have given your stomach a nasty shock with that first heave."

Lord Greyson bit his lip. "This is humiliating."

"While you have every right to feel that way, I'm actually grateful to you." Lionel couldn't help but chuckle. "With your sudden illness, all the gossip about this week's council meeting will focus on you. No one will have time to complain about the Bowtown situation or criticize the speed of Captain Laurel's investigation."

A small smile flitted across Lord Greyson's lips. "Then I'm honored to have been of service."

Lionel returned his grin. "Come on, let's get you back to your estate. The doctor will be waiting, and I'm sure Lady Greyson will be worried."

Lord Collingwood bent down to help Lord Greyson stand, but the duke waved him away. With wincing eyes and a quiet groan, he pulled himself up and walked toward the door. The two other men followed behind, close enough to help if Lord Greyson stumbled but far enough back to allow him what dignity he had left.

Lionel caught his uncle's eye. "We need to get him quarantined as soon as possible," he whispered. "That blood, it can't be a good sign."

"No." Lord Collingwood glanced back at the table. "It most definitely is not."

4
------

*A*fter staying up half the night to wait for Dr. Engel's diagnosis and spending the other half tossing in sleepless agony, Lionel couldn't wait to get out of the palace and into some fresh air. Through the early dawn hours, he lay in bed, staring up at the royal-blue canopy that was draped above him. In these silent moments, his thoughts always drifted to Aya and the night they had shared in this same bed. He smiled to himself, thinking of the delicious flush of her skin, of the way her eyes had lit up with pleasure at every touch. More than anything, he wanted to share that intimacy with her again.

For that reason, Lionel had insisted upon keeping the bed —and the rest of his bedroom furniture—when he moved into the king's chambers. Eldric had grumbled at first, but once Lionel divulged his secret, the valet had rolled his eyes and muttered "young love" with a smile.

A faint knock sounded on Lionel's door. With a groan, he retrieved his robe from the intricately carved armoire next to the bed and shuffled into the sitting area to answer the caller. A look through the peephole revealed Eldric, breakfast tray at the ready.

Lionel opened the door and moved aside to let in the valet. "You're early this morning."

"I figured you weren't sleeping anyway." Eldric's forehead wrinkled in concern. "Did I wake you, Your Majesty?"

"No, no." Lionel yawned and plopped onto the plush, paisley sofa.

Eldric sat the silver tray on the coffee table then took his usual place in the matching armchair across from Lionel. "How are you feeling?"

"Fine." Lionel chomped on a strip of bacon—no need to stand on ceremony with just the two of them present. "When we arrived at Lord Greyson's estate, we learned that Lady Greyson had become sick, too. Dr. Engel believes it was merely a bad cut of meat." Lionel shook his head. He'd never seen someone vomit blood from simple food poisoning, but he supposed the doctor would know best.

"That's a relief." Eldric looked around the sitting room, his eyes tracing the alternating emerald and mint-green stripes on the wallpaper. "You have a free day today. I rescheduled all your appointments in case you fell ill. It might be a good opportunity to meet with the palace decorator."

Lionel shook his head. "I redecorated the bedroom."

"To look exactly like your old chambers." Eldric raised an eyebrow and gestured in front of them to the fireplace built into the wall that the bedroom and sitting room shared. "Don't you want to redesign the frame? Or put up a new mantel or painting?"

Lionel shrugged.

"What about the interior wall?" Eldric gestured to their right. "Surely, you don't have the same taste as King Archon. You could restock the bookshelves with volumes from the royal library or select some new glassware or drinks for the bar cabinet."

Zedara's suggestion echoed in Lionel's mind, and that same sense of dread crept up his spine. "I'm perfectly well supplied with books, thank you. I have two bookshelves of my own and a reading couch in my bedroom. And I don't drink enough to justify restocking the bar." Lionel pointed to the other side of the room. Soft light filtered in from the window, which allowed a pleasant view of Portside. Glass-paned cabinets rested on either side. "And I have no idea what I would do with those ridiculous cabinets if I replaced their old trinkets."

Eldric sighed. "It's not about the decor, Your Majesty. It's about you accepting this room as yours, making it your own."

Lionel shuddered, his imagination streaming through all the poor women his father had paraded through these chambers. "If it bothers you so much, Eldric, you have my permission to redesign every surface of the sitting room. I don't intend to bother. No amount of new furniture will erase my father's memory from this place."

"Are you sure it's not worth a try?" Eldric's lips pressed into a tight smile, which was almost obscured under his mustache. "I imagine it's even more difficult for you to be here than it is for me."

Lionel frowned. "Why is it difficult for you?"

"I served as King Archon's valet since he was your age. In all those years, he was kind, fair, and treated me with more respect than he gave to most others." Eldric's eyes turned steely. "At the same time, I loathed him. After your mother died, Benevolent Queen bless her, he became a different person. He hardened, started abusing his powers, went from flirting with young women to actually taking advantage of them…"

A lump swelled in Lionel's throat. "Everyone knew what a horrible person my father was, or became, whichever the case might have been. I understand that the nobles feared him too much to stop his injustices and that the villagers would have been helpless to meddle in palace affairs. I myself felt scared of and powerless against him. But why did they pay him so much respect? The whole kingdom treated my father better than they ever have me, and all I've done is bend over backward to improve everyone's lives."

Lionel hung his head in his hands to hide his watering eyes.

Eldric moved to sit next to Lionel and clapped him on the back. "When it comes down to it, people care more about their well-being than anything else. It's true that your father was a tyrant, and it's also true that you're a better man than he ever was. But while your father committed heinous acts, he ensured the kingdom ran smoothly. He never questioned the system, and he kept the nobles rich and the poor just prosperous enough to avoid complaint. Under his firm hand, the citizens rarely dared break a law, and when they did, he brought them to swift punishment. For all his cruelty, he ruled consistently."

Lionel slumped back against the couch. "And I don't."

"Put yourself in the people's shoes. You assumed power after having your father executed, which was right but still shocking." Eldric waited for Lionel to nod. "Then you immediately started changing laws, you created a council to advise you, and to top it all off, you fell in love with a commoner. When you were prince, how would you have viewed a king like that?"

Lionel grimaced. He'd thought as much to himself, but hearing Eldric list his eccentricities still hurt. "I suppose I would have believed he acted rashly and showed poor judgment."

Eldric nodded.

"So what do I do now?" Lionel searched Eldric's eyes for a clue.

Eldric shrugged. "It's not my place to tell you."

The silence hung heavily between them, until a chirping sound floated out of the bedroom.

"Ah, time to wake up." Lionel smiled wryly and followed the noise.

Penelope, Lionel's treasured mechanical bird, sat perched in her wire cage, which Lionel had hung next to the bedroom window. Her wings creaked up and down as she sang a stilted but still pretty tune. While her body was scratched and dented, and the leg he had previously used as a bedroom key kept falling off, Lionel still felt awe every time she wound to life. Short of loving him, repairing Penelope was the greatest gift Aya had given the king.

Lionel opened Penelope's cage and lifted her out, careful not to disturb her flapping wings. He pinched the winder on her back between his fingers and wound it backward until her movements ceased. After giving Penelope a gentle pat on the head, he placed her back in the cage.

Eldric watched the exchange from the doorway with an amused grin. "You treat that toy as if it were a real pet."

"She's more than a toy, Eldric. We both know that." Lionel cast his eyes to the carpet, remembering the day King Archon had smashed Penelope against the wall. It was the same day he had sentenced Aya's father, the cogsmith at the time, to execution for his inability to fix her.

"You should finish your breakfast." Eldric straightened his cravat. "Since you're feeling well and uninterested in my proposal, would you like me to reschedule your appointments for the day?"

Lionel arched an eyebrow. *We both know what I'm going to do with my freedom.*

Eldric pursed his lips, and Lionel assumed he was disappointed that the king wouldn't be acting upon his counsel straight away. "Very well, Your Majesty. Have a restful day, and do let me know if you need anything."

Lionel tapped his chin in a pretense of thought. *Time for that shave.* "As a matter of fact, could you deliver a message to Theo? Madam Rutt has requested an extra guard to be stationed outside the Rudder."

"Of course. Anything else?"

"After he's handled that, would you ask him to come up here?" Lionel frowned. "That is, if he's able to leave the investigation."

"I'll send him up in an hour so you have time to eat and dress." Eldric nodded toward the wooden vanity, where Lionel always sat to shave. "There's a clean straight razor in the top drawer. I'll have a maid bring a fresh basin of water."

Lionel couldn't help but smile and shake his head. "What would I do without you, Eldric?"

The valet shrugged playfully then departed to complete his errands. Before returning to his breakfast, Lionel dressed so that he would be decent when the maid arrived. Some of the servants still acted jittery in his presence, no doubt a leftover anxiety from years of serving his father. The maid came shortly after he had finished eating, and Lionel took his time shaving, making sure his cheeks and jawline were smooth to the touch.

With all the necessary tasks accomplished, Lionel glanced at the grandfather clock across from his bed. *Why do I always do that—you're not fixed yet.* Sighing at himself, he retrieved his pocket watch from the bedside table—still fifteen minutes until he could expect Theo to arrive. Every time he held the watch, pride swelled in his chest at Aya's success as the kingdom's cogsmith. As a young prince, he'd been arrogant enough to assume his future wife would be beautiful, but he had never imagined she would be so intelligent and resourceful. For not the first time, he wondered what he had done to deserve her.

Tucking the watch into his vest pocket, Lionel returned to the sitting room. He stared around the space, and his lips formed a snarl. Eldric was right—Lionel should redecorate. But he couldn't bring himself to do it. Lionel needed to steep in his father's belongings. Each item reminded him of the kind of king he never wanted to become and punished him for the years he had stayed silent while his father executed dozens of innocent people.

Lionel wandered over to the bookshelf and perused the books. He'd done this before, hoping the titles would somehow give him a peek into King Archon's mind or, for that matter, what it meant to be king. His fingers traced the dusty spines. *The Lineage of the Royal Family. Courtly Customs and Behaviors. The Key to the Kingdom.*

Something about the last title gave Lionel pause—it sounded like the secret he'd been searching for. He slid the book out from the shelf. Despite being two inches thick, the book felt light in Lionel's hand. With steady fingers but a knotted stomach, he opened the book. The title page appeared normal, as did the table of contents. Lionel flipped through the rest of the pages, and about a third of the way through, he stopped.

Page 237 had a large hole cut in the center, as did the next hundred or so pages. Lionel peered inside the cavern, and as the title had suggested, he saw a brass key hidden inside. The handle stretched about the length of Lionel's forefinger and was nearly as thick, too. At its end, three golden hoops formed an impressive triangular design, and a sapphire rested in its center. Instead of a traditional blade with teeth cut into it, the key had four small nubs that extended out from its round stem every ninety degrees.

Lionel lifted the key from the book, relishing its weight in his hand. Though the thought made him grimace, he wished he could speak to his father, if only to ask him whether he had known about the key and what it unlocked. A brief gaze around the room proved useless. As far as Lionel knew, the sitting room held no trunks or safes nor any hidden doors.

The door.

Tossing the book on the couch, Lionel clutched the key and hurried out of the sitting room. He emerged into the greeting hall, a circular area outside of the king's chambers, where he could receive guests without inviting them into his private space. Paintings hung on the wall nearest Lionel's room, and a bookshelf with fake books sat on the other side, obscuring a tunnel that led to the ship's deck. Next to Lionel's door was an ancient, broken grandfather clock, and on its other side stood *the* door.

Like many who visited this corridor, Lionel had always wondered what lay behind the door. King Archon had sworn he had no idea where it led or how to open it. With a quick glance down the corridor to ensure no palace staff lurked nearby, Lionel walked over to the mysterious entryway.

It stood eight feet tall, the same height as the grandfather clock, and just over a head taller than Lionel when he wore his king's top hat. There was no doorknob, so Lionel looked over the smooth, metal surface for a keyhole. At the top left corner, Lionel spied an almost unnoticeable change in the metal. It appeared that this portion of the surface had been patched. Lionel dug at the seam with his fingernail, but it wouldn't budge.

With a frustrated sigh, Lionel stepped back and inspected the door from a new angle. Nothing. Not a single hole. No weaknesses in sight.

Lionel clenched the key in his fist. Fine, then. Maybe the key didn't open that particular door, but it had to belong to something important. The palace was littered with secret rooms—Lord Collingwood owned one with a painting as an entrance—so maybe Lionel, as king, had one too. After all, why would the key be hidden inside a book in a room only the king could access if it wasn't meant for Lionel?

"Eager to get going, are we?" Theo's voice made Lionel jump. He hadn't even heard the captain approaching.

Lionel slipped the key in his inside jacket pocket. "What?"

"You're waiting out here for me, aren't you?" Theo looked the king up and down, and Lionel squirmed under his scrutiny. Theo sighed. "Why do you do this to yourself?"

Lionel's face burned with guilt. "Do what?"

Theo motioned toward the center of the marble floor, which was marred with scuff marks, where a fainting couch had once rested. "This is where it happened, right? Where Aya's scheme almost failed? Where Zedara had King Archon arrested?"

At the reminder, Lionel's stomach churned with acid. He opened his mouth to tell Theo he hadn't been thinking about that night, but instead, he closed it and nodded. Until Lionel knew more about the key—or failed to find out its purpose by himself—he didn't want to tell anyone about it. If it were valuable enough to be hidden, it might also be valuable enough to steal, and Lionel wouldn't risk his friend's safety on an unknown.

Lionel squared his shoulders. "Are you sure you have time to act as chaperone today? I can ask Eldric."

Theo stretched his arms. "You're not serious? I've been cooped up in that dungeon or the Rudder or Sternville hovels too long. I could use a nice trip to Portside." He pulled a lump of sheep's wool from his pocket. "See? I even brought earplugs —just in case."

Lionel gave his friend a playful punch on the arm. "You're hilarious."

"I know." Theo winked. "Ready to go?"

Lionel glanced toward his chambers. No one else had access to them, but he didn't want to risk someone finding the book. "Give me a minute."

After motioning for Theo to wait outside, Lionel ducked back into his sitting room. He replaced *The Key to the Kingdom* on the shelf but kept the key in his interior pocket. A clean streak marked where Lionel had removed the book, so he hastily wiped the front of the shelves with his pocket square. Satisfied that the book looked inconspicuous, Lionel headed to the door. His top hat waited on the coat rack next to the exit, but he decided to leave it where it hung and locked the door behind him.

Though Lionel knew he could never escape the title, he didn't want to feel like the king today. King Lionel had the day off, and he would leave that part of himself behind in these chambers. Today, he would be the man who stole the cogsmith's heart. He would be Willem.

5

"It's open!" Aya's voice sang out from within her cogsmith shop, and Lionel's heart beat harder in his chest. Even though he'd come to court her weekly in the months since Mr. Rutt and Lord Varick's trial, his body still buzzed with a mixture of nerves and excitement.

Pushing open the door, Lionel stepped into the front room of the shop with Theo in tow as chaperone. Aya had cleaned it since his last visit. Instead of machines scattered about the floor, each item to be sold or repaired sat in its place on one of the many shelves.

"I'll be right with you," Aya called out. Lionel figured she must have been in her bedroom, as he didn't see her in the workspace at the back of the shop. He leaned against the counter, and Theo seated himself at the simple wooden table in the front room.

After a few moments, Lionel heard a door click shut, and Aya emerged from the corridor that led to her private quarters. "How can I help—" When she saw him, her emerald eyes lit up. "Oh, Lionel. What a wonderful surprise! I didn't expect to see you until tomorrow."

"I managed to get free a day early." Lionel smiled as Aya stepped into his embrace. He wrapped one arm around her slender waist, while the other reached up to cup her cheek. Her soft lips met his, and he felt her smiling into their kiss. Though he wanted nothing more than to deepen the moment, he pulled away out of respect for Theo.

"It's so good to see you." Aya patted his chest with her hands, and a jolt of fear coursed through Lionel when her palm landed on the key. But if Aya noticed anything hiding inside his jacket, she didn't let on. Instead, she walked over to Theo, who rose from his chair to receive her hug.

When they separated, Aya had a smirk plastered on her face. "Theo, I can't believe you let him talk you into chaperoning duty again."

"Nonsense. You know I can't resist the opportunity to see what you're working on." Theo grinned, and Aya blushed a delicious shade of pink.

"Oh, it's not *that* exciting."

Theo rolled his eyes. "Compared to bossing around a bunch of guards all day, it is."

Lionel nodded. "It beats dealing with the nobles and all of Desertera's problems, too."

"You're really selling this queen position." Aya poked Lionel in the side. "Come on, I'll show you what I've been doing this morning."

Aya led them behind the counter into her cluttered workspace. As they approached the back of the shop, a warm breeze drifted through the open windows. Lionel caught a glimpse of the forge she shared with the glassblower next door, pleased to see no fire glowing inside. If Aya wasn't metalworking, there was a better chance that Lionel could get her to take part of the day off.

"Here it is." Aya stopped in front of the large workbench that stood in the center of the room. On top rested a strange metal contraption about three feet wide and two feet tall. It was unlike anything Lionel had ever seen. Aya laughed, no doubt at the perplexed looks on his and Theo's faces. "It's an engine. Or it will be, anyway."

Lionel's eyes widened, and he saw Theo's do the same. "I

get it now. We have artifacts like this decorating the halls in the palace."

"Exactly." Aya beamed. "I remembered seeing similar machines in the ship, and ever since I visited the engine room, I couldn't stop puzzling over how all those pistons and pulleys would work together to spin the propellers. There wasn't anything about them in the cogsmithing books you gave me, but the mechanics and engineering books have been helpful. They allowed me to build the wheelchair Dellwyn used at the trial." Aya tucked a brown curl behind her ear. "Of course, this engine is more complicated than that, and I'm having a difficult time making it work."

Lionel smiled at the crinkle between Aya's brows and the inquisitive squint of her eyes. "You'll figure it out."

Aya had been beautiful all dolled up in the palace, but Lionel thought she was flawless in her workshop, dressed in a plain blue skirt, long-sleeved blouse, and simple corset belt, complete with calluses on her hands.

Theo leaned over to inspect the engine. "In theory, how would it work?"

Aya motioned to the back end of the engine, which looked like two metal cubes stacked on top of each other. "In this bottom box, you create a fire to burn and heat up the water, which is in the boiler, this top box. Once it's hot enough, the water will make steam. Unlike the wheelchair, which ran on a combination of boiling water and mechanical momentum, kind of like the wind-up toys I build, this would run on steam alone."

Lionel and Theo nodded to show their understanding.

"The steam from this tank would flow through the inlet valve into this cylinder here." Aya pointed at a tube that connected the boiler to the front part of the engine. "This would cause the piston to move forward and backward. When a machine is attached to the piston—for example, a pump to draw water from the wells—the engine will power that machine. Or just as a steam generator, the engine itself would make a good humidifier for the palace greenhouses." Aya shrugged. "That's an oversimplified explanation, and I still have a lot to figure out."

Lionel motioned to a pipe at the top of the contraption. "So the steam comes out here?"

"Sure does." Aya cupped her hands over the pipe. "Since water is scarce, my next project is to build some kind of canopy that will catch the steam and condense it back into liquid form. Some of the water will be lost in the process, but it's better than not conserving any at all."

Theo shook his head. "You think of everything, don't you?"

"I try." Aya's brow furrowed. "I can *think* of it all. Question is, can I *do* it all?"

Lionel reached across the table and squeezed Aya's hand, running his thumb over her rough knuckles. "Of course you can."

The shop's main door creaked open, spoiling the moment. Lionel looked over his shoulder to see a hunched elderly man enter, accompanied by a young woman carrying a pair of leather shoes.

Aya strolled to the front of the shop and shook their hands. "Mr. Cobbler, Miss Cobbler, good morning."

Mr. Cobbler's eyes narrowed as he gazed toward the workspace. "Should we come back later?"

Lionel squared his shoulders, unsure whether the old man couldn't see well or disapproved of his courtship of Aya.

The young woman followed her companion's stare and gasped. She dropped to a curtsy. "Forgive us, Your Majesty. We didn't realize that was you."

"I beg your pardon, Your Majesty." Mr. Cobbler bowed, a slight motion with his bent frame.

As Lionel walked to the front of the shop, he waved his hands. "No apologies necessary. Please rise."

"I've been showing the king my latest invention—or re-vention, as it were." Aya touched Lionel's arm in an unthinking display of affection, and both customers' eyes widened. She motioned to the shoes. "Might I try them on?"

"Certainly, Miss Cogsmith." Mr. Cobbler nudged the young woman forward, and she handed them to Aya.

Aya sat at the table to try the shoes, and while she did, she nodded her head toward the counter. "That's your locket there, if you want to give it a go."

Miss Cobbler's face lit up, and she snatched up the necklace. Shaped like a heart, the bronze locket fit snugly in the woman's cupped hand. With the tips of her thumb and forefinger, she wound the crown at the top of the locket, where it attached to a matching bronze chain.

Lionel watched in awe as the heart opened to reveal a metal desert landscape. The bottom half of the scene was the same bronze as the locket's exterior, with its top edge—the horizon—cut to depict the silhouettes of cacti and small shrubs. In the top half hung a golden sun, which slowly arced from one side of the horizon to the other. As it dipped below the bronze plate, a silver crescent moon and tiny, jeweled stars rose to take its place.

"It's stunning." Miss Cobbler's voice came out breathy. "I can't believe you fixed it."

Mr. Cobbler shuffled over to examine the locket, and his eyes glassed over with tears. "It's a family heirloom," he explained to Lionel. "My grandmother gave it to me as I give it to my granddaughter now."

Lionel grinned at the family's joy and at Aya's successful handiwork. "It's a true treasure. You all should be proud."

Aya stood and walked over, her new shoes clacking against the worn wooden floorboards. "These fit perfectly. Thank you both for repairing them so quickly."

"Are you sure it's enough? I feel like you did so much more for us." Miss Cobbler's eyes shone sincere, but her fist closed around the locket.

"A repair for a repair. It's a fair trade." Aya patted both Cobblers on the shoulder. "Unlike the farmers, I can keep my prices steady for now."

Mr. Cobbler scoffed. "You're lucky. With animal hide

taking a hike, the tanners are about to raise rates on leather. Those shoes of yours might cost double in a week."

"Well, I'm glad I sent them to you when I did." Aya wiggled her toe for emphasis. "Now, you take care of that locket, and please let me know if there's anything else I can do for you."

The pair gave Aya their thanks, and with one more curious look between the cogsmith and the king, they left the shop.

Lionel rubbed the back of his neck. "Things are really getting bad, huh? With Bowtown, I mean."

"Not yet." Aya pursed her lips. "Most of the price increases have come from concern more than necessity. If more farmers stop tending their land and animals, that's when we'll have real problems."

Lionel nodded. "It seems like your relationships with the other merchants are improving, at least."

"One at a time." Aya sighed. "As I get better at my craft and complete more meaningful projects like that, they slowly realize that I'm committed to cogsmithing. Though, obviously, they still don't know how to feel about your courtship."

Lionel smirked and snaked his arm around her waist. "As long as you know how to feel about it."

"Of course I do." Aya tilted her head up and kissed him. "I don't know how many times I have to say it, Lionel."

Lionel winked. "Maybe just one more."

Aya flashed a crooked smile. "I'm not going to run away. I'm ready for this. For us."

Lionel captured her lips in a kiss again, warmth spreading through his chest.

Theo cleared his throat, and Lionel pulled away, sharing a guilty grin with Aya.

"Do you have any more customers today?" Lionel asked.

Aya squinted. "None scheduled. What did you have in mind?"

"I have the entire day to myself. I thought we could go for a walk, maybe have lunch." He leaned in closer until his lips grazed her ear. "Or we could stay in."

Aya laughed and pushed Lionel away. "I think a walk sounds like the best idea for all of us. Don't you, Theo?"

The captain chuckled. "Whatever you say, Miss Cogsmith."

Lionel lifted Aya's hand to his lips. "A walk it is then, love."

"Fantastic. Let me fetch a hat." Aya ducked down the short corridor that led to her private chambers.

Lionel and Theo waited in amicable silence. When Aya didn't reappear after a few moments, Lionel gave in to his desire to follow her. He walked past the tiny kitchen area then paused to peek into the first bedroom, which had belonged to Aya as a child. It now served as her sitting room and cogsmithing library, complete with a reading sofa, coffee table, and single bookshelf. As his eyes landed on the room's only decoration, Lionel smiled. He had known Aya would love that painting of a frog drifting on a lily pad.

When he reached the second bedroom, which Aya had taken upon reclaiming the shop, Lionel stopped in the doorway. Aya crouched next to the bed, her hand stretched under it as if reaching for her hat.

Lionel couldn't help but snicker. "Need a hand?"

"Oh!" Aya started, and a thump sounded under the bed. "No, no, I found it." She pulled the hat out and stood.

"You know, they make these nifty racks that hold hats and coats off the floor," Lionel teased. "You should get one."

"Ah, there's my charming Willem." Aya wrinkled her nose at him. "This room is small. Storing things under the bed works fine."

"To quote the wise Captain Laurel, 'whatever you say, Miss Cogsmith.'" Lionel performed a mock salute. As she walked toward him, her body moved out from in front of the nightstand, and he noticed Charlie, Aya's mechanical frog, resting upon it. Next to him sat another familiar item. "Lord Collingwood has a music box just like that. Do its flower petals dance when wound? His do."

Aya froze. "Um, that is... was his."

Lionel furrowed his brow. "Why do you have it?"

Aya's face flushed. "I don't. I mean, it's not mine. He gave it to Dellwyn, but Sybil accidentally knocked it off her desk. I've managed to restore its outward appearance, but I'm still having trouble with the mechanics."

Lionel nodded. "I see."

Something in Aya's voice rang hollow, as if she weren't telling Lionel the whole truth. After putting on her straw hat— a boater hat, his mother used to call them—Aya led him out of the bedroom and locked the door behind them. She slipped the key down the front of her blouse, snugging it under her corset belt, and giggled. "Old habits."

"Better safe than sorry, they say." Lionel smiled, hoping Aya didn't detect his own secrecy, and held out his arm for her to take. As they walked to the front room, Lionel dared a glance back toward the door. "Why do you keep the music box in your bedroom?"

Aya's eyes darted around the shop, and Lionel couldn't decide whether she was mustering up a lie or thought his questions were nosy. "The same reason I don't show off Charlie. It's too valuable to be left out here. All it takes is one look to know it's more precious than anything anyone in Portside owns. I can't risk it getting stolen."

Lionel squeezed Aya's arm. "That makes sense."

And it did. Aya's words sounded logical, but her tone had a defensive edge. Lionel wondered what she was holding back. Maybe Dellwyn had asked Aya to keep quiet about the music box, or perhaps Aya was embarrassed that she didn't know how to fix it. He wanted to ask her more but thought again of the key tucked against his heart. As long as he kept a secret from Aya—even for her own safety—he couldn't expect her to divulge one of her own. He would simply have to wait until she was ready to tell him or until he could judge himself worthy of knowing the truth.

---

6

*L*ionel and Aya walked arm in arm through the streets of Portside, with Theo following a few paces behind. Each time the group turned a corner, the villagers met them with curious eyes and poorly concealed whispers. While Lionel and Aya had courted in public before, every date drew more legitimacy to—and created more rumors about—their romance.

For his part, Lionel gritted his teeth through the rudeness and put on his charming, protective smile. Although he never enjoyed being the center of attention, he had grown used to people gossiping about and judging his every move. The only thing he could do was act graciously, be kind, and hope the merchants would return the favor.

Aya, on the other hand, gripped Lionel's arm until it throbbed beneath her fingers. As they strolled down Baker Street, with its tidy storefronts and sweet aromas, she leaned up to whisper in his ear. "Why did I suggest this?"

"It's not that bad." Lionel patted Aya's hand. "Other than the fact that I've lost all feeling below my elbow."

"Shit, sorry!" Aya loosened her grasp then used her free hand to pinch the bridge of her nose. "Damn it. I've been trying to watch my cursing. I know the nobles frown upon it."

That means she's been thinking about being queen. Lionel bit his bottom lip to avoid grinning. "True. But they also frown upon changing centuries-old laws, so I doubt a foul word or two will cause a stir."

Aya's lips tugged up into a small smile. "Thank you for saying so."

Before Lionel could ask Aya more regarding her feelings about joining the monarchy, a man ran past them, bumping into Aya and showering dust all over her skirt. Aya stumbled, but Lionel grabbed her by the shoulders and steadied her. Theo charged forward to catch the careless offender, but Lionel held out his arm to stop him. "Look."

The man had joined a small crowd, which slowly formed a circle at the intersection of Baker Street and Blacksmith Lane. A voice rang out from within the center of the group, and Lionel swallowed down the anxious lump in his throat.

"Theo, will you go ahead and see what the fuss is about?" Lionel put his arm around Aya. "We'll stay here."

Theo nodded, already striding toward the cluster of villagers. "I'll be right back."

Lionel and Aya waited in silence as Theo approached the intersection. While Lionel kept scanning the area, watching for any sign of danger, Aya raised herself up on tiptoe for a better view of the commotion.

She landed on her heels with a huff. "I can't see anything. We should move closer."

Lionel shook his head. "I know this is your village, but it's not mine. If this is a show of dissent or civil unrest, I could be targeted. And so could you."

Aya fiddled with the collar of her blouse. "I hadn't thought about that. I'm sorry."

"It's fine." Lionel smirked to lighten the moment. "Add caution to your list of queenly habits to adopt."

Theo returned then, a frown plastered on his face. "It's Rykart Farmer. He's come to speak to the people of Portside."

"Really?" Aya's eyebrows rose. "He's never preached here before, only in Sternville and on the outskirts of Bowtown."

Theo turned to Lionel, his posture squared and attentive. "What should we do, Your Majesty?"

"Well, we can't stop him. He hasn't done anything wrong." Lionel looked from Theo's defensive stance to Aya's curious gaze. While he didn't want to put Aya or himself in danger, he had to admit that he had wondered about the farmer. The only times Lionel had seen the self-proclaimed prophet, Rykart had been a prisoner. As king, maybe Lionel had a duty to witness what had his subjects riled up.

He took a deep breath. "Let's go listen to what this farmer-prophet has to say."

They headed toward the crowd with slow, cautious steps then found a place to stand at the back, out of the farmer's line of sight. Rykart stood in the center of the group with his arms stretched out to either side and his smiling face pointed up at the sky. If Lionel hadn't known better, he might have thought a bright beam of light shone down on the so-called prophet from the Benevolent Queen's kingdom above.

Beside Lionel, Aya laced her fingers with his, and he gave her hand an encouraging squeeze. Once again, she stood on tiptoe, craning for a better view. Although Lionel didn't look back, he could feel Theo behind them, pushed closer by another layer of curious villagers.

After a moment, Rykart lowered his chin and opened his mismatched eyes. In the dungeon, they had made the farmer appear crazy. Out in the hot sunshine—one eye piercing green, the other cloudy gray—he looked otherworldly. Lionel found himself drawn to the farmer's gaze, and he could only imagine the effect it would have on a weaker-minded individual.

"People of Portside!" Rykart's voice rang out over the crowd, bringing the villagers to a respectful—or perhaps awestruck—silence. "My message is short. The Benevolent Queen has beckoned me to appeal to you on Her behalf, as She did in Sternville and Bowtown before you."

"You're crazy!" a man hollered. He threw a roll at the farmer, and it smacked against his head.

Rykart caught the roll before it fell to the ground then took a large bite out of it. Much of the crowd roared with laughter, and Lionel caught himself chuckling, as well.

"The Benevolent Queen demands your faithfulness. To Her and to each other." Rykart stuffed the roll into one of the many bags that hung around his tool belt, and his scythe caught Lionel's eye as it glinted in the sunlight. The farmer turned to face a new part of the group. "If you act with loyalty and fidelity, She will send the salvation rains. She will restore Desertera to the paradise it once was."

Lionel snorted. He didn't know much about the world before the great flood, but he knew that people always had and always would have problems—whether king or peasant.

"Sternville first rejected Her offer. They chose to support a cruel, adulterous institution and continue their servitude of the sinful nobles. For their disobedience, they bathed in the blood of the corrupt Madam Huxley, then of her murderer, the dastardly Augustus Rutt." Rykart ran his gloved hands from his cheeks down to his chest, as if washing himself in blood.

Lionel glanced around the crowd to gauge the people's reactions. Most seemed interested, but a few had their noses wrinkled in disgust. One elderly woman caught Lionel's stare, and her eyes widened in recognition. Before she could get a better look, Lionel ducked down to hide his face and found himself level with Aya. She stood with her body rigid and lips pursed.

"Are you okay?" Lionel moved his hand to rest on her lower back. "We can leave if you want."

"I'm fine." Aya rubbed her temples. "I just... I still don't know how to feel. Madam Huxley took me in, and Augustus was always nice to me. To know their true natures, and now to have them exploited for Rykart's message, it's... confusing, to say the least."

Lionel nodded and risked standing at his full height again, but he kept his hand firm on Aya's back.

"Do you know what will happen to *them* now?" Rykart pointed south toward Sternville, his outstretched arm trembling. "The Benevolent Queen will punish them. Her wrath will sweep through the village like a wildfire, turning all who would ignore Her grace to ash. Their sinful desires may be sated, but their bodies will starve for salvation."

Lionel tapped his fingers against Aya's back to get her attention then whispered, "Has Dellwyn mentioned anything about Sternville to you? Has the farmer caused any more trouble?"

Aya shook her head, her eyes downcast. "Not that I know of, but we haven't had time to speak much since she took the post as madam. Why? Do you think Rykart plans to do something?"

"Difficult to say." Lionel shrugged. "What he claims often sounds ridiculous, but it seems to come true one way or another."

Rykart paced his circular patch of ground, his brow drenched in sweat from exertion and, more likely, his all-black ensemble. "Bowtown, however, is obeying the Benevolent Queen's commandments. Every day, more people devote their lives to fidelity and truth. More farmers abandon the plots owned by the wicked nobles, the ones who will never be faithful. More good, hardworking people join Her cause—and move closer to their ultimate reward."

Rykart's voice cracked, and he paused to take a swig of water from the canteen hanging from his tool belt. "What will *you* do, Portside? Will you stay in your landlords' shops, performing your craft so the unfaithful might grow richer? Or will you gather your belongings and join the Benevolent Queen's true followers? Will you serve Her with your craft instead?"

So that was Rykart's mission. He viewed the nobles as the least faithful of all, the biggest violators of the Benevolent Queen's commandments. And only when the common people abandoned and disassociated from the nobles would their divine queen save them. Lionel thought back over his life, remembering all the true adulterers his father had sent to execution and the long list of married nobles who frequented the Rudder. While Lionel had no concept of how many peasants committed adultery, the nobles did set the bar high in terms of that particular sin.

"Lionel, we need to get out of here." Theo growled the words, and Lionel felt his friend's hand grasp his bicep.

The crowd shuffled and murmured around them, and Lionel realized that the people had recognized him. Wary or angry faces met him on all sides, and Lionel pulled Aya closer, positioning her between him and Theo. For the briefest second, he wondered whether the farmer's words had swayed the crowd against him so soon or whether the anonymity of the mob freed individuals to show their true disdain.

A hush fell over the group, but it was broken moments later by a brave outcry. "It's the king!"

"Make him answer for the nobles!" another man shouted.

"No! Make him answer for *himself*!" That time, the heckler was a woman.

Lionel stood as tall and straight as he could. Despite the heat- and fear-induced sweat that rolled down his face and back, he hoped to preserve some of his dignity. With only Theo to guard him and no sympathetic faces in sight, all Lionel had to protect himself were words and bravado. "If you would allow me—"

"He'll just lie to us!" It was the first voice again. "You think he's any better than King Archon?"

Lionel clenched his jaw. "Disrespecting me will only—"

"He's as corrupt as the rest!" the second voice said. "He stole that shop from Emil Tanner and gave it to the cogsmith."

"Well, it's only fair after what *she* gave *him*!" the woman cackled.

The villagers erupted into laughter, and Lionel felt Aya tremble against his back. But it wasn't the whole crowd against them. Only a few people had spoken out. The realization strengthened Lionel's courage, and he took a deep breath. "That is enough!"

Lionel pushed through the crowd and made his way toward the center. He heard Aya holler after him, but Theo must have held her back, because neither of them followed. As Lionel reached the inner edge of the crowd, the final row of people parted to allow him passage.

Rykart met him with a deep, respectful bow. "Your Majesty, the Benevolent Queen is pleased that you have heard Her message."

Lionel waved his hand to encourage Rykart to stand. "Pardon me, Mr. Farmer, but I clearly need to address my people."

"Of course, Your Majesty." Rykart tapped his chest. "The Benevolent Queen can only speak to their hearts. You must speak to their ears."

"Right." Lionel hoped his confusion didn't pervade his tone. He had expected the farmer to lash out at him, not to willingly give him the floor. With a conscious effort to smooth his brow and flatten his frown into a semblance of composure, Lionel faced the crowd. "Mr. Farmer is right. There are nobles who have been unfaithful."

The crowd's reactions varied from stunned silence to gasps to claps.

Lionel waited for the noisemakers to quiet. "There are nobles who have betrayed their marriage vows, who have broken already-unfair arrangements with their tenant farmers and with you." He took a deep breath, steeling himself for an angry outburst. "But there are also merchants—your families and friends and neighbors—who have ignored marriage vows, who have cheated customers and colleagues with price hikes and poor deals."

Throughout the last sentence, rumblings in the crowd grew louder. Rykart raised his hand to regain the villagers' attention. "King Lionel speaks the truth, Her truth. Let him finish."

When the crowd quieted, the farmer deferred to the king with another bow.

Lionel swallowed. Rykart's words might have spared him trouble with the Portside villagers, but once they spread to the palace, they would shatter what little respect the nobles had for him. It was bad enough for Lionel to change ancient laws and court a commoner. But to be championed by a street prophet

—one who had the potential to send Desertera's economy into upheaval and destroy the social order—would be unforgivable.

"My point is"—Lionel paused to lick his dry lips—"the guiltless among you do not deserve to be punished for the sins of the few. Nor should you harden your hearts to all the nobles when many of them are as innocent—or as flawed—as you."

Most of the villagers nodded or clapped in approval, though a few still held their arms crossed and kept their eyes narrowed. Over their heads, Lionel could just make out Aya and Theo, who had moved to stand safely outside the group. He let out a sigh of relief.

Before Lionel could get too comfortable, a surly, hook-nosed man stepped forward into the circle. "Excuse me, Your Majesty, but you ain't done nothin' for us and you ain't done nothin' for the Benevolent Queen, either. I'm not gonna stand here and obey a hypocrite."

Though Lionel stood a head taller than him, the man's wide shoulders and thick, sculpted muscles rendered him silent. If the man decided to act with violence, there was no way Lionel could outmatch him and no way Theo could come to his aid in time.

"You will not obey a hypocrite." Rykart stepped between Lionel and his challenger. "You will obey your king."

The man balked. "But he—"

The farmer poked the man in the chest, and Lionel's eyes must have bulged as far as Rykart's had during his speech. "King Lionel is the most devout king we've *ever* had."

Rykart whirled on the crowd, his voice growing hoarse with passion. "King Lionel punished King Archon—his own father —for abusing the adultery law. Then he revoked the useless law so that we would be faithful out of love and belief, not out of fear, and so that no more blood would be shed over human weakness. Until *you* do as much for the Benevolent Queen's cause, you have no right to speak to him that way!"

As Rykart spoke the words, a weight lifted from Lionel's chest, and it took all his strength not to shout with joy. Finally, someone understood why he had abolished the adultery law.

For months, the nobles had whispered about how Lionel wanted adultery decriminalized so that he could return to his playboy ways once he was married. Others speculated that he was simply lashing out against the kingdom or showing favor to Dellwyn and the Rudder.

Though she had never said it, Lionel knew Aya thought the ruling had been for her benefit, a reparation for King Archon's actions and an assurance that Lionel would never become like his father. But none of those theories were correct. Lionel wanted to give his people the freedom of choice and save those who chose poorly or were wrongly accused. He wanted to rule from a place of compassion, not fear. Even if Rykart thought Lionel's purpose was religious, at least he understood the intent of his actions.

"Thank you for your kind words, Mr. Farmer." Lionel clasped his hands behind his back to keep himself composed. "However, I'm afraid I don't deserve them."

A hush fell over the crowd. Dozens of faces stared at Lionel, but with curiosity or skepticism, not the disapproval to which he'd grown accustomed with the nobles.

"As embarrassed as I am to admit it, I have not made a single ruling with the Benevolent Queen in mind." Lionel dared a glance at Rykart—the farmer's face remained impassive. "Every decision I make is based on two simple questions: is this right, and will this improve the lives of my people? As blasphemous as it may be, first and foremost, my duty is to serve all of you."

A split second of stunned silence hung over the crowd, then the villagers burst into applause. Although he pressed his lips together in an attempt at solemnity, Lionel couldn't help but smile. At long last, he'd made a breakthrough with his subjects. The nobles might not understand or respect his actions yet, but the people of Portside did. With any luck, they would extend their newfound respect to Aya, too.

Rykart showed his approval with a final bow. As he rose, he turned his face upward to the sky once more. "Brave words, Your Majesty, but wrong. The Benevolent Queen works through you, albeit quietly. If you listen, you will learn to separate Her voice from your own."

Lionel could barely make out the farmer's words over the clapping, and he hoped that meant he alone had heard the message. "I will try to do that, if only to better understand what you are trying to do."

"You are hungry for understanding, Your Majesty." Rykart tapped his chin. "It is not the worst thing you could be hungry for in these times—or in the times to come."

Lionel's brow furrowed. "What are you saying?"

Rykart shrugged and stretched out his arms. Once again, he closed his eyes and turned his face upward to the sun. A tightness curled in Lionel's stomach, but he didn't press the farmer. Even if Rykart would respond, Lionel knew he wouldn't understand the message.

Instead, Lionel headed to rejoin Aya and Theo. This time, the crowd parted for him, each person bowing or curtsying as he passed. He returned the gestures by inclining his head or waving, all the while biting his lip to keep his smile subdued.

When Lionel reached the edge of the crowd, Aya rushed forward to greet him with a beaming grin. She placed a hand on his arm in a reserved show of affection. "You did wonderfully. I've never seen anyone capture the hearts of Portside like that."

Theo stood straight and tall, but his jaw was clenched. "A fine speech, Your Majesty."

An unspoken "but" hung in the air, and Lionel knew Theo was also worried how the nobles would react to his impromptu speech. It might take a day or two for word to trickle back up to the palace, but once it did, the council—especially the bishop—would demand answers.

But Lionel didn't want to think about that inevitability at the moment. That morning, he had promised himself he would be Willem for the day, and while resuming his role as king had won him a small victory with the people of Portside, it had also reminded him of his failings. He never seemed able to escape them, even with Aya at his side. But for a few more hours, he could still pretend to be just her Willem.

Lionel pushed the thoughts away and looked around the street. Rykart had left, and most of the villagers had dissipated, though a few still lurked nearby to watch the trio. "I don't know about you two, but I've had enough excitement for one day." He wrapped an arm around Aya's waist. "How about we head back to the shop and have some lunch?"

"That sounds nice." Aya pressed herself closer to Lionel's side, her body melting seamlessly into his. She slipped her hand around his back and traced her fingers up and down his spine.

Lionel withheld a smirk and released Aya, half pleased that his speech had had that effect on her, half concerned that the entire village had witnessed her boldness.

He dug in his pocket for a handful of coins and passed them to Theo. "Would you mind fetching us all something to eat?"

The captain's lips spread into a cheeky grin, and he lowered his voice. "As your chaperone, I expect you both to be waiting patiently—and separately—in the front room when I return."

Aya blushed and looked away.

Lionel winked and clapped his friend on the shoulder. "You better take your time, then."

7

*T*hat night, Lionel couldn't sleep. He lay in bed, staring up into darkness and gripping the comforter in frustration. The afternoon with Aya had relaxed him, utterly and completely, and he'd collapsed into bed with every expectation of sleep overtaking him as passionately as Aya had. But the minutes had grown into hours, and Lionel had accepted his sleepless fate. What he hadn't determined was what to do about it.

With a groan, Lionel sat up and fumbled for the candle on his nightstand. His fingers wrapped around the brass handle of the candleholder, and he lit the candle with shaky hands. The orange glow stung his tired eyes, enveloping him in a contained brightness and casting shadows just beyond his reach. A quick glance at his pocket watch, also resting on the nightstand, told him it was three in the morning. There was at least another hour before the earliest risers of the palace staff began their duties.

Unsure of what to do, Lionel shuffled into the sitting room and took *The Key to the Kingdom* down from the bookshelf. After returning to his chambers that evening, he had placed the key back in its hiding spot. He hadn't thought of a better place to put it, and he figured if it had survived there for at least the months since his father's death, maybe longer, it must have been a good enough place to keep it.

Carrying the book in one hand and the candle in the other, Lionel sat down on the paisley sofa. *This hideous pattern looks much better in candlelight.* He placed the candle on the coffee table then flipped open the book.

The title page appeared innocent enough, bearing the subtitle, *A Monarch's Guide to a Successful Reign*, and the author's archaic name, Sir Harold Walker. Lionel found it odd that a guard—a knight, he corrected himself with a nod to his history lessons—would have written a book on ruling. Then again, the book might have been created for the express purpose of hiding the key, and the craftsman had not taken proper care with the details. Or maybe the name was a pseudonym, or this Sir Harold may have recorded it as one of Lionel's ancestors dictated to him. Or perhaps the knight had considered himself more fit to rule than the monarch he served and had written the book for satire or spite.

He certainly wouldn't be the only one to hold such arrogant beliefs. Lionel winced, thinking about his own unpreparedness at taking the throne. *Okay, maybe Sir Harold had a point.*

Turning the thin, yellowed pages, Lionel examined the table of contents. Again, it seemed normal. Each chapter focused on a different kingly duty, from how to dress for a ball to how to knight a soldier to how to conduct a mounted foxhunt. These ancient traditions held no place in Lionel's life, but he still felt connected to the text. Whether real or fake, written by a knight or not, this book could have guided one of his ancestors. Holding it gave him hope for himself.

Lionel continued to flip through the pages, sometimes pausing when a word or phrase caught his eye, but mostly scanning them without reading. The book was written in an old style of language, with antiquated sentence structures and wasteful embellishments on the letters. *All that ink and paper they could have saved.* When the whole pages ended and the cutout section that hid the key began, Lionel took greater care in turning each page. Still, he found nothing useful. He sighed and started to close the book, when he noticed a marking.

Through the thin paper of the page, Lionel saw faded spots where a dark-gray scrawl had bled through the margin. He turned the page to reveal a handwritten note, carefully transcribed in what had once been black ink. Time seemed to stop around Lionel—even the candle flame ceased its flickering—and he stared at the note with bated breath. It was written in the same style as the book, with excessive flourishes and an old-fashioned cadence. While it was possible that a more recent ancestor might have emulated the style, the effortlessness of the words made Lionel think they had been written by someone from the world before, or at least by one of the first or second generations to live on the *Queen Hildegard*.

Lionel squinted at the text and tried to discern the basic letters hiding beneath the intricate handwriting. The author had connected each letter to the next—a technique called curling or curstive or something—Lionel couldn't remember. It took him a few moments to sort out what he had to do, but once he did, that all-too-familiar dread crept up his spine.

One must scour every inch of QH to find the lock. It will take time.

❧

MINUTES LATER, Lionel stood in front of the door to the royal library. Clothed only in his robe and pajama bottoms, with *The Key to the Kingdom* cradled in the crook of his arm and the candle held in his trembling hand, he wrapped his fingers around the cold brass handle and pushed the heavy door open. It glided inward without a sound, and candlelight spilled into the space.

With a deep, unsteady breath, Lionel stepped into the room. His fingers slid along the wall, searching for the first lantern. He found it a few feet in, lit the candle from his own, then repeated the process, feeling his way across the bookshelves to the empty patches of wall where the lanterns hung.

Once he had lit them all, Lionel allowed himself to look at the library in full.

It was smaller than he remembered. That fact alone eased some of the tension in his chest. He crossed the well-worn carpeted floor to the center of the room and placed his candle and the book on the low wooden table. As children, he and Lady Greyson had been tutored at that table, along with Theo when King Archon had felt generous. But that was only for the beginning of their schooling. After his mother died, Lionel had demanded their tutor move the lessons to his private chambers.

Lionel turned and walked to the bookshelf nearest the door, making a wide berth around the two armchairs across from the tutoring table. As he reached the bookshelf, he instinctively grabbed onto the rolling wooden ladder and stepped onto the first rung. The wood creaked under his weight, and Lionel frowned—not only was he probably too heavy for the ladder as an adult, but he realized he no longer needed it. He could easily reach the top shelf, which had once seemed as high as the wispy desert clouds, by standing on tiptoe. With a sigh, Lionel rolled the ladder aside, and it suddenly felt as distant to him as all the other memories he kept locked in the library.

A thin layer of dust covered the shelves, but not as much as Lionel would have expected to accumulate over the months since his father's execution. *The staff must still clean in here.* He browsed the subjects, each stamped on a small plaque on the edge of the shelf. *Anatomy. Biology. Ceremonies.*

Lionel rolled his eyes, making a note to return to that shelf later. Still focused on the key, he sidestepped along each tall bookshelf, his hands clasped behind his back like a window shopper avoiding the temptation of purchase. The cogsmithing and engineering shelves were empty, and Lionel smiled as he thought of those books tucked safely away in Aya's sitting room.

Etiquette. Forestry and Hunting. Journals. Literature.

That section went on for several shelves, and Lionel skipped over them without letting his eyes rest on any particular book. He had read, or rather listened to, many of them as a child and couldn't bear to get sucked in by them. He walked faster.

Meteorology and Modification. Obstetrics. Royal lineages. Ship-building.

There. He crouched down to examine the shelf. Most of the books detailed the craft of shipbuilding itself, but he remembered that at least one described the building of the *Queen Hildegard* and contained a blueprint of the ship. In the handwritten note, *QH* had to mean the palace, and what better way to know every inch of it than to start at its construction?

Squinting in the candlelight, Lionel scanned the titles. Halfway through the shelf, he found the one: *Her Majesty's Ship, Queen Hildegard: Design, Construction & Voyage.* With shaky hands, Lionel slid the book out from the shelf and blew the dust from the finely cut pages. His fingers traced the title on the cover, embossed in metallic gold letters. Each one turned brighter under his touch, practically glinting in the flickering orange glow, and Lionel felt as if the book were sighing with relief. Finally, after years on the shelf, someone had come along to rescue it from uselessness.

Lionel stood and carried the book over to the tutoring table. Still inspecting the cover, he pulled out his former chair and sat down. With a yelp at the sensation of falling, Lionel landed in the chair—much nearer to the ground than he had expected. His knees bent nearly to his chest, and he realized, with an embarrassed laugh, that the chair was made for children. *Of course I can't sit here anymore.*

Standing once again, Lionel pushed in the wooden chair and turned to the armchairs. As he stepped toward them, the hairs on the back of his neck prickled. *Stop being foolish. They're just chairs. You're the king, for goodness sake.*

He wouldn't sit in the lavender one—no, that one belonged to the queen—but he eased himself into the blue one. Like everything else in the library, this seat had shrunk with the years. For some reason, he couldn't think of himself as having grown.

The book opened with a cracking sound and a small puff of dust. Lionel blew on the pages again, noting that they appeared as yellowed and fragile as the ones from *The Key to the Kingdom*. If the books were around the same age, that made it more likely that the handwritten note referred to this one. It was a stretch, Lionel knew, but it was also his only lead.

As he had with the first book, Lionel checked over the table of contents then leafed through the pages. The beginning of the book detailed the life of the architect and his intentions for the design—*to build the world's largest steamship, one built to last through the ages.* Then the subject changed to the construction of the palace, from technical instructions to illustrations of machinery and individual portions of the ship. *Aya would love this—I'll have to show it to her later.*

In the center of the book, Lionel found what he'd hoped. Two folded pages read, *H.M.S. Queen Hildegard: Blueprints.* Resting the book flat on his lap, Lionel unfolded the pages, carefully so as not to rip the worn creases. As the palace took shape before his eyes, Lionel couldn't help but smile. He looked up at the lavender chair before him with an instinctive craving for approval then frowned and shook his head. *She's not here, you imbecile.*

Once again feeling the emptiness in the room, Lionel turned his attention back to the blueprints. He wasn't sure why they were called blueprints—the paper that held them was larger than the rest of the book but still the same yellowed color as the other pages. They contained several diagrams. Two showed the palace from the port and starboard sides, while the others each showed a different level from a bird's-eye view. None of them offered a complete picture of the ship, but together, they showed all the levels and the bulk of the rooms.

Lionel found the top view that showed level seven. Toward the bow of the ship, he found the royal chambers—labeled *Her Majesty's Quarters*—and the round greeting hall that rested outside them. To the side of that area, where the fake bookcase currently sat, two short lines indicated the secret hallway. It was labeled, *Deck Access.* But that was it. No reference to the mysterious door or indication that a room existed beyond it. From there, the map showed empty space leading to the bow of the ship until it met up with the boundaries of the rooms from the starboard side. A quick glance at the diagram of level six showed Lord Collingwood's secret room. *The blueprints must reveal the hidden areas.*

Lionel's brow furrowed as he considered the blueprints. *Maybe the door is simply a patch left over from the construction of the bow. That would explain why there's no handle… but then why are there no similar patches elsewhere?* He tapped his finger on the empty space. *Or maybe whatever lies beyond is too important to label on the blueprints. Perhaps, like the key, it was hidden from everyone but the ruling monarch.*

As Lionel considered the implications, bright light flooded the room. He held up his hand to shield his eyes, only to be met with a loud shriek.

"Oh, Your Majesty! Please forgive me." A maid stood silhouetted in the doorway, the pink light of early morning framing her figure. Once Lionel's eyes adjusted, he noticed that she was covering her eyes with a dust rag.

Lionel peered down at himself and fastened his robe tighter to cover his bare chest. "It's all right. Please come in."

"O-okay." The maid tiptoed into the room, her eyes still shielded.

Lionel chuckled. "I'm decent now. I apologize for startling you."

The maid lowered her arm, revealing a pale and lightly wrinkled face. "I should have knocked." She offered the customary curtsy then rose on uncertain feet. "It's just… well, the library is always…"

"Empty." Lionel looked down again and busied himself with folding the blueprints back into the book. "I thought I would be finished before anyone came to clean. I guess I lost track of time."

The maid nodded. "Would you like me to come back later?"

"No, that's fine." Lionel closed the book. "I'm done." As he moved to put the book away, the maid started dusting the bookshelf nearest the door. When he rose, Lionel noticed her glancing at him over her shoulder. "Am I making you uncomfortable, being in here while you work?"

The maid shook her head. "Of course not." She spoke more to the shelves than to him. "I'm embarrassed to have interrupted you. I knew you came in here occasionally. I just never knew when."

Lionel frowned. He hadn't, in fact, visited the library since he was a child. "If you've never seen me reading, how do you know I visit?"

The maid's eyes widened, and a blush crept up her neck. "Pardon me, Your Majesty, this is going to sound… well, it's not like I pry. It's just, sometimes certain spots on the shelves are clean, where you've pulled books out. You notice these things in my line of work, or at least, I notice them."

"No, not at all." Lionel arched an eyebrow and sent a nervous glance toward the study table. "In fact, I think it speaks to the quality of your work that you'd pay attention to details like that. Does a lot of dust gather between your cleanings?"

The maid sighed. "We can't escape it, all that sand and dirt. Even in a week, the shelves are always lined with dust again."

Lionel nodded then moved to the study table to retrieve his candle and *The Key to the Kingdom*. As he gathered his belongings, the maid glanced at him once more. He caught her eye, and that time, she smiled.

"May I speak frankly, Your Majesty? There's something I've always wanted to say to you." The maid turned around and waited for Lionel to nod. When he did, she wrung the dust rag in her hand. "When I was about your age, I was one of Her Highness, Queen Lisandra's handmaidens."

Lionel felt his body stiffen but tried to keep the surprise from his face.

"She was a wonderful woman and a gracious queen, your mother. I know how much she adored you." The maid's voice cracked. "Sometimes, when I finished my duties early, I would linger in the doorway and listen to her read to you."

Lionel put a fist over his mouth. It was exactly what he had been trying not to remember.

The maid's face turned paler. "I'm sorry. I know that it was wrong to eavesdrop. Her Highness just... she had such a lovely, expressive voice."

Lionel moved his hand away and offered a small smile to show the maid that he wasn't mad. "Yes, she did."

"Whenever I dust the library, I think of Her Highness and how kind she was to me." The maid ran her rag over the bookshelf as if to demonstrate. "You must be grateful to have this place. It must hold so many nice memories for you."

Lionel's brow furrowed. He had never thought about the library that way before. For him, it had always brought to mind what he had lost, not what he'd had. "Thank you." Lionel paused and swallowed the emotion in his voice. "Now that I think about it, it does."

The maid returned to her dusting, and Lionel made to exit. As he reached the door, he paused and turned back to her. "I didn't catch your name."

"Mrs. Maude Butler, Your Majesty." She curtsied again.

"It was nice to meet you properly, Mrs. Butler." Lionel inclined his head. "Please don't feel guilty or awkward about noticing what I read. Like you said, it's part of your job."

"I won't, Your Majesty. Thank you."

With a final nod, Lionel walked out of the library, leaving the door open behind him. With every step he took back toward his chambers, an unease grew tighter in the pit of his stomach. Someone had been visiting the library since King Archon's execution. It might have been Zedara taking liberties with her queen dowager title, or perhaps Eldric had been researching royal duties in Lionel's stead. Or maybe one of the other palace staff had a harmless interest in science or literature. Lionel wished he could have asked Mrs. Butler what books had been read without raising her suspicion.

Regardless, Lionel needed to find out who had been

snooping around the library. If it were a friend or innocent knowledge seeker, he would allow them to keep visiting. But if someone was searching for answers—be they secret passage-ways or keys hidden in ancient tomes—Lionel had to stop them. For all he knew, the security of his crown, or even the entire kingdom, could depend upon it.

8

———

*A*s Lionel stood waiting on the palace deck, a thin sheen of sweat broke out along his forehead. Though the sun had begun to set over Portside, its rays still cast a hot glow over Desertera. Lionel told himself to appreciate the warmth while it lasted, as when night fell, he would wish for more sunlight.

The double doors to the deck opened, and Zedara and her maid, Sybil Tanner, stepped out into the fading light.

"How are you ladies this evening?" Lionel offered the customary bow. "I hope your walk from Starboardshire was pleasant."

Zedara curtsied. "Great, actually. We let the horses do the walking."

"Really?" Lionel turned to Sybil as she rose from her curtsy. "How do you like riding, Miss Tanner?"

"I love it, Your Majesty." Sybil blushed, and Lionel tried not to smile at her girlish crush. "Any excuse to ride is always welcome."

"I'm just grateful to be out of the house." Zedara looped her arm through Lionel's and led him toward the dinner table, which waited in its normal place near the center of the deck. "If my father allows one more ridiculous nobleman to propose to me, I think my head will explode."

Lionel chuckled, and he heard Sybil snicker behind them.

"This makes number three, doesn't it? Who dared ask for your hand now?"

"The widowed Lord Aster, Duke of the Bilge." Zedara mocked the nobleman's haughty tone. "Do you know his daughter is nearly my age?"

"She's friends with my cousin." Lionel raised his eyebrows. "Not that you aren't a desirable bride, but I wonder why the duke thought he had a chance with you? Yes, you've been widowed too, but you're still young and childless. You may as well be a maiden."

Zedara rolled her eyes. "My father said it's because I've already turned down two suitors. He thinks that the more I turn down, the less prestigious my options will become."

"Could you play the grieving widow card?"

"Not for a second." Zedara smirked. "I'm pretty sure I blew my shot with that when I helped send my husband to execution."

Lionel scratched the back of his neck with his free hand. "Does your father know?"

"That I can only love women or about Isadona?" When Lionel shrugged, Zedara shook her head. "I haven't told him about either outright, but even if I did, it wouldn't matter. He wants me to continue the family line."

"Would you?" Lionel couldn't hide the skepticism in his voice. "With the repeal of the adultery law, you could do your duty as a wife and have a female lover."

Zedara scoffed. "If the situation were reversed, would you marry and bed a man?"

Lionel cringed.

"I thought not." Zedara pursed her lips. "My father could force me into a marriage. He has that right—unless you feel like changing that law as well, not that I'm asking. It might not be horrible with a good man, maybe someone of the same orientation." Zedara's gaze drifted across the horizon. "But I won't love again, man or woman. I had my one."

Lionel squeezed Zedara's arm but let the conversation

come to a close. Even if he knew what to say, it wouldn't comfort his friend or change her situation.

The pair reached the table, already set with plates, cutlery, glasses, and a carafe of water resting atop a crisp white tablecloth. As his mother had taught him, Lionel pulled out Zedara's chair for her. She smiled her thanks and sat, smoothing out her skirt around her. Lionel stepped around the table and pulled out the seat next to Zedara. "Please join us, Sybil."

The maid held up her hands. "I shouldn't."

"Probably not, but since when do the three of us stand on ceremony?" Lionel pulled out the chair another inch.

Sybil grinned and allowed him to seat her. "Thank you, Your Majesty."

"You're welcome." Lionel took his own seat across from Zedara.

The palace doors swung open again, and Stefan Chef came bustling out, a line of cooks in tow. Each carried a covered silver tray.

Sybil gasped. "Oh, my."

"See why we need you here?" Lionel winked. "There's no way Zedara and I could eat all that by ourselves."

Zedara chuckled. "But Stefan will make us try."

"You know me so well, Your Highness." Stefan stood along the empty side of the table and clapped his hands together. "I do apologize. Had I known this dinner was for three, I would have prepared more food, Your Majesty."

Lionel waved his hand. "I'm sure you made plenty, Stefan."

"Though you limit my portion sizes, Your Majesty, I'm sure your mouth will still water at tonight's feast." Stefan inclined his head toward his staff, and they each removed the lid from their trays.

Instead of admiring the food, Lionel glanced at Sybil. Her hazel eyes widened, and she leaned forward, toward the dishes. Lionel caught Zedara peeking at Sybil as well, and the two shared a smile. Sybil didn't speak about her childhood, but Lionel knew her time at the Rudder had ended with abuse, despite Dellwyn's attempts to shield her. He hoped that by following Zedara's lead and treating her more as a friend than a maid, he could offer some small recompense for her struggles.

Stefan snapped his fingers to reclaim their attention. "Dinner will start with a simple salad. For the main course, you'll have a leg of lamb with rolls and cooked vegetables." He paused, giving his mustache a playful twirl. "And for the grand finale, blueberry yogurt, made from fresh goat's milk."

"Everything looks delicious." Lionel's stomach rumbled, as if to agree.

"It is my pleasure, Your Majesty, Your Highness, Miss." Stefan bowed to each of them. When he rose, he held out his arm, and the staff placed the dishes on the table. "Please enjoy yourselves. If you need anything, my staff will be waiting inside."

"Thank you, Stefan," Lionel said.

After a final bow from the chef and his staff, the cooks filed back into the palace and left the trio alone to savor their meal. They took turns filling their plates in amicable silence, and Lionel considered how he might bring up the topic of the library. Earlier in the day, he'd asked Eldric whether he still used the library, and the valet had replied in the negative. If Zedara wasn't visiting it to read, then Lionel would have a real reason to be concerned.

Zedara dabbed her mouth with a cloth napkin. "I'm surprised you asked us to dinner."

Lionel frowned. While he did have an ulterior motive, he appreciated Zedara's company and didn't want her to feel used. "Why wouldn't I? We're still friends, aren't we, Stepmother?"

Zedara narrowed her eyes. "Of course. I meant, aren't you worried that dining with me and Sybil will perpetuate the rumors about us?"

"Oh." Lionel shook his head. "Not really. The whole of Portside saw me courting Aya yesterday. I figure that will take the heat off you."

Sybil covered her mouth to hide her chewing. "So *that* rumor is true."

Lionel's shoulders slumped. If news of his impromptu speech had reached the Starboardshire maids, it might already be circulating around the palace.

"What rumor?" Zedara straightened in her chair. "Did you get caught romancing in the street?"

"Not with Aya." Lionel smirked at Zedara's furrowed brow. "But I'm sure many will say I was letting Rykart Farmer romance me. He held one of his sermons, and I got caught in the middle of it."

Zedara took a slow drink of her water. "You spoke to him, didn't you?"

"Him…" Lionel felt himself blush. "And all the villagers gathered."

"Gracious, Lionel, how stupid are you?" Zedara ran her fingers through her blond hair. "The bishop is going to be livid."

"I didn't have a choice." Lionel tried to act casual by taking a slow bite of his lamb. "Besides, Aya and Theo said I gave a fine speech."

Sybil reached out a tentative hand and patted Lionel's arm. "I'm sure you did."

Lionel rewarded her with a wink. "Thank you, Miss Tanner."

"Well, don't tell me anything else." Zedara pointed her fork at the king. "If I have any more details, the bishop will think I'm an accomplice. My father already has him sniffing around to guilt me about remarriage. My reputation can't bear another social crime."

"Don't worry. I'm sure he'll demand a council meeting and force me to tell all of you the gritty details." Lionel shrugged. "Maybe Miss Baker will stand up for me. I really think I made a good impression on the villagers."

Sybil nodded. "I'm sure you did. The Rudder workers like you, since you've made their lives safer and let Dellwyn run things. Everyone else will come around. Some Starboardshire workers already have."

"Well, that's good to hear." Lionel's heartbeat quickened. *This is my chance.* "I've been trying to make more of an effort. I even went to the library this morning."

Zedara arched an eyebrow. "Really?" If she realized what the experience had meant to Lionel, she didn't show it. Eldric hadn't said anything either, but he had watched Lionel more closely for the rest of the day, which gave the king the impression that he knew. "Did you learn anything helpful?"

"A few things." Lionel paused to chew. *Just that the secret room I always thought existed probably isn't real—or it's even more dangerous than I imagined. Oh, and I discovered the location of every other hidden chasm in the palace.* "Have you been to the library lately?"

Zedara frowned. "Why would I? I'm not queen anymore… well, not really. The royal corridor isn't for me."

Shit. Lionel tried to keep his face neutral. *If Eldric and Zedara haven't been using the library, that means someone is sneaking around.* While logic reminded Lionel that the person might simply be a curious scholar, the tightness in his chest told him otherwise.

"What was that?" Sybil straightened and cocked her ear toward Portside. "Did you guys hear something?"

Lionel and Zedara replied that they hadn't.

"Listen." Sybil held out her hand and made a patting motion, as if she could quiet the world around them. "It's coming from Portside, or maybe Bowtown. It sounds like a loud group of people."

Lionel and Zedara locked eyes. A large gathering in Desertera, especially in the villages, rarely meant anything good.

The trio rose from the table and crossed the deck to the Portside railing. As they approached, the cacophony of voices grew louder, but from that height, it remained incomprehensible. Sybil rushed to the railing, grabbed on, and leaned over to peer farther down the ship.

At seeing the girl half hanging over the railing, Lionel froze. His heart hammered in his chest, and a cold sensation flooded his veins. It was all real again—his mother arching her body over the distant ground, his father stalking toward her, a glimpse of her shoe as she fell headfirst, then a dull and deafening thump.

"Sybil, get back!" Zedara clutched the maid's elbow and pulled her down from the railing. With a worried glance at Lionel, Zedara shook Sybil by the shoulders. "What were you thinking? You could have slipped."

Sybil's face flushed. "I'm sorry. I wanted to see better."

Lionel took a deep breath. "Let's move closer to Bowtown. Maybe Sybil can see there without putting her life in jeopardy."

Sybil walked on ahead, but Zedara lingered back with Lionel. "Are you okay?"

Lionel cleared his throat. "I'm fine."

Zedara touched his arm. "Is it difficult for you? Being up here?"

"Not as much as other places." Lionel rubbed his temple. "The deck is so large that I can separate it into sections in my head. As long as I stay away from the railings, especially near where... then it doesn't bother me too much. It's the only place I can be safely outside."

Zedara sighed. "I understand." She squeezed his arm then hastened to catch up with Sybil.

The ladies stood at the railing, but Lionel stopped a step behind them. His height still allowed him a decent view, and what he saw made his stomach turn. A mass of people had gathered under the anchor chain that stretched down from the deck, next to where the trio stood, marking the border between Portside and Bowtown.

Although the villagers appeared small from his vantage point, Lionel could make out the distinct differences in the group. On the Bowtown side, the individuals formed a black cluster—farmers dressed in their traditional dark attire. The other part of the group appeared to be a mixture of merchants. Lionel could see white bakers' and butchers' aprons and the tan leather protective gear worn by blacksmiths, tanners, and others who worked with hazardous tools. Among them were splashes of muddy red—wellmen. And in between both lines were patches of dark brown—the leather armor worn by guards.

"What's happening?" Sybil's voice came out breathy.

Lionel thought about Rykart's cryptic words, and a chill slipped down his spine. *What has he done?*

"I don't know." Zedara glanced back over her shoulder. "Lionel?"

The king shook his head and walked farther toward the bow. With squinting eyes, he surveyed the edges of Bowtown, where Rykart had set up a camp for his followers. Lionel could see the ramshackle tents but no people. *Are they too far away to see, or are they the ones causing trouble?*

Zedara joined him. "What are you looking at?"

"The farmer's camp." Lionel pointed toward it.

Zedara narrowed her eyes. "It looks empty."

Lionel nodded. "That's what I was afraid of."

"Hey!" Sybil shook her hand over the railing, the way Lionel had seen noblewomen frantically gesture toward spiders. "They're fighting now."

Lionel and Zedara rushed to Sybil's side. In his concern for his people, Lionel pushed through his fear and stood against the railing, grasping it with both hands to combat the sensation of falling. Sure enough, the cluster of villagers had morphed from two divided lines into a mash of bodies and colors. The noise, though still distant, grew louder. Lionel squinted against the light of the setting sun and could just make out the flailing of limbs.

"I should alert more guards." Lionel's voice didn't sound like his own. It sounded timid, faraway, like an echo from a long-dead monarch.

"You don't need to. Look." Zedara pointed down the side of the ship.

Lionel craned his neck to see the Portside gangway lowering from the side of the palace. When the metal bridge hit the ground, a stream of guards flowed out—both palace guards and the guards supported by various noblemen. Lionel let out a breath of relief. Theo must have been on top of the situation.

The guards jogged toward the mob and circled around it. A few of the villagers near the edge of the brawl must have noticed the impending intervention, for they backed away from the crowd and were allowed to slip out between the guards. The rest of the group kept fighting, even as the guards closed ranks around them.

Lionel's jaw clenched as the guards subdued the villagers. With the sun partially blocked by the horizon, the shapes of the people became more blurred. Lionel saw the guards cut through the crowd, tearing people from the mob and casting them back out into the village. In the center of the group, bodies jostled against each other, and Lionel watched as people left the swarm in twos. These pairs stayed nearby, and Lionel realized that the guards had begun to arrest villagers.

Footsteps sounded on the deck, and Lionel turned to see Theo striding toward him. When the captain reached the king, he made a low bow. As he rose, his eyes drifted over the side of the railing. "My men should have the rioters subdued in the next few minutes, Your Majesty."

"Thank you, Theo." Lionel glanced down at the crowd. Some villagers ran away of their own volition, no doubt to avoid detainment, while others stayed and struggled against the guards. "Are you making arrests?"

Theo placed his hands on the railing. "I've ordered my guards to hold the likely instigators until you decide what to do with them."

Sybil slid over and stood next to Theo, her eyes wide and alert. "Are you going to throw them in the dungeon?"

Theo clasped his hands behind his back. "I'm going to do whatever King Lionel commands. That's my job."

Sybil looked over her shoulder at Lionel. "What will you do with them, Your Majesty?"

Lionel rubbed the back of his neck. "Well, first I need to know what started the fight."

"Some of the farmers decided not to sell their crops to

Sternville residents and certain merchants." Theo nodded toward Bowtown. "It's the work of that prophet."

Zedara's nose wrinkled. "Why would the farmer want to deny people food? Aren't religious types supposed to be charitable?"

Lionel scoffed. "Is the bishop charitable?"

Zedara rolled her eyes. "Fair point."

Theo turned to face the king. "According to my men and the latest rumor, the prophet has convinced some of the farmers to stop selling their crops to anyone he deems unfaithful. That would include all Sternville residents and any merchants who refused to stop serving Sternville residents."

Rykart said the people of Sternville would starve for salvation. He must have meant that literally.

Lionel's brows knitted together. "What about merchants who have noble landlords or patrons? You know, those he chastised in his speech yesterday."

Theo shrugged. "I haven't heard anything. I'll instruct my men to ask about it. We'll need to interview witnesses and participants, anyway."

Lionel tugged at his jacket. The nightly chill had started to descend. "Do you know how the violence started?"

"Apparently, a group of wellmen decided to head to Bowtown to take the food by force. Some of the angry merchants joined them, and the farmers met them at the border." Theo gestured toward what was left of the crowd. "I don't think any one person can take the blame."

Lionel nodded. "Well, I could have them all arrested for inciting a riot, but that won't solve the problem, and a period in the dungeon will only make things worse on their families."

Zedara tucked a strand of hair behind her ear. "Plus, if you garnered as much goodwill in Portside as you claim, detaining merchants will erase all of it."

Theo straightened to his full height. "You can't let them all go unpunished, Lionel. If you do, everyone will think they can resort to violence without consequence."

"You're both right." Lionel weighed his options, and his

mind felt heavier with every second he pondered. "Okay, let's meet in the middle. Have your guards throw everyone they've arrested in the dungeon for one night, but don't tell the prisoners that's all it is. The guards have my permission to scare them a bit—nothing physically violent, of course. Then, when they release the prisoners in the morning, make sure it's clear that I am showing them a great mercy that will not be repeated."

Theo crossed his arms. "That takes care of the riot, but what about the farmers withholding their crops?"

Lionel's shoulders slumped. "I don't think I can do anything about that."

"Why not?" Sybil gestured from his head to his feet. "You're the king."

"Fine. I *can* do something about it. In fact, my father would have, which is why I won't." Lionel gazed out over Portside. The village was dark, save for the faint glow of candlelight and the steady light from the portable generator that Aya had repaired for the midwives and village doctors. Another subject was coming into his kingdom—or preparing to leave it.

"The farmers who own their land are private business owners," Lionel continued. "They can sell their crops and animal products to whomever they choose. Withholding goods makes them cruel but not criminals."

Theo and Zedara frowned, but their eyes told Lionel that they accepted his interpretation of the law.

"As for the tenant farmers, that depends on their agreements with their noble landlords. Some noblemen allow the farmers to sell the goods as they see fit. Others prefer to determine crop prices and broker deals with the customers themselves, and the farmers simply grow and deliver the goods." Lionel shook his head. "Either way, it's up to the noblemen to decide how to handle any violations of the tenants' agreements. If they want my help, I will gladly give it, but it's not my place to reprimand their employees."

"I should be getting back down there." Theo bowed. "I'll give my guards your orders, Your Majesty. Would you like me to have a messenger sent around Starboardshire when we find out if any of the arrested farmers have landlords?"

"In the morning." Lionel rubbed his eyes. "This doesn't need to spread any farther tonight. We'll all have clearer heads tomorrow."

"As you wish." With another quick bow, Theo turned on his heel and strode back into the palace.

The trio stood in silence for a long moment.

Finally, Sybil broke it. "Do you think it's safe to ride back to Starboardshire?" She fiddled with a lock of her copper hair.

"I'm sure it is." Zedara wrapped an arm around Sybil and squeezed her shoulders.

Lionel offered a reassuring smile. "All the trouble was on the other side of the palace, but if you're concerned, tell one of the gangway guards to escort you home on my behalf."

Sybil nodded.

"Let's head out before it gets any darker." Zedara released Sybil and gave Lionel a hug. "I daresay I'll see you tomorrow."

As they parted, Lionel rolled his eyes. "I'm sure you will. Hopefully, not too early. I haven't slept well the past few nights."

Zedara smirked. "Well, rest up, Your Majesty. You'll need all your strength to battle the council."

Lionel shook his head. "You'll back me up?"

"No matter how foolish." Zedara chuckled, but her face softened when Lionel winced. "Always."

"Thanks."

The trio entered the palace together then parted ways when the corridor forked off to the east and west. As Lionel walked back to his chambers, his feet felt heavier with each step. While the knowledge that Zedara would stand up for him offered some comfort, perhaps enough to allow his troubled mind a few hours of rest, it wasn't the comfort he craved.

More than anything, Lionel wished he could open his bedroom door to find Aya inside, tinkering with her latest creation as she waited for him to come home. He would take her in his arms, soak up her warmth, and she would murmur reassurances in his ear. They would curl up in bed and enjoy each other's embrace, no desperate rushing to make the most of every second together. Then he would fall into a long, dreamless sleep.

Lionel sighed. He knew the future would reward his patience, that he only needed to wait a little while longer, then he could live out his dream. For the time being, he would crawl into bed alone, knowing that he held Aya's heart and that her hand would soon follow.

———

9

The bishop accosted Lionel the moment the king walked into Lord Greyson's parlor. "Your Majesty, we must put an end to the farmer's violent regime at once!"

Lionel clenched his jaw but otherwise refused to satisfy the bishop with a response. All morning, he had steeled himself to face the council, imagining every outburst the bishop might have and forcing his features to stay smooth and calm. He motioned for the other representatives, who had stood upon his arrival, to retake their seats, then he walked over to shake the duke's hand. "Thank you for agreeing to host, Lord Greyson. I'm sorry you have to attend a council meeting while on the mend."

"Nonsense." Against the dark leather of his armchair, Lord Greyson's tan skin appeared even paler than it had when he had first taken ill, and deep shadows hung under his usually bright eyes. "It is my honor to have you all here this afternoon."

The duke's hand was hot and clammy, and it took all of Lionel's self-control not to cringe and wipe his palm on his trousers.

"We appreciate it." Lionel took a seat in the matching armchair next to Lord Greyson's.

A pale-yellow sand-clay vase stood in the middle of the

rectangular coffee table, filled with stalks of tiny, tightly clustered purple flowers that grew at the tips of the stems in a cone shape. Around it, Lady Greyson or the maid had arranged a tea set, painted in the same yellow as the vase. Steam filtered from the pot's spout, but the coordinating cups remained untouched on their saucers. Miss Baker perched on the edge of a sunken velvet couch, between Mrs. Farmer and Zedara. Her eyes kept flitting to the cups, but she held her hands in her lap.

Lionel nodded a greeting to Miss Baker and poured himself a cup of tea. She followed suit, and her lips tugged into a grateful smile. Across from the ladies, Lord Collingwood and Mr. Wellman shuffled as Mr. Chef leaned forward to take the pot from Miss Baker. Lionel sipped his tea to avoid chuckling at the odd sight of the three men seated on the couch. As the tea's warmth spread to his chest, Lionel couldn't help but feel proud at bringing so many diverse people together. At least he'd done one thing right as king.

After everyone had served themselves—except for the bishop, who paced before a massive landscape portrait—Lionel cleared his throat. "As you all know, a fight broke out along the Portside–Bowtown border last night. Captain Laurel Theophilus informed me that the feud began over a handful of farmers refusing to provide their goods to Sternville residents and the Portside merchants who sell to them."

"This is exactly what I feared would happen." The bishop stopped pacing and stood in front of the portrait's center, his small figure framed on either side by thick ancient trees and a wide rushing river. "That *heretic* has brainwashed the farmers. He's going to starve anyone who won't follow his false commandments."

Lord Collingwood stroked his goatee. "If you don't mind my asking, what are the farmer's false commandments, Bishop? You always rail against his heresy, but you've never mentioned any specifics."

The bishop's eyes widened, and Lionel couldn't tell if he were aghast at Lord Collingwood's ignorance or fearful at the prospect of having to explain himself. "Where do I even begin?

He thinks he speaks to the Benevolent Queen directly, when we all know She has stopped speaking to us for our sins. He perverts Her divine laws, using them for his wicked agenda."

Zedara cocked her head to one side, a smile playing at the corners of her lips. "Which is?"

"Obviously, the heretic seeks to overthrow the religious order and banish us all to eternity in this wretched desert." The bishop rolled his eyes. "And of course, the legions of devoted followers who worship him like a god aren't a bad perk, either."

So, the bishop hasn't heard Rykart's true plan. Lionel sneaked a glance at the other council members over the rim of his teacup. The nobles and Mr. Chef seemed to accept the bishop's interpretation, meaning they too probably didn't know that Rykart believed the villagers would receive salvation by breaking away from the nobles.

As for the commoners, Lionel thought he detected a hint of tension in the way they held themselves, but none of them spoke up to correct the bishop. The three had to know Rykart's plan. Mrs. Farmer was his cousin, Miss Baker lived on the street where Rykart gave his Portside speech, and Mr. Wellman caught all the gossip at the well where he worked. Were they staying silent out of fear of the bishop? Or were they simply pretending to ally themselves with the council, keeping their enemies closer as it were? Regardless, Lionel wouldn't expose the truth, either. After the respect Rykart had shown him the other day, he owed the farmer-prophet that much.

Lionel frowned. "I think that's a bit of an exaggeration, Bishop."

"Forgive me, Your Majesty, but how can you say that?" The bishop's hands knotted into fists. "The heretic is trying to starve the entire kingdom!"

Mr. Chef raised an eyebrow. "We don't know that for sure. None of the farmers have denied food to the palace staff."

"Why would they? Didn't you hear?" The bishop raised a ringed finger and pointed at Lionel. "His Majesty is their greatest ally."

The council members reacted with a mixture of gasps and shifting glances. If the implications behind the bishop's statement hadn't been so serious, Lionel might have laughed at the dramatics.

"Bishop, we both know that isn't true." Lionel sipped his tea. "When Rykart Farmer gave his speech in Portside, I found myself trapped in a hostile crowd. I spoke to the people and did my best to create sympathy for the palace and the nobles. All the farmer did was show me my proper respect as his king. It's not my fault if he misinterpreted my words or actions somehow."

Miss Baker set down her teacup. "If I may, Your Majesty…"

Lionel nodded.

"I heard His Majesty's speech, and I've listened closely to the villagers' reactions. After meeting His Majesty, so to speak, the vast majority of Portside believes him to be a fair and honest ruler. The change is striking." Miss Baker's brow furrowed. "It's true that Mr. Farmer also favors King Lionel, but His Majesty never claimed to support him."

Mr. Wellman leaned forward. "I heard the same in Sternville. Everybody's sayin' that His Majesty is tryin' to make things better fer us." His eyes narrowed. "Ain't nobody like that farmer, though."

"Thank you both." Lionel resisted the urge to break into a grin. "I'm glad most of the villagers no longer view the monarchy as their enemy. My job is to provide for everyone, and that's exactly what I intend to keep doing."

"While I'm pleased your little speech didn't ruin your reputation, Your Majesty, you need to be careful." The bishop resumed pacing, his long white robes whipping around his arms and legs. "If you seem too sympathetic to the villagers, they might try to take advantage of your kindness. And worse yet, you might isolate yourself from the nobles."

"As a matter of fact…" Lord Greyson paused as a coughing fit overtook him. One hand clutched his chest, while the other set down his cup and retrieved a crimson handkerchief from his jacket pocket. Lionel noticed that it was stained with dark patches.

What kind of food poisoning would make a man cough this much? And cough up fluids, at that?

"Pardon me." Lord Greyson tucked the handkerchief away. "I've only heard positive remarks about King Lionel's speech to Portside. The nobles appreciate that His Majesty is trying to garner more support from the villagers."

Zedara smiled. "I can report the same."

"But would anyone dare criticize the king in the presence of his family?" The bishop smirked. "And what about the leniency His Majesty has shown the rioters? I'm sure you all know that he released them from the dungeon this morning."

Lionel gritted his teeth and set down his cup. "Would you like me to explain myself, Bishop? Or would you like to keep prattling on as if I'm not in the room?"

The bishop's face hardened. "Please, Your Majesty."

"No one person or group can be blamed for the start of the fight. If I had kept the wellmen and merchants in jail, it would have put their families' well-being in jeopardy, not to mention undone all the goodwill I've created." Lionel paused to gauge the representatives' reactions—a series of respectful nods. "As for the farmers, it is not my place to punish them. According to the law, those who own their land can sell products, or not, to whomever they choose. And those who are tenants must answer to their landlords."

Lord Collingwood tapped the edge of his cup. "That is precisely how I and the other landlords feel about this issue. In fact, His Majesty has already informed the nobles whose farmers have rebelled, and they're taking the appropriate actions."

"Fine." The bishop huffed. "But what about the *heretic*? Is he not at fault for instigating all of this? Should we not stop him before he starves half the villagers?"

Mrs. Farmer straightened in her seat. "Forgive me, Your Majesty, but I don't think it would be wise to punish Rykart. He might have given the farmers bad advice, but he did not force any of them to deny goods to anyone. And besides, not all the farmers in Bowtown believe in Rykart. Most remain loyal to their landlords."

Lionel laced his fingers together. "I'm inclined to agree with you, Mrs. Farmer. While Rykart is clearly attempting to manipulate certain people, he hasn't committed any actual crimes."

The bishop stamped his foot. "That is preposterous!"

"Oh, my! Did I come at a bad time?" Lady Madeleine Greyson bustled into the room, carrying a silver tray filled with goat cheese, fruits, and pastries. Unlike her husband, Madeleine appeared to have recovered from the food poisoning. Her eyes, though still slightly crossed from birth, appeared clear and alert, and her pale skin held a rosy glow. "Please pardon the interruption. I thought you all might be getting peckish." Madeleine placed the tray on the coffee table. As she straightened, she smoothed down her simple gown with her trademark lace gloves. Most noblewomen had long abandoned the fashion trend, but Madeleine had worn gloves for years. Lionel assumed it was her way of setting herself apart from the other ladies.

"Thank you, Lady Greyson." Miss Baker inclined her head toward the vase. "Those flowers are lovely, by the way. I might have to get some to decorate my bakery."

"Aren't they?" Madeleine grinned. "The maid picked them out in the wildflower fields."

Miss Baker nodded.

"Yes, thank you for the refreshments, Lady Greyson." Lionel tried not to frown. More than likely, his cousin had found *herself* hungry for political gossip. Her appetite had given Lionel headaches more than once, but the crowning moment had been when she told Aya that she and Lionel were courting. The idea of romance with Madeleine, cousin or not, sent bile rising up his throat.

Madeleine smiled at the king, wrapping one of her many wild, escaped curls around her finger. "It's no trouble at all. I would have sent the maid in with the tray, but I didn't want her to overhear anything confidential."

"Clever thinking." Lionel dared a moment of informality to touch her bare forearm. No sign of a fever. "How are you feeling, Cousin?"

"Much better. Thank you, Your Majesty." Madeleine moved to stand behind the duke and rubbed his shoulders. "Luckily, I didn't eat as much as Lord Greyson, so the sickness has already left me. Dr. Engel thinks my husband might have caught something new, though, while his body was fighting the initial illness."

"I'm glad to hear you're well, sweetheart." Lord Collingwood took a hunk of cheese from the tray, and the other council members followed suit. "And if Dr. Engel is right, that could explain your horrible cough, Frederick."

Lord Greyson nodded. "I think the worst of it is behind me now." His chest quivered with the effort of withholding another coughing fit. "Another few days, and I'll be back to normal."

"And we're all delighted to hear it." The bishop tapped his foot in quick, impatient beats. "But can we please return to the matter at hand?"

"Of course." Lionel waited for Madeleine to excuse herself, and when she didn't, he turned his signature grin on her. "I apologize, Lady Greyson, but I must ask you to leave the room again."

"Oh, yes, okay." Madeleine fidgeted with her gloves. "First, do you have the time, Your Majesty?"

Lionel pulled his watch from his vest pocket. "Two thirty-eight."

"Thank you." Madeleine leaned down to kiss the duke's cheek. "If you need anything, darling, just shout."

Once Madeleine had disappeared into the drawing room, the bishop resumed his tirade. "The heretic is clearly a threat to Desertera. If he continues at this rate, he'll put Sternville, Portside, and Bowtown into economic travesty, maybe even war."

Lionel held up his hand. "Bishop, I agree that there is serious cause for concern and that we must monitor this situation closely but—"

"Then why won't you act?" The bishop trembled with anger, and he curled his hands into fists again. "Your father, Benevolent Queen rest him, would have executed the heretic without a second thought. Why do you let him live?"

"Because he hasn't broken any laws!" Lionel bit his lip in hesitation, then with a haughty huff that would have made King Archon proud, he continued. "Or perhaps it's because I'm not the one whose power is threatened by him. Maybe I'm the bigger man."

The bishop's face fell, all sign of insolence gone. A touch of guilt gnawed at Lionel's gut for the petty jab, but it was overcome by a warm rush of pride. Lionel had never dared to speak to the bishop—or any rude noble—that way before, but he was tired of being disrespected by his own kind. If the mad farmer-prophet could show Lionel proper respect, so could the bishop.

"Your Majesty, I… Forgive me. Of course you know best." The bishop clasped his hands behind his back, and Lionel wondered whether he had imagined the slight edge of sarcasm in the final statement.

Lionel took a deep breath and fought the urge to apologize for his own outburst. "Thank you, Bishop. Do you have any more concerns to raise before we adjourn?"

To Lionel's surprise, the bishop bowed. "Just one, Your Majesty. Another rumor has gained strength after your speech in Portside, and I hoped you might answer it."

Lionel rubbed his temples. *What else could I have possibly done wrong?* "Go ahead."

The bishop shot a conspicuous glance at Zedara. "Is it true that you were in Portside that day to court Miss Cogsmith?"

Lionel let the question hang between them for a moment. The other representatives avoided looking at both the king and the bishop, probably fearing another outburst or trying to disguise their own curiosity. While every nerve in Lionel's body screamed that his relationship was none of the bishop's business, he knew that it was. Although the queen served as more of a figurehead than a ruler, her character still meant a great deal to the people of Desertera.

Lionel leaned back in his chair, preparing for a barrage of objections. "Do you disapprove of Miss Cogsmith, Bishop?"

The bishop shook his head. "It is not my place to comment on who you court, Your Majesty."

"Indeed it's not, but I'll answer your question, anyway." Lionel ran his fingers through his hair, his voice softening as his thoughts turned to Aya. "The rumors are true. I am courting Miss Cogsmith. As most of you probably know or surmised, our romance began under less-than-ideal circumstances. I think it's important that she and I take the proper time to get to know each other before committing to a marriage, and that's all I will say about it for now."

Lord Collingwood grinned at Lionel, and Lord Greyson clapped him on the shoulder. Zedara leaned over to squeeze his hand, and Lionel returned the gesture with a small smile.

The bishop looked between the queen dowager and the king, disappointment clear in his furrowed brow. He sighed. "Thank you for your honesty, Your Majesty. I hope that when you are ready to seal the engagement, you will seek my spiritual counsel as the kings before you have."

Another wave of guilt washed over Lionel—both for scolding the bishop and for his inability to be a model king and marry a noblewoman like Zedara. His relationship with the bishop had never been perfect, but it had at least been cordial. Lionel suspected that after the meeting ended, it would be more strained than ever. No matter how hard he tried, it seemed as if Lionel would never strike the balance between friendliness and respect.

"Of course, Bishop." Lionel inclined his head. "I would never deny you your duty as our religious leader."

"Thank you, Your Majesty." The bishop fiddled with the end of his sleeves. "Might I make a parting request to the council?"

Lionel motioned for the bishop to continue.

"I apologize for my part in making this meeting tense, but I feel very strongly about last night's act of violence." The lines in the bishop's face deepened, and he looked as if he had not slept in days. "I would ask that we remain vigilant as regards the heretic, especially those of us who live outside of noble society. While his actions may remain *legally* innocent for the time being, I cannot emphasize enough how much they concern me. We would all be wise to learn as much about his beliefs and plans as we can, lest he or his followers catch us by surprise again."

As Lionel watched the bishop's imploring gaze linger over Mr. Wellman, Miss Baker, and Mrs. Farmer, his earlier revelation resurfaced. Whether the council members had taken sides in this religious dispute or not, they'd chosen to withhold Rykart's true cause from the rest of the representatives. They were keeping both the farmer and the council close, hedging their bets and waiting to see who would have their best interests at heart.

The thought sent a jolt through Lionel. For better or worse, he had direct access to the bishop and knew his every religious and practical concern. When it came to Rykart, Lionel had spent weeks relying on reports from Mrs. Farmer and gossip from various corners of the kingdom. Yet he'd learned more about the farmer-prophet during their brief encounter in Portside than he had in countless secondhand conversations. Maybe it was time to sit down and have a proper chat with Rykart.

10

*L*ionel and Eldric strolled along the wide corridor that held the palace's shops. Designed to look like a regular village street, the hallway had two long rows of stores that stood facing each other. Narrow alleyways cut in between them, allowing the merchants a private entrance for goods or workers. Lionel lowered the brim of his top hat to shield his eyes against the bright sunlight that streamed in from the open gangway. Though unpleasant at that time of day, the rays added much-needed warmth to the rigid metal walls and cold marble floors of the ship.

While Lionel preferred to visit the stores in Portside—not just for Aya but also for the semblance of freedom the outside allowed—he still counted his weekly trip to the starboard shops among his favorite duties as king. Surrounding himself with the cheery merchants and bustling nobles made him feel like a true part of Desertera. Hidden away in his quarters or perched high on his throne, he was a body unto himself. Here, he was just another drop of blood coursing through the beating heart of commerce.

"I don't know about you, Your Majesty, but I think a walk through the shops is exactly what I needed after yesterday." Eldric popped the last bite of his scone into his mouth. "Mmm. I could eat these all day."

Lionel grinned. "I agree to both."

While he had invited Eldric along to seek his counsel about meeting with Rykart Farmer, Lionel was glad he could also lift the valet's spirits. Eldric had spent much of the previous day addressing staff rumors about the Bowtown violence and helping make sure commerce ran smoothly as merchants paid their usual visits to the palace through the Portside gangway. Luckily, no one had seen fit to take their hostilities out on the nobles, at least not yet.

"I've said it before, but I'm pleased you decided to keep up this particular tradition, Your Majesty. I think it does the nobles and shop owners good to see you active in the community." Eldric swerved aside to allow a young man carrying a stack of garment bags to pass. "And I must admit, the walking helps my stiff joints."

"Your joints are fine, old man." Lionel chuckled and patted Eldric on the back. "But I like these walks, too. The stores make me feel connected to noble society in a way ceremonies don't—maybe because everyone is in such a good mood from shopping and eating."

Eldric tucked his hands into his pockets. "King Archon used to say the shops offered the best of both worlds. A king could be wholly present among his people and yet still manage to get lost in the hustle."

A coldness crept through Lionel's veins, and he surveyed the crowd through his father's discerning eyes. Sure enough, the nobles offered bows or curtsies as he approached, but once he tipped his hat in reply, they hurried along to the next shop. However, if Lionel feigned interest in a window display or stopped to chat with anyone other than Eldric, the nobles slowed their paces or stalled to retie a shoelace. For what felt like the thousandth time, he wondered how many other little revelations he had been missing as king.

As the pair reached a familiar, mask-shaped awning, Lionel shook the thoughts from his head. "Let's make one final stop before we depart. I'd like to call on Abrim."

Eldric held open the door, and Lionel stepped inside. As his gaze fell on the blue ottoman in the center of the mask shop, he remembered how beautiful Aya had looked seated there. Enveloped in the warm glow of sunlight sifting through the window and surrounded by dozens of false faces, she had seemed at once otherworldly and irresistibly real. It had been the first time Lionel had felt more than lust for her.

Abrim shuffled out of his cramped workspace, his back bent in a permanent bow. "Good afternoon, Your Majesty. What brings you to my shop today?"

Lionel motioned to the mounted displays, only half full. "Thought I'd see how your latest batch of masks is coming along."

"A fine excuse, Your Majesty." Abrim nodded, and his long white beard shimmied against his paint-stained apron. "I have about half of them made, but you can't rush the art. Each mask has its own personality, and I must wait for it to be revealed to me as I craft."

"That's an interesting philosophy. And what do you mean 'excuse'?" Lionel arched an eyebrow. "You make it sound like I have an ulterior motive for visiting you."

"Don't you?" Abrim waved his hand at Lionel's puzzled brow. "Ah, the gift of self-ignorance."

Eldric stepped forward to protest, but Lionel put out his arm to stop him. Abrim lifted a mask from the wall and held it to his face. It was painted like a clock, complete with moving hands that spun around the wearer's nose.

With a delicate but shaky finger, Abrim pushed the hands to form midnight. "This was your favorite shop, growing up. Do you remember why?"

Lionel thought back to his childhood. As a young boy, he had loved to try on different masks and speak in funny voices. Then, when he neared adolescence, he'd enjoyed watching the young women preen in the mirrors, imagining how he would ask them to dance when he grew old enough to attend the masquerade.

"The masks let me be someone else for a while." Lionel's

lips tugged up into a sad smile. "Sometimes I feel like I'm still trying to be someone else."

"And there is your first reason for seeking refuge from the crowd here." Abrim slid the mask's hands to ten minutes before two o'clock. "And the second?"

Lionel rubbed the back of his neck. He had reached this realization all on his own. "Aya."

Abrim winked. "You know more than you give yourself credit for, Your Majesty."

As Abrim put the clock mask back on its peg, Lionel removed his top hat and ran his fingers through his hair. "Can I ask you a question, Abrim?"

The old mask maker turned around with a sly smile. "You *are* the king."

Lionel playfully narrowed his eyes. "Being an artist, studying people and helping them disguise or reveal their true selves, you must be a good judge of character."

Abrim raised his brows. "That is a fact, not a question."

"What do you make of Aya's character?" Lionel pinched the bridge of his nose. "Not of herself, but of her potential as queen? Of us together? Do you think the rest of the nobles are right?"

"That is many questions." Abrim stroked his beard. "I must answer with one of my own. Why do you ask me?"

Lionel frowned. "Well, the bishop expressed his disappointment in my courting Aya yesterday. And I've heard comments from other nobles over the past few months. You're one of the few people who has seen Aya and me together. So I thought, maybe, you might be a good person to ask."

"You're missing the point." Abrim shook his head. "The answer to each of your questions is the same, and the only one who can give it is Aya."

Lionel put his top hat back on. "But you like her?"

Abrim laughed. "You know I do."

With a relieved smile, Lionel gazed out the shop window to see the nobles heading toward the gangway. He checked his pocket watch and confirmed that lunchtime had passed. The bulk of the nobles would be heading back to their homes for an afternoon nap or other restful activities. For a few hours, the palace corridors would stand empty and silent while nobles and staff waited out the hottest hours of the day.

"We should be on our way." Lionel traced his thumb across the back of the watch then tucked it back into his vest pocket. "I'm glad to see that your art is going well, Abrim."

Abrim inclined his head, as much of a bow as the old man could manage. "Thank you, Your Majesty. I always enjoy our visits, whatever the reason. Please come again, and do bring Miss Cogsmith next time. I'd like to hear her answers."

"Me too." As Lionel left the mask maker's shop, something in Abrim's words stuck with him. He locked the idea away in the back of his mind, saving it for when Aya was ready.

Lionel and Eldric returned to the corridor and saw the rush of nobles had slowed to a trickle. A few individuals loitered near the shop entrances, conversing with merchants or wrapping up business deals. Near the gangway, a group of adolescents fidgeted with sunbonnets and suit jackets, clearly torn between the duty of returning home for tutoring and the desire to socialize with the opposite sex. Lionel cringed as he remembered all the tutoring sessions he had skipped to flirt with girls or to explore the palace with Theo. What he wouldn't give to have those lessons back.

The pair strolled past the final shop and emerged back into the main corridors of the palace. As Lionel had hoped, the hallways stood empty.

"Do you care if we take the long way?" Lionel racked his brain for a valid reason and settled on a simplified version of the truth. "I have a lot on my mind, and walking helps me sort through it all."

"Of course, Your Majesty." Eldric clasped his hands behind his back as they ambled along, a sign of self-restraint.

Lionel could sense that Eldric wanted to ask what was troubling him, but he knew the valet would wait for him to share. Eldric's deference benefitted Lionel, as he needed a few moments to gather his thoughts and decide how to broach the subject. In the meantime, the king busied himself with observing the portraits on the walls and the various ancient artifacts that rested along the corridor. His eyes searched each one for a hidden keyhole or other secret use. Despite everything happening with Bowtown, the key remained firmly fixed in Lionel's mind. He figured if he thought on it enough, a revelation would come to him eventually.

"How many secret rooms and passageways do you think the palace holds?" Lionel counted off the few he had personally discovered on his fingers. "I've seen three."

Eldric blew out a long breath. "Many more than that, I'm sure. Most of the noble families who reside in the palace claim to own a hidden chamber, and the staff have special corridors they use to traverse the floors quickly or store clean uniforms."

"Huh. That answers so many questions." Lionel had always wondered how the palace workers seemed to be everywhere at once. His eyes darted around the hallway, and he began to second-guess his plan to seek Eldric's counsel during their walk.

Eldric's forehead wrinkled. "Why do you ask, Your Majesty?"

Lionel considered telling Eldric about the key. After all, if anyone knew what it opened, it would be the king's valet. However, that same nagging sensation held him back. If the key were important enough to hide from everyone else, he should protect it until he learned more.

"Well"—Lionel glanced around the corridor again—"I was wondering where the safest place to talk would be."

"Here is fine." Eldric stopped walking and looked Lionel up and down, as if his secrets were sewn into his clothing. "What did you want to discuss, Your Majesty?"

Lionel steeled himself for Eldric's disapproval. "I would like to ask your advice on something. And to be clear, I'm not asking whether I *should* do it. I'm asking *how* to do it."

There was the look—the same one the valet had given Lionel as a boy. Eldric's eyes narrowed, and his lips pursed so tightly, they disappeared under his mustache. "I'm listening."

"I want to speak to Rykart Farmer directly." Lionel held up his hand to prevent Eldric from interrupting, a power he had not had as a child. "Though Rykart did not participate in yesterday's fight, his request to the farmers made the brawl possible. From what Rykart said in Portside the other day, I think withholding food from Sternville is only the beginning."

Eldric raised an eyebrow. "And what does talking to the farmer accomplish?"

"Maybe I could negotiate a compromise or, if nothing else, figure out what his future plans might be so we can prepare for them." Lionel shrugged. "Rykart showed me a great deal of respect when I spoke to the villagers. I think he would listen to me, if I could talk to him privately."

Eldric resumed walking, his demeanor as carefree as if they were discussing the unchanging weather. His voice, however, deepened under the gravity of Lionel's intentions. "The way I see it, you have three options, Your Majesty. You could summon the farmer to the *Queen Hildegard*, meet him on neutral ground, or venture to his territory. Each presents unique advantages and challenges."

"I don't think I can bring him here." Lionel lifted his top hat to run his fingers through his hair. "If I invite him on friendly terms, it will communicate to the people that I support him and legitimate his cause. But if I drag him here under threat, I risk angering the farmers who support him and ruining any chance of peaceful dialogue."

"My thoughts precisely. Meeting him somewhere in the villages, perhaps at a pub in Portside or at one of your uncle's farms, would give a more neutral impression—not an alliance or an attack." Eldric scowled. "Though I worry holding the visit outside of the palace might make you appear too approachable."

Lionel furrowed his brow. "What's wrong with being approachable? I want to be available for the people."

Eldric sighed. "That's not the same thing. A king who is available listens to his subjects, but there is no expectation that he will bend to their will. A king who is approachable appears to be on the same level as his subjects, and that gives them untoward ideas."

"What do you mean?" Lionel glanced down an open corridor as they walked by. No one in sight. *But is it really empty?*

"If you can be approached, you can be touched. And if you can be touched, you can be hurt." Eldric squeezed Lionel's shoulder—a little tighter than necessary—to prove his point.

Lionel winced and pulled away. "I think you're taking this too literally."

Eldric clasped his hands behind his back again. "Am I?"

Lionel resisted the urge to roll his eyes. "I assume you don't think I should visit the farmer's camp either, then?"

"Of course not." Eldric let out a dry laugh. "Even more so than summoning him to you on good terms, you paying the visit to him would legitimize him as a religious authority and threat to Desertera. Not to mention, it would—"

"Make me look weak. I know." Lionel rubbed the palm of his hand against his forehead, wondering if his brow would ever relax. "I guess it comes down to which is the lesser of the evils."

Eldric sighed. "I'm not going to change your mind, am I?"

"No, but I don't blame you for trying." Lionel smirked. "It's your job to keep me from making stupid decisions."

"Indeed it is." Eldric's eyes appeared distant, as if he were imagining a life in which he didn't have to play caretaker to insolent kings.

Lionel, too, pondered what a normal life would be like, and that was when it hit him. He snapped his fingers. "What if it wasn't me who went to meet with Rykart Farmer?"

Eldric ran his fingers along the top of one of the machines they passed. "Wouldn't sending a proxy defeat the whole purpose of this scheme?"

"It wouldn't really be someone else." Lionel grinned. "It would be me in disguise."

"Oh, Lionel." Eldric stopped walking and screwed his eyes shut. "You can't be serious."

"I am." Lionel nearly shook with excitement. "I'll dress up

like a commoner and meet the farmer somewhere outside of the palace where I'm least likely to be recognized."

"There are so many flaws with this plan that I don't even know where to begin my objections." Eldric crossed his arms. "Why would the farmer agree to meet if he doesn't know that you're the one arranging the meeting?"

"I'll say that I'm an influential merchant who is interested in joining his movement."

"Mhmm." Eldric shook his head. "And if this is all to be secret, how will you exchange correspondence and organize this meeting without telling anyone your plan?"

"You'll do it." Lionel shrugged. "You already know the plan."

Eldric scoffed. "Ah, yes. The king's valet arranging a meeting between an unnamed merchant and a known heretic. That won't raise suspicion at all."

Lionel's chest deflated, and he sighed. "Point taken." Tapping his chin, he considered another angle. "What if we brought Rykart here in secret, then? We could have Dellwyn sneak him into the palace through the Rudder. I could meet him somewhere secluded—the old cargo hold, maybe."

"It's not the worst idea you've presented today." Eldric resumed walking, and Lionel took his movement as a positive sign. They had almost reached the royal corridor, so they needed to decide in the next few minutes. "Two questions. First, what excuse will you use for visiting the cargo hold should someone catch you down there?"

Lionel's brow furrowed. "What if I took Aya along? I could say I'm helping her find more cogsmithing relics. Worst case, people think we're sneaking off for a tryst."

"Again, not the worst thing you've ever done." Eldric pursed his lips. "And I assume it goes without saying that you trust her to stay silent about this meeting."

Lionel nodded.

They rounded a corner and emerged into one of the palace's main corridors. At the end stood the famous statue of Queen Hildegard. On either side of her, the hallway forked.

One side headed toward the stern, the other to the royal family's private chambers, library, and other rooms.

"Final question." Eldric glanced around the corridor to confirm they were still alone. "Why would Rykart agree to go to the Rudder? He must be worried about outside threats, and the people of Sternville have made it clear that he's not welcome there, not even on the outskirts near the palace."

"He'll go for Dellwyn." The conviction in his voice surprised Lionel, but he realized the words were true. "Her stubbornness and commitment to finding Madam Huxley's killer are the only reasons Rykart kept his head. He owes her his life, and he's not one to take that kind of debt lightly."

"Very well." Eldric's shoulders slumped, and Lionel withheld a smile at his victory. "Please give me some warning before you hold this meeting. I'll need to reassign a few staff members to make sure no one is working near the corridors that connect the Rudder and the cargo hold."

Lionel clasped the valet's shoulder. "Thank you, Eldric."

"Don't thank me. I'm only helping to keep you from getting caught." Eldric shook his head. "To be clear, this is an idiotic plan."

"I know it is." Lionel looked up at the statue of Queen Hildegard. The cold stone immortalized the queen in a pose of rigid determination, her eyes narrowed as if staring over a tempest sea. Pride swelled in Lionel's chest, and for the first time, he felt a kinship with his legendary ancestor. "But I'm the king, and my people's lives could be in jeopardy. I have to try."

11

---

*A*s far as Lionel knew, no one had ventured into the cargo hold in years. It took both himself and Aya to wrench open the rusty metal door, and the groan it made sent a shiver down Lionel's spine. The couple picked up their lanterns and held them high above their heads, trying to cast as much light into the cavernous space as possible.

"If I would have thought about how dark it would be down here, I would have borrowed the generator." Aya squinted against the darkness as her voice echoed back to them from distant walls.

"Oh, I don't know." Lionel slipped his arm around Aya's waist, relishing the feel of the soft fabric under his fingertips, and she turned to allow her body to meld against his. "I think it's kind of romantic."

Aya laughed and patted his chest with her free hand. "Of course you do."

Lionel grinned. "What's that supposed to mean?"

Aya playfully rolled her eyes and wiggled out of his grasp. "You know what it means."

Lionel let Aya go, his fingers trailing down her arm to clasp her hand. She squeezed back, and together, they waited in comfortable silence for Dellwyn and Rykart to arrive. When they finally heard footsteps approach, Lionel gave Aya's hand one last squeeze before releasing it.

As Dellwyn and Rykart's forms took shape in the darkness, accompanied by the glow of their own lantern, Lionel straightened his top hat and tugged down the sleeves of his jacket.

"Don't worry," Aya whispered. "Everything is going to be fine. No need to be nervous."

Lionel placed his hand over his heart in mock dramatics. "You're right. It's only a food protest, riot, and potential economic crisis at stake. Nothing serious."

"Hey." Aya nudged Lionel in the ribs. "Why did you ask me to come along if you weren't going to listen to me?"

"I am." Lionel shook his head. "It's all business with you merchants, isn't it?"

"You're damn right it is." Aya winked. "Now, try to act a little less like your Willem self and a little more like your king self."

Lionel smoothed down his jacket. "Yes, ma'am."

Dellwyn and Rykart stepped into full view. Even in the weak light of the lanterns, Lionel found Dellwyn's bright smile contagious.

Lionel inclined his head. "Welcome, Madam Rutt, Mr. Farmer."

Rykart bowed, low and respectful, but otherwise remained silent. He seemed content to gaze around the dark corridor.

The madam curtsied in greeting. "Good evening, Your Majesty. It's good to see you again." As she rose, Dellwyn turned to Aya with a mischievous smirk. "And you too, Your Highness."

Aya narrowed her eyes, but a smile played at her lips. "Oh, starting right in with the wit, are we?"

Dellwyn made an exaggerated shrug, and the two friends laughed and hugged each other.

Lionel couldn't help but grin. He knew how concerned Aya had been about losing Dellwyn's friendship when she moved to Portside. He was glad they'd remained close.

Lionel motioned to the lantern that Rykart held. "Did you find the way all right?"

"Sure." Dellwyn craned her neck to peer past Aya into the cargo hold. "Oh, wow. There's plenty of room to expand the Rudder back here. We'll have to talk about a real estate venture, Your Majesty."

"Next time." Lionel chuckled and turned his attention to Rykart, who still inspected the walls of the corridor. "Mr. Farmer, thank you for accepting my invitation to meet. It seems we have much to discuss."

Rykart's stare shifted to Lionel, and the king's skin crawled. "Words travel only as far as sound. We can see actions from greater distances."

Lionel resisted the urge to groan. "Yes, but words worked well enough to spread the news of your food strike and the fight your followers caused."

"I appease one monarch and anger another." Rykart's shoulders slumped. "If it pleases you, we can try to use our words."

"It does. Let's go inside the cargo hold. Your words will travel better than you think through this tight corridor, and we can't take the risk." Lionel picked up the extra lantern and handed it to Dellwyn. The group entered the cargo hold, and Lionel wrenched the door shut behind them. "Better safe than sorry."

Aya touched Lionel's arm. "If you don't need us, Dellwyn and I will do a little exploring while you chat."

Lionel nodded. "Shout if you need me."

Aya glanced from the king to Rykart. "Same."

"Come on, then." Dellwyn held the lantern aloft. "Let's see how many rooms I could fit in this wasted space."

Lionel chuckled and watched the women wander away. When the darkness obscured their shapes, he turned back to Rykart. "You should know that my council wants me to arrest you, possibly even have you executed for the commotion you've created."

Rykart's face remained still, betraying no surprise or

emotion. It seemed to Lionel that the farmer-prophet's face was the only part that stood before him. With his all-black clothing and the flickering light, Rykart's body melted into the darkness of the cargo hold.

"Doesn't that concern you?" Lionel rubbed his forehead. "Don't you care to live?"

"I will live as long as the Benevolent Queen wants me to live." Rykart shrugged. "When my work has pleased Her, She will retire me. Until then, I must continue."

Lionel pursed his lips. *So, no, then.* "Why did the Benevolent Queen choose you, Rykart? She has never spoken to any bishop, at least as far back as the palace records go. She never makes Her presence felt among Her other children. What makes you so special?"

"I like to think it is because I listen to Her." Rykart cupped a gloved hand to his ear. "But really, I do not know. I must simply trust in Her the way She has trusted in me."

"I see." Lionel pinched the bridge of his nose. *He must be crazy. Why do the other farmers not realize this?* "Did the Benevolent Queen order you and the other farmers to stop providing food to Sternville?"

"Only the farmers who would listen."

"Yes, of course." Lionel shifted his weight, trying to consider another angle from which to approach the issue. "Are you sure you heard correctly? Why would the Benevolent Queen want Her children to suffer? Wouldn't She want you to help them hear Her message?"

Rykart's gaze flitted around the room, as if the goddess might be eavesdropping. He whispered, "You must remember, Your Majesty, the Benevolent Queen destroyed the world out of anger at us. She is showing great mercy and patience by allowing only the wicked to starve."

Lionel crossed his arms to keep himself from shaking the farmer by the shoulders. "Fine. But here is what you must understand. I believe that *you* believe you're doing good for the spiritual well-being of the people."

Rykart bowed. "Thank you, Your Majesty."

"However, it is my job to care for the people's physical well-being. I can't have you starving my subjects and inciting them to riot in the streets."

Rykart stroked his stubbled chin, as if he were considering the king's words. *Finally, we're getting somewhere.*

Lionel uncrossed his arms. "Have you ever heard the phrase, 'you catch more lizards with candied flies'?"

Rykart shook his head.

"It means that treating people well and being kind works better than punishment." Lionel inspected the farmer's face for some sign of understanding. "Your speeches might have worked in Bowtown, but they've been ineffective in the other villages. Likewise, denying food to Sternville residents and some Portside merchants resulted in anger and violence."

"It takes a long time to break a person's spirit." Rykart smiled, which made his words all the more chilling. "They need time to feel the hunger in their bellies, to see their muscles wither, to realize that their denial of Her is the root of their suffering."

Lionel's jaw clenched, and it took several deep breaths before he could formulate an unemotional response. "Mr. Farmer, why did you praise my repeal of the adultery law?"

"Because it gave the people a choice." Rykart placed a hand over his heart. "You allow us to choose fidelity out of desire instead of fear."

"Precisely." Lionel tapped his lips with his forefinger. "And what of your actions? Do they not force the starved villagers to turn to the Benevolent Queen out of fear and desperation? Then what happens when they're fed again? Do you think they will stay loyal to the goddess and prophet who nearly starved them and their families?"

Even in the lantern light, Lionel could see Rykart's face pale. The prophet's hands started to tremble, followed by his arms, his chest, and his entire body. With a mournful cry, he dropped to his knees and placed his head in his hands.

Lionel crouched beside Rykart and took the lantern away from him so that he wouldn't hurt himself. "Are you okay?"

"I can hear Her now." Rykart's voice quavered. "I misunderstood. She didn't want me to starve them. She wanted me to feed them."

Since the farmer's hands still covered his face, Lionel allowed himself an eye roll. *Oh, what a convenient revelation.* "And how will you do that?"

Rykart let his hands fall to his sides. "I will host a feast at my camp for the entire kingdom. Everyone who comes will hear the message of the Benevolent Queen, will be offered the opportunity to regain Her favor and live as She commands."

"Well, that certainly sounds better than what you've been doing." Lionel placed Rykart's lantern on the ground. "But how do you know that anyone will come? Or that those who attend won't use it as a chance for revenge?"

"If they want to fight more, they know where my followers and I live." Rykart wrinkled his nose. "Besides, it takes a cruel person to spit on an apology. I must believe Her children are better than that."

"I would like to think so." Lionel lifted his top hat and ran his fingers through his hair. "Do you mind if I handle the announcement of this feast?"

Rykart shrugged. "It matters not who takes the credit."

"No, I don't want credit." Lionel shook his head. "But I do want to make sure the kingdom understands that you're making an apology. That this is an act of community service."

"A punishment?" Rykart cocked his ear, as if he heard someone whispering to him. "You want the villagers to feel I am sanctioned?"

"Yes and no." Lionel sighed. *What do I want from this?* "People need to understand that you regret your past transgressions and are taking a new course. And honestly, it would be good for my reputation if everyone thought I had some control over your actions—however ridiculous that concept might seem."

"I see." Rykart tapped his temple. "The villagers are more likely to follow me if I serve both monarchs equally."

Lionel let out a surprised chuckle. *That works, too.* "If that is how you see it, then yes."

Rykart scrunched up his face and nodded, like an elder nobleman agreeing on the quality of pipe tobacco. "Leave it to me."

Lionel handed Rykart's lantern back, and the two men rose. "You'll keep me informed, though? Of your plans?"

The farmer bowed. "Completely. I'll use the words you like when all is settled, then the announcement will be made."

Their business concluded, the two men rejoined Aya and Dellwyn farther in the cargo hold. The friends glanced cautiously between the king and the farmer then smiled.

"We found some shit." Dellwyn waved her hand toward a vast expanse of darkness. "Way in the back there. We couldn't see well enough to sort through it with these lanterns, but we'll revisit it when you and I talk property, Your Majesty."

Lionel smirked. "If you say so, Madam Rutt."

"All finished settling the kingdom's problems?" Aya's voice sounded cheery on the surface, but Lionel detected a waver of concern on the last syllable.

"We've come to an arrangement." If the farmer had been anyone else, Lionel might have clapped him on the back to demonstrate their goodwill. As it was, he kept his arms at his sides. "Do you feel good about it, Mr. Farmer?"

"She does, yes." Rykart lifted his gaze toward the ceiling. "She has waited many years for a terrestrial monarch to listen."

Dellwyn scoffed. "Oh, you're talking to Her now, too?"

Lionel put on his trademark smile. "I'm not important enough to speak with Her directly, but we've started a dialogue with our intermediary."

"Shall we go, then?" Aya stepped forward and looped her free arm through Lionel's. "It'll be suspicious if either Rykart or I leave the palace too late into the night."

"It's already going to be suspicious." Dellwyn put her hand over her heart in mock horror. "The prophet and the future queen, both spending hours at the Rudder. Just wait until that gossip hits noble society."

Lionel groaned and led the group back toward the entrance. "Don't even joke about that."

Dellwyn snickered. "Don't worry. I know the owner. She'll make sure they both get out unseen."

"She sounds like a lovely lady." Aya narrowed her eyes at Dellwyn. "Maybe she could teach you some manners."

They reached the entrance then, and Lionel wrenched the door back open. The hinges still whined but not as loudly as before. Dellwyn and Rykart paid their respects and departed, with Aya promising to head to the Rudder shortly after.

Once the pair had disappeared down the hallway and their footsteps faded to silence, Aya turned to Lionel. "How was your conversation really?"

He let out a long breath. "Do you mind if we walk and talk? Or do you need to head back now?"

"I can stay a while longer. I shouldn't leave at the same time as Rykart, anyway." Aya retook Lionel's arm, and the two headed back into the cargo hold. "Let's go this way. To para-phrase the ever-eloquent Dellwyn, we might find some more shit."

"Fair enough." Lionel chuckled, and the couple held their lanterns higher. "For the most part, the conversation went well. Rykart agreed to try more peaceful tactics, and we decided that I would announce them so that it appears I have him under control."

Aya arched an eyebrow. "Was that a good idea?"

"If everything goes according to plan, it will be fine." Lionel kicked a loose scrap of debris into the darkness. "It might not help me with the nobles, but it would likely secure the respect of the villagers."

"Okay." Aya bit her lip. "And if it goes poorly?"

"Honestly?" Lionel winced. "It'll be a good thing that I'm the king, because my title is all I'll have left."

Aya leaned into Lionel's side and squeezed his arm. "And me. You'll always have me."

"Thank you. That's the most important thing." Lionel unlaced their arms so he could tuck a curl behind her ear.

"Though not being the worst king in all of Desertera's history wouldn't be terrible."

Aya's eyes hardened. "You're already not the worst."

"I know." Lionel wrapped his arm around Aya's side and drew her close. He placed a soft kiss on her temple and held his lips there until her brow relaxed once again. *But right now, I'm a damn close second.*

With a sigh, Aya pulled away, and Lionel knew she wanted to change the topic.

"What all is supposed to be down here, anyway?" Aya took a sharp turn to the right and raised her lantern. A black shape rested on the perimeter of the light.

"Not much, I'm afraid." Lionel swung his lantern around to help illuminate the mystery object. "The ship's cargo manifest says most of the items stored here were removed over a century ago, though obviously, a few must remain. Some of them served a practical purpose, while others were stripped for their materials and used to build the villages."

"After looking at this place, I'd believe it." Aya crouched to examine the object. Four metal rings, two large and two small, lay in a heap. Around and between them rested rotted wood, which crumbled against Aya's inquiring touch. "There's a stain on the floor. This must have held liquid, wine maybe."

Lionel frowned and gave Aya his arm as she rose. "It seems strange that they'd leave a barrel behind."

Aya shrugged. "Who knows? Maybe the contents were bad, or it was already busted, and they never bothered to clean it up."

"True, or maybe there's more back with that other shit you two found." Lionel smirked. He rarely cursed, but he knew it amused Aya when he mimicked her and Dellwyn's rougher speech.

Aya grinned and slipped her hand into Lionel's as they walked on. "I haven't had the chance to ask about the council meeting. Did everything go okay? Is that why you wanted to talk with Rykart?"

Lionel's brow furrowed. "How did you know we had one?"

Aya gave him a pointed look.

"Yeah, okay." Lionel shrugged. "I guess it's pretty obvious we'd have one after everything that's happened."

"You're stalling." Aya leaned into his side and kissed his shoulder. "That bad?"

Lionel's chest warmed at the gesture. *How does she always know what I need?* "No, not too bad. It's really just the bishop. He thinks I should have Rykart imprisoned before anything else happens."

"And you don't." It wasn't a question.

"I thought I owed him a chance to explain and negotiate." Lionel traced his thumb in circles over Aya's hand. "Do you think I did the right thing?"

Aya let out a *whoosh*. "We both saw how well my attempts at political cunning worked out. I don't think I'm the best person to give you advice."

"True, but you misunderstand me." Lionel stopped walking and pulled Aya to him so they stood face to face. "I'm not asking the fake ward who nearly got herself executed by playing along with Lord Varick's schemes."

Aya blushed and looked away.

Lionel took her chin in his fingertips and gently directed her gaze back to his. "I'm asking the girl who survived in excruciating circumstances, the woman who charmed me with her passion, and most importantly, the cogsmith who can fix anything with enough study and determination."

Aya's eyes shone with tears, but none fell. She reached up and pressed Lionel's palm against her cheek. "You really think so highly of me?"

"Of course I do." Lionel rubbed his thumb against her skin. "You're the most amazing person I've ever known. I would trust you with any decision because I know you would give it the same care as your craft and the same tenderness as you show those you love."

"I trust you, too." Aya bit her lip. "I know it seems crazy— we've been together such a short amount of time in the grand scheme of things—but when I'm with you, everything feels right. From the moment I met you, I noticed a shift, deep down in my core, as if my life had finally turned back in the proper direction."

Lionel grinned. "I know exactly what you mean. Every moment before you is shrouded in a haze, like the heat shimmering on the horizon."

Aya's voice lowered to a whisper. "And the ones after me?"

"They're fresh and crisp, bathed in the new light of dawn." Lionel pressed Aya's hand to his lips. "Now that we've established how amazing you are, would you answer my question?"

"When you put it like that..." Aya smirked. "I think you made the right decision in meeting with Rykart. I also think you already knew that, whether you admitted it to yourself or not."

Lionel furrowed his brow. "What do you mean?"

"You always do the right thing, Lionel." Aya rolled her eyes in mock annoyance. "Even when the rest of Desertera disagrees and gives you shit for it, you always choose what's right over what's easy."

Lionel shrugged. "There's nothing else I can do."

Aya leaned forward and pressed her lips against his. When she pulled away, she whispered, "And that's why I love you."

A spark danced on Lionel's lips, and warmth spread through his body. In all the months of their courtship, Lionel hadn't dared say those words. He knew that if he spoke them, Aya would reply in kind, and he didn't want her to feel obligated. For once they had been spoken—in Lionel's mind at least —they sealed his and Aya's future together. Hearing Aya say the words made his knees weak with joy.

"I love you, too." Lionel let his lantern fall, the light snuffing out as it clattered against the metal floor. He took Aya's face in both hands and crashed his lips into hers, smiling against the kiss as she returned his enthusiasm. Her lantern fell too, and the two of them stood in darkness, the quiet of the cargo hold pressing in around them.

Lionel entwined one hand through Aya's curls and let the other slide down her body, from breast to hip, before settling tight around her waist. As Aya's arms wrapped around him, a shiver slipped down his spine, but that familiar hunger didn't rouse in the pit of his stomach. For the first time in his life, Lionel was perfectly, blissfully happy to kiss, and only kiss, the woman he loved.

Aya must have felt the same way, because she pulled away and laid her head against his chest. "I'm so relieved I finally said it."

Lionel laughed and stroked her hair. "Me too."

"Why did *I* have to say it, anyway?" Aya playfully slapped him on the chest. "Aren't *you* supposed to woo *me*?"

"Perhaps." Lionel kissed the crown of her head. "But when has our relationship been anything close to normal?"

"Fair point." Aya's breath tickled Lionel's neck as they held each other in the dark. "Promise me that it will always be like this."

Lionel cleared his throat to calm the emotion swelling up in him. "Like this?"

"Honest. Open." Aya sighed. "I know we have a kingdom to run, and I know that means we can't always put ourselves first, but promise me we'll try."

She said we.

Lionel slid his hand from Aya's curls to her cheek, his thumb feeling for her lips in the dark. Once he found them, he leaned down and gave her the tenderest kiss he could stand. "I promise. I love you, Aya."

The corner of Aya's mouth lifted into a smile beneath his thumb. "I love you too, Lionel."

12

---

*L*ionel cringed and resisted the urge to cover his nose with his cravat. The rank, metallic odor of Lord Greyson's vomit had started to make him queasy, but he refused to insult the duke or appear weak. Lord Greyson heaved, and his body contorted into a trembling arch over the side of the bed. A thin stream of blood dribbled from his mouth and splattered into the metal bucket.

"Dr. Engel should be here any moment, Freddy, darling." Madeleine sat on her husband's other side, a wet rag in hand.

Lionel couldn't help but frown at Dr. Engel's name. It seemed so strange to him that the doctor used her profession as a title rather than a surname like the merchants, farmers, and wellmen. He supposed that, centuries ago, it must have been treated as an honorary title, the way the nobles used "Lord" and "Lady" before their family names.

Lord Collingwood paced at the foot of the ornate bed, and Lionel could imagine him wearing a trail into the patterned carpet underfoot. "What is taking her so long?"

"Calm down, Uncle." Lionel glanced at the clock that was perched atop the armoire—his wedding gift to the couple, fixed by Aya, of course. "Madeleine only sent for her an hour ago. If she was with another patient, it might be a while longer."

"Stop fussing over me." Frederick collapsed back against

the colorful pile of pillows—Madeleine had ordered the maid to bring every single one in the estate for the duke's comfort—and took a shaky breath. "It's a cold. That's all."

"I'm sure you're right, darling. Father is just anxious for you to get better, as we all are." Madeleine dabbed the rag against Frederick's forehead. His pallor had grown even paler in the few days since the last council meeting. For once, Madeleine had removed her lace gloves, and Lionel noticed a pink scar on her palm. *She didn't have that as a child. No wonder she always wears gloves now.*

"That's right." Lionel nodded his agreement. In an automatic fashion, he pulled his pocket square out of his jacket, shook it, refolded it, and stuffed it back in his pocket. He knew the action was ridiculous the first time he'd done it, let alone the fifth, but he had to keep his hands moving. It was all he could do.

After a few moments of strained silence, Frederick heaved again. The action must have caught him by surprise, for his eyes bulged and his hands flew to his mouth in shock. Luckily, he only spat a few drops of blood into his palms, and Madeleine wiped them off without a word.

Frederick leaned back and squinted at his wife. "Can you draw the curtain? My head is throbbing."

Lionel hurried over to assist. "You stay there, Madeleine." He pulled the bed's canopy curtain closed behind her, shielding Frederick from the offending light of the candles on the bedside table.

As Lionel retook his spot on the other side of the bed, he heard a knocking sound, followed by footsteps and hushed voices. "I think the doctor has arrived."

Sure enough, the older woman strode into the bedroom with her trademark pigskin satchel in hand. She gave Lionel the obligatory greeting—a bow, not a curtsy, he noticed—then turned to her charge. "Lord Greyson, we simply must stop meeting this way."

The duke managed a chuckle, but it elicited a wet cough.

Madeleine patted his head again with a clean section of the

rag. "Thank you for coming, Dr. Engel. I believe he's far worse than yesterday."

"Of course." Dr. Engel arched a slender gray eyebrow at Lionel and Lord Collingwood. "While I understand you are concerned for Lord Greyson's health, Your Majesty, my lord, the two of you shouldn't be here. From his previous symptoms, I believe Lord Greyson might have developed influenza, and it is highly contagious."

Lionel smiled, tight-lipped. "We'll take our chances."

Lord Collingwood nodded his agreement.

"Very well. My conscience is clear." Dr. Engel shrugged, retrieved a scarf from her satchel, and wrapped it around her nose and mouth. Then, perching on the edge of the bed, she shooed Madeleine's rag away and dabbed the duke's brow dry with her sleeve. The doctor placed the back of her hand against his forehead then felt his cheeks and neck. "Well, my lord, you most definitely have a fever."

Lord Collingwood stopped pacing and stood at the foot of the bed with his arms crossed. "What does that mean?"

Dr. Engel rolled up her sleeves, revealing pale arms lined with thin green veins and brown age spots. "Not much by itself, simply that his body is fighting something. Please be quiet for a moment." She pressed two fingers to Lord Greyson's neck, paused, then felt for the pulse on his wrist. With each passing second, the creases in her brow deepened.

Lionel took a step toward the bed. "What's wrong, Doctor?"

"His heartbeat is irregular, Your Majesty." Dr. Engel smoothed her hands over her gray bun. "Lord Greyson, have you noticed any chest pains or shortness of breath?"

Frederick's brow furrowed. "Both, yes."

"He's also complained of a headache." Madeleine hung the rag over the bed frame then turned back to her husband and rubbed his arm. "And sensitivity to light. Even the bedside candles hurt his head."

"That could be connected to the nausea. Those two symptoms often go hand in hand." The doctor motioned to Frederick's chest. "May I?"

The duke nodded.

Dr. Engel unbuttoned Frederick's sleeping shirt and rested her ear against his chest. "Deep breath in." She paused to listen. "Deep breath out." Another pause. "Okay, good. Can you sit up for me?"

Madeleine scooted toward the head of the bed and helped the doctor lift Frederick to a sitting position. Dr. Engel removed his shirt the rest of the way then leaned her ear against his back. "Deep breath in." She paused. "And out. All right, you can help your husband dress, Lady Greyson."

Lionel tapped his foot against the carpet. *I don't know how Madeleine can be so patient. If Aya were this sick…*

"Well, your breathing does sound a bit uneven, but that's not uncommon for someone who is ill or in pain." Dr. Engel rolled down her sleeves. "I didn't hear any fluids, but if I had, you'd probably already be drowning in them." At Madeleine's gasp, the doctor smiled. "Don't worry, my lady. The sickness isn't in his lungs."

Frederick made a noise between a cough and a heave. "What's wrong with me, then?"

"If I didn't know better, I'd think you still have food poisoning. However, the illness couldn't have survived in your system this long. Like I said before, I believe it's influenza, made extra nasty since your body was weak when you caught it." Dr. Engel stooped to pick up her satchel. After rifling through it, she pulled out two small bags and handed them to Madeleine. "I'd like you to add these herbs to Lord Greyson's tonic. A pinch of each should do the trick, same as the others. You've been giving it to him, right?"

Madeleine's crossed eyes narrowed ever so slightly. "Twice a day, as you prescribed."

Lionel noticed a defensive edge in his cousin's voice, and for once, he pitied her. Of course she would do whatever the doctor had ordered. *Madeleine might be stubborn and manipulative, but she isn't stupid.*

"Let's up it to three." Dr. Engel slung the satchel over her shoulder. "One cup with each meal, piping hot, as you'd take your tea."

"What will the herbs do?" Lord Collingwood leaned forward to examine the plants, but Madeleine kept the bags closed and firmly clenched in her hands.

Dr. Engel pointed at one of the bags. "The black elder should help break the fever. Lord Greyson, your wife can feel your forehead, but you will probably be the best judge of when your fever breaks. Do you know the sensation?"

Frederick nodded.

"Good. When you no longer feel feverish—no chills, no burning skin, fewer inexplicable aches—have Lady Greyson stop administering the elder." Dr. Engel inclined her head toward the second bag. "The other herb I've given you is ginger root. It should help with the fever as well, but it will be most effective in calming your stomach."

Frederick motioned to the bucket. "Did you see?"

"I did." Dr. Engel let out a series of *tsks*. "Your body keeps telling your stomach that something bad is stuck inside, but your stomach has already expunged all the food and bile. That leaves your blood."

Lionel frowned. "Can't that damage his stomach?"

"Oh, yes, Your Majesty." Dr. Engel's eyes widened. "That's why the ginger root is so important. It's also crucial, Lord Greyson, that you drink plenty of water and tea and eat soft foods. Better to vomit them up than your stomach lining."

The four nobles winced.

"Thank you for your advice, Dr. Engel." Madeleine bowed her head from the bed. "Do you mind seeing yourself out?"

"No trouble. I know the way." The doctor bowed to the group then removed her scarf and tucked it back into her satchel. "I'll check in on you in a day or so, Lord Greyson. Lady Greyson, do call me if his condition worsens before then."

Madeleine replied that she would, then the group fell silent while Dr. Engel departed. Once he heard the door to the estate click shut, Lionel let out a long breath. If the doctor didn't seem overly excited about Frederick's condition, then perhaps they were all worried for nothing.

The duke tried to sit up against the pillows, but Madeleine pushed him back down with a gentle but firm hand. "You need to rest, darling. Sitting up for the doctor was enough for now."

Frederick shook his head. "I can't discuss business from my back. I feel like an invalid."

Lord Collingwood chuckled. "Today, you are, Son."

"What business could you possibly have to discuss, anyway?" Lionel glanced between the duke and Lord Collingwood. "Surely Uncle has all of your tenants managed."

"Of course." Lord Collingwood turned his cuff links. "Everything is in order. Nothing to worry about."

"I know that." Frederick's chest heaved, and he let out a deep, wet cough. "Lionel, I'm afraid I cannot remain on your council in this state."

A coldness slipped through Lionel's veins as he realized the implications of Frederick's statement. *What are the odds of finding another Starboardshire-approved noble who will support my decisions? And even if I do, will the other representatives stand for a second replacement when a simple command could release Lord Varick from house arrest and restore the "proper" council?*

"I don't think that's necessary." Lionel waved his hand. "It's only the flu. The worst will pass in a few more days, then you'll be fit to attend meetings again in a week or two. Surely, the kingdom can survive short of one council member."

Lord Collingwood stroked his goatee. "Without a Starboardshire representative, the council has an even number. If anything important goes to a vote, and the vote ties, that could be problematic."

Lionel shrugged. "I don't think that's likely to happen in the next week or so, but even still, I could always exercise my monarchical authority to break it."

"I have a suggestion." Madeleine rubbed the duke's arm. "Darling, couldn't you stay on the council and just not attend the meetings? You're still sound of mind. Why not appoint someone to sit in on the meetings for you then bring the information back here?"

Frederick squinted in thought. "Would that be allowed, Lionel?"

"It seems like a logical solution to me." Lionel turned to Lord Collingwood. "What do you think?"

"Obviously, I'm fine with it because I want to keep our familial alliance intact." Lord Collingwood crossed his arms. "But you need to be careful, Lionel. Whatever decision you make about this situation will set a precedent, and it might not always be wise to allow a proxy when future council members are temporarily incapacitated."

Lionel rubbed the back of his neck. "True. Perhaps we stipulate that the majority of the council must approve the proxy? That way, the person chosen has at least some social vetting."

Madeleine scooted toward the end of the bed. "Why not make the decision yourself, Lionel? Do you really need to get the rest of the council involved?"

"*I* would feel comfortable with this responsibility, but what about future kings?" Lionel looked down at the floor. "We all know how some men like to twist the law to their advantage. And that's exactly what I created the council to prevent."

"Fair point." Lord Collingwood squeezed Lionel's shoulder, and the action pulled the king out of his mournful thoughts.

Frederick heaved again, but nothing came out. He wiped his mouth with his sleeve. "I suppose all that's left is to decide who to nominate."

Lord Collingwood nodded. "It needs to be someone with a good memory who will listen carefully and repeat conversations back to you as accurately as possible."

"It would be best if they were unbiased about the other council members, too." Lionel shifted his feet. "Or at least they would need to share your biases so they could observe and report from as close to your perspective as possible."

"And you'd have to trust him completely, as would the rest of the council." Lord Collingwood added. "In these times especially, we can't afford any doubt about whether he's giving *you* accurate information and giving *us* your truthful opinions and votes."

Lionel crossed his arms. "That's right. Another good reason to allow the council to vote on the proxy. We can't have the other members worrying about the exchange of information."

"What about your valet?" Madeleine fiddled with the strings on the herb bags. "He's served you since you were a child. Surely, he would be able to view the council meetings through your eyes. And you trust him with all your other business."

Frederick knitted his eyebrows. "True, but it doesn't feel right to send a servant in my place." Another retching cough erupted. "Even though he wouldn't be a proper representative, the council and the people still expect a nobleman in that position."

"I agree." Lord Collingwood glanced toward the open bedroom door. "And while I'm sure your valet is trustworthy, I could see the other council members expressing concern over gossip spreading through the staff."

Lionel lifted his top hat to run his fingers through his hair. "Do you have any friends in Starboardshire that you trust?" It seemed inappropriate to give Frederick's council spot to a friend, but Lionel knew the duke didn't have much other family. His parents had died a few years back, and a feud over the inheritance had left him estranged from his younger brother.

"I would trust my best friend." Frederick took his wife's hand. "What do you say, Madeleine?"

"Me?" The noblewoman's eyes widened, and for the first time in Lionel's memory, she was stunned silent. After a long moment and a deep breath, she said, "I don't know. While I fancy myself to have *some* political savvy, I worry I wouldn't fully understand what the council discusses."

Lord Collingwood scoffed. "You're smarter than half the noblemen in the palace, sweetheart. Besides, if a wellman can follow along, I'm sure you'll do fine."

Lionel frowned at his uncle's classism but bit his tongue.

"You don't think the council would mind swapping a cousin for a cousin?" Madeleine scrunched her nose. "I know I'm not replacing Freddy, but I don't want them to accuse you of nepotism. Again."

"As you say, you're not a permanent replacement, so it shouldn't matter." Lionel shrugged. "Besides, who knows a man's temperament and wishes better than his wife? That's the perspective we'll encourage the council to take."

Madeleine nodded and turned back to the duke. "And you're sure, darling? I won't be offended if you change your mind."

"Nonsense." Frederick screwed his eyes shut and took a sharp breath. The veins on his temple stood out, and Lionel imagined that they were throbbing in pain. "I trust you, Madeleine. Besides, it would do you good to get out of this estate and take a break from caring for me every once in a while."

"If you insist, then I accept." Madeleine smiled down at her husband and patted his arm. "For now, though, you should rest. No more business."

Frederick made to speak then leaned over the bed and spat another trickle of blood into the bucket.

"I think that's our cue." Lionel bowed to the Greysons. "Feel better, Cousin. Madeleine, I'll call a council meeting tomorrow to vote on your temporary appointment."

"Thank you, Lionel." Madeleine reached out a hand, and Lionel squeezed it.

Lord Collingwood bowed to his son-in-law then kissed Madeleine on the forehead. "You be sure to get your rest too, sweetheart."

"I promise, Father." Madeleine waved. "Until tomorrow."

As Lionel and Lord Collingwood emerged into the streets of Starboardshire, Lionel couldn't help but shake his head. "I must say, Madeleine has matured over the last few months. Sometimes I hardly recognize her."

Lord Collingwood nodded. "Frederick's been a fantastic

influence on her. As I always said, all my daughter needed was the right husband to straighten her out."

"Do you think they're really in love?" Lionel scratched the back of his neck. "It looks like it to me, but it's so difficult to know."

Lord Collingwood grinned. "I have no doubt."

Lionel glanced back toward the estate. "At least someone in this family had an easy time of it."

"Not every marriage is like mine." Lord Collingwood's face fell. "Or your mother's."

Lionel frowned. "Where is Aunt, by the way?"

Lord Collingwood cocked an eyebrow.

"Ah." Lionel formed a tight-lipped smile. At least his aunt and uncle had managed a compromise after the abolishment of the adultery law. Lord Collingwood passed his nights with Dellwyn at the Rudder, and Lady Collingwood kept her own lover, who remained a mystery to Lionel. "Well, Madeleine seems happy. Maybe our generation will come out better from the start."

"I think you will." Lord Collingwood clapped Lionel on the back. "A decade from now, you'll watch your own child run through the palace corridors, and you'll realize you worried for nothing."

"Thank you, Uncle." Lionel's shoulders sagged, and he took off his top hat. Even after only a few months, he could hardly remember what it felt like to be so carefree. But Lord Collingwood had lived much longer than the king. If he promised better times would come back around, Lionel trusted him. "I'm sure you're right."

$\mathcal{P}$erched on his elevated throne in the ballroom, Lionel felt beads of sweat spread across his brow as Theo and the other palace guards opened the double doors. Two lines of subjects streamed inside. The nobles walked in from the east, while the residents of Sternville, Portside, and Bowtown entered from the west. At Theo's command, the petitioners stopped a respectful distance from the throne, but Lionel's chest still tightened, as if they crowded around him.

While Lionel hated everything about holding court— looking down on his people from his throne, sitting on display for their own judgmental gazes, the unpredictability of the problems they would present—he had insisted on reviving the tradition after his coronation. King Archon had stopped holding court over a decade ago, around the time he married his third wife and started abusing Desertera's laws. By reinstating the practice, Lionel had hoped to make himself available to his people and regain some of their favor.

So far, holding court hadn't seemed to influence the public's opinion of Lionel or improve the people's morale. But that session would be the first since Lionel's impromptu speech in Portside. Maybe the goodwill he'd earned would continue despite the recent fight at the border. Judging by the nobles' narrowed eyes and upturned noses, he doubted that he had gained any ground with them. However, most of the merchants seemed to appraise the king and the palace with curious eyes and genial smiles. That much was an improvement.

Lionel glanced to his left. While the queen's throne sat empty, Zedara stood off to its side, along with Lord Collingwood, the bishop, and the newly appointed Lady Greyson. In a quick gathering before court had opened, the other representatives approved Lionel's proposed precedent and Lady Greyson's position as proxy for her husband. With a quiet chuckle, Lionel wondered whether Madeleine had realized her first duty would be to stand in on court and pondered how quickly she would come to regret joining the council.

On Lionel's right, beyond the empty throne for the king's heir, stood Miss Baker, Mrs. Farmer, Mr. Wellman, and Mr. Chef. As the noble council members were present to help Lionel address the concerns of the noble subjects, so would the common-born representatives assist in solving the problems of the villagers. Each of them inclined their head toward Lionel to indicate their readiness to begin.

Lionel cleared his throat and attempted his steadiest, most royal voice. "Captain Laurel, please send forward the first petitioner."

Theo bowed then turned to the line on his left. He motioned for the first noble to step forward.

Lord Meeran strode up to the throne and bowed to Lionel. "Good morning, Your Majesty. First and foremost, I want to convey my gratitude for the lovely ceremony you held for my son last week."

Lionel tipped his top hat. "You and the countess are most welcome. I'm sure I speak for the bishop as well when I say it was our pleasure."

The bishop placed a hand over his heart. "My greatest joy as religious overseer is welcoming new life into our ranks."

"Well, thank you." Lord Meeran clasped his hands behind his back. "Unfortunately, though, I now have a grievance for Your Majesty."

Lionel nodded. "What can I do for you?"

"I know it's petty, but some of the horse fencing is down in Starboardshire, and our neighbors' horse keeps crossing into our yard." Lord Meeran sighed, and Lionel detected a hint of embarrassment in the way the nobleman refused to meet his eyes. "It wouldn't be a problem, other than my wife is terrified of the beast and refuses to leave the house until it's confined."

Out of the corner of his eye, Lionel saw Zedara break into silent giggles. He, too, had to press his lips together to avoid laughing. After a deep breath, he replied, "Regardless of your wife's feelings, you're right. The horses are supposed to be penned." He turned to Zedara, whose cheeks glowed suspiciously pink. "Your Highness, could you convey my orders to have the fence repaired? Perhaps you could also recommend the builder who constructed your personal pen?"

Zedara smirked, and her eyes still danced with laughter. "Absolutely, Your Majesty. Lord Meeran, if the countess would like, I could also help her with her phobia. She has nothing to worry about from any of the horses in Starboardshire."

Lord Meeran chuckled. "I appreciate the offer, Your Highness, but trust me, it'll be a rainy day in Desertera before she steps near any livestock." The count turned back to Lionel and bowed. "Thank you, Your Majesty."

Lionel smiled. "You're welcome."

As Lord Meeran exited the ballroom, Lionel let out a sigh of relief. One problem solved without any nasty remarks or unexpected complications. Judging by the lines, it looked as though it would be an easier day so far as listening to petitions went—only a few dozen more subjects waited to address the council.

Theo motioned to the next individual, a merchant from the right-hand line.

The woman approached Lionel with short, cautious steps, so Lionel widened his smile and opted to greet her first. "Good morning, ma'am. Can I help you?"

With a wince, the woman stopped and dipped into an awkward curtsy. "I hope so, Your Majesty." As she rose, she pulled her skirt up to reveal her ankle, bruised purple and swollen to twice the proper size.

Lionel cringed, and he heard some of the council members gasp around him. "You must be in terrible pain. Would you like to sit on the edge of the platform?"

The woman straightened her stance as much as she could while keeping her weight on her good foot and let her skirt fall to cover the injury. "That's all right, Your Majesty."

Lionel scooted forward on his throne, ready to jump to the woman's aid should she need to sit. "Have you seen a doctor?"

"That's why I'm here, Your Majesty. I can't afford it." The woman's eyes watered, and she made a gulping sound as she choked back her tears. "I'm a tailor, you see, and the farmer who sells me the animal and plant materials to make my sewing supplies has cut me off. I brokered a hasty deal with a new farmer, but he's charging me double. I can barely put food on the table for my family."

Lionel's hand balled into a fist. Hearing that the farmers might capitalize on Rykart's disruptions hadn't prepared him for seeing the physical result. "I'm sorry you've been put in this situation, Miss Tailor. If the council agrees that it is fair, I'll start by declaring that all farmers who take on new customers should honor the customers' previous arrangements for at least the first month. Greed has no place in this crisis."

The council members nodded, and Mrs. Farmer stepped forward. "I'll make the announcement when I get home, Your Majesty."

"Thank you, Mrs. Farmer." Lionel inclined his head. As he turned back to the front, he noticed a few individuals step out of the western line and leave the ballroom. *I wonder how many farmers have formed unfair deals over the past few days?*

Lionel shook his head. "If you don't mind my asking, Miss Tailor, how did you get hurt?"

Miss Tailor wrinkled her nose. "It was my own fault, Your Majesty. I tripped and rolled my ankle while carrying water home from the well."

Lionel nodded. "Did you spill the water, too?"

"No. My jug has a tight lid."

"Good." Lionel leaned back on his throne. "Well, I have a proposition for you."

Miss Tailor knitted her brows. "Okay."

"I will pay for all your medical expenses until your ankle is healed." Lionel resisted a smile at the tailor's jaw drop. "In return, you can alter a suit for me. How does that sound?"

"Very generous, Your Majesty." Miss Tailor blushed. "But I'm hesitant to accept. I'm sure your suit is far finer quality than any I've worked with before, and I'd hate to ruin it."

Lionel waved his hand. "As your customer, I'm prepared to take that risk. Though I have no doubt that you will treat my suit with the utmost care and skill."

"Of course." Miss Tailor attempted another curtsy. "Thank you, Your Majesty. I cannot tell you how much this means to me."

"Show me with your sewing skills." Lionel smiled at the tailor. If the rest of the court petitions went like the first two, he would have a fantastic day. "Theo, please have a palace guard escort Miss Tailor directly to a doctor and make sure she is treated today."

Theo signaled one of the guards who stood at the doors, and he hurried over to Miss Tailor. With a final "thank you," she allowed the guard to support her and limped toward the exit.

Without waiting for Theo's cue, the next noble stomped up to the throne. Miss Blanche Frieson, daughter of the Viscount of the Crow's Nest. As cold as the "freeze" in her name, the young noblewoman and her family had a reputation for their snobbish attitudes. Lionel knew Miss Frieson better than he would have liked—she and Madeleine had been friends since childhood.

Maybe having Madeleine on the council will soften Blanche up a bit.

Instead of offering a curtsy, Miss Frieson put her fists on her hips and glowered up at Lionel through slitted eyes. "Hello, Your Majesty."

And then again, maybe not.

Lionel clenched his jaw. "Good morning, Miss Frieson. What can I do for you?"

Miss Frieson huffed. "Well, to begin, you can explain why you have allowed a perfectly innocent, upstanding nobleman like Lord Varick to remain under house arrest for six months."

Lionel withheld a frustrated sigh. "As I have said every time I've held court, the council agreed to a one-year sentence. I cannot release Lord Varick until Captain Laurel has closed the investigation."

Miss Frieson glared at Theo over her shoulder. "Pardon me, Your Majesty, but you're being unfair. Just a few days ago, you allowed a group of *proven* violent criminals to go free after only one night in the dungeon. How can you possibly justify—"

A clattering sound out in the hallway interrupted the noble-woman, and she stomped her foot.

Lionel had to purse his lips to keep from snickering. "I'm sure it's nothing, Miss Frieson. Please continue."

Miss Frieson rolled her eyes. "As I was saying, why, in all of Desertera, would you show those violent criminals more respect than—"

A series of shouts echoed throughout the corridor, and Miss Frieson groaned. Some of the petitioners crowded toward the doors to look down the hallway, while the others backed farther into the ballroom. Lionel stood for a better view, but if there was anything to see, he couldn't glimpse it through the mass of bodies.

"Your Majesty, please sit." Theo waved for the guards at the door to investigate the commotion, which grew louder each second, then jogged over to stand on the throne platform next to Lionel. He motioned for the council members to gather closer. "Until we know what's happening, you all need to stay right here. If it's another brawl, we'll head for the back door as a group, His Majesty first, of course."

While Lionel had never seen the back door to the ball-room, he trusted Theo and nodded to show he understood. The other representatives replied in kind, their faces a mixture of anxious curiosity and downright fear. As the shouting and scuffling noises drew nearer, Lionel balanced himself on the edge of the throne, his leg muscles shaking with tension.

Theo moved to stand in front of Lionel, one hand clutching his dagger, the other held aloft, ready to signal the council members to run. Lionel leaned around him to see. The crowd had grown tighter near the doors, more people competing for a view of the fight in the hallway. For a moment, the bodies jostled together. Then, with an uproar of shrieks and gasps, the crowd flooded back into the ballroom, and the people instinctively retreated to their designated sides of the room.

Through the divide, Rykart Farmer emerged, restrained by two palace guards. A third guard walked behind with Rykart's tool belt slung over his shoulder and the farmer's trademark scythe clutched in his fist. As Lionel stood and pushed past Theo, he saw that the farmer had a cut on his lip, and a bruise was developing over his gray eye, which was nearly swollen shut. *Why is he here? And what have the guards done to him?*

Lionel stepped down from his throne and met the guards in the center of the crowd. "What's the meaning of this?"

The guard holding the tools bowed. "We caught the farmer sneaking in through the Rudder stairwell, Your Majesty." He held out the scythe. "He was armed."

Lionel wanted to tell the guard that Rykart always carried his scythe, but he held his tongue. The last thing he needed was to look as though he were defending the man. "I see. And since when does trespassing justify beating a man?"

"He was armed," the guard repeated, enunciating each word.

Lionel's jaw clenched. "I heard you the first time. Did Mr. Farmer attack you? Did he resist detainment?"

The guard frowned. "No."

"Okay." Lionel narrowed his eyes, mimicking the guard's condescending tone. "Why. Did. You. Beat. Him?"

The guard swallowed. "He's dangerous."

"Yes, he looks very threatening." Lionel gestured to the farmer's bruised face. "Unhand him, please."

With a nervous glance over Lionel's shoulder, no doubt to get Theo's approval, the guards let Rykart go and returned his belongings.

The farmer bowed. "Thank you, Your Majesty."

Lionel crossed his arms. "Why were you skulking around the stern, Mr. Farmer?"

"I wasn't." Rykart rubbed his elbows where the guards had grabbed him. "I came to use my words."

Heat spread through Lionel's chest, and his body went rigid. *So much for letting me make the announcement. No one will ever agree to this feast now.* He took a deep breath and blew it out with a near growl. "You came to speak with me?"

Rykart nodded. "We did."

Lionel rolled his eyes. "And you thought the best way to reach me was to sneak in through the Rudder's stairwell?"

"You're holding court." Rykart looked past Lionel to his throne. "The palace is open to all when the king holds court. Why should the journey matter when the destination is the same?"

"Very well. Council members, please retake your positions." Lionel turned on his heel and strode back up to his throne. Once seated, he straightened his back and waved the farmer forward. "Use your words, then. And be quick—these good people are waiting their turns."

Rykart bowed again. "Please accept my apology for the behavior of my fellow farmers, Your Majesty. The Benevolent Queen does not want Her children to suffer violence any longer."

Out of the corner of his eye, Lionel saw the bishop's hands clench into fists. Lionel waited to catch the bishop's gaze then gave a small shake of his head. "I accept your apology, Mr. Farmer. None of us want any more violence."

Rykart turned to the rest of the crowd, who had more or less reformed their lines but at a greater distance from the thrones and the farmer. "I also apologize for anyone whose body or well-being our actions harmed. We were wrong, and we are sorry."

A murmur coursed through the group, but no one dared speak out individually. As realization dawned upon Lionel, he rubbed his chin to hide his smile. *He's humbling himself before the people, demonstrating his respect and deference for me as his true ruler. He understood what I meant after all.*

Lionel cleared his throat to soften his voice. "Thank you, Mr. Farmer." He hoped Rykart could detect the sincerity in his tone. "Do you have anything else to say?"

Rykart held out his arms, but instead of turning his face upward, he kept his stare locked on Lionel. "With Your Majesty's permission, we would like to show our apology is true by hosting a feast. All of Desertera may come and dine and share in the glory of our divine monarch."

Lionel clasped his hands together. "That's quite generous of you, Mr. Farmer. I think a little goodwill is exactly what the kingdom needs."

Before Rykart could reply, the bishop stepped forward. "Excuse me, Your Majesty, but I'm not sure this feast is a good idea."

The crowd burst into whispers—some of the nobles smirking at the bishop's public chastising of the king.

Lionel held up his hand to silence the people, and out of either respect for him or thirst for more drama, they obeyed. "Go ahead, Bishop. Share your concerns."

"Thank you, Your Majesty." The bishop put his hands together as if he were praying. "On a spiritual level, I worry about exposing more of the kingdom to this man's ideas." He wheeled around to face the crowd, his eyes wide and imploring. "Make no mistake, neither the king nor I support this heretic or his supposed connection to the Benevolent Queen. She does not speak to Her children and will not until we earn Her affection."

Lionel waited with bated breath for Rykart to react, but the farmer-prophet merely smiled at the bishop, the way adults patronize foolish youngsters.

If the bishop noticed Rykart's expression, he didn't show it. "On a practical level, I worry for the safety of our people. How do we know that Mr. Farmer and his followers aren't leading us into a violent trap? After the fight they so carelessly started, after all the other stunts this man has orchestrated in the villages, after what he did *just now*, how can we trust him? Or his people?"

As much as it pained him to admit it, Lionel knew the bishop had a point. Even though Lionel believed Rykart to be harmless and had arranged this idea with him, the farmer's followers might ignore his commands and incite violence on their own. But Rykart had made a smart move in publicly asking for Lionel's permission to hold the feast. If Lionel agreed to it before the kingdom, then he could assist in the planning and provide his guards to ensure the event remained safe.

Rykart walked toward the bishop and knelt in front of him. As the crowd gasped, the bishop took a hurried step backward. *Now what is he playing at?*

"Bishop, I give you two reasons to trust me." Rykart's voice trembled. "First, I open myself to you here and now. If you have any desire to do ill to me, to retaliate or punish me for the sins I've committed, you may have your retribution."

The bishop's face paled, and he took another step back. "I'm a man of faith. I would *never* lay a finger against another of the Benevolent Queen's children."

"I trusted you would not, as I hope you will trust me." Rykart placed a hand over his heart. "The second reason is simple. I swear to you, on the grace of the Benevolent Queen, that I will not allow any of Her children to come to harm during this feast."

"How can I believe anything you say?" The bishop nearly spat the words. "You're a heretic. You think you worship the Benevolent Queen, when really you pervert Her commandments for your own use."

Lionel leaned forward on his throne and scanned the crowd. While the facial expressions varied from smug grins to blank stares to grimaces, he couldn't tell who agreed with which religious leader. And if he were being honest, Lionel didn't trust either of them himself.

Rykart's lips reformed his patronizing smile. "As I said to His Majesty, why should the journey matter when our destination is the same? We worship the same goddess. We both want Her to bless the kingdom with the salvation rains and the magnificence of Her love. What can it hurt if we both try to please Her in different ways?"

"It matters because you're wrong." The bishop's skin flushed red, a violent shade against his pristine white robes. "By worshiping Her incorrectly, you invite Her scorn. You create a greater insult than those who ignore Her teachings altogether."

"And what is the correct way to worship Her, Bishop?" Rykart stood to tower over the short man. "Is it to hide yourself away in the palace? Is it to act superior to Her other children? Or is it to enjoy the fine clothing and jewelry associated with the title of bishop while others soil their clothes and callus their hands to survive?"

Rykart held out his hands, palms up, to reveal dirt caked into the lines and rough scabs under the fingers. "Even though I have freed myself from my noble landlord, I still work to eat."

Lionel dared a glance at Lord Collingwood, who had been Rykart's landlord. His uncle watched the debate with interested but impassive eyes. *He's found a new farmer. I suppose he's no longer upset that Rykart abandoned his land.*

Rykart's words grew louder as his passion mounted. "I still strive to prove myself worthy to Her. I go out into the streets to try to reform the wicked. What have *you* ever done to show your devotion?"

"I gave up my life for her!" The bishop's voiced boomed throughout the ballroom and silenced the quiet chatter that had continued within the crowd. "I was a nobleman before I put on this robe. I had a family name, a title, a beautiful woman who wanted to marry me. And I gave it all up for the

Benevolent Queen." The bishop's lips trembled, and his eyes shone with angry tears.

Though Lionel had known that the bishop hadn't always served as Desertera's religious leader, he'd never considered what the man had given up. He'd just assumed the bishop had been without family or so full of devotional ardor that he hadn't minded leaving his old life behind. The king shook his head. *How thoughtless, Lionel.*

The bishop paused to take a deep breath, and when he spoke again, his voice was so soft that Lionel had to lean farther forward to hear it. "I bless these people when they enter the world. The king only blesses the nobles, but I bless them all. Then, when they die, I burn their bodies and send their spirits into the stars. I sit on the king's council and assist in the ruling of the kingdom. And when I retire at night, I pray for hours that She will show us—you, especially—mercy."

Rykart's forehead smoothed, and his lips curved into a smile—no patronization evident. "Exactly. Don't you see, Bishop? This is why She needs us both, why we need one another. We each do what the other cannot."

A heavy silence hung throughout the ballroom, and Lionel clutched the arms of his throne until his knuckles turned white. How the bishop replied would set the tone for the future of religion in Desertera, and whatever that might be, Lionel would be the one to lead the people through it.

"It's not right." The bishop shook his head. "I appreciate that you think you are doing Her work, but you're not. You're just another misguided street prophet—one in a long line of lost souls."

Rykart's shoulders slumped, and he backed away from the bishop. When he turned to face Lionel again, the king saw the glassy shimmer in his unscathed green eye. "Your Majesty, I would still like to host my feast. Do I have your permission?"

Lionel lifted his top hat to run his fingers through his hair. If he denied Rykart's request, he would be going back on their deal and denying the villages of Desertera the chance to heal. If he approved Rykart's request, he would be taking the risks the bishop mentioned and supporting, however infinitesimally, the farmer's cause.

Replacing his hat, Lionel looked to the common council representatives. "Do any of you object to this feast?"

Miss Baker shook her head. "It's the least the farmer can do after the trouble he's caused."

Mr. Wellman scratched the back of his neck. "My people don't care nothin' for his preachin', but they won't turn down a free meal. I'll try to make sure there's no fightin'."

Mr. Chef shrugged. "It seems harmless enough to me."

Mrs. Farmer wrung her hands. "It's the only way he knows how to make peace."

"Thank you for your honesty." Lionel shifted to face the noble council members. "Bishop, I understand and respect your concerns, but I'd like to hear what the rest of the noble representatives think."

Zedara crossed her arms. "He doesn't really need your permission to host a feast, Your Majesty. The fact that he's here, asking for it, shows me he's trying to do right by the kingdom."

Lord Collingwood nodded. "Her Highness makes a good point. Though I do share the bishop's fear that another fight could break out. If you grant this request, I would ensure guards attend to discourage any more violence."

Madeleine fiddled with the cuffs of her lace gloves. "I think Lord Greyson would support and trust whatever decision you make, Your Majesty." She paused, brows knitted together. "However, if I'm speaking for myself, I agree with the bishop. This man is a heretic and has betrayed the people's trust time and again. You owe him nothing."

Lionel pursed his lips. *That isn't true.* After another moment of thought, he sighed. "Mr. Farmer, I will grant your request to host a feast on two conditions."

Out of the corner of his eye, Lionel saw the bishop hang his head and Madeleine scowl.

For his part, the farmer kept a solemn face. "Yes, Your Majesty?"

"First, as Lord Collingwood suggested, you must allow guards to police the event." Lionel waited for Rykart to nod. "And second, to assuage the bishop's other concern, you must promise that there will be no preaching or talk of religion. You've proposed this feast as an apology and an act of service, and that's all it will be."

"Thank you, Your Majesty." Rykart bowed. "I accept, and I invite Your Majesty and your council to help plan the feast and attend as guests of honor."

Lionel inclined his head. "We will discuss it more later. Thank you, Mr. Farmer."

After a final bow, Rykart turned and left the ballroom. Whispers erupted among the people gathered, but the voice that struck Lionel the loudest was the bishop's. He had retaken his place at the side of the throne and stood with his head bowed in prayer. His furtive words were just a blur of breathy sound to Lionel. It was the first time, outside of ceremonies, that Lionel had seen the bishop pray, and guilt simmered in the bottom of his stomach.

Though most of the council had approved of or been indifferent toward the feast, Lionel couldn't help but feel as if he'd deceived them. He had met with Rykart in secret and planned the event. He'd acted the part of the impartial monarch during court. And he'd ultimately made the decision to allow the feast.

If anything *did* go wrong, Lionel knew he would shoulder the blame. But if it all went *right*, then Lionel would take on an even bigger burden—that he had successfully manipulated his people, deceived his council, and acted out of a sense of self-preservation. And that, despite all his efforts to prove the contrary, he was indeed like King Archon.

14

The next few days passed in relative peace. Once news about the feast spread throughout the kingdom, the people chattered with excitement, and Lionel received a much-needed reprieve from being the center of attention. As he approached the farmer's camp on the outskirts of Bowtown, Theo in tow for company and protection, his body buzzed with curiosity. After all the gossip and warnings, he longed to see the source of the commotion with his own eyes. And more importantly, he could hardly wait to know how the feast preparations were shaping up.

Squinting against the morning light, Lionel saw the other council members gathered outside the ring of shabby tents, and his enthusiasm deflated when he realized the bishop wasn't among them. From his own perspective, Lionel appreciated that the bishop's absence meant less chance for conflict, but he couldn't understand why the religious leader would pass up an opportunity to scope out the farmer's territory. How did the bishop expect to fight against Rykart's influence if he hadn't even seen what the farmer offered people?

Lionel took his place next to the representatives and tipped his top hat in greeting. After they replied with bows and curtsies, most of them met him with excited smiles or glittering eyes. But Lord Collingwood and Madeleine stood together to the side, their arms crossed and lips pressed into skeptical frowns. *At least they came.*

Zedara stepped forward and looped her arm through Lionel's. "We weren't sure if we should enter the camp, so we waited for you."

"No worries. Probably best we all go in together." Lionel took a deep breath and looked over his motley crew. "Is everyone ready?"

The council members responded with nods varying from enthusiastic to curt. With a deep breath, Lionel led the representatives forward and into the camp.

As they walked between two of the small, ill-constructed tents, Lionel and Zedara had to jump to the side to avoid a line of children carrying empty buckets to fill at the Bowtown well. A woman called after them, reminding them not to spill a single drop and holding a hunk of fresh-cut cacti in her hand. When she noticed Lionel and Zedara, the woman scurried back to the front of the tent and retook her seat between two other women.

Emerging from behind the tents, Lionel craned his neck to see what the women were doing. That trio plucked cacti needles from the husks, while other clusters shucked wheat stalks or sharpened sickles.

Zedara shuddered at his side. "I don't envy them that work."

Beyond the tents on the other side of the camp, Lionel could see men tending to the livestock and the fields. Some of the fields contained tall plants and straight rows, indicating to Lionel that they had been owned by the farmers for years, because noble landlords wouldn't have allowed their fields to support Rykart's cause. Other fields had barely sprouted, and Lionel surmised that these must have been planted when the farmer-prophet first broke off from the main village.

Unsure where Rykart might be, Lionel stopped in the center of the tents, next to a fire pit circled with large, flat seating stones. Though the women and children watched the council members with wide eyes, none of them paused from their tasks to offer hospitality. Lionel busied himself by attempting to count the number of people working for Rykart, but the flurry of activity made it impossible to keep track. At any rate, Lionel knew the farmer had recruited more followers than any of the representatives had expected.

Rykart threw back a tent flap and stepped forward to greet the council. "Welcome, Your Majesty, respected council members, and Captain Laurel!" After giving a reverent bow, he rose with a grin. "The Benevolent Queen is so pleased you're here to help with Her feast."

Lionel inclined his head. "Thank you, Mr. Farmer, but I thought we agreed to forgo the religious talk."

"At the feast, yes." Rykart looked from Lionel to the other representatives and back. Though bruises still tinged his skin, his gray eye was no longer swollen, and his gaze had regained its penetrating quality. "But I see it is not welcome now, either. I will refrain."

Zedara's lips formed a tight smile. "Much appreciated."

Rykart pointed to the sky with one hand and placed the other to the side of his mouth. "I can't make promises for Her, though," he whispered.

Mrs. Farmer offered a polite chuckle, but the rest of the council stayed silent. Lionel hoped that Rykart didn't notice Madeleine's eye roll.

"Okay. The feast will be on the other side of the camp." Rykart's beam betrayed no offense. "Follow me, please."

The farmer-prophet led the group between the tents and back outside the encampment. A long row of mismatched tables stood before the group, with a collection of chairs, barrels, crates, and large rocks placed around it to serve as seating.

"Many villagers have been generous enough to lend us their furniture. If we run out of chairs, my people will stand first." Rykart gestured beyond the tables to the young fields. "I thought this would be a good spot. So few people take the time to visit where their food grows."

As the tiny plants rippled in the hot breeze, Lionel took a

deep inhale. Unlike the palace, which smelled dusty and metallic, the air outside the camp reeked of life—dry stalks, tilled sand, fresh manure. It should have disgusted Lionel's noble sensibilities, but instead, it thrilled him. Somehow, year after year, the farmers coaxed the land to life and kept the kingdom fed. It was the greatest miracle in all of Desertera.

Lionel nodded. "Good thinking, Mr. Farmer."

Lord Collingwood held his cravat over his nose. "The odor's a bit pungent, no?"

Next to him, Madeleine held her father's handkerchief over her face. With her free hand, she pointed at a sled piled high with brown sludge. "That better not be what I think it is."

Mr. Wellman snickered. "What did ya think happens when yer maid empties yer chamber pot? This land ain't gonna fertilize itself."

"That's vile." Madeleine backed up, bumping into Mrs. Farmer in the process. "I cannot breathe under these conditions, let alone eat."

"You won't, my lady. I've been keeping track of the time…" Rykart pulled a circular golden device from one of the bags that hung on his tool belt. Holding it up to his eye, he adjusted the bar that bisected the circle until it lined up with the sun. With a satisfied nod, he replaced the device in the bag. "I'll make sure all the fertilizer is spread before it rains. The scent will wash away, and you will breathe easy at the feast."

"Rain?" Lionel glanced at the sky but didn't see a cloud in sight. "It showered a few weeks ago. What makes you think it would rain again so soon?"

Rykart smirked. "You asked me not to speak of Her grace."

"Right." Lionel's jaw clenched. *Just when I forget that I'm talking to a mad man…* "The feast, then. Do you have everything you need?"

"Plenty of meat, cacti, and vegetables." Rykart frowned. "Though, no bread or rolls."

Miss Baker crossed her arms. "None of the other bakers have offered to donate?"

Rykart shook his head.

"Figures." Miss Baker huffed. "I'll make some rolls for you. Send your people around to get them the morning of the feast."

"Thank you." Rykart wiggled a finger toward the sky and whispered, "From both of us."

Mr. Chef stroked his mustache. "And what about dessert? Any nobles who attend will be expecting dessert."

Rykart's eyebrows knitted together, as if Mr. Chef had whinnied instead of spoken, and Lionel nearly chuckled.

"I thought so." Mr. Chef waved his hand. "Don't worry about it. I'll have my cooks whip up some yogurt. It'll change your life."

At that, Lionel and Zedara did laugh. Rykart smiled and repeated his thanks.

Theo stepped forward and stood at attention. "As far as security is concerned, I've hand-selected the guards who will attend the feast. We'll do a separate survey of the area before the event to assess any possible risks and emergency exit routes."

"Thank you, Captain." Rykart bowed again. "We trust you and your guards to keep us safe."

With a polite nod, Theo returned to his place behind the representatives.

Lionel looked around the area. "Do you need our assistance with anything else?"

Rykart cocked his head. "Nothing comes to mind."

"Then, we'll let you get back to the preparations." Lionel turned to the council members. "Unless you all have anything else to discuss with Mr. Farmer, you're free to go."

With the requisite bows and curtsies to Lionel, and a squeeze on the arm from Zedara, the representatives took their leave. Once they had walked passed the encampment, Theo joined Lionel's side, and the king turned his attention back to the farmer.

"Do you know how the villagers feel about the feast?" Lionel scratched the back of his neck. "What I mean is, do you think it's creating goodwill like we hoped?"

Theo arched an eyebrow at Lionel, but he didn't comment.

"I believe so." Rykart patted one of the tables. "Many in the community have shown their support, and my followers seem in brighter spirits."

"That's good. Nothing like free food to bring out the best in people." Lionel chuckled. "Well, if you think of anything you need in the next two days, please let me know. No pressure, but I need this feast to be a success."

Rykart glanced up at the sky. "As does She, Your Majesty."

LIONEL COULD SEE the agitated clench of Theo's jaw out of the corner of his eye, but to the captain's credit, he remained silent until the pair had passed the farmer's encampment and reentered Bowtown proper.

When they turned down one of the village's wide streets to find it empty, Theo spoke. "What was all that about?"

"You're too observant." Lionel smiled to break the tension. "Let's just say, rather than imprison the farmer like *some* council members asked, I helped him come up with a peaceful way to make amends with the kingdom."

Theo rubbed his chin, but the tightness had left it. "That's why you were so calm when he petitioned you the other day. You already knew about the feast."

Lionel nodded.

"Huh. Well played." Theo clapped Lionel on the back. "And here I thought you weren't any good at politics."

"Let's not get ahead of ourselves." Lionel sighed, and a heaviness settled in his chest. He knew he needed to discuss another political issue with Theo, but he couldn't bring himself to ask a question to which he already knew the answer.

Instead, Lionel craned his neck to look farther down a curved row of tiny but neat houses. "I can't remember the last time I visited Bowtown. I'd forgotten how quiet it is."

Theo nodded. "It's a much slower pace of life than Portside. No hustle and bustle."

"Do you know why they concentrate all the houses closer to the palace and their well?" Lionel inclined his head to the wellman as they passed through the middle of the village. Best to wait until they were out of Bowtown to have a serious conversation, anyway. "It seems like it would be more sensible to build houses near the fields."

"My father told me that the fields came later." Theo hitched his thumb the way they had come. "The lands were more fertile back when the water had first receded, but it still took time for the crops to grow. While our ancestors waited and divided up the land, they built their houses near the palace, which was still the center of all life. Until the villages were fully established, people ate and slept in their quarters aboard the ship."

"I see." Lionel tapped his chin. "And I suppose it's too expensive to rebuild the houses out near the fields now."

"True." Theo narrowed his eyes against the sun, which had started its arch over the ship. "One of my men used to be a farmer, or his father was anyway, and he said they like where the houses are. Leaving the fields physically at the end of the day allows them to leave the work behind mentally, too."

Lionel considered the relief he experienced when he left the palace to visit Aya in Portside. "I understand that."

Theo fell into a respectful silence, and the conversation lulled. As they reached the last row of houses, Lionel stopped. They stood together in the shadow of the palace, and despite the cool of the shade, Lionel felt his forehead break out into a sweat. *Now or never, then.*

"I've been meaning to ask you…" Lionel sighed. "There's only two days left."

Theo frowned. "The investigation into Lord Varick. I know."

"I'm sure you've been busy with everything else that's happened." Lionel took off his top hat and fanned his face. "Have you had any breaks at all?"

"Not really." Theo let out a long *whoosh*. "I spoke to the potter again, and she reconfirmed that the shard is porcelain, but she has no record of who made it or purchased it. Of course, it had to belong to a noble, but how or when Mr. Rutt acquired it remains a mystery. As for Lord Varick, I had my guards search his estate again, and we still came up empty-handed."

Lionel shook his head. "That's not your fault. If there was any evidence left after the first search, Lord Varick wouldn't have been stupid enough to keep it around."

"I know." Theo ran his fingers through his shaggy blond hair. "I hate to say it, Lionel, but I think we need to accept that we're never going to have an answer. As far as history is concerned, Mr. Rutt killed himself rather than face trial and death by the executioner's ax."

"I figured you'd say that, and as much as I want to ask you to stall for the rest of Lord Varick's sentence, I know the kingdom won't stand for it. That, and if the investigation has failed, I might as well continue my streak of earning goodwill." Lionel replaced his top hat. "Thank you for trying, Theo. You're a good captain and an even better friend."

Theo offered a sad smile. "I'm sorry I couldn't find what you needed."

"You can't find what doesn't exist." Lionel watched his people walk in the shade of the palace, where they had once been forbidden to pass. His eyes trailed up the side of the ship, past the worn letters that used to spell its name, and for the briefest second, he had the distinct sensation that it would fall over and crush them all.

He shook the thought from his mind. "This is still my kingdom. One day, Lord Varick will make a mistake, and when he does, we'll be there to catch him."

Theo straightened. "And until then?"

"For starters, I'll let Lord Varick rot in his estate for two more days. He doesn't need to attend the feast." Lionel pressed his lips together to keep from smiling. "In the meantime, I'm going to pay a visit to the bishop. I made him a promise, and I need to fulfill it before I forgo yet another royal tradition."

---

15

*T*he bishop's chambers lay on the starboard side of the *Queen Hildegard*, near the bow. As Lionel approached the door, which was distinguished by a simple painting of a compass, his stomach twisted into knots. He knew the bishop wouldn't approve of his decision, but Lionel hoped to avoid a lecture. The seamless feast preparations had boosted his confidence, and he didn't want the bishop dragging down his mood.

With a deep breath and steady hand, Lionel knocked on the door. He heard heavy footsteps approach then stop on the other side.

"My apologies, but I'm not hosting prayers until this afternoon." Even through the thick metal of the door, the bishop's voice sounded deep and authoritative. "Please return after lunch."

Lionel cleared his throat. "I'm here to seek private counsel, Bishop. It should only take a few minutes."

The door wrenched open to reveal the bishop, clothed in a plain white shirt and trousers. He bowed. "Forgive me, Your Majesty. I wasn't expecting you."

"Think nothing of it. I should have made an appointment." Lionel tried not to stare. The bishop looked strange, smaller perhaps, without his ceremonial garb. "Would you like me to come back later?"

"No, no." The bishop swung open the door the rest of the way. "Please come in."

Lionel tipped his top hat before stepping inside. "Thank you."

The bishop led the king across the room to the seating area, and Lionel settled into one of four leather armchairs arranged around a low table. The bishop lingered near a second doorway. "Would you like anything to eat or drink?"

Lionel shook his head. "I won't stay long."

"Very well." The bishop seated himself across from Lionel then folded his hands in his lap. He wore no ceremonial rings, either.

Feeling overdressed, Lionel removed his top hat and balanced it on the arm of his chair. "We missed you in Bowtown this morning."

The bishop raised his eyebrows. "I didn't realize my attendance was mandatory, Your Majesty."

Lionel frowned. "It wasn't, but I would have welcomed your critical voice. You might have noticed a flaw in the feast preparations that the rest of us overlooked."

"Perhaps." The bishop crossed his ankles. "But I grow tired of inserting my opinions where I know they are not wanted."

Feeling his cheeks grow hot, Lionel stalled by gazing around the room, which appeared as bare as the bishop. No paintings, trinkets, or decorations—only the simple furniture, a tall potted plant next to the small window, and two plain doors that must have led to the bishop's kitchen and private bedroom.

Lionel rubbed the back of his neck. "It's not that I don't want or value your opinion, Bishop. I just wish you would show a bit more open-mindedness. *Sometimes*, breaks from tradition don't threaten the *entire* kingdom."

As Lionel had hoped, the bishop chuckled. "That may be so, Your Majesty. However, the reverse is also true. Not all traditions threaten Desertera, either."

"Fair point." Lionel leaned back in the chair. "Can I assume that you will not be attending the feast, then?"

The bishop sighed. "At first, I intended to stay home. However, I remembered I have a duty to the people. Though the heretic claims he will keep his religious beliefs to himself at the feast, I cannot allow him to be the only spiritual counsel present should the issue arise."

"I'm glad to hear it." Lionel grinned. "While we're on the topic of your counsel, what other advice would you offer me?"

The bishop waved his hand. "It's not my place to tell you *how* to govern, Your Majesty, only to advise on specific actions."

Lionel tapped his fingers on the brim of his top hat. "Well, hopefully you can help me with this particular action. As I said, I've come to seek your spiritual counsel."

"Ah." The bishop's eyes widened in understanding. "When I asked about your courtship the other day, I didn't realize it was so advanced. But I'm pleased you've decided to discuss your plans with me, anyway."

"Of course." Lionel rubbed the tops of his thighs. "So, how does this work?"

"It's quite simple." The bishop straightened in his chair, resuming his air of authority. "I will ask you three questions: one about you, one about Miss Cogsmith, and one about your relationship. Based on your answers, I'll assess whether I think you are ready to enter into the sacred pact of marriage and whether she will make a fitting queen."

"Okay." Lionel took a deep breath. "What's the first question?"

"What is the most difficult aspect of ruling Desertera?"

Lionel furrowed his brow. "What does that have to do with me?"

The bishop smiled. "Answer, please."

"Fine." Lionel considered all the challenges he'd faced since becoming king—the constant judgment, reconciling social expectations with his true self, the loneliness of ultimate authority. "I think the toughest part for me is balancing what is best for the kingdom with what is morally right."

The bishop nodded. "Why is that so important to you?"

Lionel scoffed. "You knew my father—his impatience, cruelty, selfishness. I promised myself I would never make my people live in fear, and I make every decision with that vow in mind."

"But don't the people live in fear still?" The bishop put up his hand to stay Lionel's objection. "The people may not live in fear of you or the law, but they still have concerns. What will the heretic do next? What if the wells dry up? How will I support my family if I get hurt? The fear might change, but it is always present."

Lionel raked his fingers through his hair. "So you're saying my whole mission as king is useless."

"Not useless." The bishop laced his hands together. "However, my *advice* to you would be to manage your expectations. I'm afraid that what's best for the kingdom isn't always just and vice versa. The longer you rule, the easier the balance will become."

"Thank you." Lionel's chest tightened. "What does that tell you about me?"

The bishop made a *tsk*. "I'm asking the questions for now. As for Miss Cogsmith, what makes her worthy of being queen?"

Lionel pressed his lips together to withhold a frustrated grunt. Though he didn't know the third question, he assumed that, given Aya's heritage, the answer he provided next would be the most important in garnering the bishop's support. More than anything, he wanted a noble who wasn't family to back his choice of queen, to understand and respect the quality of Aya's character.

"I know you don't approve of Aya because she's a commoner." A warm conviction spread through Lionel, and in his mind's eye, he could envision Aya before him. "But she's not common at all—she's intelligent and modest, compassionate and beautiful. She cares deeply about doing her part for Desertera and helping its people—all of us—live better lives. If I knew nothing else about her, that alone would make her a worthy queen in my eyes."

The bishop placed his hand over his heart. "Your words might be true, Your Majesty, but I'm afraid we must take into consideration Miss Cogsmith's prior actions. She lied about her identity to infiltrate the palace and join the nobility, she flirted shamelessly with King Archon, and most damning of all, she spent a decade working at the Rudder—while adultery was still a punishable crime, no less. You might not have a problem with her indiscretions, but do you really think your subjects will accept such a woman as their queen?"

To his credit, the bishop kept his voice soft and slow, and Lionel could see the apology in his eyes. It was a genuine concern, one that Lionel guessed most of the nobles shared. However, suspecting that his subjects thought ill of Aya and hearing her character criticized aloud were two different experiences.

Lionel sighed. "That's a fair question. The simplest answer is that I don't know how the people will react to Aya as their queen. But quite frankly, it doesn't matter. If she will have me, I intend to marry her."

The bishop pulled in his lips and nodded without comment.

Lionel leaned forward, elbows resting on his knees. "That being said, I would hope that the people—you and your fellow council members, especially—could find it in your hearts to give Aya a second chance. She worked at the Rudder out of necessity after King Archon wrongly ordered her father's execution. She accepted Lord Varick's offer of refuge because she loathed working at the Rudder, and she only lied about her identity to avoid scorn for her father's alleged treason."

As Lionel thought of King Archon's actions and Aya's lengthy struggle, his hands trembled, and he balled them into fists. "Show me a person, noble or peasant, who has never committed adultery, who has never lied, who has no moral indiscretions to their name. You show me that person, and I'll make them queen or give them my crown. But until you can do that, I know of no one more worthy than Aya to rule by my side."

The bishop smoothed his trousers. "I admire your conviction, Your Majesty. For my part, I will try to think more kindly toward Miss Cogsmith."

"I appreciate it." Lionel closed his eyes for a moment, feeling as though he had won a battle. When he opened them, the king saw the bishop watching him with his impassive stare. "Will Aya be the first commoner made queen?"

The bishop shook his head. "As far back as I can trace the royal lineage, it's occurred once before. Granted, the woman happened to be the daughter of the kingdom's wealthiest merchant."

Lionel chuckled—at that fact and with relief. "That's not surprising." *At least Aya won't have the pressure of being the first.* "And the final question?"

"This is my favorite." The bishop broke into a proper grin. "How does each of you make the other a better person?"

A wave of relief washed over Lionel. *Where do I even begin?* "In the short time we've known each other, Aya has done so much for me. She's opened my eyes to how the villagers live, and she's exemplified what it means to act in service for others, both of which I hope have made me a more compassionate king.

"But, most importantly, Aya has shown me what it means to love with all of yourself. I look at the sacrifices she's made, her dedication to her father after his reputation was wrongfully ruined, her ability for forgiveness, and I want to be like that. I want to love as wholly and unabashedly as she does."

The bishop nodded, his face smooth with neutrality. "And how do you believe you've bettered Miss Cogsmith?"

Lionel let out a long breath. "Honestly? I don't know if I have. I like to think that I've helped Aya find more joy in life, but that might be her improved circumstances more than me."

The king rubbed his chin. "I guess... I hope I've shown her that she doesn't have to be what everyone thinks she'll be. I mean, I'm not exactly what the people expect in a king, but as time goes on, they're starting to understand that maybe that's a good thing. Likewise, Aya's not what the people expect in a queen, but that doesn't mean she won't leave them pleasantly surprised in her own way."

For a long moment, the pair sat in silence while the bishop's eyes lingered on Lionel's features. The king felt his complexion warm, and he avoided the bishop's gaze by fiddling with one of the metal cogs on his top hat.

Finally, the bishop cleared his throat. "While I still feel that choosing a commoner for your queen is a risk, especially with all the other changes you've implemented in the kingdom, I understand your decision. You do not have my approval, but you have my respect, and I sincerely hope Miss Cogsmith proves me wrong."

Lionel nodded. *That's about the best I could have hoped for.* "Thank you, Bishop."

As Lionel rose to stand, the bishop held out a hand to stop him. "Might I advise you on one more point, Your Majesty?"

"Of course." Lionel lowered himself back into the armchair but stayed perched on the edge. "What is it?"

"Given all that has happened, and the fact that Miss Cogsmith is an untraditional choice for queen, I think it would be wise to keep with tradition in all other possible ways." The bishop's face cringed into an apology. "Do you understand what I'm saying?"

Lionel shook his head.

The bishop sighed. "It's custom to ask for the woman's hand, even if you are the king."

"How can I ask for Aya's hand?" Lionel's eyebrows knitted together. "Both of her parents are dead, and she has no extended family." *That's the whole reason she got into the mess with... no.*

"Absolutely not!" Lionel stood again, towering over the seated bishop. *It's bad enough that I have to let him go free.* "Even if Aya was Lord Varick's ward, for all of a few weeks, you can't expect me to ask for her hand from a suspected criminal."

"Is he, though?" The bishop rose as well, probably trying to reduce Lionel's physical domination. "My friend on the palace guard informed me that Captain Laurel is all but ready to give up the investigation."

Lionel's body burned with rage, and his jaw clenched tight. "He has two more days before his next report."

"Yes, of course, Your Majesty." The bishop clasped his hands behind his back. "I only meant to ease your concern about appearing subservient to a criminal. Do you have another objection to speaking to Lord Varick?"

The twinkle in the bishop's eye made Lionel wonder whether he knew the whole truth of Aya's introduction to the palace. But even if the bishop confirmed that he knew about Lord Varick and Aya's plot against King Archon as well as Lord Varick's betrayal of Aya, Lionel would never have admitted his distaste for the nobleman. *If there's one thing I've learned from that man, it's never to expose evidence—in any form.*

Lionel put his top hat back on. "No. I can't say that I do."

"Good." The bishop led Lionel to the door. "If you need a pretense for visiting Lord Varick's estate before his name is cleared, you could update him on the investigation. Or, better yet, you could get him caught up on recent events so that he's ready to retake his council seat."

The blood drained from Lionel's face, and he felt the sensation of falling grip his stomach. He'd completely forgotten that Lord Varick's absolution from the crime would also mean his reinstatement on the council. *How could I have let this happen?*

"Your Majesty?" The bishop placed a hand on Lionel's arm. "Are you feeling all right? You've gone pale."

"Yes." Lionel jerked back to the present. "I think I need to eat something. My energy has started to run low."

"I think that would be a good idea." The bishop's lips curved into a smile, and while it appeared kind on the surface, Lionel sensed an edge of satisfaction lurking underneath.

Lionel tipped his top hat. "Thank you for your counsel, Bishop. I'll take it under advisement."

"Any time, Your Majesty." The bishop opened the door for the king. "Oh, and when you speak with Lord Varick, please tell him to come see me for prayer after he's released. I'm sure he'll have conflicting emotions to process, and I'd hate for him to express them in an unhealthy way."

Lionel's breath hitched. *Was that a warning to look out for Lord Varick or a prediction that I'll suffer for "wrongly" accusing him?*

"*If* I decide to visit Lord Varick, I'll give him your best." Lionel inclined his head as a goodbye, and the bishop gave him a parting bow.

The king might have had the last word, but between the defeated tone of his voice and the bishop's tight smirk, they both knew his statement had been all bravado. Lionel would go see Lord Varick—not to request Aya's hand or welcome the nobleman back onto his council—but to issue his own final, unquestionable warning.

16

"**Your** Majesty, what a pleasant surprise!" Lord Varick greeted Lionel with a low bow, smoothing out his velvet suit as he rose. "I'm so pleased to finally host you at my estate."

Lionel gritted his teeth and put on his most charming smile. If Lord Varick intended to act congenial, then so would he. "Thank you, Lord Varick. Might I take a seat?" Lionel gestured to the sitting room, where two couches and a plush armchair sat around a wooden coffee table.

"Actually, would you mind if we chatted on the balcony? After being cooped up inside for so long, I've come to appreciate the freedom of fresh air." Lord Varick twirled his ivory walking cane, and Lionel noticed that the nobleman's skin had paled to almost the same shade.

"Very well." Lionel looked over his shoulder at Theo, who stood guard inside the estate's doorway. With a quick jerk of his head, Lionel indicated that the captain should follow them. He didn't trust Lord Varick under the best of circumstances, let alone at staggering heights.

The pair walked past the sitting area and through the sliding glass door that led to the balcony. Once outside, Lord Varick stood at the metal railing and lit his pipe. Before taking a puff, he held it out to the king. "A breath, Your Majesty?"

"No, thank you." Lionel stayed toward the center of the small balcony, within an arm's length of Theo, who positioned himself in the doorway. "Yours is the only palace estate with a balcony, correct?"

"I believe so." Lord Varick took a deep inhale from his pipe. "The family legends are conflicted about its origins. My grandfather told me it was an observation deck during the *Queen Hildegard*'s construction, but my mother claimed a curmudgeon of an ancestor insisted on building it for a slice of sunshine. Either way, I'm grateful to have it."

"I don't blame you."

As the hot desert air blew the smoke in Lionel's face, he stifled a cough and turned to look out over Sternville. Though Lord Varick's balcony was lower than the deck, Lionel found his knees shaking as he gazed down at the tiny hovels below. The railing only came up to their waists, and Lionel imagined the simple misstep it would take to topple over it and plummet to the ground.

Lord Varick faced Lionel, his beady eyes narrowed against the afternoon sun. "Well, Your Majesty, to what do I owe the pleasure of your company?"

Lionel smirked. "What? Can't pay you a social call?"

"Why, of course you can." Lord Varick's lips curled back to reveal his pointed teeth. "Though you can't blame me for hoping for news about the investigation. I haven't slept a full night, knowing my dear Augustus's murderer is still loose in Desertera."

Lionel arched an eyebrow. "I thought you believed Mr. Rutt committed suicide?"

"I did. Maybe I still do." Lord Varick's gaze drifted back out over Sternville, and he let out a long breath of smoke. "But you and Madam Rutt seem so convinced that Augustus was killed, part of me has grown to believe it, too. While I might have known him most *intimately*, I'm sure Madam Rutt knew his character best."

After all this time, he's sticking to the lover alibi.

"I suppose she did." Lionel pressed his lips together,

debating whether to satisfy Lord Varick's curiosity. Regardless of what Lionel did, the ruling would be revealed soon, but he couldn't bring himself to admit defeat to Lord Varick directly, even in private. "At any rate, you're right. I'm not here for a social visit."

Lord Varick straightened his cravat. "You do have news about the investigation, then."

"No." Lionel took a deep breath. *Don't let him rile you up.* "Actually, I've come to discuss a personal matter."

"Oh?" Lord Varick's brow lifted. "What personal business could you and I possibly have to discuss?"

Lionel pushed his shoulders back and stood at his full height. "As you have probably heard, I've been courting Miss Cogsmith. Now that I'm ready to take the next step, the bishop believes that I should ask you, as her last guardian, for her hand."

Lord Varick let out a melodious laugh. "Goodness, the bishop's a stickler for custom, isn't he?"

"Always." Lionel kept his tone light and matter-of-fact. The last thing he needed was for Lord Varick to sense discord between him and the bishop. "With Miss Cogsmith being a commoner and my other unconventional decisions as king, the bishop feels it would be best for me to keep to this tradition. He seems to think your support for my and Aya's engagement would help the nobles accept her as their queen."

"I see." Lord Varick tapped the end of his pipe against his chin. "Well, I would love to grant your request, Your Majesty, but I'm not sure I agree that you're the right man for my Miss Aya."

Lionel clenched his jaw. "You realize that I came here for the pretense, correct? We both know you have no authority over me or Aya."

"Pretense is good and well, as long as I'm locked away in my estate." Lord Varick grinned at Lionel, then Theo, then back. "But I daresay I'll be released before your wedding, and while I could never stop your marriage, I couldn't live with myself if I did not make my concerns as Aya's guardian public."

"Fine. I'll humor you." Lionel crossed his arms. "What are your concerns?"

"Most prominently, Miss Aya's life." Lord Varick placed his pipe hand over his heart. "As you know, I agreed to let my blood daughter, Isadona, marry your father. And look how being queen worked out for her."

"We both know I'm nothing like King Archon." Lionel scoffed. "If I were, you wouldn't be standing here."

Lord Varick arched an eyebrow. "Is that a threat, Your Majesty?"

Lionel shook his head. "Merely an observation on my father's style of ruling. Do you have any actual concerns?"

"Several, Your Majesty." Lord Varick counted them off on his fingers. "Would Miss Aya be happy when her role as queen takes her away from her craft? Do you really love her, or do you think you owe her for her father's execution? Can Miss Aya's kind heart handle the scrutiny she will face? Will you grow tired of each other and start to dally?"

As Lord Varick rattled off more concerns, Lionel repeated the truth in his head. *Aya and I will be happy together. He's trying to create doubt in my mind and destroy our relationship. None of this is real.*

When Lord Varick stopped, Lionel forced his lips into a smile. "Have you raised all of your concerns?"

"I believe so." Lord Varick traced tiny circles on the balcony with his walking cane. "For pretense, this is the part where you reassure me that my worries are unfounded."

"You know that they are, as well as I know that you don't care about Aya." Lionel rolled his eyes. "But, for pretense, I can assure you that my feelings for her are genuine. Whether she'll be happy as queen is up to her, but I will do everything in my power to help her with the transition."

Lord Varick nodded and took a puff from his pipe, as if he needed time to consider Lionel's words. They stood in silence on the balcony, and with each passing minute, the nobleman's smug smirk grew wider. *Why did you give him the satisfaction, Lionel?*

As the king prepared to give in and ask for Aya's hand a final time, a bird swooped at the pair and let out a loud *caw*. The sound broke the spell, and Lord Varick blinked. "While I still harbor concerns, I give you my blessing to ask for Miss Aya's hand in marriage. Who am I to stand in the way of your happiness?"

Lionel bit his tongue to prevent himself from saying "thank you." Instead, he straightened his stance again. "A wise decision, Lord Varick. You would have looked like a rather incompetent guardian if Aya had married me without your consent."

"Hmm. Indeed." Lord Varick's eyes scanned Lionel from top hat to shoes, and the king repressed a shiver. "Is that all you have to discuss with me, Your Majesty? If so, I will show you to the door."

A tightness curled in Lionel's chest. "Actually, now that I've kept my promise to the bishop, there's one more thing I would like to say to you."

Lord Varick pursed his lips. "And that is?"

"I'm watching you. This lonely widower act might have the rest of the kingdom fooled, but I know what you truly are." Lionel closed the distance between them and towered over Lord Varick. "Sooner or later, you're going to slip up, and when you do, I'll be there to expose every crack in your *porcelain* façade."

Lord Varick didn't even flinch. Instead, he glanced at Theo, who glowered at him, then he broke into a smile. "The investigation has failed, I see. Thank you for telling me, Your Majesty."

Lionel frowned. "I didn't say that."

"You didn't have to." Lord Varick tapped his cane on the floor. "If I wasn't close to release, why would you bother warning me to behave?"

Lionel huffed. *So much for that idea.* That time, it was his turn to stall by staring out over Sternville. His gaze landed on the anchor chain, where two people exchanged goods at the border, meeting in the middle so that neither party had to make the full walk in the unrelenting sun.

"If I were to offer you a deal, would you be honest with me?" Lionel held up his hand. "And I mean really honest. None of your half truths or twisted phrases, but a plain answer in plain language."

"Perhaps." Lord Varick's eyes narrowed. "Though that depends on the question..." He inclined his head toward Theo. "And the company."

Lionel nodded. "How about an exchange of information? I'll answer two of your questions about the investigation. In return, you'll answer two of mine about your actions. What is said will not leave this balcony—it's for our own peace of mind."

Lord Varick chewed the end of his pipe. "And how will I know that *you* are being honest with *me*, Your Majesty?"

"You'll have to take me at my word." Lionel shrugged. "As I will have to trust yours."

"And how do I know that this is not some elaborate trap?" Lord Varick looked Theo up and down. "While I have nothing to hide, I know how words can be manipulated—or misheard —by witnesses."

"Theo, please step inside and close the door behind you."

The guard's brow creased. "Your Majesty, I—"

"It's fine, Theo." Lionel lowered his tone. "Lord Varick isn't stupid enough to cause me any harm, especially not when he believes he is so close to release."

Theo glared at Lord Varick before bowing to Lionel and reentering the estate as instructed. He stood a few steps inside the door, one hand resting on his dagger, his eyes locked on Lord Varick.

"Satisfied?" Lionel waited for Lord Varick to nod. "To prove that I'm sincere, I'll allow you to ask the first question."

The nobleman angled his body outward to Sternville, probably so Theo couldn't read his lips. "How was Augustus's body found?"

Lionel frowned. *Is he trying to act as if he doesn't know, or is he making sure his accomplice did a good job in hiding the evidence?*

"Propped up in the corner of his cell. His forearms had been slashed open, and a sharp object lay near his hand."

Lord Varick placed the back of his pipe hand over his mouth. If Lionel hadn't known the nobleman better, he would have thought Lord Varick actually cared for Augustus.

"My turn." Lionel smirked. *What lie will it be this time?* "Did you supply Augustus with the money to buy the Rudder?"

"Yes."

Lionel's breath hitched.

Lord Varick offered a wry chuckle. "Don't look so surprised, Your Majesty. You asked for blunt honesty."

"So I did." Lionel lifted his top hat to wipe the sweat from his brow.

"For my second question, I'd like to know exactly how much longer I'll be under house arrest." Lord Varick snuffed out his pipe. "I have it on good authority that there's no evidence linking me to the crime, but I'm fully aware that you could detain me for another six months."

Lionel nodded. "As much as I would like to keep you locked up in here, my conscience won't allow it. With my mercy, you'll be released in two days."

Lord Varick broke into a genuine smile, perhaps the first Lionel had ever seen grace his features. "Thank you, Your Majesty. And your final question?"

"I'll repeat my promise: your answer will remain between us. It's useless without evidence, anyway." Lionel tugged down his jacket. "How did you orchestrate Mr. Rutt's death?"

"I thought you might ask that." Lord Varick dumped the ashes from his pipe over the balcony. "You won't believe me."

"Try me." Lionel cocked an eyebrow. "I know what you're capable of."

Lord Varick sighed. "The truth is that I didn't orchestrate Mr. Rutt's death. And before you accuse me of linguistic trickery, know I mean it in the simplest way. I did not kill him, convince him to kill himself, hire an assassin, or cause an accident."

Lionel's jaw clenched, and his body flushed with a hot rage. "You're lying."

"I'm not." Lord Varick stared Lionel in the face, his eyes unblinking. "To be honest, I greeted Augustus's death as a great stroke of luck, but I never would have arranged it. Though he murdered Madam Huxley, he had never wronged me, and I cannot bring myself to harm anyone who has not harmed me. Granted, I can see how you came to the conclusion you did. Eliminating my alleged accomplice would have been a clever idea."

Lionel cringed in disgust. *How can he speak so nonchalantly about life and death?* But after that initial reaction left his system, his heart started to hammer. If Lord Varick was telling the truth, then there were only two alternatives. Either Mr. Rutt had killed himself—and Lionel had made a fool of his authority by accusing and arresting Lord Varick—or the murderer remained free.

As the balcony began to swirl, Lionel pressed a trembling hand to his abdomen to hold himself steady. Heat flushed his cheeks from fear and embarrassment. He took an unsteady step backward and groped for the door. Without warning, it slid out from under his fingers as Theo wrenched it open and grabbed Lionel by the arm. "Are you all right, Your Majesty?"

"Yes, fine." Lionel rubbed his temples. "He didn't do it, Theo."

Theo looked between Lionel and Lord Varick with narrowed eyes. "What do you mean?"

Lord Varick scoffed. "He means I didn't kill Augustus Rutt, but surely your investigation already led you to that conclusion."

"So it was a suicide?" Theo pursed his lips. "I guess now we know."

Having steadied himself with Theo's support, Lionel straightened and brushed off his jacket. "Pardon me, gentlemen. I think the height must have gotten to me." He turned to Lord Varick on shaky legs. "If you don't mind a third question, what do *you* think happened to Mr. Rutt?"

"Honestly?" Lord Varick tapped the top of his cane. "As much as I admired Augustus's ambition, I don't think he had the conviction to take his own life, even if it meant saving himself from a more gruesome fate. And had your guards been completely innocent in the matter, Captain Laurel, one of them would have spoken up by now."

Lord Varick pushed his shoulders back. "No, I think someone manipulated their way past the guard and into Augustus's cell. Someone he wouldn't have viewed as a threat, who could kill him quietly and without struggle—maybe so quietly that your guards didn't even know he was dead until much later."

Lionel frowned. "That's incredibly specific."

Lord Varick shrugged. "I've had six months to work it out. And besides, it's what I would have done, had I done it."

"Fair enough." Lionel smirked. "Since you *are* innocent, you wouldn't want to help with the investigation, would you? Obviously, you have a keen insight into the criminal mind, and it would be a good way to clear your name, once and for all."

Lord Varick laughed. "Not for all the water in Desertera, Your Majesty. I'll leave the conspiring and political maneuvering to you for a while."

Lionel raised an eyebrow. "For how long?"

Another chuckle. "Well, for now."

17

$\mathcal{W}$armth flooded Lionel as Aya's dark-brown curls emerged from the Rudder stairwell. She peeked her head cautiously through the doorway to look for passersby. When her emerald eyes landed on Lionel, she broke into a grin and hurried over to meet him.

Lionel took off his top hat in greeting. When Aya reached him, he gently kissed her lips, smiling against them as her fingers wrapped around his lapels. "Good evening, Miss Cogsmith."

"Good evening, Your Majesty." Aya glanced over her shoulder, checking for bystanders again. "I didn't expect to see you here. I thought we were meeting in your old chambers?"

"I couldn't wait that long." Lionel tucked a curl behind her ear then trailed his hand down her shoulder and the smooth sleeve of her dress. As promised, Aya had worn the gown he'd given her a few months ago, which she'd never had occasion to wear. The plaid pattern, crisscrossed in shades of red, brought out the richness of her tanned skin, and the fabric clung to her in just the right way—sexy, but still elegant.

Lionel fiddled with the brass buckle of the dress's exterior corset. "How does it fit?"

"You tell me." Aya performed a little spin, sending the full skirt billowing around her.

"It looks perfect." Lionel took Aya's hand in his. "But do you like it?"

"I love it." Aya nudged his side. "Even if it is ridiculous and unnecessary."

Lionel chuckled and put his top hat back on with his free hand. Then he started to lead Aya down the corridor. "And here I thought I'd selected a casual walking dress that you could wear in Portside. Shows you how much I know about women's fashion, I suppose."

"Indeed." Aya laughed, but her eyes still darted around the hallway. As the pair passed the door to Lord Varick's estate, Aya's gaze avoided it.

"You don't need to be so nervous, you know." Lionel squeezed her hand. "It's not trespassing if you're my guest."

"I know that." Aya rolled her eyes. "It's just… I thought we were trying to keep our courtship quiet, and here we are, walking down the corridors of the palace for everyone to see."

Lionel frowned. "Would it be such a bad thing if someone did see us? Are you embarrassed to be with me?"

"No, not at all." Aya's cheeks flushed red. "I figured you wouldn't want to be seen with me. I know how the other nobles disapprove."

"I don't care what they think. If I did, would I visit you in Portside in the middle of the day?" Lionel gave Aya a pointed look, and she shook her head. "Exactly. But if it eases your mind, we won't be seen tonight. I have guards stationed in the corridors to make sure we're not interrupted."

Aya raised her eyebrows. "Dress, privacy—you've thought of everything."

"Almost." As the pair approached the statue of Queen Hildegard, Lionel slapped his hand against his forehead. "I forgot about Queen Hildegard, though. She's such a gossip. Our secret will be all over the palace by dawn."

"Okay, let it go. You've made your point." Aya snickered and tugged Lionel toward the royal corridor. When he stopped and inclined his head toward the other hallway, her brow furrowed. "We're not going to your old chambers?"

Lionel pressed his lips together to prevent himself from beaming, but the mischievous smile still lifted the corners of his mouth. "Change of plans, love. I hope that's all right?"

Aya nodded, but her body stiffened. "What's going on, Lionel?"

The king shrugged and led her down the corridor. "Nothing. I had a better date idea."

"You're a worse liar than I am." Aya poked his side. "You better not have gotten me another gift. You promised."

Lionel held up his free hand. "I remember. Gracious, I've never met a person who so despises presents."

Aya chuckled, then they walked in comfortable silence to the end of the corridor. As Lionel turned them to the right, back toward the ship's stern, Aya's eyes narrowed at her surroundings. Lionel knew she was trying to figure out where they were headed, and he hoped she wouldn't catch on before they arrived.

"This looks familiar." Aya scrunched her nose. "Or I thought it did. I guess all the hallways look similar."

"You learn to tell them apart, eventually. It only took me the first ten or so years of my life." Lionel's joke earned a smile from Aya, and his chest swelled. "We're almost there."

"Great." Aya squeezed Lionel's hand, and the pair fell back into silence.

As they neared their destination, Lionel's stomach fluttered. He thought over his plans in his head, reciting each detail so he would get everything right. After all Aya had been through, he wanted the night to go perfectly.

"Are you okay?" Aya's brows knitted together. "You look upset."

Lionel made an effort to smooth out his features. "How could I be upset when I'm with you?"

Aya smirked, but a grin quickly replaced it. "I know where we are. We're near the Starboardshire shops, right?"

Afraid of spoiling the surprise, Lionel answered with a simple "Mhmm."

"You're not going to make me drink that nasty plant water,

are you?" Aya frowned. "No, they're not open this late. Are we going into the village, then?"

Lionel sighed. "Would you be patient and trust me?"

"Fine. I *suppose* I can do that."

As they rounded the corner and entered the shopping hall-way, Aya released Lionel's hand and discreetly wiped her own on the fabric of her skirt. Lionel cringed—he hadn't realized he'd started to sweat—and rubbed his palms against his trousers. With slow, careful steps, he allowed himself to fall a few paces behind Aya and watched her browse the shops' window displays.

Exactly as Lionel had hoped, when Aya reached the mask maker's shop, she stopped and cupped her hands to the glass to peer inside. Lionel bit his lip to keep from smiling and placed his hand on her lower back. "See anything you like?"

Aya's breath fogged the glass. "The new masks look beauti-ful. Abrim's outdone himself."

"Should we take a closer look?"

Aya pulled away from the window and frowned. "It's closed."

Lionel raised his eyebrows in mock innocence and backed toward the doorway. As he knew it would, the handle turned, and the door swung open.

"What did you do?" Aya squinted. "Lionel, what's going on?"

"I thought you'd enjoy a peek at what Abrim's working on, and this is the only way we can do that and have privacy." Lionel swept his arm across the threshold. "After you."

Though Aya's face was still scrunched in skepticism, she entered the shop without further comment. Lionel closed the door behind them then lit the lantern that Abrim had left inside the doorway for him. Its light bathed the masks in a soft orange glow and cast long, face-like shadows on the walls.

Aya's fingers slid along the outline of the clock mask Abrim had shown Lionel before. "I like this one." With great care, she spun the hands of the clock around the nose. "How adorable."

Lionel chuckled. "Leave it to the cogsmith to pick out the

clock mask." He walked past a section of empty pegs and held the lantern over a different row. "I'm fond of the animal masks, myself."

Aya moved to stand next to him. "That's right. You were my frog prince, not that I knew it at the time."

Lionel sucked in a breath. *This is your opening.* "I've always loved Abrim's shop, but ever since the day I ran into you here, it's held a special meaning to me."

"Me too." Aya touched Lionel's arm. "When I think about how we met, my mind always ends up here rather than the Rudder stairwell."

"Agreed." Lionel led Aya over to the ottoman and placed the lantern on the ground. They sat next to each other, facing the window, precisely as they had nearly a year before. "How did you feel about me when we first met?"

Aya wrinkled her nose. "You know how I felt."

Lionel took her hand and squeezed it. "Humor me."

"Well, I've never believed in love at first sight." Aya bit her lip. "But I know I lusted for you from the beginning."

Even in the flickering light of the lantern, Lionel could see Aya blush. He leaned over and whispered in her ear. "As did I for you."

Aya shivered and pulled away with a smile. "In those first encounters, you represented a chance at true feeling. I'd never had that before. It was like you fell from the sky—handsome and charming and genuinely kind—a gift for all my years of emptiness at the Rudder. I couldn't resist the temptation to feel alive."

Lionel's top hat suddenly felt heavy on his head, and he wished he hadn't worn it. "Is that how you still feel about me?"

"Yes and no." Aya gazed up at the ceiling, and Lionel knew she was choosing her words carefully. "I'm still attracted to you, obviously, but it's not the same—it's deeper. When we met, you were a handsome shell that I could fill up with my own imaginings and desires. Now, you're *you*. You're witty, thoughtful, too compassionate for your own good, and you're better than anything I ever dreamed."

With a sigh, Lionel took off his top hat and held it over their clasped hands. "And this?"

Aya traced one of the metal cogs. "What about it?"

"You fell in love with a nobleman, not with a king." Lionel shook his head to keep Aya from protesting. "I know what this crown meant to you for so long. Can you truly say that seeing me wear it doesn't affect you? Doesn't fill you with anger or dread or anything you once felt toward the king?"

Aya took a deep breath. "I used to feel those things, and the first few times I saw you wearing that hat, it made me uncomfortable. But now I know it's just another part of you." Her lips curved into a smile. "I might have fallen for Willem, but I love *you*, Lionel. All of you."

Emotion swelled in Lionel's throat, but he swallowed it down. After replacing his hat on his head, he whispered, "I love you too, Aya."

The cogsmith held up her hands to display fingertips stained gray from metalworking. "Even these? I'm not the almost-noble ward you fell for, either."

"Especially those." Lionel took her hands between his and kissed her fingertips. "You know I don't care that you're not noble born. I'm proud that you're a successful merchant."

Aya cocked her head. "And how have your feelings about me changed through our courtship?"

Lionel broke into a sheepish grin as he noticed his hands had begun to shake around hers. "When I first saw you, you were this scared and broken doll of a girl. But then, before my eyes, you transformed into a fiery, stubborn seductress." Lionel allowed his eyes to drift over Aya's frame, once again appreciating the way her dress clung to her figure. "A few years ago, I would have been happy if that's all you proved to be."

Aya chuckled. "And now?"

"Now…" Lionel's heartbeat sped up, and he kissed Aya's hands again. "Now, I know that you're the strongest woman I've ever met. That you're exceedingly intelligent and insatiably curious. That you will do anything for the people you love. And I am so lucky to count myself among them."

Aya's eyes welled with tears, and her lower lip trembled, as if she wanted to speak but didn't want to lose control of her emotions.

Lionel reached up and cupped her face, his thumb resting on the corner of her mouth. "I have to ask something of you. It's not a fair question, and I want you to think carefully about your answer."

Aya swallowed. "Okay."

With his heart hammering in his chest, Lionel slid off the ottoman and lowered himself onto one knee before Aya. Her hands flew to cover her mouth, and the tears in her eyes spilled down her cheeks.

The king took a deep breath. "Aya, loving you has been the greatest privilege of my life. And if you'll have me, I'd like nothing more than to keep loving you as your husband."

"Lionel…" Aya reached down to him, and he took her hands in his again.

"Wait. Let me finish." Lionel's brow furrowed as his mind raced to remember the words he had prepared. "When I ask you the question, I'm asking you for more than love and marriage. I'm asking you to be my queen and all that the title entails. Your life will never again be fully your own. You'll become a moral example to the people, be expected to attend ceremonies and arrange charitable acts, provide the kingdom with an heir. Thousands of lives will depend upon your wisdom and compassion."

Aya frowned. "Lionel—"

"One more thing. Please, I need to get this out." The king squeezed her hand, and Aya nodded. "I didn't have a choice in becoming king, but you do in becoming queen. I mean it, Aya. If you don't want this title, but you still want me, I'll be with you. I won't take a queen, I won't have an heir, I won't—"

"Lionel." The strength of Aya's voice gave Lionel the courage to fall silent. As he stared up at her, Aya's lips curved into a gentle smile. "Just ask me."

With a deep breath, Lionel let go of Aya's hands and reached inside his jacket. From his breast pocket, he withdrew the small velvet box and held it up for her. His fingers shook as he opened the lid. "Aya Cogsmith, will you marry me?"

Aya beamed. "Yes."

As if an anchor had broken away, Lionel floated up to standing, pulling Aya with him. He crashed his lips into hers, and a warmth spread through his chest as she wrapped her arms around him. His free hand slipped behind her head, tilting it back to deepen the kiss. Aya responded by pressing her body fully against his, and Lionel forgot where she ended and where he began.

After a long moment, Aya pulled away and pressed her forehead against his. "You didn't let me finish."

"I'm sorry." Lionel brushed a wild curl away from her face. "Please do."

"I'll be your wife." Aya gave him a quick peck on the lips. "I'll be Desertera's queen." Another kiss. "I'll be the mother of the next monarch." A third kiss. "And I'll be the cogsmith."

Relief flooded Lionel, and for the first time that night, he stopped buzzing and subsided into complete calmness. He smiled. "I'd hoped you'd say that."

Lionel held the box up to Aya again and took out the ring. As he had planned, the ruby matched Aya's dress. Situated inside a golden cog, which glimmered in the faint lantern light, the stone shone a blood red. With an even wider smile, he slipped the ring on Aya's finger—a perfect fit.

"I love it." Aya poked the prongs of the cog. "Did the jeweler make it?"

"He added the cog for me, but the ruby and the golden band are original." Lionel placed the box back in his pocket and bit his lip. "It was my mother's. A dress ring, given to her by my grandfather. I wouldn't give you anything my father—"

Aya held a finger to Lionel's lips. "I'm honored. Thank you."

Lionel rubbed the back of his neck. "How would you feel about wearing it to the feast tomorrow?"

"You mean…" Aya turned her hand, watching with wide eyes as the light danced off the ring.

"Yes. I want you to attend the feast as my betrothed." Lionel wrapped his arms around her waist. "That is, if you're comfortable sharing our news with the kingdom."

"I am." Aya wrinkled her nose. "But what about the nobles? Aren't you supposed to have some kind of party to announce it?"

"That's why tomorrow is perfect." Lionel snugged her in closer. "Most monarchs hold a feast to celebrate. Well, why not co-opt the one that's already planned? And this way, all the villagers will be able to attend. You are, more than any woman in decades, their queen, too."

Aya pressed her lips together. "I hadn't thought of that, but you're right. Okay, the feast it is."

Lionel nodded. "I can't wait."

"So, what now?" Aya leaned further into Lionel's embrace. "How do you end the best night of our lives?"

Lionel brushed Aya's hair off her neck. "Who says it has to end yet?"

Aya shivered. "Not me."

"Good." Lionel placed a kiss on her bare skin. "How about we take this visit to my previous chambers, then? Once more, for old time's sake?"

Aya pulled back. As she ran her hands from Lionel's shoulders to his chest, sparks shot across his skin. "That sounds perfect."

"It will be." Lionel took Aya's hand in his and kissed her ring. "*Everything* will be now that we're really, truly, completely in this together."

18

*L*ionel and Aya walked hand in hand through the feast grounds, turning heads and inciting whispers with every step. As they approached new clusters of people, the villagers parted to allow them passage and bowed or curtsied before them. With Aya on his arm and his subjects showing such great respect, Lionel's chest swelled with pride. *This is how it was always supposed to be.*

Aya pushed back her wide-brimmed straw hat to wipe sweat from her brow. Turning her face from the crowd, she whispered to Lionel, "How long does it take to get used to all the attention?"

The king chuckled and fished his pocket watch out of his vest pocket. With an exaggerated squint, he pretended to check the time. "Until about half past eternity."

"Lovely." Aya straightened her hat. "Is it just me, or is it hotter than it was at noon?"

Lionel tucked the watch back into his pocket and frowned. The sun arched far over Portside, and a warm breeze drifted by —the day's final yawn before giving way to a cool night. He rubbed Aya's arm. "Don't be so nervous."

"Easy for you to say," Aya grumbled.

As the pair reached the long line of tables, which seemed to have tripled in number since the meeting, Rykart greeted them with a low bow. "Your Majesty, Miss Cogsmith, we're so pleased you've arrived."

Lionel tipped his top hat. "Thank you for hosting us, Mr. Farmer."

Aya started to curtsy, but Lionel held her arm to keep her from dipping. With wide eyes, she straightened then inclined her head to the farmer. "We're happy to be here, Rykart."

The farmer looked between the couple, and his mismatched eyes seemed to peer through Lionel and into his heart. "Come. You must seat yourselves so that your kingdom will follow." Rykart frowned. "Some must sit on the ground, but you will not."

Lionel thanked the farmer and allowed him to lead them to the head table, where the rest of the council stood waiting. Once he'd delivered them, Rykart dismissed himself to attend to the other guests.

Zedara's eyes landed on the couple first, flitting between their faces and Aya's left hand. She rushed forward to greet them and wrapped Aya in a hug, which the cogsmith returned with her free arm. Lionel hugged Zedara next, and when he pulled away, she beamed up at him.

Lionel mirrored her smile. "Good afternoon, Zedara."

"Indeed it is, Your Majesty." Zedara turned to Aya. "It's wonderful to see you again, Aya. I hoped you'd be here."

Aya leaned closer to Zedara. "I'm glad you're here, too. It's nice to have a friend present."

"Oh, you have more than one." Zedara craned her neck. "Sybil and Dellwyn are here somewhere. Not that we'll get much chance to see them."

Lionel squeezed Aya's hand and jutted his head toward the rest of the council, who stood behind Zedara with expectant faces.

Aya nodded. "We'll talk later. Sit by me?"

The queen dowager winked and lowered her voice. "Of course, Your Grace."

As Lionel led Aya over to the other council members, she leaned in closer to whisper, "Will that be my title as queen?"

"You'll be Your Highness as queen. For now, it's Your Grace, as it is for any transitory royal position." Lionel put on his wide smile for the other representatives and waited while they performed the customary bows and curtsies. "Hello, everyone. I'm pleased to see you all here. Miss Cogsmith, have you met all of the council members before?"

Aya clasped her hands, covering her ring in the process. "Almost. I had the pleasure of meeting Lord Collingwood, Miss Coll—I mean, Lady Greyson—Bishop, and Mr. Chef as a ward of the palace. And Lady Ollessen, of course." Aya's cheeks reddened an even deeper shade. "I used to live a few houses down from Mr. Wellman, and I've enjoyed many of Miss Baker's fine creations. But I haven't met our Bowtown representative."

Mrs. Farmer stepped forward and curtsied. "Mrs. Eveline Farmer. Pleased to meet you."

Aya's eyes lit up with recognition. "Likewise, Mrs. Farmer."

Lionel rubbed Aya's back. "Good. Now that we're all acquainted, should we take our seats? Mr. Farmer seems eager to begin the festivities."

The council members nodded, and the group headed to their chairs. While the village representatives walked farther down the tables to dine with their families and neighbors, the nobles stayed toward the end. Lionel seated himself at the head, with Aya on his right and the bishop on his left. As promised, Zedara sat next to Aya, and Lionel could just hear the queen dowager whispering the rules of noble table etiquette over the buzz of the gathering crowd.

As the rest of the subjects who dared to attend the feast seated themselves, Madeleine leaned over to address Aya. "Miss Cogsmith, it's so nice to see you again. I'm sorry it has to be in such dreadful conditions." She wrinkled her nose. "I told the farmer the fertilizer stench would ruin the feast."

The bishop scoffed, scooting his chair to distance himself from Madeleine's intrusion. "Yes, we see how accurate the heretic's rain prediction has proved. Some prophet."

Aya lifted her nose. "I don't smell anything."

"No?" Madeleine clutched her chest with a gloved hand. "Well, I suppose you must be used to it."

Lionel clenched his fist and opened his mouth to retort, but Aya gripped his knee under the table.

"I have had the privilege of spending time among the people of Bowtown." Aya smiled. "And I'm very grateful they're hosting us."

Lord Collingwood nodded from Madeleine's other side. "That's a fantastic attitude to have, my dear."

Aya blushed again. "Thank you, Lord Collingwood."

Lionel squeezed Aya's hand under the table then shot his uncle a grateful smile. The nobleman waved his hand as if shooing away a fly.

"Oh, it's a lovely act of charity and a wonderful excuse to socialize." Madeleine widened her crossed eyes. "And I'm thrilled you're doing well. You look much healthier and happier than the last time I saw you."

"Thank you, Lady Greyson. You look precisely as I remember." Aya kept her tone cool, and Lionel resisted the urge to kiss her.

Madeleine gave a tight-lipped smile. "A lot has changed since your, well, departure from the palace. Has my cousin told you that I'm a duchess now? Married to Lord Frederick Greyson, Duke of the Stacks."

"Congratulations." Aya's lips twisted into a smirk. "I know you had other marital ambitions, but I'm pleased to hear you're happily settled down."

Lionel pretended to cough to hide the cringe that overtook his features. *How did Madeleine ever think I would marry her—cousin or not?*

"Indeed. I wish I could say the same to you." Madeleine sneaked a sideways glance at Lionel, and he feigned interest in the slender clouds that drifted overhead. "Still, Miss Cogsmith, I hope as a working woman, you don't think me a boring married lady. I assure you, I still find plenty of projects to keep my mind in shape."

Aya raised her eyebrows. "Oh, I have no doubt about that."

As Lionel continued to avoid Madeleine's scrutinizing gaze, his eyes landed on Rykart. The farmer hustled toward him, carrying something that looked like a metal funnel with the thinnest part sliced off. When he reached Lionel, he held the object out as if bestowing him with a great gift. "So that your words might travel farther than their sight."

Lionel furrowed his brow but took the object without question. The other nobles looked on with narrowed eyes, but Aya beamed.

"How thoughtful, Rykart!" Aya turned the object in Lionel's hands so that the skinnier end faced him. "Speak in the small opening. The shape will amplify your voice so the crowd can hear you better."

"I see." Lionel cleared his throat, both in preparation to speak and to choke down his embarrassment at not immediately understanding the simple device. He turned to the farmer. "Are we ready to begin, then?"

Rykart nodded. "When you have used all your words, the other farmers and Mr. Chef's servers will bring out the food."

Lionel swallowed again. "Do you think there's enough for everyone?"

"Yes." The farmer's face fell. "Many did not come. They send anger from Sternville, indignation from Portside, superiority from Starboardshire, and fear from Bowtown proper."

"You did the best you could." Lionel stood and patted the farmer's shoulder. As the king looked out over the full tables and the masses seated on the ground around them, his breath hitched. Rykart may have been disappointed that the entire kingdom hadn't shown, but it appeared as if nearly half of it had. He scanned the perimeter of the feast area then sighed with relief as he spotted his guards encircling the crowd.

"And it looks like your best was pretty impressive." Lionel turned back to Rykart, but he'd already started to walk away.

As the people noticed Lionel standing, quiet descended over the tables like a cloud casting shade over the ground.

When the noise died to a whisper, Lionel held the funnel before his mouth and spoke in the loudest, clearest voice he could muster. "Thank you all for coming this late afternoon. Your presence here shows your compassion in accepting Mr. Rykart Farmer's apology and your commitment to creating a safe and peaceful kingdom for all."

The crowd clapped politely, and Lionel took a deep breath. *So far, so good.*

"Before we dine together, I would like to make two announcements. First, please remember that this is not a religious occasion. Any spiritual questions may be directed, in private, to the bishop, seated at my left." Lionel motioned to the bishop, who stood to wave to the crowd—not that anyone could see his tiny frame from more than three chairs down. "Second, I have some personal news that I hope you all will be happy to receive."

Lionel held out his hand to Aya. She took it and, with trembling knees, rose to stand next to him. "As of last night, Miss Aya Cogsmith and I are betrothed. Please join us in celebrating her first outing as the future queen of Desertera."

Though the crowd burst into applause, mixed reactions greeted Lionel. Zedara and Lord Collingwood grinned, of course, but the bishop and Madeleine pursed their lips. Farther down the row of tables, some subjects had leapt from their seats to give Aya a standing ovation, while others exchanged whispers and eye rolls. Lionel knew some of the villagers still thought Aya had manipulated her way into being queen, but he hoped that, in time, they would realize what an asset a common-born queen could be to their own affairs.

When the crowd quieted down again, Aya sat, and Lionel adjusted his grip on the funnel. "Mr. Farmer, his companions, and many charitable persons throughout the kingdom have worked hard to prepare this meal. Please enjoy it and thank our hosts when you see them."

On Lionel's last words, farmers and palace workers streamed out from between the tents of Rykart's camp, carrying trays of food and carafes of water, milk, beer, and wine.

Before Lionel could retake his seat, Lord Collingwood walked around the table to hug him. "I'm so proud of you, Son."

"Thank you, Uncle." Lionel squeezed him back, relieved no one else could hear the crack in his voice.

Lord Collingwood released him then took Aya's hand and placed a courtly kiss on her knuckles. "Welcome to the family, Your Grace. I'm honored to see you're wearing my sister's ring. I know she would have loved you."

Aya's lips quivered. "Thank you, Lord Collingwood." Then, taking a deep breath, she composed herself enough to chuckle. "Though I haven't married Lionel yet. I still have some time to wise up."

The nobleman mock whispered, "Get out while you can."

Lionel narrowed his eyes. "Oh, very funny."

Madeleine came over next, wrapping Lionel in a stiff hug. "Congratulations, Cousin." Then she whispered so that only he could hear. "I hope she's worth the trouble. I thought you were smarter than your father."

Heat flooded Lionel's face, and he shifted his body to the side, blocking Madeleine's path to Aya.

With another of her tight-lipped smiles, the noblewoman leaned around the king. One hand squeezed his shoulder, while the other lingered at his waist. "My best wishes for a long and happy union, Your Grace. You'll have to come over for tea and tell me all about your engagement."

Aya squinted between Lionel and Madeleine. "Thank you."

As Madeleine returned to her seat, Lionel retook his own. Aya patted his knee, and Lionel smiled to show that he was okay.

The bishop inclined his head to both Lionel and Aya. "Congratulations, Your Majesty, Your Grace. May your reign be long and your kingdom prosperous."

Zedara nudged Aya's side. "And may your marriage be swift to free me of this title all the sooner."

Aya laughed.

Lionel shook his head at Zedara's joke and turned back to the bishop. "Thank you, Bishop. With your guidance, and the rest of the council's, I have every faith that Aya and I will govern well."

As the servers reached the table, they placed trays and carafes in front of the group. Lionel poured himself a glass of water and took a grateful gulp. Setting his clay cup back on the table, the king breathed deeply. The air was filled with the delicious scent of steaming, whole-roasted chicken and freshly baked bread. Even the golden corncobs, not a kernel puckered or blackened, made Lionel's mouth water.

The rest of the council members glanced between Lionel and the food with hungry eyes, and Lionel realized the entire kingdom waited on him to start the feast.

With an unceremonious crack and a little help from the serving knife, he broke off a drumstick and placed it on his plate. "Dinner is served."

As Lionel finished his meal, the sun started to set over Portside, its base slipping beneath the roofs of the shops and houses. From his position at the head table, Lionel peered down the rows of chairs and around to the people who stood or sat on the ground nearby. Most of their plates appeared empty, and they chatted and laughed with those around them, while the brewer and his band of Portside merchants played joyful tunes in the background. Warmth spread through Lionel's chest. His and Rykart's plan to restore goodwill—at least for those in attendance—had worked.

The bishop caught Lionel's eye, frowning at the king's satisfied smile. With a huff, he stood. "Excuse me, Your Majesty. I'm going to walk amongst the people." He didn't wait for Lionel to respond.

Furrowing his brow, the king watched the bishop's small, white-clad frame weave through the crowd. His departure created a ripple effect, and the rest of the group stirred.

Yawning, Zedara leaned back in her chair to survey the grounds. "After that meal, I'm nearly ready for bed. I should find Sybil to relieve her for the night."

Though his body still buzzed from all the activity, Lionel yawned, too. "It was a satisfying feast. Mr. Farmer and his people did a good job."

Aya and Lord Collingwood nodded their agreement.

Madeleine stood and pressed her shoulders back in a lady-like stretch. "I'm glad the feast was successful, Your Majesty. If you don't mind, I'll head home now. I don't like to leave Lord Greyson for long in his current condition."

Although his cousin had been on her best behavior throughout dinner, Lionel's jaw clenched as he addressed her. "That's a good idea. Has Frederick improved at all?"

"More of the same, I'm afraid." Madeleine swept a loose curl away from her face. "But don't let this dour topic spoil your evening, not when there's so much to celebrate. My congratulations again, Your Majesty, Your Grace."

Aya took Lionel's hand in hers, angling the ring toward Madeleine. "Thank you."

Lionel tipped his top hat but said nothing more.

Lord Collingwood moved to stand. "Do you want me to walk you home, sweetheart?"

"Oh no, Father." Madeleine patted Lord Collingwood's shoulder to keep him seated. "I'll find one of Frederick's guards to escort me. You stay and enjoy yourself."

Lord Collingwood nodded and served himself a second helping of chicken, and Madeleine left without another word.

Aya rubbed her thumb over Lionel's hand. "I'm proud of you."

Lionel arched an eyebrow. "Is that so?"

"Yes." Aya grinned and gazed out over the crowd. Though most of the subjects still sat in groups, some had started to dance, while others mingled with people from different villages.

"You helped bring everyone together tonight. Those who attended will appreciate what you've done, and those who didn't will experience the positive effects of the peace you've created."

"I hope you're right." Lionel squinted against the setting sun. "It's going to be dark soon. Do you know if Mr. Farmer thought about lanterns or something to light the grounds?"

Aya shrugged. "He borrowed a couple of the generators. I actually had to have Mr. Glassblower make new bulbs. Luckily, between the two of us and another metalworker, we figured out how to do it. Hopefully, the wiring holds up."

Lionel leaned over and kissed Aya's temple. "You're amazing. I envy that mind of yours."

The future queen blushed.

"Ask, and you shall receive." Zedara pointed toward the farmer's camp. "It looks like someone has lit a fire."

Sure enough, an orange glow emanated from the tents, and smoke drifted into the darkening sky. The thick column blended into the blanket of gray clouds.

Lionel tilted back his head. "At least the cloud cover will keep things warmer tonight."

Voices on the other side of the camp grew louder, punctuated by shrieks and cackles.

Aya laughed and shook her head. "Sounds like they broke into another batch of liquor."

"Maybe." Lord Collingwood stood, placing one hand over his brow. "Lionel, your eyesight is better than mine. What's going on down there?"

Lionel rose and mimicked his uncle's stance. The crowd farther down the row of tables moved to check out the commotion, but at least half of the people doubled back in a jog. Sending his gaze past the feast, Lionel focused on the horizon, and that was when he saw it.

Smoke billowed from the farmer's camp, and sparks danced into the sky. A shred of smoking fabric broke away from one of the shabby tents, and Lionel watched with held breath as it landed in the nearest of the young crop fields. In seconds, an ember sputtered to life, and a line of orange flames flared across the horizon.

"We need to get out of here." Lionel's voice quavered, and he lifted a shaky hand to his mouth. "The camp. The fields. It's all on fire."

19

*L*ionel's hands trembled as he grabbed Aya's shoulders. "You and Zedara need to get out of here. Head to your shop and wait for my uncle and me there."

Aya shook her head. "I'm not leaving you. Besides, the fire's on the other side of the camp. We're fine here."

"It's not worth the risk." Lionel tucked a curl behind Aya's ear, and for that one second, the world faded away, and all he saw was her. "Please, if you love me, do as I ask."

Aya bit her lip. "Promise me you won't do anything brave."

Despite the chaos erupting around them, Lionel scoffed. "No worries there, love."

Zedara looped her arm through Aya's. "Come on. I saw Sybil and Dellwyn heading toward the village. If we hurry, we can catch them."

"Okay, fine." Aya stood on tiptoe and pressed her lips to Lionel's. "Be safe. Please."

Lionel gave her another quick kiss then handed her his top hat—it would only get in his way. "I will. Now, go."

With Zedara pulling her along, Aya jogged toward Bowtown proper and away from harm. Lionel's chest tightened as her figure faded into the darkening light, but he knew she would be safest away from the blaze. The other villagers had split into two groups—some gathering what leftover food they could and scrambling to safety, a more courageous few staying to face the fire.

Lord Collingwood rubbed the back of his neck. "What can we do, Lionel?"

"I don't know." Lionel glanced between his uncle and the flames. Already, they'd spread to a second field, and Lionel could see the silhouettes of the villagers darting helplessly around the edges.

A farmer ran past them, a single jug of water sloshing in his arms.

That won't be enough.

Lionel jogged after the farmer, waving for Lord Collingwood to follow. As he matched the farmer's pace, Lionel shouted, "How many buckets can the well fill at once?"

The farmer didn't even look at the king, but through labored pants, he replied, "One."

"Thanks." Lionel stopped and turned back to Lord Collingwood, who trotted a few paces behind. "Head into Bowtown, toward the well. Find as much rope or chain as you can and get everyone to fill up as many buckets and jugs as possible."

Lord Collingwood frowned. "It won't be enough to put out the fire."

"No." Lionel coughed as the first cloud of smoke blew over them. "But if we soak the edges, it might contain the flames to what they're already burning—save the other fields."

With a quick nod, Lord Collingwood turned on his heel and bolted toward the well. As he moved away, Lionel could hear him yelling for ropes and buckets. Covering his mouth and nose with his cravat, Lionel jogged through the smoke toward the fire. Though the smoke remained thin, thanks to the same warm wind that helped fan the flames, the heat intensified with every step Lionel took.

As Lionel reached the nearest field, the roaring of the fire and the shouts of his subjects flooded his ears. All along the rows of crops, farmers bent over the flames, attempting to smother them by beating blankets and coats at their edges.

Unsure of what else to do, Lionel spotted a gap in the line and ran over to help.

Lionel peeled off his jacket, which had grown damp with sweat, and patted at the flames. The first time, the scalding heat of the fire caused him to gasp. With a lungful of smoke, he reeled back from the blaze and wheezed into his cravat. Then, squinting against the flames, he wheeled back around and slammed his jacket to the ground.

Over and over, Lionel smashed the expensive fabric against the dirt. With each stroke, the consequences of the fire flashed before his mind—Rykart and his people roaming Bowtown, homeless; blackened fields; food prices soaring; and skeletal children begging on Baker Street. Each vision hardened his resolve, and though his efforts only won back one inch of field at a time, he kept pounding away at the flames.

A cry startled Lionel out of his trance. He straightened and craned his neck toward the noise, wiping the sweat from his brow with a damp sleeve. On the other side of the field, closer to the farmer's camp, a man whipped around a blanket that had caught on fire. As he spun with the burning fabric, his shrieks grew louder. Lionel frowned. *Why doesn't he throw it on the ground and stamp out the flames with his boots?*

In his distraction, Lionel's arms fell to his sides. His fingers grew hot, and he looked down at his own jacket to see flames licking up its back. With something between a shriek and a groan, Lionel threw his jacket to the ground and stomped the fire out, singeing the bottom of his pants. Then he pulled off his vest and beat it into the ground. A few slaps told him it was too small to be of any use, and as the fire crept up its edges, he discarded it, too.

No longer able to fight the fire in the fields, Lionel left his useless clothing behind and ran toward the man in distress. Other villagers rushed to the man's side, and the way they bobbed and weaved around the man and his blanket filled Lionel with an internal fire.

Through ragged breaths, he shouted, "Help him! Someone help him!"

As Lionel drew nearer, the man released the blanket, and it fell to the ground in a fiery heap. A guard ran over and doused the blanket with a bucket of water, but the man still screamed. Flames shrouded his legs, which danced and scrambled like two flickering torches. Within seconds, they had spread to his abdomen, and the man flung himself on the ground.

Someone crouched next to the man, attempting to roll him and smother the fire. Other individuals gathered around, beating the flames with their cloaks. The man yelled louder, grabbing at his stomach and kicking as if the people were the ones who were hurting him.

Lionel reached the scene and dropped to the ground to help hold down the man's arms. At Lionel's touch, the man fell silent and stared up at the king with wide, fearful eyes. Lionel muttered reassurances but kept his gaze focused on the diminishing flames. After a few moments, the villagers had put out the fire, and Lionel relaxed his grip on the man.

The king looked down at him with a smile. "The fire's out. You're going to be…"

The man's eyes had gone blank, and his mouth hung open, a thin line of blood dripping from the corner. Risking a glance at the man's body, Lionel saw blackened fabric melded with blistered skin. His stomach retched, but he forced the bile back down his throat.

Silence fell over the gathered villagers, and their cloaks hung limp in their hands. Lionel staggered to a standing position, his knees quivering with the effort. He backed away from the corpse, covering his mouth with a shaking hand. *I allowed this feast to happen. That man died because of me. I'm responsible for all of this.*

As Lionel's eyes focused again on the rest of the feast grounds, his senses opened back up and flooded him with horror. The fire had consumed the second field—the spot where Lionel had fought had become engulfed in flames—and threatened to spread to a third. A deep breath through his cravat caused Lionel to cough and brought him scents he'd never smelled—charred earth, singed metal, and roasted flesh that reminded him of suckling pig.

With another retch, Lionel bent over and gripped his thighs. The gulps of air he pulled in burned his lungs, but he kept breathing, over and over, until his sickness subsided.

Someone clapped him on the back. "Are you all right, boy?"

"Yeah." Lionel stood and wiped his mouth. Though black soot coated the man's face, Lionel recognized his hooked nose and stocky muscular build. It was the villager who had challenged him during Rykart's Portside speech.

"Yer Majesty." The man's eyes widened. "What are yeh doing here? It's not safe."

"I have to help." Lionel coughed. "I can't leave my people like this."

The man nodded, and Lionel detected a grudging respect in the upturn of his mouth. "Yeh stay safe, out o' the fire, okay? We need yeh in the palace more than them fields."

"I have no right to rule." Lionel shook his head. "Look what I've done—the fields, that poor man. It's all my fault."

"Don't talk like that, Yer Majesty." The man frowned. "Accidents happen. Yeh get on back to the palace now. Yer fiancée'll be worried."

"You're right." Lionel took another deep breath and straightened. "I should get out of the way."

The man bowed quickly then ran off to rejoin the other villagers. Surrounded by running people, deafening shouts, and flying embers, Lionel blinked back the tears that welled in his eyes. *He can't save Bowtown any more than I could save that man.*

With his stomach sick from guilt, Lionel hurried back toward the farmer's camp. The surly man was right—whether Lionel thought he deserved the title or not, he was the king. If he couldn't be of any use at the feast grounds, maybe he could help his subjects from the palace. When the fire burned itself out, someone would have to lead the people through the ash. And for better or worse, that someone was him.

Every structure in Rykart's encampment had either

succumbed to the flame or been blackened with smoke, so Lionel made a wide berth around it. The tents crackled, some caving in on themselves, and though he was already far enough away, Lionel leapt back to avoid the falling debris.

As he rounded the other side of the camp, Lionel collided with a young woman. Her eyes were wide and wild, and she screamed and thrashed against Lionel.

The king grabbed the woman by the shoulders, looking her over for flames or signs of injury. "Are you okay?"

The woman clutched Lionel's shirt and shook him. "My son!"

"Where is he?" Lionel scanned the area but saw no children. "Miss? Where's your son?"

"He went in." The woman let out a hoarse cough. "You have to save him. He went in."

Lionel furrowed his brow. "Went in where?"

The woman dragged Lionel closer to the camp and pointed with a trembling finger. "Our tent. There!"

Narrowing his eyes against the brightness of the burning camp, Lionel followed the line of the woman's finger to a blackened but unburned tent. Even if Lionel could make it through the flames unscathed, the smoke that billowed from the structures would surely suffocate him. He looked around again, but no one else was in sight.

Lionel clenched his jaw. Part of him wanted to run for help. After all, if he and several villagers couldn't save a man right in front of them, how could he save this poor boy alone? But that would waste the boy's precious time and cast other innocent subjects into danger. No, Lionel was responsible for this carnage, and he had wanted to help. This was his chance to atone.

"Are you sure?" Lionel tugged off his cravat. "He's in there?"

"Yes!" The veins in the woman's throat bulged as she screamed. "Please! Please save him!"

Lionel held his cravat over his nose and mouth, thankful that his sweat had moistened it to create a slightly more effective filter for the smoke. As he braced himself, Aya's words echoed in his mind—*Promise me you won't do anything brave*—and a pang stung his heart. He sent a thought toward Portside. *I'm sorry, love. I can't allow any more of my people to die.* Then, with a final breath of almost-clean air, the king charged into the camp.

Running sideways to make himself as thin as possible, Lionel skirted between two tents—one engulfed in flame and one collapsed but unburned. The heat of the fire flushed his skin and sent a new sheen of sweat racing down his chest. *Keep moving. You're not in danger yet.*

Once inside the encampment, Lionel found the cooking pit unlit, a lonely pile of ash in a circle of bare ground. Though he remained safe from the flames themselves, the air hung thick with heat and smoke, and Lionel's lungs burned. Crouching as low to the ground as possible, Lionel hurried over to the woman's tent. He couldn't hear anyone inside—though he couldn't detect any sounds over the roar of the fire—and the tent appeared stable despite its smoke-blackened exterior.

With a tentative hand, Lionel pulled back the tent flap and peeked inside. A little boy lay curled on the ground, eyes closed, clean streaks marking his sooty cheeks where he had cried. In his hand, he clutched a plush bird toy. Lionel crawled inside, closing the entrance behind him to prevent any more smoke from seeping through the gaps in the fabric. Despite the blaze outside, the tent had protected the boy from most of the smoke.

Lionel knelt next to the boy and shook him by the shoulder. "Hey! Can you hear me?"

The boy didn't stir.

More gently, Lionel placed two fingers on the boy's neck as he had watched Dr. Engel do to Frederick. A faint pulse beat against Lionel's fingertips, so he moved his hand in front of the boy's nose. He was still breathing.

Releasing a sigh he hadn't realized he'd been holding, Lionel ripped off his shirt, popping the buttons in the process.

He lifted the boy's head and carefully tied the shirt around the child's nose and mouth to help shield him from the smoke. Then Lionel stuffed the bird in his pocket, scooped the boy over his shoulder, and shuffled to the exit.

As Lionel opened the tent, a wave of heat washed over him, nearly sending him staggering back inside. He pushed through and squinted against the light of the flames. Though it might have been his imagination, he would have sworn the smoke had thickened and more tents had caught fire. He strode toward the area where he'd entered the encampment then stopped short. The burning tent had bent over to touch the collapsed one, and they combined to form a wall of fire.

Lionel's heart hammered as he spun around, searching for a new escape route. He headed back toward the boy's tent, but the flames from its neighboring structures licked too close to its walls for him to slip through, even without the boy. At the next unburned tent, the problem was the same, as it was at the next.

With a frustrated scream, Lionel stopped pacing around the camp. His head spun, and he lowered himself to the ground again. Cradling the boy to his chest with one hand, Lionel used his other to press his cravat closer to his nose. It didn't make his lungs burn any less.

Think, Lionel. There must be a way out.

Lionel looked around the camp. His vision had started to blur, but he could still make out basic shapes. A roasting spit. A bag of shucked wheat. A sickle. A large sharpening stone.

A sickle, you fucking idiot!

With renewed hope swelling in his chest, Lionel scooped the boy over his shoulder again, dropped his cravat, and shuffled toward the sickle. One of the women must have left it out from when she was sharpening the tools the other day, and Lionel swore that if he lived to discover her identity, he would give her a duchy. Though the tent nearest the sickle burned, the tool lay safely away from the flames. As Lionel's fingers grasped the handle, he couldn't help but smile.

Scurrying back to the boy's tent, Lionel pushed aside the flap with the sickle's blade and entered. Smoke hung thick in the air, thanks to Lionel's repeated disturbance of the shelter. Lionel's bare chest and arms had turned bright red, and in the confined space, the intense heat threatened to blister his skin.

Using all the strength he could muster, Lionel raised his arm and stabbed the tent wall with the sickle. A hole tore in the fabric, but the tent wobbled against the pull. Lionel shrugged the boy up his shoulder and glanced around them. One side of the tent curled at the bottom, and the flames from the neighboring structure caught hold of the fabric.

Cursing under his breath, Lionel clutched the tent wall to pull the fabric taut then slashed the sickle toward the ground. His efforts created a hole just large enough for the pair, but before Lionel could squeeze through, the tent collapsed on them. Staggering under the weight of the boy and the tent, Lionel dropped the sickle and flailed for the hole. As he did, he could hear the crackling of the fire grow closer and feel its heat radiating from only a few feet away.

Please. It can't end like this. I have to marry Aya. I have to rule. I have to live.

In the next moment, Lionel's fingers hit a wave of cool air. He'd found the hole. Pushing his arm through, he followed with the rest of the body, lugging the boy with him. As he emerged outside of the camp, Lionel sucked in a deep, almost clear breath. His body convulsed with coughs, but he strengthened his grip on the boy and kicked the tent fabric away from his legs. With what little energy he had left, Lionel dragged the boy away from the burning camp just as flames engulfed the rest of the tent.

"Help!" Lionel's voice cracked, and he sucked in another large breath. "Help us!"

The boy's mother came running from the other side of the camp, a few other villagers in tow. When she saw her son, she burst into tears and flung herself on the ground next to him. She pulled Lionel's shirt away from the boy's face and checked for a pulse and breath.

"He's alive!" The woman sobbed over her son, stroking his face with her shaking hands. "Thank you! Thank you!"

Lionel couldn't bring himself to speak, so he nodded. A wave of relief spread through his body, and with his task completed, he allowed himself to lie down next to the boy. The other villagers crowded around him, checking his body for burns or wounds, but Lionel couldn't make out their faces. In fact, everything seemed even blurrier than before, and darkness closed in around the edges of his vision.

One of the villagers gasped. "It's the king! The king saved the boy!"

Lionel's lips moved, but if any sound came out, he couldn't hear it. The world grew quiet around him, the voices muffled, and the fire became silent. He thought he heard a low rumbling sound, but that might have been his own voice gurgling uselessly in his throat or perhaps his lungs straining for clean air.

Wetness dotted Lionel's skin, and his vision focused for a second. He searched for the person who had sprinkled the water, but no buckets or jugs hovered over him, only worried, blackened faces. Then he saw it—a streak of lightning cracked across the sky, and the thunder growled again. Lionel smiled as a downpour of rain bathed his skin in cold, pure water. Then everything went black.

20

*a*s Lionel's eyes opened, bright light flooded his vision, and he let out a ragged scream. Squeezing his eyes shut again, he waited to feel the fire. Heat flushed his skin, and the sound of flames crackled all around him and in him. Pressure closed around his arms, and he realized they were empty. Where had the boy gone? Had he escaped? Or had Lionel dropped him?

"Shh. You're safe now." Aya's voice cut through the smoke in Lionel's mind, and he risked another peek into the light.

That time, Aya sat before him, her figure silhouetted against the window. Eyes still narrowed, Lionel surveyed at his surroundings. A steamer trunk, a nightstand, a mechanical frog. He was in Aya's bed.

His gaze drifted back to Aya, who smiled down at him. "How are you feeling?"

Lionel pushed himself to a sitting position, wincing as his sore muscles flexed. Though he and Aya remained alone, he pulled the blanket up to cover his bare chest in case someone else came in.

"I'm…" Lionel's lips moved, but only a squeak came out, and he realized his own wheezing breaths made the crackling sound.

Aya handed him a cup of water from the nightstand, and

Lionel noticed that Dellwyn's flower music box no longer rested next to Charlie. *Aya must have fixed it.* With a grateful smile, Lionel gulped down the entire cup. The effort of drinking made his throat burn, but the water soothed the dryness enough for him to speak.

After handing the cup back, Lionel cleared his throat. "The boy?"

"He's alive." Aya took Lionel's hand and rubbed her thumb over it in small circles. "Last I heard, he hadn't woken up, but the doctor remains optimistic."

Lionel nodded. "The fire?"

"The rain put it all out." Aya shook her head. "Even the bishop has called it a miracle."

Attempting to chuckle hurt his chest, so Lionel smiled. Instinctively, he reached for his pocket watch with his free hand then cursed as he remembered discarding his burnt vest and jacket in the field. "I lost my watch last night."

Aya pursed her lips. "I figured as much when they brought you here shirtless. But that's okay. I can repair another watch, but I can't replace you."

Lionel squeezed Aya's hand. "What time is it?"

"About seven in the morning. You only slept through the night." Aya looked over her shoulder toward the doorway. "Eldric's asleep in the sitting room. Theo slept here overnight too, but he left for Bowtown at dawn. Zedara and Lord Collingwood wanted to stay, but I sent them home after Dr. Engel saw you. She says your throat and chest might be sore from the smoke, but you'll recover in a few days."

"How long…" Lionel cringed against the ache and swallowed. "How long was I in the fire?"

"Only a couple minutes, thank the Benevolent Queen." Aya raised her gaze to the heavens. "Dr. Engel said if you or the boy had been in there even five minutes longer, you both would have died."

Lionel coughed. "I'm sorry, Aya. I had to."

"I know." Aya reached over and cupped Lionel's face. "I would have done the same thing. I'm just glad you're okay."

"Me too." Lionel put his hand over Aya's, leaning his cheek into her palm. Emotion swelled in his chest, and he fought back the tears that threatened to spill from his eyes. He was safe. Aya was safe. Everything was going to be fine.

A quiet "Ahem" sounded in the doorway, and Lionel peeked past Aya to see Eldric. His white hair stuck out on all sides, and the wrinkles around his eyes seemed to have deepened.

Lionel waved for the valet to come closer.

"Good morning, Your Majesty." Eldric's forehead creased, right between his brows, and Lionel could tell he fought against his own emotion. "I'm relieved to see you looking well after your ordeal."

"I'm relieved to see you at all." Lionel sighed and ran his fingers through his hair. The action released a burnt odor into the air, and fear jolted Lionel's heart, followed quickly by embarrassment. "Ah, I stink. I'm sorry."

"Of all the things to worry about." Aya narrowed her eyes in a playful glare. "If you're feeling up to it, there's a basin of water in my shop. It's not big enough to sit in, but you could bathe with a rag."

Lionel let out a long sigh. "That would be great. Thank you."

Eldric smoothed down his rumpled clothes. "While you bathe, Your Majesty, I'll return to the palace to fetch a fresh change of clothes and some breakfast. Dr. Engel said soft foods only for the next few days, and I'm sure Stefan can whip up something for both of you."

"That's not necessary, Eldric." Aya tucked a curl behind her ear. "I'm sure Stefan has enough on his plate this morning."

"Trust me, Your Grace, Stefan will want to cook." Eldric held up his forefinger. "One thing you'll learn as queen is that everyone has their own role to play. Stefan can't help rebuild Bowtown, but he can feed the palace. Taking away his contribution would be crueler than sparing him the work."

Lionel watched as Aya's brow furrowed then relaxed. He

hoped Eldric hadn't offended her with the unsolicited advice. While he and Aya both needed the counsel, what Aya needed even more was confidence in her own judgment.

"I understand." Aya's lips twisted into a smirk. "And I'm grateful. Stefan's cooking is leagues better than mine, anyway."

Eldric chuckled, and Lionel smiled, struggling to withhold his own snicker.

"Later this morning"—Lionel paused to swallow—"I want to go to Bowtown."

Aya and Eldric shared a skeptical glance.

"Are you sure that's wise, Your Majesty?" Eldric's mustache twitched. "You should take time to recover."

"I'm well enough." Lionel pushed himself straighter to demonstrate his fitness. "Besides, I allowed the feast to happen, so I must take responsibility for the fire. The people need to see me trying to help."

"You helped plenty last night." Aya shook her head. "You saved a little boy from a fiery death. I'm sure the people of Bowtown would agree that you deserve one day of rest."

Lionel tightened his grip on Aya's hand. "You're right. I do deserve the rest, but my—*our*—people deserve answers and new homes and food. I can't give them any of that from this bed."

Aya rolled her eyes. "Fine. But one hour in Bowtown, that's it. Then you go back to bed."

Lionel pulled Aya down to his level and kissed the top of her head. "You have a deal, Your Grace."

WHEN LIONEL, Aya, and Eldric arrived in Bowtown, they found the village quiet and closed. The houses had their doors and windows shut. No farmers were sitting outside or working in their private gardens. Even the well had been left unattended. As the group reached the outskirts, the scene changed. Rykart's camp had collapsed into a scorched pile of debris, and palace guards and farmers worked side by side, loading up sleds with rubble and ash to haul away.

Lionel shielded his eyes from the sun and searched for Theo among the workers. He spotted the captain standing at the edge of a blackened field, talking to Rykart. A sinking sensation pulled at his stomach, and Lionel realized it was the same field he had tried to protect during the fire. With a gentle nudge to Aya, Lionel led her and Eldric over to the two men.

Rykart bowed as they approached. "Good morning, Your Majesty, Your Grace."

Theo did the same. "I didn't expect to see you so soon. Are you feeling all right?"

Lionel's gaze drifted from the field to an isolated patch of black ground, where he'd watched a man burn to death. In his concern for the boy, Lionel had forgotten about the dead man, and acid welled in his throat.

Aya squeezed the king's shoulder. "Lionel?"

"I'm fine, thank you." Lionel rubbed his forehead, trying to push the memory of the man's blistered skin from his mind. "How is everything here?"

Theo straightened his leather armor. "In terms of damage, Mr. Farmer and his followers have lost their camp and all possessions it contained. The main buildings of Bowtown remained unscathed, but five fields burned to the ground."

"The fields will thrive." Rykart tapped his temple. "Fire brings rebirth in the soil. In a few months, we will have all our fields again."

Lionel stared at the burnt earth—barren for nearly as far as he could see. With a shake of his head, he replied, "I suppose you would know best, Mr. Farmer. You predicted the rain somehow."

"You know how." Rykart scratched inside his ear. "Though I heard wrong by a couple days. I must listen better next time."

Eldric scoffed.

Aya bit her lip. "What about the people, Theo? How many were harmed?"

The captain hung his head. "Three dead. About two dozen

reported injured."

Lionel's hands balled into fists, while Aya's covered her mouth.

Rykart offered a sad smile. "May the Benevolent Queen's merciful waters rush over them."

"Praise be to Her," Aya whispered.

"This is all my fault." Lionel clenched his jaw. "I knew there might be trouble when I agreed to the feast, but I never imagined…"

"You didn't start the fire." Eldric's haughty tone told Lionel that he would not tolerate any objections, so the king held his tongue. "In fact, Captain Laurel, I think we're all eager to learn the cause."

Theo glanced around the area then stepped closer to the trio. "I haven't made the announcement public yet, but I believe someone set the fire intentionally."

Lionel's mind raced through everyone who opposed the feast, Rykart Farmer, or himself in some way—it made for a long list of suspects. He cleared his throat. "What led you to that conclusion?"

"It's the only one that makes sense." Theo shrugged. "The camp ignited first, but nothing had been burning inside. Several of Rykart's followers testified to smothering all the cooking fires, and they don't use candles or lanterns."

Lionel crossed his arms. "Was anyone sighted near the camp around the time the fire started?"

"You know we never get that lucky." Theo ran his hands through his hair. "Though one of my men did find something strange in the camp. I've sworn him to secrecy, but I fear someone might have seen or overheard the evidence."

Lionel swallowed, his throat suddenly drier and achier than when he'd awoken. "What is it?"

Theo inclined his head toward Rykart.

Lionel sighed. "Mr. Farmer, as the other person responsible for this fire, can I trust you to stay silent about what you witness in this conversation?"

Rykart clasped his hands together. "As my monarchs, both

you and Her have my word."

"Thank you." Lionel straightened. "Tell us, Theo."

The captain cringed and reached into his pocket. As he pulled out the circular object, Lionel's heart leapt up into his throat. His pocket watch.

Without thinking, Lionel reached out and snatched the watch from Theo's hand. "I can't believe it survived the fire. Where was it?"

Theo scratched the back of his neck. "Right outside the camp, on the far side of the tents."

"I wonder how it got all the way over there." Lionel wound the bronze crown then held the watch up to better inspect the gears through the glass panel.

Aya leaned over and angled Lionel's hand so the watch faced her. "It's in perfect condition. It must not have had any exposure to the fire."

"How is that possible?" Lionel slipped the watch inside the pocket of the clean vest Eldric had brought him. "Maybe it fell out of my vest before I went to the fields?"

"Lionel, there's more." The severity of Theo's tone made the king stand at attention. "Your watch was found next to a shattered lantern. And both laid near the first tent to catch flame."

"What?" Lionel's stomach dropped to his feet. "How?"

Eldric huffed. "You can't be implying…"

Theo pursed his lips. "I know that Lionel would never endanger his people, or the crop fields, for that matter. But you have to think like his enemies will if they catch wind of this."

Rykart cocked his head toward the sky. "She knows you are innocent, Your Majesty. The kingdom will, too."

"Of course he is." Aya rubbed Lionel's back. "Lionel was at the head table for the entire feast. At least a dozen people, most of them nobles, can testify to that."

"Yes, but think about the precedent Lionel and I have set with the investigation into Lord Varick." Theo's face reddened, and Lionel felt his own skin burn hot with shame and fear. "We've held Lord Varick under house arrest for months, based on next to no evidence and the possibility that he acted through an emissary."

Eldric huffed. "Perhaps our culprit has a similar thought in framing His Majesty. In theory, the king could have instructed someone to set fire to the camp. He could have even lent them his watch to time when to ignite the blaze."

Theo nodded. "You see my concern."

Lionel clutched his chest—his nerves intensified the ache in his lungs. "It's awfully poetic, isn't it? I'm responsible for the fire. I allowed the feast to happen. Now someone has decided to make my blame literal."

"Don't say that. This isn't some divine justice. Someone is out to get you for political or personal reasons, plain and simple." Aya lowered her voice as a pair of farmers passed the group to enter the ashy fields. "However, your self-admonishing brings up a good point. What motive could you have for starting the fire? You gain nothing but blame and ill will."

"Does he?" Eldric raised an eyebrow. "His Majesty publicly aligned himself with the bishop, so eradicating Mr. Farmer's camp could be viewed as religiously inspired."

"Or political." Rykart stubbed his boot into the ground. "We hurt so many people. If you hurt us, it would be to protect others."

Lionel scoffed. "And, of course, being such an adamant supporter of the feast and jumping in to help fight the fire would be the perfect cover... and will only make me look even more suspicious to anyone searching for guilt."

Theo put his hands on his hips. "What do you want me to do with all this? The council, if not the people, will expect an explanation for the fire."

Eldric stepped forward. "If I may, Your Majesty, I suggest keeping this information private. You are innocent, so there's no need to breed any false suspicion or concern in the king-dom. Maybe the fire *was* an accident."

"We all know it wasn't." Aya frowned. "Lionel, you can't let the real criminal get away with this. People got hurt. They died."

"I know, love. Everyone harmed deserves justice, and they can't have that without the clues we have, however misleading they might be." Lionel gazed out across the field, where two farmers stooped over, likely searching for debris or maybe surviving roots. "Besides, what happens if the evidence was seen or overheard as Theo fears? If I cover it up and it becomes known anyway, that's even worse than if I were honest from the start."

Theo let out a long breath. "You want me to report it, then? In full?"

"It's the right thing to do." Lionel coughed, and a sharp pain shot down his throat and into his chest. "Tell them that I thought I lost my watch when I removed my vest in the fields. For all I know, it fell out of my pocket during the commotion or someone found it and moved it."

Eldric wriggled his mustache. "That sounds like an excuse, and a flimsy one at that."

Lionel shrugged. "I don't have a better explanation."

"You need no other." Rykart tapped his temple. "You are the king, the most honest one we've ever had. The people will know the truth when they hear it. They listen with their hearts, and you will speak to their ears."

Aya, Eldric, and Theo scrunched up their faces, as if Rykart had spoken in tongues. But Lionel understood. His chest swelled with hope, and he clapped the farmer on the shoulder. "Thank you, Rykart. I think that's the most sensible thing you've ever said to me."

In the face of this tragedy and someone's brazen attempt to frame him, Lionel had to trust that his people would remember all the good he had done as king. He had freed their romantic choices from the punishment of adultery. He had opened their trading options. He had listened to their concerns every month. And however disastrously it had ended, he had arranged the feast to offer recompense for allowing the farmer's misdeeds. For the time being, Lionel would appeal to their logic, and sooner or later, the truth would triumph.

21

*T*hough Lionel's new seat at the round council table was only two spots down from his previous position, his stomach fluttered with nerves. He had been cast over to Lord Collingwood's chair, and from that vantage point, the courtroom seemed somehow more foreboding, the table wider, the other representatives taller and sterner. He wished he had encouraged everyone to trade places at each meeting, then perhaps his mutiny wouldn't ring out so loudly with every creak of the chair.

Lord Collingwood sat in Lionel's seat at the table's head, which Lionel hadn't thought existed until the bishop instructed him to trade places with his uncle. All the other council members retained their customary positions, though an extra chair had been added to the table for Lord Varick, who sat between the bishop and Mrs. Farmer. While seeing Lord Varick return to the council made Lionel's sore chest tighten even further, to the nobleman's credit, he remained the only representative brave enough to look the king in the eye.

Placing a fist over his mouth, Lord Collingwood cleared his throat. "Shall we get started, then?" He paused, though his question was rhetorical. "In light of the... the evidence that arose during Captain Laurel's investigation yesterday, the core council members have seen fit to ask His Majesty to relinquish control of this meeting. As the next of kin, I will preside over the session."

Lord Collingwood shot Lionel an apologetic glance, and the king lowered his head. From the moment he first saw the blaze, Lionel knew he would have to take responsibility for the fire. And he had. In the past twenty-four hours, hardly a minute had passed without his mind flitting to the burnt man, the still-unconscious little boy, or the faceless others harmed in the chaos. Their suffering hung like a yoke around Lionel's shoulders, and in quiet moments, he wondered if he didn't deserve, just a tiny bit, to be framed for the disaster.

"I'd like to begin by welcoming Lord Varick back to the council and society at large." Lord Collingwood bowed his head. "As you all know, after months of thorough investigating, Captain Laurel and his team found no evidence linking Lord Varick to Mr. Rutt's death. Per His Majesty's mercy and fair judgment, Lord Varick has been released from house arrest early, and all charges have been dropped."

Most of the council members greeted Lord Varick with polite smiles and nods.

However, Madeleine huffed. "It should have been brought to the council for a vote." Then, as if remembering her place, she held up her gloved hands. "I'm sorry, Lord Varick. Of course I'm pleased that you've been proved innocent and freed, but these kinds of inconsistencies are why this council has been so ineffective."

Despite the precariousness of his situation, a smug satisfaction swelled in Lionel. After how Madeleine had treated him and Aya at the feast, Lionel derived a juvenile pleasure from watching her useless scramble to hang onto her power on the council.

"No offense taken, my lady. I would have wanted to help make the decision too if I were in your position." Lord Varick placed a hand over his heart. "Thank you for your kind words, Lord Collingwood. And thank you for agreeing to halve my sentence, Your Majesty. I only hope that one day we can all discover the truth about what happened to Mr. Rutt."

"As do I, Lord Varick." Lionel scanned the nobleman's features for any hint of a lie—a twitching lip, a tapping finger, a vein bulging in his neck—but he gave away nothing. *Can I trust what Lord Varick said in confidence? Is he really innocent?*

Lord Collingwood stroked his goatee. "Lady Greyson brings up a good point. Because the council is new, relatively speaking, we still have rules and regulations to sort out. That's part of what we will do here today."

Lionel shifted in his seat, and the movement of his torso sent a stabbing pain through his chest. Though he knew Lord Collingwood was on his side, Lionel couldn't help but feel like he had as a child when his uncle had placed him in time-out for arguing with Madeleine.

"To begin, I would like to explain why both Lord Varick and Lady Greyson are attending this meeting." Lord Collingwood's brow furrowed. "As the fairly elected Starboardshire representative, Lord Varick has resumed his proper position on the council. However, since I am acting in His Majesty's place today, I needed someone to fill my spot on the council's core. Given Lady Greyson's recent experience on the council, she seemed the correct choice."

The representatives nodded, while Lionel bit his tongue. He couldn't fault the logic, but he could curse himself, and he mentally shouted a string of obscenities. The system he had created might have been fair for a guilty person, but for an innocent one, it was infuriating. A twinge of empathy stirred in his gut for Lord Varick, and Lionel cursed himself again.

Lord Collingwood laced his fingers and placed his hands atop the table. "The core of the council made the executive decision to restructure for this one meeting. However, we would like everyone to vote on how we should proceed from here."

Zedara scoffed, and Lionel had to press his lips together to keep from smiling. At least he could live vicariously through her open discontent.

Miss Baker leaned forward in her chair. "Excuse me, Lord Collingwood, but what do you mean?"

Lord Collingwood sighed. "I'm sure you all know that

Captain Laurel has opened an investigation into the cause of the fire. So far, the only evidence he has uncovered points to His Majesty as the culprit. The king's pocket watch and a broken lantern were found near where the fire started."

"That's absurd." Mrs. Farmer stuck out her chin as defiantly as any disgruntled noblewoman. "His Majesty remained at the head table throughout the entire feast."

"Yes, he did." Lord Collingwood shook his head. "Her Highness, Lady Greyson, the bishop, and I all sat with him. However, no other suspects have arisen."

Lord Varick pursed his lips. "Forgive me, Your Majesty, Lord Collingwood, but if Captain Laurel treats this investigation as he did mine, I'm sure he's considered that His Majesty could have had an accomplice who lit the fire for him."

"That has been suggested." Lord Collingwood's jaw clenched, and Lionel's did the same.

Of course, Lord Varick would take every care to point out the similarities to the council. Whether Lord Varick had been guilty or innocent, Lionel's situation made for the perfect revenge. A shock coursed through Lionel, and his body went rigid. *This* is *the perfect revenge. But how could Lord Varick have pulled this off when he'd been locked in his estate on the feast night?*

Mr. Wellman hocked something up in his throat, sounding as though he was about to spit on the floor. "Pardon, my lord, but what exactly are we decidin' today? I can't make head nor tails of this sideways talk."

"You're right, Mr. Wellman. I should be more direct." Lord Collingwood drew his brows together. "We're voting on two issues. First, whether His Majesty should retain his position on the council, pending the investigation into the fire. Second, whether His Majesty should retain his full responsibilities as king until he's found innocent."

Lionel's heart leapt into his throat, and an instinctive swallow made him wince in pain. After Lord Varick's displacement, Lionel knew his position on the council would be threatened... but his title as king? Was it even possible to remove a monarch from power? And more importantly, would the council members betray him like that?

Lord Collingwood cleared his throat again. "Before we vote on His Majesty's council seat, does everyone understand the evidence against him?"

Most of the council members nodded.

Mr. Chef tapped his fingers on the table. "The evidence makes sense, but what are the charges exactly? I mean, should His Majesty be charged?"

Lionel pinched the bridge of his nose. *Do we really need to entertain this outrageous falsehood? And do I really need to sit here and listen to my character be dragged through the dirt?*

"Good question." Lord Collingwood pulled in his lips and rubbed them together before continuing. "According to Captain Laurel, *whoever* caused the fire will be charged with property damage, reckless endangerment, and three counts of manslaughter."

Squinting at the table, Lionel racked his brain for the penalty for manslaughter. His father had held a trial for the crime once before after one wellman had punched another too hard in a drunken fight. A nagging sensation told Lionel that King Archon had sentenced the man to death—*No use in clogging up the dungeon with Desertera's trash, Son*—but execution might not be the official punishment.

The bishop scooted closer to the table. "For the record, the punishments for those crimes are as follows: property damage results in a fine for the value lost, while reckless endangerment earns a stint in the dungeon." He paused, giving Lionel a small, apologetic smile. "And manslaughter ranges from life imprisonment to execution, depending on the situation and the ruling party's judgment."

Lionel coughed as the wind left his sore chest. *Life imprisonment? If this sadistic asshole succeeds in framing me, I'll spend my life locked away in the dungeon or under house arrest? Absolutely not—I'd rather be executed.*

Zedara's hand found Lionel's under the table, and she squeezed it. He risked a glance at her. With narrowed eyes and a near-imperceptible shake of her head, Zedara said what Lionel already knew. No matter what happened, she would never stop fighting for him. Lionel squeezed her hand in return, and for the briefest moment, he wished King Archon were still alive. Zedara could only do so much in her limited role as queen dowager. His father could have put an end to the entire investigation with a snap of his fingers. *Maybe ruling with a harder fist wasn't always such a bad thing.*

Lord Collingwood sighed. "Is everyone ready to vote?"

Another round of silent nods.

"Good." Lord Collingwood tugged down his jacket. "First, we will vote on whether His Majesty should retain his council seat during the investigation. Please say 'yes' or 'no' as I call on you. You may start us off, Your Highness."

"Absolutely," Zedara growled through clenched teeth. Then, at Lord Collingwood's insistent stare, she rolled her eyes. "Yes."

Lionel inclined his head toward the queen dowager.

Lord Collingwood continued. "Lady Greyson."

"No. I'm sorry, Cousin." Madeleine wrinkled her nose. "But it's only fair that you give up your seat as Lord Varick was forced to abdicate his. Temporarily, of course."

You mean so that you can keep your new spot on the council's core.

Mr. Wellman, Miss Baker, and Mr. Chef all agreed that Lionel should surrender his council position until the investigation ended.

Mrs. Farmer shook her head. "I can't believe you all. Yes, His Majesty should keep his seat. The evidence against him is obviously false, planted by Rykart's enemies."

Lionel mouthed a "thank you" across the table, and Mrs. Farmer replied with a stubborn nod.

Lord Collingwood turned to the next representative. "Lord Varick?"

"No." Lord Varick raised a slender, gloved finger in the air. "Though, for the record, I would like to say that I know you are as innocent as I am, Your Majesty. I hope Captain Laurel doesn't take as long to decide this time."

How comforting. Lionel gave the nobleman a polite nod.

The bishop didn't wait to be asked. "No."

Lionel shook his head. He thought they'd come to a mutual respect after he'd sought the bishop's counsel regarding his proposal to Aya. *I guess not.*

Lord Collingwood smoothed down his lapels. "Very well, then. My vote is yes, but the noes have the majority." He turned to Lionel. "Your Majesty, you are hereby freed from further council meetings until Captain Laurel concludes his investigation."

Lionel took a deep breath and let it out in a long whoosh. "I understand."

He'd expected the council to vote as they had, and if Lionel were being honest, a tiny place deep down in his gut shuddered with relief. Council meetings had always been stressful. He could use a break.

"And"—the bishop shot a sideways glare at Lord Collingwood—"if the conclusion of the investigation results in your innocence."

"I believe that was implied, Bishop." Lord Collingwood nearly spat the words, and Lionel struggled to keep his lip from curling into a snarl. "Now then, are we all ready to vote on the second issue?"

Around the table, there was another series of silent nods.

Lord Collingwood sighed. "To reiterate, this vote will determine whether His Majesty will retain his full responsibilities as king. If we vote no, then His Majesty will only perform ceremonial duties. If we vote yes, he will still hold court for the villages, act as judge during trials, and perform all regular acts of governing, other than sitting in on council meetings."

Lord Varick cocked an eyebrow. "And you, as next of kin, would rule in His Majesty's stead?" His gaze drifted between Lionel and Lord Collingwood.

"That is correct." Lord Collingwood fiddled with his cuff links. "Until His Majesty's innocence is officially declared, I would be interim ruler of Desertera."

Mrs. Farmer frowned. "What if His Majesty were found guilty and charged with the crimes? Would you become king?"

"I hope it never comes to that." Lord Collingwood bowed his head. "But yes, according to the law of succession, since His Majesty has no heirs and no siblings, the monarchy would default to me."

A thick silence hung in the air, and all Lionel could hear was the pounding of his own heart. Just a few months ago, the prospect of foregoing his royal responsibilities—temporarily, of course, to quote Madeleine—would have given Lionel the same modicum of relief as briefly abdicating his council seat. But losing his royal power after all the good he had done, after betrothing himself to Aya, after one of the worst disasters in Desertera's history, made Lionel sick. Yes, his decisions had created opportunity for the fire, but his blame also gave him the duty to assist Bowtown. Shouldn't he get to keep his power as king, if only so he could use it to help fix what he'd broken?

Lord Collingwood took a deep breath. "Since this decision carries more serious implications, please feel free to cast your vote whenever you are ready. I don't want anyone to rush to a decision." He paused while the council signaled their understanding. "For my part, I vote yes. Removing His Majesty from power will only stir fear and distrust throughout Desertera and lend credence to these heinous lies."

Lionel nodded to his uncle.

"Yes." Zedara smacked her hand against the table. "The fact that we are even having this vote is a disgrace to the kingdom."

That time, Lionel allowed his lips to form a tight smile.

The bishop shook his head. "I disagree. His Majesty has always emphasized fairness in ruling. If we bend the rules for him, it goes against everything he stands for." He turned to Lionel with wide eyes. "I'm sorry, Your Majesty, but as you took King Archon's place when evidence arose against him, so should Lord Collingwood take yours until you're no longer deemed unfit to rule. My vote is no."

Lionel crossed his arms and stared down at the table. He

didn't know which stung worse—that the bishop would vote to strip him of his power or that his own sense of justice had been used against him.

Mr. Wellman leaned forward. "No."

The representatives waited for him to say more, but when he didn't, Miss Baker took her turn. "I think the bishop is right. If you allow yourself to be reprimanded now, Your Majesty, I'm sure my people will respect you even more when your innocence is proved. I vote no."

Three negative votes already. Two more would remove him from power. Lionel forced his face to stay neutral, though under the table, he clasped his knees until his knuckles turned white.

"You're all making a mistake." Mrs. Farmer tightened her ponytail. "Perceived innocence doesn't matter. True innocence does. I say yes."

Lionel inclined his head toward Mrs. Farmer, and she replied in kind.

Mr. Chef played with the end of his mustache. "I have to vote no. After all the crimes I watched King Archon commit, I couldn't live with myself if I did nothing now. I believe you're innocent, Your Majesty, but given the evidence, my conscience can't take the chance."

Tears welled in Lionel's eyes. During his time as king, he'd done everything in his power to prove he wasn't like his father. To Stefan alone, he'd ordered small meals that created no waste, never made special requests, and always complimented the food. Even after all that, the chef valued Lionel's title and heritage more than his actions. *Will I never be anything more than the tyrant's heir?*

The representatives glanced between Lord Varick and Madeleine. With a sigh, Lionel started to think through what he would say. While he trusted Madeleine to vote with the family—he knew she just wanted the last word for dramatics— he also trusted Lord Varick to dole out his payback. It would only take one more "no" vote to reduce Lionel to a figurehead, and he could practically feel Lord Varick's glee emanating from across the table.

Finally, Lord Varick tapped his cane against the floor. "If I were to stick with the bishop's logic, then I would have to vote no."

Lionel bit his bottom lip to keep from cursing.

Lord Varick grinned at the king. "But I must follow my own logic."

Lionel withheld a gasp. *He won't...*

"When I was wrongfully suspected of murder, His Majesty wisely chose to remove me from the council." Lord Varick spun his cane. "However, since my guilt remained unestablished, His Majesty did not strip me of my title, estate, or holdings. I could never return such generosity with cruelty, so I must vote yes. His Majesty should retain his full power as king."

Lionel bit down on his lip harder to suppress his grin. Despite what Lionel had done to him, Lord Varick kept his composure and voted with fairness and reason. Once Madeleine delivered her vote, Lionel's title and responsibilities would be safe, and he could help find the true arsonist and repair the damage to Bowtown.

As all eyes turned to Madeleine, she tucked a wild curl back into her bun. "The evidence against His Majesty seems a little too convenient to me, and I have spent many hours pondering why he might want to sabotage the event he so enthusiastically allowed to happen."

The group met Madeleine's thoughts with nods. Lionel forced himself to take long, steady breaths, and he prayed the others couldn't hear how loudly his heart pounded in his chest. *Just a few more seconds. You're almost free of this ridiculous meeting.*

"That being said, I did come up with a couple theories. Ruining the feast would further discredit the farmer and, therefore, reinforce the true faith led by the bishop." Madeleine tapped her chin. "And if His Majesty both allowed the feast to happen and acted as the people's savior after things went awry, he would receive double the goodwill."

Madeleine sighed and turned to Lionel. "That's all

desperate speculation, me trying to make sense of a nonsensical situation. I don't think you have it in you to hurt anyone, Your Majesty, not even a fly."

Lionel offered a tight-lipped smile. *Then hurry up and vote already.*

"However, given the existing evidence and some of your other decisions as king, I have to do what I think is best for the kingdom." Madeleine paused, and Lionel's heart nearly beat through his rib cage. "Forgive me, Cousin, but my vote is no."

Sound dulled, and a hazy numbness washed over Lionel. *How can she do this to me? To Desertera?*

Zedara slammed her hands against the table and stood up, leaning over Lionel to glower at Madeleine. "How dare you, you selfish little brat! You want what's best for the kingdom? In what world is civil unrest and no king best for the kingdom?"

Mr. Wellman pointed at Lord Collingwood. "We still have a king."

"An interim ruler, you ignorant—" Zedara stopped short and took a deep breath. "After all the shit this kingdom's been through, this was the last thing we needed. I hope you all are happy."

With that, Zedara squeezed Lionel's shoulder then turned and stormed out of the courtroom. The door slammed behind her, and its echo washed over the group. They sat in silence, and Lionel found each member unwilling to meet his gaze.

After a few moments, Lord Collingwood stood. "Your Majesty, do you understand the council's judgment?"

Lionel nodded, too stunned to speak.

"Good." Lord Collingwood pursed his lips. "If no one else has anything to say, this meeting is adjourned."

Keeping their eyes toward the floor, the representatives rose from their seats and filed out of the courtroom. Only Lord Varick paused to bow to Lionel.

Once they had left, Lord Collingwood walked over and sat in Zedara's empty chair. "I'm sorry it has to be me, Son. I feel like I'm betraying you."

Lionel shook his head. "I'm glad it's you. You're the only

man I would trust to rule in my stead."

Lord Collingwood clapped Lionel on the shoulder. "That's kind of you to say. I'll seek your counsel whenever possible and do my best to rule as you would."

Hot tears slipped down Lionel's cheeks, and he put his head in his hands. "Maybe you shouldn't. I tried so hard not to be like my father, to be fair and just and merciful. And look where it got me."

"True." Lord Collingwood chuckled. "But look where being cruel got him."

Lionel raised his head and managed a dry laugh, though the action hurt his chest. As the pain reverberated in his lungs, Lionel's mind sobered. "You don't think they'll get away with framing me, do you?"

"No, I don't. You know Theo will work tirelessly to prove your innocence." Lord Collingwood's eyes hardened. "And if he can't, it doesn't matter. The one good thing to come from this meeting is that I have the power to protect you now. I won't let anything happen to you, Lionel."

"I know, Uncle." Lionel rubbed the back of his neck. "But you shouldn't have to. I should have been smart enough to protect myself."

Lord Collingwood's gaze dropped to the floor.

Lionel lifted his eyes upward and looked around the tiered seating in the courtroom. Even when he presided over trials, the whispering and cackling of the spectators made his conscience squirm with guilt. He couldn't imagine what it would feel like to be the one on trial, to face the brunt of the kingdom's judgment.

With a defiant nod, Lionel promised it would never happen. No matter what social codes he had to break or what laws he had to bend, Lionel would clear his name and reclaim his place as king. And once he had returned to the throne, Lionel's first action would be to set up more safeguards for his title and to protect himself and Aya from any future attempts at treason. He couldn't—he *wouldn't*—ever let himself become this helpless again.

22

"Thank you all for letting me speak with you today." Lionel took off his top hat and rested it on his knees. He stared into each face in turn—the two wives who had lost husbands, the father who had lost his grown daughter, and the grandfather of the little boy Lionel had saved. In the tiny, undecorated living room of the latter's Bowtown home, they all sat close together in two lines—the grieving on one side, and Lionel and Aya on the other, with Theo standing guard. While Lionel had refused Mr. Farmer's offer of water upon entry, his eyes flitted to the kitchen area, wishing he'd thought about his dry throat.

Instead, Lionel pressed his hand to his chest. Feeling the mysterious key tucked safely inside his jacket pocket, Lionel took a deep breath, as if he could draw strength from its presence. After being removed from the council and losing his full power as king, Lionel's first act had been to take the key from *The Key to the Kingdom* and place it on his person. That way, if he lost his chambers or rights to his possessions, the key would remain hidden and safe.

Aya reached over and squeezed Lionel's hand, her soft smile encouraging him to continue. Theo stood with his hands clasped behind his back, and Lionel could tell by the incremental twitches of his lips that he struggled not to look irritated. Like Eldric, Theo had argued with Lionel about visiting with the families of the people who had died—and the boy who still might die—because of the Bowtown fire. However, also like Eldric, Theo respected Lionel enough, even in his new status of figurehead king, not to stop his ill-advised plan.

"I wanted to come here to apologize to all of you." Lionel took another breath, wincing as his lungs stretched. "As your king, I allowed the feast to happen, and therefore, I take responsibility for the tragic way it ended. I cannot imagine the pain you all must be going through, and I'm deeply sorry for my part in it."

The younger of the two wives—she looked to be in her early twenties, like Aya and Lionel themselves—leaned forward. With puffy, red-stained eyes, she glared at Lionel. "The rumors are true, aren't they, Your Majesty? You helped start the fire. That's why you're here."

Lionel flinched at the malice in her voice then recovered and shook his head. "No, I had nothing to do with—"

"How dare you accuse His Majesty! He saved my grandson!" The grandfather smacked a leathery hand against his thigh. "The coward who lit that fire wouldn't have run back into it for a little boy."

The father, a middle-aged man with a back already bent from a lifetime of labor, crossed his arms. "Sure he might have. Wanting to destroy the heretic's camp is different than wanting to kill a little boy. Though he woulda been smart to do it when the camp was empty."

"Excuse me." Lionel cleared his throat, using all his strength to avoid a second cringe in front of the farmers. "If you would like to exchange theories about my guilt and besmirch my character, you can do so when I leave. Until then, please direct all your comments and questions to my face, and I'll give you the same courtesy."

Though the farmers tensed at Lionel's words, they each offered a begrudging nod.

"Fine, then." The father leaned back in his chair. "If you didn't start the fire, who did?"

Lionel motioned to Theo. "Captain Laurel and his men are conducting a thorough investigation into the fire. In fact, when we're done speaking here, I would ask that you all answer his questions. Anything you might have seen or heard, however insignificant it seems, could help bring justice for your loved ones."

"These investigations never go anywhere. You still don't know what happened to that male whore." The father gritted his teeth. "Why should we believe this time will be any different?"

The king started to answer, but Aya held out her hand to stop him. She smoothed down the fabric of her dress and looked the father square in the eye. "Because, often, justice takes a long time. Do you know who I am, Mr. Farmer?"

He nodded. "The cogsmith's daughter."

"That's right." Aya smirked. "King Archon unfairly sent my father to execution, and I had to grieve in private, as the child of a traitor, for ten years. His Majesty's first act as king was to clear my father's name and provide restitution for my suffering."

The younger Mrs. Farmer inclined her head toward Aya's ring. "Yes, but His Majesty obviously had a special interest in you, *Your Grace*."

Anger flared within Lionel, and he bit his tongue. *Aya can handle this. She's faced worse from Madeleine and the other merchants.*

"You're right." Aya shrugged. "But His Majesty didn't have to give me justice. In fact, it would have been easier for him to coerce me into marriage when I was at my most vulnerable."

Lionel frowned. Such a thought had never even crossed his mind, but it was exactly what his father had done with Zedara and some of his other wives.

"But it's not just me," Aya continued. "His Majesty worked tirelessly to acquit Rykart Farmer of Madam Huxley's murder. He's still working to solve Mr. Rutt's death. And most importantly, he doesn't have to be here now."

Aya met the farmers' furrowed brows with an eye roll. "The whole kingdom has gotten so used to Lionel's kindness already. But think—what would King Archon have done if your husbands or children died at one of his events? Nothing, except maybe ensure that your noble landlords had new farmers to work their land."

Lionel withheld a scoff. That sounded like his father, all right.

"Instead, Lionel's here, in one of *your* homes, giving his condolences and listening to you attack his character without punishment." Aya shook her head. "Does that sound like the kind of man who would risk countless lives and the kingdom's food supply by setting Bowtown on fire?"

The younger Mrs. Farmer looked at the unlevel floor, her cheeks as red as the gemstone in Aya's ring.

With tears in his eyes, the father shook his head. "Forgive me, Your Majesty. It was unfair of me to accuse you."

"I accept your apology." Though anger still burned in his chest, the empathy Lionel felt for the farmers overpowered it. "Everyone in this room has lost, or nearly lost, someone they love in unjust circumstances. That grief clouds our judgment and directs our thoughts. In your situation, I would be looking for someone to blame, as well."

A heavy silence hung in the air, and after a moment, the creaking of Theo's leather armor broke it as he straightened. "Does anyone else have questions for His Majesty? He needs to return to the palace soon."

The older Mrs. Farmer, who had remained quiet and still throughout the arguing, placed a hand at the base of her throat. "Is it true, Your Majesty?" She drew in a ragged breath. "Were you there when my husband died?"

Lionel closed his eyes for a brief moment, trying to push away memories of the burning man's bubbling flesh. "Yes. I and a few other men tried to save him, but the fire had already done too much damage."

"Did he…" The woman swallowed hard. "Did he suffer?"

With a sigh, Lionel ran his fingers through his hair. "Yes, ma'am." At the older wife's gulping sob and the other farmers' gasps, Lionel drew his brows together. "I won't lie to you. Any of you. I'm sorry, Mrs. Farmer. Your husband was in great pain, but only for a few moments. He passed quickly, and I believe, right before the end, he no longer felt the torment of his body."

The older Mrs. Farmer dabbed her sleeve under her eyes, and Lionel pulled out his pocket square and handed it to her. Its colorful paisley pattern stood out against the woman's dusty black clothing, and Lionel did his best not to flush. Being around the villagers always reminded him of the frivolities of noble life, and he hoped Aya would help set a more restrained example for the ladies of the kingdom… that was, if she still got to be queen.

"Thank you, Your Majesty." The older Mrs. Farmer wrung his pocket square in her hands. "I appreciate your honesty. The other men, well, they had different stories to tell."

"I'm sure they were trying to protect you, Mrs. Farmer, but I understand why you wanted to know." Lionel rubbed the back of his neck. "There's actually another reason I came here today. In addition to my sincerest condolences, I'd also like to offer you help. I know you all, especially you ladies, will face added financial strain during the coming months. If there is anything I can do to ease that burden, please don't hesitate to ask now or to send word via one of my guards later."

Though the farmers' eyes widened, none of them spoke up. Aya had cautioned Lionel that their pride might prevent them from taking his aid, at least in front of each other, so he kept his face smooth and his pause short.

"Okay. Captain Laurel has some questions about the investigation, if you would be so kind as to answer them." Lionel turned to the grandfather. "If you wouldn't mind, Mr. Farmer, could Her Grace and I visit your grandson? I'd like to see how he and his mother are doing."

"Of course, Your Majesty." The old man pointed to one of the small house's interior doors. "They're in the bedroom."

"Thank you." Lionel replaced his top hat on his head then stood to leave the living room, with Aya following behind. As he walked past the older Mrs. Farmer, she held his pocket square out for him, and he took it with a small incline of his head.

At the door, Lionel knocked softly, waiting until the boy's mother called out, "Come in." He opened the door for Aya and allowed her to go in first. As he shut the door behind him, he could hear Theo's voice reciting the investigation procedure for the farmers in an almost mechanical fashion. *Poor Theo. I hope he finds a strong lead soon, for him as much as me.*

Turning back around, Lionel bowed to the mother. When her eyes met his, they widened with recognition. She pushed herself off the steamer trunk—the only piece of furniture in the room besides the narrow bed on which her son slept—and gave a small curtsy. "Your Majesty, Your Grace, welcome."

Lionel tried not to wince at the cracking of the mother's voice, even more bedraggled sounding than his own had been after the fire. "Thank you, Miss Farmer. We've come to see how your son is doing."

Miss Farmer sighed and looked over her shoulder at the boy. Even from where he stood, Lionel could see her son's chest rattle with the effort of breathing.

"The doctor is surprised he's survived this long." Miss Farmer retook her seat on the trunk. With a trembling hand, she stroked the boy's blond hair away from his forehead. "He sleeps most of the time, partly because he's weak, but also because of the tonic the doctor gives him. She says sleeping will help his body heal faster."

Aya offered a kind smile. "I'm sure she knows best."

"Is the doctor optimistic that he'll pull through?" Lionel put his hand over his mouth, trying to quell the sadness and guilt that welled inside him.

"At this point, she still doubts he'll live." Miss Farmer rubbed her thumb against the boy's cheek. "But even if he does, he'll never be my son again."

Lionel sucked in a breath. "What do you mean?"

"He hasn't been awake long enough to know for sure." Miss Farmer stared at the blanket as she spoke, her eyes and voice expressionless. "But the doctor says severe smoke inhalation can cause chronic symptoms. At best, she thinks he'll wheeze and cough for the rest of his life. At worst, he could have trouble walking or controlling his body, or even be dumb-stricken."

Tears stung Lionel's eyes, and the rage that pulled at his chest turned inward to fester in the pit of his stomach. "I'm so sorry. I wish… I should have run right into the camp when you told me. I wasted time asking questions. I could have saved him faster."

Aya's hand traced up and down his back. "It's not your fault, Lionel."

Miss Farmer met Lionel's gaze with her empty eyes. "Her Grace is right. I'm the one to blame. I should have kept a better watch over him. He never should have gone back into the camp in the first place. And now, because of my neglect as a mother, what quality of life can he possibly have?"

A small part of Lionel shivered with relief—he would never have forgiven himself if Miss Farmer could not—but a greater part of him surged with anger again. "That night was chaos, Miss Farmer. The fire separated families from every side. What happened to you and your son could have happened to anyone."

"And he can still have a good life." Aya tucked a curl behind her ear. "He has a roof over his head. He has a family who loves him. Never underestimate the power of the little things."

"Is that enough?" Miss Farmer rubbed her forehead. "If he can't work the land, can't even sit with the wives and prepare the plants or feed the livestock, how will he earn a living? If he's dumb-stricken, what woman will marry him and bear his children? Who will support him when my father and I are gone? How will he find joy and fulfillment in life when so much could be denied him?"

Lionel crossed the room and knelt on one knee before Miss Farmer, taking her hand in his. "You can't worry about all that yet. Right now, you need to make sure he has a life. Then, once you know he'll have one, you can worry about the quality."

"I just… the doctor seems so certain he'll have problems. I can't help but wonder…" Miss Farmer stared deeper into Lionel's eyes, and he saw the wall within her break as tears streamed down her cheeks. "What if… would it have been better if you hadn't saved him, Your Majesty? If he had fainted and passed painlessly in the tent? If he passed now rather than face whatever cruel future his body has prepared?"

"You'll never know. You have to trust that your son will be strong enough to find meaning in his life and that you will be strong enough to help him." Lionel released Miss Farmer's hand but remained kneeling in front of her. "As for the financial concerns, I made this offer to your father and the others already, but I extend it to you, too. Say the word, and your family will never have to worry about money again. Whether your son can work or not, I'll make sure he is provided for."

Miss Farmer's lips parted, and she looked between Lionel and Aya with a furrowed brow. "I couldn't… I would never ask or expect that, Your Majesty."

Lionel shook his head. "I know, but I'm offering. At the very least, would you consider allowing me to pay for his visits from the doctor? You asked me to save your son, and from what I can see, he's not been saved yet."

"I—"

The boy coughed, and his eyes fluttered open. With a racing heart, Lionel stood and backed away, allowing Miss Farmer to attend to her son.

She grabbed a cup of water from the floor between the trunk and the bed and raised it to the boy's lips. He took a series of tiny sips, wincing with each swallow. Then, as if exhausted from the effort, his eyes slipped shut and his breathing resumed its regular but shaky pattern.

"Okay." Miss Farmer set the cup back down then leaned over to place a kiss on her son's forehead. When she straightened, she took a deep breath. "In Bowtown, we don't often accept charity. We prefer to barter and trade favors. But since I lost everything in the fire, and I doubt my skills would be of much use to you, I have nothing to give you."

Lionel frowned. "I'm not asking—"

Aya placed her hand on his arm, and Lionel fell silent. He looked between the two women, and he saw an unspoken understanding in the soft upturn of their lips.

"I will accept your offer to help, Your Majesty." Miss Farmer held up a finger to keep Lionel quiet, and he bit his tongue. "But you must promise me, if you ever require a favor from a farmer, you'll seek me out first so that I can repay this debt, as uneven as my payment might be."

"A fair deal." Lionel tipped his top hat. "Between us, I'm not normally one to pray, but I'll say a few words for your son."

"Thank you." Miss Farmer bowed her head. "I hope your prayers are answered more quickly than mine."

"Can I ask…" Aya sucked in her bottom lip. "I'm sorry, I know it doesn't change anything, but do you know why he ran back into the camp?"

Miss Farmer smiled sadly and pulled back the blanket. Underneath, the boy clutched the stuffed bird toy between his tiny hands.

"It's all he has left of his father." Miss Farmer tucked the blanket back around her son. "Just as he's all I have left of my lover."

Aya's hand slipped into Lionel's. "I'm so sorry."

Lionel squeezed Aya's hand and pulled her toward the door. "Take care, Miss Farmer. I hope to hear good news from you soon."

As Lionel reached for the doorknob, the young mother cleared her throat. "Your Majesty?"

Lionel stopped. "Yes?"

Miss Farmer pursed her lips. "Word has reached me, even hidden away as I am, about the evidence against you."

Her hand balled into a fist, and though he was innocent, a cold shame washed over Lionel. He swallowed. "And?"

"I don't believe it." Miss Farmer tapped her clenched fist against her knee. "And I'm telling anyone who will listen that it's all a lie. You're a good man, Your Majesty."

Tears welled in Lionel's eyes again, and he blinked them

away. "Thank you, Miss Farmer. You have no idea how much I needed to hear that today."

The young mother nodded, and Lionel and Aya left the bedroom. As Lionel shut the door behind him, he paused with his hand still on the doorknob and closed his eyes. No matter how foolish it felt, he had to keep his word.

I don't think you're out there, and if you are, I doubt you're listening. At least, you're probably not listening to me after how easily I stopped believing in you. But just in case, Your Divine Highness, please heal Miss Farmer's son. Don't do it for me. Do it for their family. They're good people, and they don't deserve to be punished for having a pushover for a king. None of your children do.

A thought struck Lionel then, ringing out in his mind as clear and sonorous as an early morning bell. The people might deserve a just king, as he'd tried to be, but they didn't deserve the pushover he'd become. Whoever had framed him for the crime must have known that Lionel would allow himself to be removed from power, maybe even sent to trial over the false evidence. After all, that was the *fair* thing to do, especially after Lord Varick's house arrest.

In his attempts to rule with fairness, Lionel had put himself —and, by extension, the entire kingdom—into jeopardy. More than anything, Lionel wanted his people to live full, happy lives, free from the fear that had hung over them during King Archon's rule. Though Lionel trusted Lord Collingwood, the only way to guarantee the people were treated right was by regaining his power. Lionel would have to get tough—he might even have to be ruthless—but he was willing to do what it took. For the good of his subjects, Lionel wouldn't allow himself to be pushed around anymore.

23

"Your Majesty, Your Grace, please come in." Madeleine curtsied as Lionel and Aya entered the Greyson estate's lavish parlor. With a gloved hand, she waved away the maid. "Miss Valet, make some tea for our guests."

Lionel quirked an eyebrow. "Are we using titles, Lady Greyson? I thought you said this was a family invitation."

The noblewoman blushed. "It is, yes." Stepping forward, she took Lionel's hands in hers and squeezed them. "Forgive me, Cousin. And thank you for coming. I'm pleased you changed your mind."

Lionel forced his lips into a tight smile. "You're welcome."

When Madeleine's maid had first conveyed the invitation to tea, Lionel had rejected it. However, Aya insisted they recant, on account of keeping an eye on the council and maintaining familial alliances. Once Lionel's blood had stopped boiling, he realized she was right.

Madeleine released Lionel's hands and repeated the gesture with Aya. "Welcome to our home. If it's all right, I'd like for you to call me Madeleine in familiar company."

"Very well." Aya nodded, but Lionel detected a flicker of distrust in her emerald eyes. "You may call me Aya, then."

"Splendid." Madeleine let go of Aya's hands and clapped hers together. "Please make yourselves comfortable. Lord Greyson—Frederick, I should say—will be along any moment. He was freshening up when you arrived."

Lionel and Aya seated themselves on one of the plush couches, and Madeleine sat opposite them. While they waited for Frederick to make his entrance, an awkward silence descended over the group. Out of the corner of his eye, Lionel could see Aya sizing up the estate—no doubt appalled at its opulence—and Madeleine sizing up Aya.

Before Lionel could think of something congenial to say to distract the women from their thoughts, Frederick strolled into the room. When Lionel turned to face the duke, his jaw nearly dropped. Though bags still hung under his eyes and he appeared thin, Frederick's pallor had been restored to its regular tan glow, and he carried himself with a confident gait.

"You look like a new man, Frederick." Lionel reached his hand over the back of the couch, and the duke shook it. "You're feeling better?"

"Much, thank you." Frederick walked around to his leather armchair, but before he sat, he presented Aya with a deep bow. "I'm thrilled to finally meet you, Your Grace. I've heard many good things about you from the rest of the family."

"You're too kind." Aya inclined her head in return. "And I understand this is a familial visit, so please, call me Aya."

Frederick grinned and eased into his chair, his leg muscles shaking slightly with the effort. "Congratulations on your engagement. I'm sorry I wasn't there when you announced it."

"Think nothing of it." Lionel offered a dry laugh. "In fact, I wish I hadn't been at the feast either"

"Yes." Frederick cleared his throat. "Well…"

Madeleine leaned forward. "I'd like to give you both my congratulations again, too." Looking down at her lap, she sighed. "I'd also like to apologize for the way I reacted to your news at the feast. While no excuse justifies my rudeness, between the conditions at that gathering and Frederick still being ill, I wasn't in a good frame of mind, and I shouldn't have allowed my frustrations to get the better of me. I'm deeply sorry."

For the second time, Lionel had to tighten his jaw to keep it from dropping. He rubbed the back of his neck. "Thank you, Madeleine. That means a lot to me—to us."

"Yes, thank you." Aya's voice conveyed warmth, but Lionel felt the couch shift as she tensed at his side. "I appreciate your honesty. If Lionel were sick, I'm sure I'd be out of sorts, too." Aya's hand wrapped around Lionel's, and he smiled. *How can I ever deserve her?*

"You both must be excited to have the courtship phase over with—all that uncertainty and behavioral politics." Madeleine shivered in mock disgust. "The two months Frederick courted me felt like the longest of my life."

"Courting was fine, actually. We both knew what we wanted before we took that step." Aya's gaze drifted to Lionel, and his chest swelled at the love and surety he saw in her eyes. "Though I am relieved that we won't have to deal with the engagement rumors anymore."

Lionel chuckled. "I'm afraid there will always be rumors, love. First, it'll be about the wedding—when it is, what dress you'll wear, who's invited."

"Right." Frederick smirked. "Then, the pregnancy bidding will begin."

"Oh, for fu—" Aya flushed a delicious shade of pink. "I mean, I suppose I should have figured. I've been trying to take this all one day at a time."

"That's smart. If you let it, the wedding planning will over-whelm you." Madeleine fiddled with the lace cuff of her glove. "If you need any help with the wedding—well, I'm sure you'll have Zedara—but if you'd like a second opinion, I'd be happy to offer mine."

Aya grinned, genuinely that time. "That would be nice. Thanks, Madeleine."

The maid bustled back in then, carrying a silver tray. Clinking sounds filled the room as the bright-pink tea set and

matching serving plates—complete with the traditional assort-
ment of bread, fruits, and goat cheeses—shifted with Miss
Valet's steps. As she set the tray down on the low coffee table,
Lionel noticed that the yellow vase and its flowers had been
removed, and he snickered to himself. *What, Madeleine? No hot-
pink vase to match?*

"In the large pot, we have tea, and the smaller one contains
hot chocolate." Madeleine winked at Aya. "I remembered
that's what you ordered when we dined at the Starboardshire
tea room. You don't have a taste for tea, right?"

"Right." Aya scooted to the edge of the couch and poured
herself a cup. "This is perfect. Thank you for thinking of me."

Lionel looked at the two women in turn, and he swore he
saw an unspoken understanding pass between them. Their
bodies shifted toward each other, their brows relaxed, and the
intangible tension in the air dissipated. With a sigh, he tried to
push down his own negative feelings and distrust toward his
cousin. Madeleine was making a real effort at reconciliation,
and if Aya could be receptive to it, then so could he.

The group fell quiet for a few moments, and the only
sounds in the room were the cascading of liquid from spouts
and the clinking of spoons against cups. As Lionel lifted his tea
to his lips, the steam filled his nostrils and sent a warm calm
through his body. He enjoyed drinking tea—not as much as
Madeleine—but the aroma and the temptation before the sip
were his favorite parts.

Frederick grabbed a crust of bread from the tray and
scarfed it down. Watching made Lionel wince—though four
days had passed since the fire, his throat still ached on occasion, particularly when he ate hard foods. He took a gulp of
tea, relishing how the heat loosened his sore muscles.

"I'm glad to see you have your appetite back, Frederick."
Lionel raised his eyebrows. "Have all of your symptoms
cleared?"

Frederick nodded and held a hand over his mouth while he
chewed. "It's been a process over the last few days. My fever
broke first, and the nausea followed soon after. I still have some

aches, especially in my throat and abdomen from the illness, but my strength is returning. You wouldn't believe how feeble you become after a week in bed."

Aya took a crumble of cheese from the spread. "What did Dr. Engel say?"

"She's been impressed with the rate of my recovery." Frederick shrugged. "I'm not surprised. I told everyone it was a simple flu."

Madeleine rolled her eyes, but her smile softened the gesture. "Darling, I don't think there's such a thing as a *simple* flu. And besides, where was all that bravado when you kept asking for your tonic?"

Lionel and Aya shared a sideways glance, barely holding back their own grins.

Frederick pouted. "Why are you teasing me in front of our guests?"

"They're family." Madeleine turned back to the couple. "You were there, Lionel. Dr. Engel said to stop giving Freddy the black elder after his fever broke, which it had when I came home from the feast the other night. I still gave him the ginger root for an extra day."

"That is what the doctor said, Frederick." Lionel took another sip of his tea to hide his smile. *It's sweet how much she cares about him.*

Frederick put up a hand. "You can't blame me for wanting to make sure I got better. Though, of course, it seems Dr. Engel was right. I've healed fine without the tonic."

Aya swirled her spoon in her cup. "Does this mean you'll be taking the spot on the council's core, Frederick? Or does your father want you to stay on, Madeleine?"

Though Madeleine opened her mouth to reply, Frederick cut her off. "We haven't spoken to Stanton yet, but I'm sure he'll want me to rejoin the council. Madeleine was only acting as my emissary."

So I should blame you for all but losing my crown, then? Lionel's hand drifted up to his chest, where the key still hid inside his jacket. He glanced at Aya, and from the lines that had formed between her brows, he knew she was having the same thought.

"I had hoped to avoid this topic, but I should have known it would be inevitable." Madeleine tightened her bun and pushed away the wild curls around her face. "Lionel, I'm sorry for the way I voted at the council meeting. I didn't—"

"What Madeleine means to say is that *I* didn't have a choice." Frederick shifted in his seat. "I hope you can understand, but I didn't think it would be fair to allow you to keep your full responsibilities with the evidence against you and the precedent the council set by restricting Lord Varick's rights during his similar ordeal."

Lionel nodded. Only his clenched jaw prevented him from asking Frederick what he thought of Lord Varick's vote to allow Lionel to keep his power. Perhaps Madeleine hadn't told him for fear of making the duke feel guilty or threatening his newly restored health.

"At any rate," Frederick continued, "I thought the temporary freedom from your official duties might give you more time to help Captain Laurel catch the bastard who's framing you or, at the very least, offer some relief. I know I wouldn't want the responsibilities of the monarchy on my best day, let alone while facing a criminal investigation."

Aya made a noise between a scoff and a chuckle. "You shouldn't have voted the way you did, then. If Lionel loses his crown, it passes to Lord Collingwood, and since Madeleine doesn't have any siblings…"

She motioned up and down at Frederick with a wave of her hand, and Lionel's eyes followed the pattern. He'd always believed that the duke was on his side, but a small voice inside his mind cautioned against blind trust of Frederick—or anyone besides Aya—after the council vote. *Still, as easy as it would be to say the duke married into our family for prestige, it's clear he loves Madeleine.*

As if Frederick could read Lionel's thoughts, he reached out a hand to his wife, and she clutched it in hers. Lionel noticed that Madeleine still wore her gloves, even though she was eating. *She must be really embarrassed of that scar.*

Lionel shook his head. "It won't come to that, Aya." The words tasted sour in his mouth, but he had to say them. Part of not being a pushover meant confidence, and he would fake it until he felt it.

"Lionel's right." Frederick shrugged. "He is innocent, after all. The truth will come out, one way or another, and his power will be restored."

"I wouldn't be so sure." Madeleine held up her free hand. "I'm merely echoing Father. Before the council vote, he cautioned us to consider the worst-case scenario as a legitimate possibility. And since then, well, let's just say he's taking to his position. Did you hear he's holding court on the day after tomorrow?"

Frederick clicked his tongue. "Your father's a practical man. He wants to make sure the kingdom's needs are met, especially at such a vulnerable time."

Lionel set his teacup on the table. "It's good that Uncle has demonstrated such enthusiasm. The people should see him as a fitting replacement for me, and should the worst happen, you'll have to show the same eagerness for your new title as prince."

"I don't know about that." Frederick brushed bread crumbs off his jacket. "If the crown did fall to me and Madeleine, I'd be sorely tempted to return it to your child the moment he or she came of age."

Madeleine's eyebrows knitted together. "I don't think it works that way."

Frederick smirked. "If we're in charge, it works however we want."

Lionel frowned. *I wish I'd taken that attitude from the beginning.* Though he appreciated the duke's words, Lionel knew they couldn't be true. Even if Frederick thought he meant them, a taste of royal power would change his mind.

"It's nice of you to say." Lionel ran his fingers through his hair. "But I'm afraid I have to side with Madeleine. The monarchs have power, but even they must rule within the bounds of law and reason."

"Let's not talk about it anymore." Madeleine pulled her hand out of Frederick's and crossed her legs. "If we *must* discuss politics, let's at least focus on clearing poor Lionel's name."

"There's not much point in that conversation, either." Aya spun her engagement ring around her finger. "Lionel's innocence is in Theo's hands now, and he's got his guards working on it day and night. They'll make a breakthrough soon, maybe even before Lord Collingwood has a chance to hold court."

"Surely there's something we can do." Madeleine pursed her lips. "Couldn't we put out some kind of reward for information?"

Frederick snorted. "That would bring in a flood of false information. The poor will say anything for coins."

Anger bubbled in Lionel's throat, but he swallowed it down. The way Aya's eye twitched told him she did the same. Though Frederick's words had been insensitive, they hadn't been necessarily wrong.

"I suppose that's true." Madeleine leaned back against the couch with a huff. "I don't understand who would have done this. Anyone who detested the farmer or your ruling benefited from the fire itself but not from framing you. They have to know that even if Father would replace you, his governing style would be almost identical to yours. If it's change they want, they went about it all wrong."

"I hadn't thought about that side of it before, but you make a good argument." Lionel sighed. "Honestly, the only person who directly benefits is Uncle, but I know he'd never do this to me."

"That's good to hear." Madeleine wrinkled her nose. "I told Father that you'd never suspect him, but he's been worried you might. He says fear and greed bring out the worst in people."

Aya frowned. "He called Lionel greedy?"

"No, of course not." Madeleine rubbed her temples. "I'm

not articulating this correctly. He just—Father realizes his position. As you pointed out, Lionel, he's the one who benefits most from framing you. Captain Laurel would be dumb if he didn't place Father at the top of the suspect list."

"So he would." Lionel glanced at Frederick, who had grown quiet and turned his attention to devouring a fat strawberry. "Though, by extension, the two of you would benefit, too."

Frederick stopped mid-bite, and hurt shone in his dark eyes. "Lionel, you have to know that we would never, ever betray you like that. We're family. We must stick together."

While Lionel believed Frederick to be sincere, a coldness curled in his gut. *Right, like I stuck by my father?* With a deep breath, he pushed the thought from his mind. *That was different. He was guilty.*

Madeleine leaned forward, and her naturally crossed eyes bore into Lionel's as best they could. "Cousin, you know me as if you were my brother. If I wanted to be queen, I would have married King Archon. Don't make that face. He and I shared no direct blood. Or I would have tried harder to trap you into marriage. When have I ever displayed the patience, let alone the tact, to scheme and manipulate like this?"

Despite the gravity of the subject matter, Lionel chuckled. "Never."

"I meant it as a rhetorical question." Madeleine rolled her eyes. "But there's your answer."

Aya laughed, and Lionel could tell by the hard edge to it that she had grown uncomfortable with the conversation.

With a polite smile toward their hosts, Lionel slipped his hand back into Aya's. "I should say, Madeleine, I hope your scheming is better when it comes to wedding planning."

His cousin winked. "Decidedly so. In fact, when Frederick and I were engaged—"

"Madeleine, darling." Frederick's voice was soft and kind, if not a little patronizing. "I believe Lionel was being merciful in changing the topic. He and Aya don't really want to hear all the wedding details."

"Oh, I do, actually." Aya blushed. "I've never attended a royal wedding before, or even a regular noble one at that, so I have no idea what's expected. Anything you could tell me about them would be helpful."

"Easy. Thanks to my dear, departed uncle, I've attended my fair share of royal weddings." Madeleine smoothed her skirt. "I'm glad some good can come from the experience now."

As Madeleine launched into an explanation of the royal wedding ceremony, Lionel allowed his mind to wander. Frederick muttered something unintelligible into his tea, but he kept his lips upturned at the edges, probably as a last effort to disguise his boredom. For the second time, the duke had been right in his ill-phrased words—Lionel didn't care for the wedding chat either, but watching Aya bond with a member of his family, even Madeleine, made him smile.

After the women became fully immersed in their conversation, Lionel tried to think of something to say to Frederick. Topics slipped through his mind like sand through his fingers, and Lionel realized that he didn't know where to begin. Sure, they got along well, but they hadn't socialized much outside of the council meetings. He didn't know what the duke liked to discuss or what hobbies he practiced. *I guess now is the time to start bonding, then.*

Before Lionel could decide on an opener, Frederick leaned over and whispered, "The ladies could go on like this for a while. Fancy a game of checkers?"

Lionel rubbed his hands against his thighs. "I've never been much for strategy games, but it sounds better than discussing the merits of different lace patterns."

"That's my man." Frederick clapped Lionel on the back. "Maybe I can teach you a thing or two. Checkers has always been my game."

"Sounds fun." Lionel touched Aya's arm and inclined his head toward the drawing room. When she waved him away without a show of concern, he rose and followed Frederick.

As they sat down at the game table, Lionel's heart started to beat faster. His eyes scanned the checkerboard, playing out the moves in his head. Though he hated to admit it—like King Archon, Madeleine, and even Lord Collingwood in the right situation—Lionel had always had a competitive streak. And as foolish as it was to conflate the two, after losing his full power as king, he didn't intend to lose this game of checkers. Though he lacked the skill and experience, somehow he would arise victorious. *No more being a pushover, remember? Don't let Frederick outmatch you now.*

$\mathcal{L}$ionel nodded to the gangway guard as he and Aya reentered the palace and began walking toward the royal corridor. The Starboardshire shops had closed for the evening, and Lionel smiled as the empty hallway reminded him of their engagement.

"How did your game of checkers go?" Aya asked. "I didn't want to ask in front of Frederick. You both looked pretty intense when you came out of the drawing room."

Lionel chuckled. "It was a tough match, but I beat him in the end." With an exaggerated flourish, he retrieved a white checker piece from his trouser pocket and held it up for Aya's inspection. "The token of my victory. Frederick says to present it anytime for a rematch."

"That's nice." Aya looped her arm through Lionel's. "I'm glad you two get along. Who knew Madeleine would end up having good taste in a husband, after all?"

"Not me." Lionel faked a shudder and pocketed the checker piece. "How was the wedding talk? Did you get along as well by yourselves?"

"Surprisingly, yes." Aya drew her brows together, and Lionel couldn't help but grin at the little wrinkles between them. "Am I a bad person if I don't fully trust her, though? I mean, she's always been so backhanded and condescending to me, and now she wants to act like family? Don't get me wrong. I like her when she's not being cruel, but I want to know which side is the real one."

Lionel smirked. "That's fair. Honestly, I'd worry about you if you didn't have some hesitation toward her."

The couple rounded a corner and emerged into a busier hallway. As the nobles and staff there noticed Lionel and Aya, their eyes widened. One group quieted, which made a nearby pair erupt into whispers, which made a butler pause to stare down the corridor. Watching the ripple effect raised the hairs on Lionel's neck. At least everyone in the villages kept working and moving as they scrutinized him and Aya.

With a shake of her head, Aya pulled Lionel toward one of the artifacts that lined the walls. About the size of a fat hog, the metal steam engine rested on a marble slab. Thanks to his brief tutorial from Aya, he knew where to pour the water, how it would move through the chambers, and where it would emerge as steam. He also knew the engine wouldn't have existed in isolation.

Aya squatted to examine the base of the machine, and Lionel knelt next to her. Keeping one eye on the other nobles, who had finally resumed their own walks, he whispered, "What would it have powered?"

Aya's eyebrows raised. "Look at you, Mr. Engineer."

Lionel nudged her with his elbow. "I pay attention when you explain your craft—even if I don't understand half the things you say."

Aya chuckled. "Given the size, I believe this engine would have been attached to an automobile of some kind—that is, a self-moving carriage that transported people."

Lionel rubbed his chin. "Do you think it might still work?"

"I doubt it." Aya pointed toward the creases where the machine had been welded. "There's too much rust on the outside here. I'm sure the insides, the pistons especially, are rotted too."

"It could be useful to study. Would you like me to have the

guards move it to your shop?" Lionel winced then stood. "Wait. I guess I can't make those offers anymore."

Aya rose as well and squeezed Lionel's arm. "That's okay. It would be silly to transport it before I decide what to do with my business, anyway. I've considered moving into the Starboardshire shops. I doubt I'll want to walk to Portside every day once we're married."

"True." Lionel wrapped his arm around Aya's waist. As he kissed the top of her head, he smiled against her curls. "You have plenty of time to decide."

Taking a slower pace, the couple resumed their stroll back toward the royal corridor. They fell into a comfortable silence. Aya observed the different machines, busts, and tapestries as they passed, and Lionel watched how her eyes lit up with curiosity or how her nose scrunched with distaste. Each time Aya reacted, Lionel glanced at the object, imagining what thoughts or emotions it stirred in her. While he knew Aya's body and soul, Lionel still had so much to learn about her clever mind, and he couldn't wait to spend his life unraveling it.

After a few more minutes, they passed the ballroom and came face to face with the imposing Queen Hildegard statue. Lionel moved to turn down the royal corridor, but Aya stopped and stared up at the queen. With equal intensity, Lionel's gaze washed over Aya. *What does she see when she looks into those stone eyes?*

"Do you think I'll be a good queen?" Aya kept her gaze fixed on the statue, and it took Lionel a second to realize she was speaking to him.

He frowned. "You know I do. I've told you several times."

Aya tucked a curl behind her ear. "Yes but whenever I see this statue, I can't help but think that I'll never be as strong or wise as Queen Hildegard. She must have been an amazing woman to lead our ancestors through the flood."

"You will be a wonderful queen, in your own way." Lionel glanced up at the statue, and its hard squint seemed to bear down on him. "She makes me question myself, too. However faintly, her blood runs in my veins. It's a lot to live up to, but I promise I'll get my powers restored so that we both have the chance to leave our mark on the kingdom."

"I have full faith in you, Willem." They stood side by side, and Aya leaned her head against his arm. "What should we do with the rest of our evening?"

Lionel shrugged. "Well, I don't have any responsibilities. Do you need to work?"

"No." Aya sighed. "With some of the crop fields burning, food prices have soared. Nobody has the extra coin to spend on luxuries."

"I'm sorry." Lionel scratched the back of his neck. "I wish I could help."

Aya straightened. "Me too."

"How about this?" Lionel grinned and pulled the checker piece from his pocket, hoping to lighten the mood again. "We'll flip for it. If the crown side comes up, we'll go back to my chambers and have dinner. If the blank side comes up, we'll keep walking and see where it leads us."

Aya's lips tugged up into a smile. "Flip away."

Lionel balanced the checker piece on his thumb then flicked it into the air. The piece flew off to the side, and Lionel reached out to catch it, only to knock it off course with his hand. With a tinkling sound, the piece ricocheted off the palace wall, bounced against the statue, then fell on the floor between the two.

Aya giggled. "Does it still count if it lands on the floor?"

"Only if you like the outcome." Lionel winked and walked to the rear of the statue. It rested about two inches away from the wall, and luckily, the checker piece had fallen near the corner of the statue's base. Crouching, Lionel slid his hand down the wall and reached his fingers into the narrow space. With short, quick motions, he scooted the checker piece toward himself. As he watched his progress, Lionel noticed something scratched into the surface of the statue inside the folds at the back of Queen Hildegard's skirt. He finished retrieving the checker piece, pocketed it, then leaned over to get a better look at the inscription.

Aya's own skirt rustled against Lionel's legs as she came to stand beside him. "What is it?"

Lionel's brow furrowed. "There's something written here. It's smooth, like it was carved as part of the statue, not scratched in later."

Aya's breath hitched. "What does it say?"

"It's numbers, not words." Lionel squinted to make out the shapes, a difficult task from the angle at which he crouched. "A nine, followed by a colon, then a two, and finally a seven."

"Let me see." Aya tapped her foot while Lionel stood and backed away.

9:27. Lionel racked his brain, but he couldn't remember seeing numbers written that way. Could it be the dimensions of the statue? Or maybe ancient nautical coordinates? No, both of those would have more numbers and different punctuation marks.

"It's a time." Aya rose slowly, a stiff motion with her dress's exterior corset, then smoothed down the fabric of her skirt. "That's how it's written in all the clockworking books you gave me. Hour and minutes, separated by a colon. What I don't understand is why someone would carve it into a statue."

Like the gears in one of Aya's mechanical devices, the facts locked together and spun in Lionel's mind. He clutched his chest, feeling for the key hidden in his jacket pocket. The whole time, Lionel had thought it would unlock one of the *Queen Hildegard*'s secret doors or passageways, but he had been wrong. What had someone scribbled in the margins of *The Key to the Kingdom?*

One must scour every inch of QH to find the lock. It will take time.

Every inch of the statue, not the ship. What if "it" didn't mean that the mission would take time. In grammar lessons, Lionel's tutor had taught him that pronouns referred to the previous noun. The lock. The lock takes time.

"It's not a door." Lionel fumbled in his jacket for the key. "It's a clock—the grandfather clock!"

"What?" Aya hissed, her eyes scanning the corridors. "Lionel, what are you talking about?"

Lionel's face paled, and he froze with his fingers around the key. Glancing over his shoulder, he saw other people walking near the ballroom. An icy shock flooded his veins, and he grabbed Aya's elbow with his free hand. "Come on," he whispered. "It's not safe here."

They rushed toward the end of the royal corridor as quickly as they could walk without breaking into a run. As they reached the place where the hallway narrowed, Lionel felt resistance tug at his arm. He looked back to see Aya frown, her steps growing smaller and more hesitant.

"I'm sorry." She shook her head. "I know it's foolish. We always go to your old chambers, and except when Dellwyn made me, I haven't been here since that night with King Archon."

Lionel stopped and slid his hand down to wrap around Aya's. "It's okay. I understand." He chanced a look down the corridor and saw it was empty. "I need to tell you something. I would have told you about it sooner, but I didn't think it was safe. I'm not sure it is now, either, to be honest."

"You're scaring me." Aya's body shook as she shifted her feet. "Just tell me, Lionel."

The king took a deep breath and pulled the key from his pocket. With a trembling hand, Lionel passed it to Aya. "I found this hidden inside a book in my new chambers. I figured if it was important enough to hide in a room only the king can access, then it must be dangerous. Or, at the very least, meant for me alone."

"I know how that feels." One of Aya's hands reached up to clutch her chest, while the other held the key closer toward the light streaming in from the windows.

"Inside this book, in the margins, someone had scrawled a message, a clue to what the key unlocks." Lionel nearly bounced on his heels with anticipation. "At first, I thought it meant that the key belonged to one of the palace's secret doors, or maybe a chest or box. But with the numbers…"

"You think it fits in the grandfather clock somehow?" Aya squinted as she examined the key. "I suppose that could make sense. It's awfully strange, what with having those four little nubs around a cylindrical blade instead of a line of proper teeth. It looks more like a winder to me."

With her focus absorbed in the mission, Aya walked into the circular greeting hall outside the king's chambers with slow but steady steps. "How do you know the clock takes some kind of key or winder, though? What other clues do you have?"

Lionel shrugged. "I just know. My father always told me the clock was important. He said that, even though it was broken, we had to respect its place and let it stand sentry here. I have a feeling he would have told me more about it had we gone through a normal transition of power."

As they approached the grandfather clock, the rest of the waiting area faded away, and the object seemed to tower above Lionel even more than normal. While Aya opened the cracked glass pane to search the clock's innards, Lionel looked over the dark, wooden exterior. The smooth boards flowed one into the other, and the only markings were the seams that connected the decorative trim to the main panels.

Aya poked her head around the glass pane. "Anything?"

"No." Lionel ran his fingers along the clock's edge. "Actually, help me move it. Maybe there's a keyhole behind the face."

Aya rose and positioned herself on the other side of the clock.

"On three." Lionel nodded, his fingers gripping the trim as best they could. "One, two, three."

Lionel gritted his teeth as they attempted to push the clock away from the wall. It didn't budge. As Aya's eyes met his, Lionel performed another silent count, and they tried again. He could feel the veins in his neck straining and see Aya's cheeks puffing out with effort. That time, they moved the clock a quarter of an inch.

"Shit, that's heavy." Aya panted. "We won't move it without help."

With a huff, Lionel stared into the tiny gap they had created. Though the area behind the clock's face was cast in shadow, he spied some kind of metal tubing extending from the back of the clock into the wall.

He motioned for Aya to come look. "I don't think we're supposed to move it."

Aya leaned her face against the crack and peered up toward the pipe. When she pulled away, her nose was scrunched up in thought. "That's not normal, right? The grandfather clock in your old chambers doesn't have an extension like that."

"No." Lionel ran his fingers through his hair. "I had it moved into my new room. It wasn't attached to the wall or anything else."

"Hmm." Aya tapped the key against her lips. "Come back around to the front here. I'm too short to see directly under the clock's face, but you probably can. Maybe there's something up higher."

Lionel reopened the glass pane and poked his head inside the clock's body. As Aya had declared, the bottom and the sides were smooth, unbroken wooden panels, just like the exterior. Pushing the pendulum and weights aside, Lionel peered up toward the clock's face. He gasped. There was a tiny hole—round with four notches at equal intervals around the circle—hidden beside the base of one of the weights.

Aya's voice shook. "Did you find something?"

"Pass me the key." Lionel stuck his hand out. Aya pressed the key into his palm, and he closed his fingers around the warm metal.

Given the tight space, Lionel's arm couldn't fit inside the clock's body along with his head, so he took a moment to memorize the keyhole's location. Then he popped his head out and reached his arm up, feeling with his fingertips for the hole. *Smooth, smooth, ah—there it is!* Pushing the key upward along the line of his finger, he fumbled for the hole. It took him a few seconds to find it again, but once he did, the key slid right into place.

"It's in!" Lionel smiled at Aya, who stood at his and the

clock's side, biting her thumbnail. "I'm going to turn it now. Will you watch the clock to see what happens?"

With a nod, she moved to stand directly in front of the clock.

Taking a deep breath, Lionel turned the key. A clicking sound issued from within the clock, but after one rotation, the key stopped and wouldn't budge. "Anything?"

"No." Aya's foot tapped, sending soft pulses throughout the rounded room. "Wait. 9:27, right?"

Lionel rolled his eyes at himself. Of course, *the lock will take time.*

Aya's skirt brushed against Lionel's back, and she leaned against him, grunting as she stretched toward the clock's face. "I can't reach."

"That's okay. Scoot back." Lionel gently released the key, and luckily, it hung in place. With a trembling finger, he reached up and spun the clock's hands until they rested at 9:27. Then, leaning back into the clock's body, he groped for the key. When his fingers found it, a cold fear slid over his body, and he craned his neck toward Aya. "Step back a bit. We don't know what might happen."

Though her nose wrinkled, Aya walked backward to stand near the center of the greeting hall, noticeably avoiding the scuff marks where the fainting couch had once rested. Satisfied that she was out of harm's way, Lionel took another large breath and turned the key. That time, it twisted without fuss, and louder clicking noises sounded.

Aya gasped. "The clock face is coming out."

Lionel looked above him. Sure enough, the face of the clock had inched forward, connected to the rest of the mechanism by a long spindle. After a few more turns, the key stopped twisting, and the clock face came to a halt. Backing away from the clock, Lionel peered up toward the gap between the face's exterior and its insides.

"Can you see anything?" Aya moved to stand next to Lionel, stretching up on tiptoe.

"Not really." Lionel sighed. "But even if I did, I wouldn't know what I'm looking at. Let me get you a chair."

While Aya alternated between examining the clock's open face and the inside, where he had left the key, Lionel unlocked the door to his chambers and rushed into his bedroom. He fetched the plain chair from his vanity and carried it to the greeting hall, pausing only to relock the door to his chambers behind him.

"Here." He placed the chair beside the clock and held his hand out to help Aya climb up.

Once in position, Aya started her investigation. First, she checked the hands of the clock face. They wouldn't turn. Then she traced her finger around the face itself—a floating white circle, perfectly aligned with the wooden frame from whence it had escaped. Next, Aya pinched the spindle, following it back to the inside of the clock. Her eyes lit up, and she turned her hand to twist the spindle. The clock face spun, and a few moments later, it shuddered loose. Aya passed it, still connected to the spindle, to Lionel, then removed a tiny screwdriver from her pocket.

He took the clock face from her and looked at it from all angles. It didn't seem remarkable to him, and maybe it wasn't. Maybe the real secret hid deeper inside the mechanism.

Spinning the spindle between his fingers, Lionel watched Aya work. Whenever her eyes lit up, his heart pounded with excitement and pride at her vastly improved skill set. But whenever her eyebrows knitted together, his stomach ached, and he stepped forward, prepared to sweep her out of harm's way if the clock somehow turned dangerous. She pulled apart the interior of the clock, one cog, screw, and metal plate at a time, placing each piece in one of her pockets.

Lionel frowned. "Will you remember how to put it back together?"

Aya shrugged. "It looks like a lot, but it's a pretty standard unit." Biting her lip, she unscrewed another part. "What's interesting is that the regular clock mechanism seems to be interlaced with something else. I'm guessing whatever feeds through the pipe into the wall."

"Is that even possible?" Lionel glanced over his shoulder to ensure they were still alone. As Aya exposed the innards of the clock, he felt more exposed, too.

"Well, it's just a theory. I've never seen anything like it before, obviously." Aya paused and bit her lip. "But yes. Though they look rigid, mechanisms like this are quite fluid. Each piece flows into the other to create one motion. Whoever designed this could have connected the clock portion to our mystery mechanism with any number of movements. I'm just not skilled enough to see—"

Aya's hands flew to her face, and she shrieked.

"What?" Lionel rushed forward, putting one hand on Aya's back. Her body quivered under his palm, so he put his other hand on her stomach to steady her. "Aya, you're going to fall."

"No… no… I'm fine." She placed a hand on Lionel's shoulder and gripped it until her knuckles turned white.

Through a clenched jaw, he whispered, "Now you're the one scaring me. And ow."

Aya looked down at her hand with wide eyes. Though she loosened her grip, she still clutched Lionel's shoulder. "I spoke too soon. I recognize the second mechanism—it's similar to how Charlie and Penelope are built. And it's missing pieces."

"Can you fix it?" Lionel searched Aya's face, trying to discern the severity of the problem from the worry lines that creased her tan skin.

"I don't know." Aya waved at the clock. "You think the key, all this, is dangerous, right?"

Lionel nodded. "I don't know why else the key would have been hidden so well—and in the king's chambers."

Aya licked her lips. "Do you remember the first time we saw each other?"

"Of course." Lionel frowned. "Why? Does Lord Varick have something to do with this?"

"No. The first day we *really* saw each other." Aya's eyes filled with tears. "When we were children…"

"Oh… yes." Lionel's mind flashed back to that day—King Archon smashing Penelope against the wall, the cold tone in his voice as he ordered Master Cogsmith's execution, and the girl outside the room, begging the king to reconsider while Alfred Butler held her back.

Aya swallowed. "King Archon didn't really care about fixing Penelope. What he wanted was the part that could do it, the vortric cog."

A sinking sensation tugged at Lionel's stomach. Though he'd always hated his father for ordering Master Cogsmith's execution because the craftsman couldn't fix Lionel's beloved toy, he'd always thought it had been his father's warped expression of love. As vain and stupid as it was, knowing that King Archon hadn't cared about Lionel's happiness and had only used him as an excuse to hunt down some cog made him even sicker.

Lionel shook the thought from his mind. "Is that what the clock needs? A vortric cog?"

"Yes." Aya peered back inside the mechanism. "Three of them."

"So it's hopeless?" Lionel's fists clenched at his side. "If Master Cogsmith didn't have or couldn't make one back then, we definitely won't find three."

Aya sighed and squeezed Lionel's shoulder, softly that time. "Don't be mad at me."

Lionel's brow furrowed as he watched Aya reach down the side of her dress. When her fingers reemerged, she clutched a gold cog between them.

"Is that…" Lionel reached out to touch the cog, and though Aya allowed him to do so, she didn't let go of it.

Aya nodded. "You understand why I couldn't tell you about it, right? If your father was willing to kill for the vortric cog, and my father was willing to die to keep it from him, I knew it had to be dangerous—like your key."

"Of course." Lionel cupped Aya's face. "You did the right thing by keeping it secret from everyone."

Aya blushed and looked down at her feet.

Pain pierced Lionel's heart. "You told someone."

"Dellwyn." Aya's eyes watered again. "Only because we lived with each other, and I couldn't hide it from her."

"It's okay." Lionel shook his head. "It doesn't matter now. What matters is that we only have one cog, and we need three."

"Actually, we have two." Aya inclined her head toward Lionel's chambers.

The realization clicked in his head. "That's how you fixed Penelope."

"I fixed her with the vortric cog from Charlie, the one my father died to protect." Aya bit her lip. "This one came from the music box Lord Collingwood gave to Dellwyn."

A wave of relief washed over Lionel. Lord Collingwood might have the power of the king, but at least he didn't have the cog anymore, whatever it might do.

"And the third one was in Penelope, but it broke."

"Gold is a soft metal." Aya tucked the vortric cog back into her corset. "It's a miracle the other two have survived this long."

Lionel clenched his jaw. "And since Charlie is still broken, I take it you haven't had any success in making a new one."

Aya shook her head. "I've tried with other metals, less rare ones, just to see if I could get the shape right, and I haven't yet. Nine teeth is a rarity, too. Most cogs have an even number."

Reaching into his jacket, Lionel retrieved his pocket watch. Dinnertime approached, and if they didn't head to the royal dining room soon—Aya refused to dine on the deck—Eldric or Stefan would come searching for them.

"We'll be expected for dinner in a half an hour." Lionel sighed. "Can you put the clock back together quickly? At least enough so it looks unchanged?"

Aya nodded. "What are we going to do? We still don't know what the clock does or where that pipe might lead."

Lionel's gaze drifted to the unmarked door to the clock's right. "I have an idea."

Aya's eyes followed Lionel's, and she smiled. "You read my mind."

"For now, though, there's nothing we can do without a third vortric cog." Lionel rubbed the back of his neck as Aya started replacing the clock's pieces. "Only you would be able to make another, and if a fourth does exist, it's been well hidden for decades, if not centuries. I'm not worried about it magically emerging anytime soon."

"So, are you saying we leave it?" Aya stopped working and glared down at him. "How can we do that, Lionel? We're so close to… to whatever it is our fathers wanted to control."

"I know." Lionel rested his hand on Aya's back again. "But if the answer were easy to find, you would have figured it out already. And even if we did discover something, I have no power to protect it. I'm not the proper king right now, remember?"

Aya's face paled. "That's true. And if anyone else found out about what we're doing, Lord Collingwood could take over our search or claim our findings for himself."

"Exactly." Lionel's stomach churned, but not from hunger. "I trust my uncle, but the things Madeleine said today worried me."

"Me too." Aya tugged at her curls. "We can't risk him getting involved, especially not if he *is* getting a taste for power."

Lionel sighed. "We're agreed, then? Our first priority is restoring my power as king so that when we do discover something, we have complete control over it."

Aya nodded and leaned down to place a gentle kiss on Lionel's lips. "But how in Desertera are we going to do that?"

"I'm not sure yet, but I know that, between the two of us, we'll figure it out." Lionel ducked under Aya and reached inside the clock's body. As he unwound the key, an idea struck him. With a grin, he pocketed the key and turned to Aya. "Actually, I think I know the perfect place to start."

25

The next morning, before sunrise, Lionel and Aya sneaked down the royal corridor. Each step they took seemed to reverberate off the palace walls. Lionel looked over his shoulder at Aya, who had one hand clutched to her chest, where he knew the vortric cog was hidden inside her corset. He did the same, feeling for the key inside his jacket pocket.

As they reached the royal library, Lionel glanced down the hallway a final time, holding his lantern up to illuminate as much of the space as possible. Aya did the same, lighting the way they had come, then nodded at him. With held breath, Lionel opened the door, allowing Aya to step inside first, then closing it behind them.

Shadows danced across the bookshelves as Lionel walked around the room and lit the lanterns that hung on the wall. With their light combined, the lanterns cast a soft glow, enough that Lionel and Aya would be able to read. Lionel took Aya's lantern from her and strolled over to the children's study table, where he placed the lights at either end.

"How do you know she'll even clean the library this morning?" Aya wiped her finger across one of the shelves. "It's dusty, but I've seen worse."

Lionel put his hands on his hips and scanned the bookshelves, searching for a promising subject. "Mrs. Butler told me that she cleans the library once a week. I checked with Eldric, and this morning is the day."

"Okay." Aya fidgeted with the ends of her hair. "What do we do, then? Wait here to ambush the poor maid?"

"We're not ambushing her." Lionel returned to Aya's side and took her hand, wrapping it in both of his. "And, more importantly, there's nothing to be nervous about."

"You know I'm a horrid liar." Aya bit her lip. "Besides, how will it look when this maid waltzes in here to do her cleaning and finds the king and his fiancée—"

"Deep in book research?" Lionel quirked an eyebrow. "We're not putting ourselves in a compromising position, Aya. And even if we were, what does it matter? The whole kingdom knows our histories. No one would be shocked or scandalized."

Aya sighed, but her lips tugged up into a smile at his comment. "You're right." Her hand relaxed in his. "Are you ready to tell me what you're thinking now? I know you wanted time to process everything last night, but I need to know before the maid gets here."

"Of course. Thank you for being patient with me." Lionel lifted her hand and kissed her knuckles before releasing it. Then he walked over to the shelf marked *Government & Governing.* "A couple weeks ago, I came into the library to do some reading around this time of day, and the maid walked in on me."

He heard Aya chuckle behind him. "You make it sound so tawdry."

"Well, I *was* in my pajamas." Lionel grabbed the first book on the shelf. *The Laws & Covenants of Desertera—seems as good a place as any to start.* He shrugged and pulled out the next, stacking it on top. "Anyway, Mrs. Butler made an offhanded comment about what I'd been reading. She'd noticed clean spots on the shelves where books had been removed. Only, I hadn't visited the library... not since..."

Aya came to stand beside him again. "Your mother."

Lionel frowned. "How did you..."

"I know that tone." Aya rubbed his arm. "It's the same one I use when I talk about my father."

"So it is." Lionel inclined his head toward the lavender reading chair in the middle of the room. "She used to read to me in here. Mostly, she'd read literature—she adored stories—but sometimes zoology or meteorology."

"That's lovely." Aya followed Lionel's lead, taking more hefty volumes from the shelf. "So if you weren't reading the books, who was?"

"Not Eldric or Zedara. I asked both of them." Lionel motioned toward the children's study table, and they walked over and set the books down on it. "It'll sound crazy, but after our conversation with Madeleine and Frederick, I have this nagging feeling that whoever is attempting to frame me for the fire knew that I would lose any real power as king during the investigation."

Aya nodded. "And you think they figured that out by doing research in the library?"

"Maybe. I mean, to my knowledge, these are the only books about the structure of Desertera's government and its laws." Lionel flipped open one of the books to reveal coarse, handwritten pages. "See? All written on pigskin, after the flood. The scribes wouldn't have wasted resources on copies. Even if a book or two has been lost, the monarch is supposed to know or make the rules, anyway."

"Just as the council has used your new rules against you." Aya lowered herself into one of the children's chairs. "Still, the two people might be unconnected. It's entirely possible a farmer wanted you to take the blame and didn't think about the consequences for you. Or who's to say the noble who framed you couldn't have guessed the punishment you'd face? If they were clever enough to try to frame you, I'd hope they could predict the ramifications."

"True." Lionel crossed to the shelf and retrieved the final few books. "That's why I want to test my theory. When Mrs. Butler comes in, she can tell me which books 'I' have read over the last couple weeks. Hopefully, there will be a connection."

Aya's brows knitted together. "And if there's not?"

Lionel eased into one of the too-small chairs and tapped a book. "Well, then at least our research time won't be wasted. We still need to figure out how I can restore myself to full power. Plus, I want to see exactly what my uncle—and anyone else—stands to gain from my dethronement. I can't believe that he would betray me like this, but if he's the only one to benefit, I have to pursue it."

"I agree. You never really know what other people are capable of until they show you." Aya stared down at her engagement ring, twirling it around her slender finger. "This is just our luck, you know. It took me nearly a year to come to terms with the idea of being queen, to reconcile my potential royal responsibilities with my cogsmithing ones, to realize how much good I could do if I combined the roles. And just as I accepted, and even grew excited about assuming the title, someone has threatened to take it away." Tears welled in her eyes. "I don't know what I'll do if they take you away, too."

A pang stung Lionel's heart, and he clasped Aya's hand across the table. He knew Aya would be afraid to lose him, but he never thought she would regret losing the chance to become Desertera's queen.

"Hey, look at me." He waited for her eyes to meet his. "No matter what, no one will take me away from you. I have faith in the people, in my friends and family. They won't stand for it."

Aya nodded, but her lip still trembled.

"As for our titles, no one has taken them yet, either." Lionel rubbed his thumb over the back of her hand. "We'll find whoever is doing this, and we'll bring them to justice. When it's over and we're married, you'll be the best queen Desertera has ever known. I can't even imagine all the wonderful things you'll do for our people."

"I hope you're right. I don't want to think about the alternative, especially now that we're so close to unlocking the grandfather clock." Aya closed her eyes and took a deep breath. When she opened them again, the tears had receded and her face, though still flushed, had relaxed. "I feel greedy for wanting to protect a title I've never held."

Lionel shook his head. "There's no shame in wanting what's best for us nor for wanting to guard the people from whatever the cogs might be hiding."

"Well, talking about it more isn't going to do us any good." Aya flipped open the book nearest to her, and Lionel could tell by the tight clench of her jaw that she was fighting to keep her emotions in check. "Let's get to work."

AFTER AN HOUR OF RESEARCH, Lionel allowed the book he'd been reading to drop to the table with a thud. Groaning, he stretched his legs, then twisted his back in either direction. "Apparently, *Noble Titles & Rights* means duke and downward."

"Shit. That one looked promising." Aya rested her chin in her hands. "I'm not getting anywhere, either. Though if you ever want to learn about the legal aspects of village planning or well digging, I can recommend a *very* detailed volume."

Lionel raised his eyebrows in mock interest. "How fascinating. I'll keep that in mind."

As the pair chuckled, a squeak sounded from the other side of the room, and Lionel turned to see Mrs. Butler enter, dust rag in hand.

With wide eyes, Mrs. Butler lowered into a curtsy. "Forgive the interruption, Your Majesty. Would you like me to come back later?"

"No, thank you, Mrs. Butler. You're welcome to clean while we read." Lionel motioned to Aya. "This is my fiancée, Miss Aya Cogsmith."

"It's a pleasure to meet you, Mrs. Butler." Aya smiled, a little too brightly, and Lionel's chest warmed at how she always tried to make everyone feel comfortable in her presence.

Mrs. Butler curtsied again. "The honor is mine, Your Grace."

Lionel turned back to the books, and Aya followed his lead.

As Mrs. Butler began dusting, Lionel could see her glancing at the table out of the corner of his eye. He wondered whether "he" had read these books before or whether the maid was simply nosy.

As Mrs. Butler reached the shelves closer to the study table, she paused to switch out her dust rag with a clean one from her apron. "Did you tire of botany, Your Majesty?"

Lionel raised his eyebrows. "Botany?" If the person sneaking into the library were only interested in learning, it foiled his whole theory.

"That was me, actually." Aya tucked a curl behind her ear. "As a matter of fact, would you happen to have noticed which book I read last? It gave me an idea for my bridal bouquet."

Mrs. Butler's brow furrowed, deepening her wrinkles. Still, she walked to the botany shelf and retrieved a book. "*The Native Flora and Fauna of Desertera*, Your Grace." She handed it to Aya. "You must be excited about the wedding."

Lionel arched an eyebrow. "What do you mean?"

"Nothing." Mrs. Butler blushed. "Pardon me, Your Grace. It's not my place to pry into your personal affairs."

"It's fine." Aya thumbed through the botany book. "I did start my research prematurely, didn't I?"

Mrs. Butler waved her hand. "It's smart to get a head start on the planning. There's so much involved in a royal wedding. No harm in being prepared."

Aya winked. "My thoughts exactly."

As Mrs. Butler resumed her dusting, Lionel grinned at his fiancée. Whoever had been reading the botany books had started well before Lionel and Aya's engagement. It was a small, probably useless clue, but it was more than they'd known an hour ago.

The library fell silent other than the sounds of Mrs. Butler's shoes as she walked along the shelves and the botany book as Aya browsed its pages. Lionel pretended to read another governmental tome, and the handwriting blurred before his eyes. He had to figure out an innocent way to ask

Mrs. Butler whether any other books had been read since his last visit to the library.

Lionel cleared his throat to get Aya's attention. When she looked up from her book, he inclined his head toward the maid. "I'm starting to think I imagined that passage, Aya. I have no idea where I read it."

Aya raised a dubious eyebrow, to which Lionel shrugged. It was a long shot, sure, but he had to say something before Mrs. Butler finished cleaning.

"I doubt that, Lionel." Aya sighed. "Could it have been categorized in a different section? Just because the part you're looking for relates to governing, that doesn't mean the entire book did."

"Maybe." Lionel clicked his tongue as if he were trying to remember. "Mrs. Butler, you haven't noticed any clean spots on the government shelf, have you?"

Mrs. Butler turned around. "I don't think so, Your Majesty." Her lips twisted in thought… or maybe suspicion. Lionel could only imagine how stupid she must have thought he and Aya were.

Lionel pinched the bridge of his nose. *What else could he say without seeming even more foolish?* "If I tell you what I'm really looking for, will you promise to keep it to yourself?"

"Of course." Mrs. Butler's eyes widened. "I swear it on my loyalty to Her Highness, Queen Lisandra."

Lionel nodded. He couldn't ask for a more serious vow than that. "I know there's a passage, somewhere in these books, that talks about how to remove or restore a monarch's power as well as describes the potential orders of succession. However, I can't for the life of me remember where it is."

"I think I know." The maid crossed the room—she'd almost dusted to the end of the shelves—and crouched before the *Royal Lineage* section. Running her fingers along the spines, she stopped at a thick brown volume and pulled it out. With a satisfied smile, she rose and passed the book to Lionel. "This book was read every single week in the first few months after

His Majesty, King Archon, was executed. I had assumed it was you."

Aya blushed and ducked her head lower towards the botany book, obviously trying to hide her surprise.

Lionel felt his cheeks grow hot. "After what happened to my mother, I found it too difficult to come in here. I often had Eldric Valet or Her Highness, Queen Zedara, do my research for me. So I knew the content but not the volume."

"Mmm." The lines around Mrs. Butler's eyes softened. "I can understand that. If you don't need anything else, Your Majesty, I'll leave you and Her Grace to your research."

"That's fine." Lionel ran his fingers over the cover of the book Mrs. Butler had given him. *Monarchical Power and Succession.* Could it have been any more obvious? "Thank you for your help, Mrs. Butler."

The maid curtsied. "You're welcome, Your Majesty, Your Grace."

Lionel bowed his head as a goodbye, and Aya did the same. He watched Mrs. Butler walk toward the door, waiting for her to leave before he dove into the text.

As she reached the exit, Mrs. Butler glanced down either side of the corridor then turned back. "For the record, I think what the council did to you was abhorrent. Anyone who has met you should know that you'd never be capable of something like that fire." She shook her head. "I hope that book helps you catch the man who's framing you."

"Thank you." Lionel offered a small smile. "Me too."

With a nod, the maid left and shut the door behind her. Lionel took a deep breath and flipped through the pages. Like the government books, it featured tight, scrawling handwriting and wavy pigskin in place of paper. Around the halfway mark, he noticed a corner turned down and smoothed it out.

Then, as Lionel's eyes took in the chapter title, he gasped. "Someone marked this page: *Procedure for Replacing an Unfit Monarch.*"

Aya scoffed. "Unfit. Where was that when King Archon was in charge?"

Lionel clenched his jaw. "Say what you want about my father, but at least he made a more formidable foe than I. Only Lord Varick was brave enough to challenge him, and even he did it in secret."

"Still, it could have been useful." Aya wrinkled her nose. "What does it say?"

"Give me a few minutes." Lionel skimmed the section. By the time he'd finished, his heart pounded in his chest. Everything written in the text fit his situation. According to the book, the council had every right to restrict his power. And one of the representatives had more to gain than Lionel had thought possible.

"What?" Aya reached across the table and snatched the book. As her eyes raced across the pages, they grew as wide as Lionel's must have been. "Oh, shit. Okay, I'm starting to come over to your side. Whoever read this knew exactly how to get you kicked off your throne."

Lionel closed his eyes, the black words flashing in his mind. *Adultery. Murder. Manslaughter. Reckless endangerment of the people. Destruction of life-sustaining natural resources or property. Complete mental or physical incapacitation.* He opened his eyes and let out a long breath. "I'm suspected of three, arguably four, of the six conditions that warrant dethroning a king. Granted, the percentage is even higher when you strike adultery from the law."

Aya squinted as she read on. "Until proved guilty, the monarch must be stripped of all governing power, which shall revert to the royal spouse, rightful heir, next of kin, or the acting bishop, respectfully. Under divine law, the monarch may retain ceremonial responsibilities, except in cases of dire spiritual need, during which, the acting bishop will assume all ceremonial duties."

"It goes on to say that if I'm proved innocent, my full power will be restored." Lionel rubbed his forehead. "No contingency plan for when a king is wrongly convicted, of course."

"Of course." Aya laid the book down. "I'm not going to

KATE M. COLBY

justify this situation by reading the punishments."

"We already knew them, anyway." Lionel pointed to the final passage in the chapter. "This is the part that's really interesting. It describes how to select the next monarch."

Aya frowned. "If a rightful heir has not been born, power transitions to the next of kin, with priority given to siblings, then uncles or aunts, then first cousins, then first cousins once-removed and so on." With knitted eyebrows, Aya glanced up at Lionel. "We know all of this."

Lionel tapped the page. "Keep reading."

"If the monarch removed is the second generation to be determined unfit, especially for spiritual reasons, the bloodline could be contested." Aya bit her lip. Though she read the final sentences in silence, Lionel could hear the words ringing in his mind.

In the case of contestation by a member of the nobility or clergy, measures must be taken to purify the bloodline. The acting bishop will become king, and the bloodline will henceforth flow from his untainted lineage.

Aya set the book down again. "You don't think…"

"The bishop used the word 'unfit' in his vote against me." Lionel ran his fingers through his hair. "Think about it. He never agreed with my repeal of the adultery law. He despises the Rudder as an institution, and therefore, you and our relationship by extension. He hates Rykart Farmer and his followers."

"In one fell swoop, framing you takes care of all those problems." Aya snapped her fingers. "And the bishop sat next to you at the feast. He had plenty of opportunities to swipe your pocket watch or distract you while someone else did it for him. He also left early, remember? The fire started not too long after."

"That's right." Lionel rubbed the back of his neck. "I can't believe I didn't see it before. He planned this all out, and now he's perfectly poised to take my kingdom away from me *and* the rest of my family."

"What are you going to do?" Aya's hands had started to

shake, and she pressed them to the table to steady them. "We have to tell someone. Lord Collingwood? Theo?"

"Not yet. First, we're going to get evidence." Lionel placed his hand on his chest, feeling for the key, which was still tucked safely away in his jacket pocket. "Then, once we're certain it's true, we'll do to the bishop what he's trying to do to me."

26

"I must say, Your Majesty, Your Grace, I was surprised to receive your request. Delighted, of course, but surprised." The bishop escorted Lionel and Aya into his modest chambers. "Please take a seat."

The couple sat in the two closest leather armchairs, while the bishop sat across from them on the other side of the small table. While the bishop arranged his white robes around himself—unlike last time, he'd had notice to prepare for company—Lionel glanced around the room, his eyes scanning each inch for clues. As before, the sitting area was sparsely furnished, save for the tall potted plant that stood in the corner near the window. *Botany. Why didn't I put it together in the library?*

"Thank you for seeing us this afternoon, Bishop." Lionel laced his fingers through Aya's, hoping her grasp would keep his hand from shaking. "As Eldric conveyed in our message, we would like to go through the traditional premarital counseling. Both of us have neglected our spiritual health over the years, and especially given the recent religious turmoil in the kingdom, we want to remedy that before we take our marriage vows."

"A wise decision, Your Majesty." The bishop clapped his hands together, and the clinking of his rings sent a shiver down

Lionel's spine. *Why couldn't he have dropped one of those gaudy things when he lit the fire?*

The bishop grinned. "I'm glad you haven't let the council's decision deter you from moving forward with your life. While I can't speak for my fellow representatives, I know that I feared you would take our vote as an attack, when our true aim is to protect the kingdom."

"I was hurt by the outcome." Lionel looked the bishop square in the eye. "But I understand that you will do anything in your power to safeguard the kingdom, and as king, I respect that—even if I don't agree with your methods."

"Thank you, Your Majesty." The bishop turned to Aya. "And what about you, Your Grace? Has the council's decision been difficult for you, as well?"

Aya shook her head. "Mostly, I'm worried about what will happen to Lionel in the long term. If Captain Laurel doesn't uncover the truth and this farce goes to trial with only the current evidence"—she pushed back her shoulders—"the man who's framing Lionel better pray to the Benevolent Queen that he's not discovered, because when we find him, it won't end well for him."

The bishop appeared undisturbed by Aya's words and the hard edge in her tone. With a sigh, he replied, "The Benevolent Queen shows no mercy for those who betray Her allies. Rest assured, Your Grace, that justice will be served to those who deserve it."

Lionel bit his tongue to avoid lashing out against the bishop's inference. If he revealed his suspicions too soon, he wouldn't get any information from the bishop. Instead, Lionel forced his lips into a tight smile. "I'm sure you're right, Bishop. If there's one thing I've learned in my short time as king, guilt always surfaces, no matter how hard you try to hide it."

"Agreed." The bishop's eyes narrowed, a near-imperceptible change. If Lionel hadn't been watching so closely, he would have missed it. "But enough of politics for one afternoon, yes? Let's focus on your spiritual selves so that when your full titles are restored, you'll be fit to rule by the Benevolent Queen's standards."

"Wonderful." Aya scooted forward in her seat, appearing every bit the anxious bride-to-be. "How do we begin?"

"It's different for every couple." The bishop leaned back in his chair. "What we discuss depends on your own spiritual journeys, as well as how confident you feel in your relationship. In the past, I spent most of the sessions warning couples against adultery, but as you can imagine, the nobles are less concerned about that topic than they once were."

Lionel squeezed Aya's hand. "Adultery is still an important topic to us. Because we are the royal couple, the Benevolent Queen holds us to the highest standards of all."

"That's true." The bishop clicked his tongue. "Even a lustful thought by one of you toward a third party could continue the punishment of all Her children."

"Really?" Aya's eyes widened, and Lionel nearly chuckled as he realized she wasn't acting. "Forgive me, Bishop, my spiritual instruction ended when I was a girl, so I missed much of the lessons about adultery. I had no idea the monarchs shouldered such a strict burden for the kingdom."

"Oh, yes. While betrayal of the flesh might be the most visible form of adultery, betrayal of the heart and mind are, in my opinion, even more severe." The bishop's gaze dropped to the floor, and he shook his head. "Complete fidelity is the cost of the crown, and so far, it has proved too expensive for even the most upstanding monarchs."

Aya frowned. "Surely, in the history of Desertera, at least one royal couple maintained full fidelity with each other."

"I would think so, as well, Your Grace." The bishop held out his arms, his white sleeves pooling at his elbows. "And yet, here we are. The fact that we are still stuck in this miserable desert shows that all our monarchs have failed each other and, therefore, us."

Lionel crossed his ankle over his knee. "Why do you think that is, Bishop? Is it a mortal failing, or is my bloodline somehow tainted?"

The bishop pursed his lips. "It's difficult to say, Your Majesty. There's no telling how a different family line might perform under the pressure of the monarchy. However, if I have learned anything from my years studying people, it's that they have little self-restraint. Given the right temptation, all will succumb to their darkest desires."

"Surely, you don't include yourself in that group?" Aya blushed a light pink, the shade she turned when attempting a white lie or to make herself look innocent. "As the kingdom's spiritual leader, haven't you forsaken all mortal and sinful lusts?"

"Sinful, perhaps, but not all mortal desires. I still eat, after all." The bishop chuckled. "Oh, how rude of me. I didn't offer you two any refreshments. Would you like something?"

"No, thank you." Lionel placed a hand over his stomach. "Stefan has been stuffing us to the brim at each meal. I think it's his way of apologizing for the council vote."

The bishop nodded. "I imagine you're right. Would you like tea, then?"

"No." Aya answered a little too quickly, and a real blush flushed her skin. "Thank you."

"Very well." The bishop crossed his legs. "Now that we've discussed the most important aspect of your spiritual responsibilities, shall we talk about where you both are in your journeys? I will better know where to take you if I know our starting points."

Lionel's jaw clenched. *What a perfect way to expose us. He'll have all our insecurities and moral failings by the end of the hour. The things he must know about the rest of the nobles...*

Aya's fingers tensed around Lionel's, and he glanced at her from the corner of his eye. Given the firm set of her lips and the slight flare of her nostrils, he knew she sensed danger, too.

The bishop looked between them with a patient smile. "Why don't we start with you, Your Majesty? I tended your spiritual education as a child, but what about your teenage years?"

Lionel shrugged. "My tutor included theology as part of my daily lessons."

"Mhmm. Good." The bishop tapped the ends of his fingers together. "And after your schooling ended, how has religion played into your adult life?"

"Well, I've always tried to remember the Benevolent Queen's teachings about treating everyone fairly and prioritizing justice above all else."

"Evident in your ruling style." The bishop pressed his lips together. "How about fidelity? Has that ever been an issue for you?"

Lionel's brow furrowed. "What do you mean? I've never been married before."

"No, but our early relationships can act as a testing ground for our moral rigor." The bishop crossed his legs in the other direction. "Given your reputation, is it fair to say that you found it difficult to remain committed to one woman?"

The king resisted the urge to roll his eyes. *As if I did anything different than any other young, single man.* "No, because I never tried. Until I met Aya, I never wanted a relationship."

"And this lack of fidelity doesn't concern you?" The bishop turned to Aya. "Either of you?"

Aya smoothed down the fabric of her dress with her free hand. "Why would it? Even before Lionel became king, exploring one's options wasn't a crime. And I think the fact that he's moved past that phase in his life to become a loyal, unwavering partner to me speaks volumes about his character."

Lionel rubbed his thumb in circles over Aya's hand. "I couldn't have said it better myself."

"Hmm." The bishop tilted his head back and forth. "Well, that's good to hear. Your perception of your sins and moral growth are almost as important as the reality. And what about your spiritual education, Your Grace? You said it ended after childhood."

"Yes." Aya squared her shoulders. "My father told me stories about the great flood and imparted the Benevolent

Queen's lessons. After his untimely death, I had to forgo any spiritual instruction in favor of survival."

The bishop nodded. "That must have been difficult for you."

"It was." Aya's eyes welled with tears, and Lionel saw their opportunity coming. They'd agreed beforehand that one of them would make an excuse to leave the sitting area to search another part of the bishop's chambers.

"Do you regret the sins you committed while at the Rudder?" The bishop's lips curled into a smile, and Lionel nearly scoffed. If the clergyman thought he looked sympathetic, he needed to spend more time practicing in his mirror. "I can only imagine how many cases of adultery to which you must have been a party."

Aya's skin flushed red, and tears spilled down her cheeks. If it hadn't been for her fingernails digging into his hand, Lionel would have thought she was crying tears of sadness, not anger.

She sucked in a shaky breath. "What would you have me say, Bishop? Of course I didn't want to commit adultery. I didn't want to have sex with any of my clients. But what else was I supposed to do? Beg on the street? Allow my body to shrivel up from thirst and die a martyr to morality? The Rudder sheltered me when nowhere else would."

"It's difficult to put our soul's needs before our body's." The bishop made a *tsking* sound. "I cannot blame you for your actions. Most young women would have done the same."

"I wasn't a young woman." Aya hissed the words through clenched teeth, and Lionel's skin crawled at the venom in her voice. "I was thirteen. *A child.* No family, no trade. If you care so much about my moral salvation, where were *you* and the Benevolent Queen when I had nowhere else to turn?"

The bishop sighed. "As brutal as the truth might be, my dear, it is this: I am responsible for every soul in the kingdom. While I would love to help everyone who needs it, I simply cannot. Be thankful that I have the opportunity to help you now."

Aya's entire body trembled, and she released Lionel's hand,

pushing herself up on unsteady legs. "If you'll excuse me, I'm going to compose myself." Then her voice rivaled even Zedara's haughtiest tone. "When I return, I expect the conversation to have changed."

Without waiting for the bishop's permission, Aya stormed out of the sitting room and through one of the doors. As it swung open, Lionel spied simple bedroom furniture, and he let out a sigh of relief. While he knew Aya had been upset by the bishop's words, he also knew she wouldn't let them distract her from the mission, and he promised himself that he would comfort her later.

A heavy silence lingered over the room. After a few moments, the bishop cleared his throat. "I apologize if I offended Her Grace, but we must push through past transgressions if we are to create spiritual growth in the present."

Lionel scoffed. "I'm not the one who needs to hear your apology."

The bishop fiddled with his rings. "Yes, well…"

Rubbing the back of his neck, Lionel struggled to think of something to say. *How do I bait the bishop without giving away how much I know? What would be sound enough evidence for the council?*

As Lionel's gaze drifted again to the plant, he motioned toward it. "I didn't realize you had a passion for botany, Bishop."

"What?" The bishop craned his neck to look where Lionel had pointed. "Oh, yes. I often get lonely, cooped up in here by myself. It's nice to have another living thing around."

The confession tugged at Lionel's chest, and he swallowed the emotion. *What's wrong with you? This is the man who's been trying to frame you, take your power, maybe even execute you. He doesn't deserve your sympathy.*

Lionel leaned back in his chair. "Have you studied much about botany?"

"No, I can't say that I have." The bishop shrugged. "It seems to be a natural skill."

"How fortunate." Lionel faked a smile. "Well, if you're ever interested in learning more, there are some books on it in the royal library. I'd be happy to lend them to you."

The bishop's eyes widened. "Oh, well, um... thank you, Your Majesty." His gaze flitted to the bedroom door. "Maybe I should prepare some tea for us, after all? It's good for the nerves."

Before Lionel could answer, the bishop stood and scurried through the second door, which presumably led to the kitchen. Lionel covered his mouth with his hand to prevent himself from grinning. While he hadn't uncovered any solid evidence, the bishop's reaction confirmed Lionel's suspicions. An innocent man wouldn't have fumbled over his words at that offer. What could he have found so shocking about being lent a book?

Aya emerged from the bedroom then, her face splotched red. With a nervous glance around the room, she hurried to sit next to Lionel.

He took her hand and searched her eyes, grateful to see that she was no longer crying. "Are you all right? Did you find anything?"

"Nothing," Aya whispered. "It's as barren in there as it is in here. That alone gives me pause. Like he's so concerned about having something to hide that he'd rather not own anything at all."

Lionel inclined his head toward the plant. "We talked about his passion for botany. I offered to lend him books from the royal library, and he practically ran out of here to fix tea."

"That's not suspicious at all." Aya rolled her eyes. "No hard evidence, though."

"Not yet, but hey..." Lionel kissed her fingers. "You didn't answer me. Are you all right?"

Aya's lips quivered, and she took a deep breath. "Let's just say it wasn't difficult to fake my emotional outburst."

"I'm sorry." The sound of clinking dishes floated from the kitchen, and Lionel glanced over his shoulder. "We won't stay much longer. It's obvious he's not going to reveal anything."

Aya nodded. "I'm okay, Lionel. A little shame is a small price to pay to clear your name and regain the kingdom."

"I know. I just wish you didn't have to do it." Lionel placed another kiss on Aya's knuckles then straightened in his chair. She did the same, and they waited in silence for the bishop to return.

Finally, the door to the kitchen swung open, and the bishop emerged, carrying a tray. As Lionel's eyes landed on the tea set, his heart leapt into his throat, and he nearly jumped out of his seat. Instead, his legs made an abrupt, jerking motion, earning him frowns from both Aya and the bishop.

"Lionel?" Aya's eyes had grown wide again. "Are you feeling well?"

The king shook his head, his gaze never leaving the tea set as the bishop placed the tray on the low table and retook his seat. In the center sat a fat white pot with a thick ring of amethyst-colored smoke painted around the middle, up the spout, and around the lid. Lined up in front of the pot stood three porcelain teacups, each with its own amethyst smoke ring painted near the top. They exactly matched the shard Theo had found in the dungeon, the shard that had slit Augustus Rutt's wrists.

"You're missing a cup." Lionel swallowed. "Where is the fourth cup?"

"There are only three of us, Your Majesty." The bishop raised an eyebrow. "Are you expecting someone else to join us?"

Lionel gritted his teeth. "Where. Is. The. Fourth. Cup?"

Aya placed her hand on Lionel's arm. Her eyes met his, and Lionel could see the unspoken question within them. When Lionel nodded, she turned to their host. "Answer your king, Bishop."

"Fine." The bishop shrugged as if the question was foolish, but his voice had escalated in pitch. "I don't have another cup. The set was given to me incomplete—the fourth had been broken."

Lionel's heart beat faster, and he could hardly hear the bishop's response over the rush of blood. "When?"

The bishop crossed his arms. "Your Majesty, why would I have asked when the cup—"

Lionel smacked his hand against the arm of his chair, and the bishop flinched. "When did you receive the tea set?"

"About… maybe…" The bishop squirmed in his seat. "Six months. Yes, six months ago."

The timeline fit. If the bishop were telling the truth, then he would have received the tea set shortly after Augustus Rutt died. Meaning whoever had owned the tea set before him, whoever had been so timely in giving it away, would have still possessed it on the night Augustus's life had ended.

Aya's breath hitched at Lionel's side. In the heat of the moment, he couldn't remember which details he had told her about Augustus's death, but from the sheen of sweat that had budded across her forehead, Lionel knew she understood what was at stake.

Lionel leaned forward. "Who gave you the tea set, Bishop?"

"Your Majesty…" The bishop fidgeted with his rings. "I don't see why that is relevant to—"

"Damn it, Bishop!" Lionel pushed himself up and stalked around the table. Placing his hands on the arms of the bishop's chair, Lionel towered over the short man. "Tell me who gave it to you."

"I was asked not to tell." The bishop's voice quaked almost as much as his body, and he curled in on himself. "It was a gift, a belated gift, for premarital counseling. But she was embarrassed that it was broken, so she asked me not to tell… not even her husband."

Lionel grabbed the bishop's robes in his fist and pulled him closer. "Who?"

The blood drained from the bishop's face, and with a whimper, he replied, "Lady Greyson."

27

The lines of nobles and villagers petitioning Lord Collingwood stretched out of the ballroom and halfway down the corridor in either direction. Despite the dirty looks he received, Lionel strolled past the other nobles with Aya at his side. Under her arm, the cogsmith clutched *The Native Flora and Fauna of Desertera* and a sprig from a fresh-picked flower. As they reached the doorway to the ballroom, the two guards on duty stopped them.

Lionel straightened his top hat. "Let us pass."

"I'm sorry, Your Majesty." One of the guards stepped forward, his arms crossed. "You must wait your turn to see His Grace, Lord Collingwood, like everyone else."

"No, I'm sorry. I should have been more direct." Lionel squared his shoulders. "You will allow Her Grace and I to pass this instant. I might not hold my full power, but I am still your king, and you *will* do as I command."

The guards shared a look, and the one before Lionel shuffled his feet. "We have orders—"

"And now you have new ones." Lionel checked his pocket watch. "I'm expecting Captain Laurel to join me any moment. If you'd like to wait for him, that's fine, but it will be the last thing you do as a palace guard."

After another wide-eyed exchange, the guards moved aside

and bowed to the royal couple. Without waiting for their apologies, Lionel strode forward between the two lines of petitioners and stopped before the raised platform. From his seat at the center throne, Lord Collingwood frowned, concern shining in his hazel eyes. As Lionel had expected, the queen's throne sat empty. The queen had no obligation to sit in when the king held court, and Lady Collingwood preferred a life of solitude.

But the heir's throne was occupied. Madeleine sat in the princess's position, her crossed eyes flitting between Lionel and Aya. Seeing Madeleine in that place of honor—poised to be queen, one degree away from blame or suspicion—made Lionel's blood boil. In his head, he stomped up to the throne and ripped her out of it by her frizzy brown bun. But in reality, he forced a tight-lipped smile.

The current petitioner—who appeared to be a farmer, like most of the waiting villagers—and the rest of the crowd had fallen silent upon Lionel's entrance. The council representatives, which once again included Frederick, shot each other suspicious looks but stood tall and straight in their places at the sides of the throne.

Lionel turned to the current petitioner. "Pardon my interruption, Mr. Farmer. If you give me a few moments, I will be happy to attend to your concerns."

Lord Collingwood cleared his throat. "Your Majesty, how can we help you?"

As Lionel stared up at his uncle, his gut trembled. The one thing he and Aya hadn't figured out in their scramble to gather evidence was the extent of Lord Collingwood's involvement in Madeleine's scheme. While Lionel had lain awake in the night, he prayed to the Benevolent Queen that Lord Collingwood was innocent. Lionel had already lost his father. He couldn't lose his uncle, too.

With a deep breath, Lionel bowed. "Your Grace, I'm here to clear my name in connection to the Bowtown fire."

Lord Collingwood's eyes lit up, and he smiled so widely that all his teeth showed. "That's wonderful news, Your Majesty. Please go ahead."

Either he's a phenomenal actor, or he's in for the worst shock of his life.

At Lord Collingwood's side, Madeleine crossed her legs and smoothed down the fabric of her dress. She slid her hand into her father's, and he shone his grin down upon her.

Guilt curled in Lionel's chest, but his rage burned the weaker emotion away before he could consider asking to speak to Lord Collingwood in private. *No, she's been hiding for too long. It's time the entire kingdom learns what she really is.*

"I know who framed me for the fire, but that's not all this person has done. They've been scheming for months, maybe more than a year, to take my crown." Lionel swallowed and lowered his voice. "I'm sorry, Uncle. This might... well... I hope this comes as a surprise to you."

Lord Collingwood furrowed his brow. "Go on, Son."

Lionel glanced at Aya, and she nodded firmly. With heavy steps, he moved to stand in front of Madeleine. "Would you like to explain, Lady Greyson, or should I?"

Madeleine gasped and tightened her grip on Lord Collingwood's hand. "What are you talking about, Lionel?"

"Do you know something about this, Madeleine?" Lord Collingwood pursed his lips. "I told you to leave the investigation to Captain Laurel."

Lionel shook his head. "Have you been meddling again, Madeleine?"

As if on cue, Theo stormed into the ballroom. On his right side, he escorted a palace guard, whose hands were bound by chains, and on his left walked Dr. Engel, Miss Valet, Mrs. Butler, and the palace potter.

"Right on time." Lionel held up a finger. "Last chance to confess to your crimes."

Madeleine pressed her lips together, and her nostrils flared from fear or anger, maybe both.

"Confess?" Lord Collingwood banged his free fist against the arm of Lionel's throne. "Have you gone mad? How dare you accuse my daughter, your own cousin, of such a heinous crime!"

"Are you sure you don't want to tell your father and the kingdom, Madeleine?" Lionel shrugged, as if Lord Collingwood's rage didn't make his skin crawl. "All right. I'll do it."

Lionel strolled back to the center of the ballroom, where Aya, Theo, and the witnesses stood waiting. After tipping his top hat to both groups of representatives, Lionel took another deep breath. "I must ask for your patience, Your Grace, esteemed council members, as the evidence you're about to hear spans a great amount of time and is, admittedly, convoluted."

Lord Collingwood scooted to the edge of his throne, and while his jaw was clenched, he nodded for Lionel to continue.

"Let's start with the fire, as that is the easiest crime to explain." Lionel motioned for Aya to move closer as they had rehearsed. "When Lady Greyson congratulated me on my engagement to Her Grace, she stole my pocket watch out of my vest pocket, like so."

Aya hugged Lionel, then lingered with one hand on his shoulder to distract him, while the other fished his watch out of his vest. She held it up for the crowd to see.

"By using an unnecessarily firm grip on my shoulder and speaking so rudely about my engagement, Lady Greyson successfully distracted me from her pickpocketing." Lionel tapped his chin. "For the record, I have considered who else might have gotten close enough to me to steal my watch that night, and the only other persons I hugged were Her Highness the Queen Dowager and you, Your Grace."

Though Lord Collingwood shot a glare at Zedara, he didn't speak. Lionel continued. "As you and the other council members will remember, Lady Greyson left the feast before the rest of us—except for the bishop, of course. The fire started a few minutes after her departure, giving her time to rush to the farmer's camp, ignite the blaze, and leave my watch on the ground."

Lionel clasped his hands behind his back. "And, to top it all off, Lady Greyson voted to remove me from the council and take away my acting power as king."

Frederick stepped forward. "Lady Greyson voted as my proxy, as *you* instructed her to do. You cannot hold her vote against her."

"Perhaps, but that depends on His Grace." Lionel turned to Lord Collingwood. "After Lord Varick reclaimed his rightful place on the council, you told the rest of us that Lady Greyson would take your position on the council's core. Isn't that correct, Your Grace?"

Lord Collingwood frowned. "Yes."

"Representatives, was it clear to you that Lady Greyson was still acting as her husband's emissary?" Lionel looked at each member in turn. "From my perspective, it seemed obvious that Lady Greyson herself received the new council seat, as Lord Greyson's name was never mentioned."

Madeleine scoffed. "Lionel, you're being ridic—"

"Ah!" Lionel held up his hand. "Forgive me, *Princess* Madeleine, but I'm speaking to the council members, not you."

On both sides of the throne, the representatives whispered among themselves. As they deliberated, Lionel's heartbeat quickened. Surely, they would remember the facts, and even if they didn't, then hopefully they would sense the transition of power crackling in the air. Lionel didn't plan on leaving the ballroom without his full title restored.

Lord Varick tapped his walking cane against the marble floor. "At the time of the vote, we understood Lady Greyson to be the sole holder of the seat on the council's core. His Grace did not reappoint Lord Greyson until this morning, and the reason given was to free up Lady Greyson to act in her role as heir to the throne."

Mrs. Farmer curtsied. "That is our conclusion, as well, Your Majesty."

"There you have it." Lionel couldn't help but break into a grin. "By legal definition, Lady Greyson acted according to her own will. With *her* vote, she stripped me of any real power and positioned herself as heir to Desertera, pending my guilt in the crime for which she framed me. If that is not motive, I don't know what is."

The ballroom fell silent again, and all eyes flitted between Lionel and Lord Collingwood. For several moments, Lord Collingwood stroked his goatee, and Lionel wondered whether he would be able to see past his love for Madeleine to the truth of her character. *Even if he can't, at least let him see enough evidence to clear my name.*

Lord Collingwood pursed his lips. "While I understand how you reached this conclusion, Your Majesty, your evidence seems circumstantial at best."

"I agree, Your Grace." Lionel clasped his hands. "Let's go back a little further. As the council will remember, Lord Greyson fell violently ill at one of our meetings a few weeks ago."

Madeleine stomped her foot. "I didn't—I got sick, too!"

Lionel nodded. "Clever thinking on your part, Lady Greyson. After all, how could you have any blame for your husband's condition when you took ill, as well? Only you didn't stay sick for long."

Lord Collingwood pulled his hand out of Madeleine's and crossed his arms. "Lady Greyson loves her husband. It's obvious to anyone who has seen them together."

"I'm not saying she doesn't—only that she loves the idea of being queen more." Lionel turned to the village representatives. "Miss Baker, do you remember the flowers that Lady Greyson kept on the coffee table in her estate?"

Miss Baker raised her eyebrows. "Yes, Your Majesty."

Aya held up the sprig of tiny purple flowers. "Were these the flowers Lady Greyson had?"

"Yes." Miss Baker looked to her fellow representatives. "Surely, I'm not the only one who remembers."

The other council members nodded to show that they recognized the flowers as well.

With a demure smile, Aya opened *The Native Flora and Fauna of Desertera* and held it up to display the drawing to the representatives and the crowd. "The Daylilithum flower, commonly known as Rattlesnake Tail, is a vibrant purple shade, with clusters of tiny flowers arranged in a cone shape around the top of the stem. While harmless to grow and display in the household, if ingested, it can cause severe symptoms, including paleness, loss of appetite, nausea, vomiting, stomach bleeding, high fever, and, over prolonged periods, even death."

Frederick's face paled, and he clutched his stomach.

Lionel waved to a witness. "Dr. Engel, would you please approach the thrones?"

The doctor stepped forward, her face scrunched in disgust.

"Dr. Engel, are the symptoms Her Grace read congruent with those you diagnosed in Lord Greyson?"

"Yes." The doctor bent her head. "As I said when the duke took a turn for the worse, if I didn't know better, I would have thought his food poisoning continued, as his symptoms seemed odd for the flu. Given the new evidence, I'm confident Lord Greyson was poisoned with Rattlesnake Tail."

"Thank you. Please stay here a moment longer." Lionel motioned to the next witness. "Miss Valet, it's your turn."

As the maid approached the throne, Lionel saw Madeleine's hands ball into fists.

"Miss Valet, did Lady Greyson allow you or anyone else in the estate to administer Lord Greyson's tonic while he was ill?"

The maid shook her head. "Lady Greyson always prepared and served Lord Greyson's tonic herself. She even wanted to inspect his meals to make sure I served him exactly what she instructed."

"Thank you, Miss Valet." Lionel turned to Aya. "Your Grace, when we visited the Greyson estate yesterday, did you notice any Daylilithum flowers?"

Aya pursed her lips. "No, there were no plants to speak of. And I distinctly remember Lady Greyson mentioning that she had stopped administering Lord Greyson's tonic on the night of the fire."

"As do I." Lionel looked at Dr. Engel again. "Doctor, how long does it take to recover after the poison has stopped being administered?"

Dr. Engel laced her hands together. "It depends on the patient and the dosage of poison. However, the fever would subside in a matter of hours, a day at the most. The nausea and vomiting would take a few days to fully dissipate, as the body would need a while to purge the remaining poison from its system. After that, the patient would experience muscle weakness and some mild disorientation but would be more or less recovered in a week."

Lionel nodded. "Her Grace and I saw Lord Greyson three days after the fire—after Lady Greyson had stopped poisoning him, that is—and his fever, vomiting, and nausea had disappeared." The king motioned to the duke. "Six days after the fire, he's more or less recovered, as you all can see."

Frederick walked toward the throne on shaky legs. "How could you, Madeleine? Why?"

Madeleine's mouth flopped open and shut, but she didn't say anything.

Lord Collingwood looked between his daughter and son-in-law, and deep creases formed across his forehead. "All of this is still circumstantial. So Madeleine happened to have a dangerous flower in her home? That doesn't mean she used it to poison Lord Greyson."

"Then why was I sick, Your Grace?" Frederick nearly spat the words. "The *flu*?"

Dr. Engel made a *tsking* noise. "Absolutely not. The flu is severely contagious, and it is near impossible that you wouldn't have infected at least one other member of your household."

"There you have it." Lionel held out his hands. "Only I'm not finished yet. If you'll allow me another moment, Your Grace, I have one final accusation that will tie everything together."

"Father, you can't let this go on." Madeleine grabbed Lord Collingwood's arm. "Please, can't you see what Lionel's doing? He's looking for someone to blame. It's a desperate attempt to reclaim his power."

Lord Collingwood pulled his arm away. "I have to hear him out, Madeleine. And I think it's best if you stay quiet for now."

Lionel waited for Lord Collingwood to motion for him to

continue. Once he received the signal, Lionel excused Dr. Engel and Miss Valet then waved Theo, the arrested palace guard, Mrs. Butler, and the potter forward.

Removing his top hat, Lionel held it over his heart. "Captain Laurel wanted to be the one to tell you, Uncle, but I couldn't allow you to hear this from anyone but me." Lionel took a deep breath. "Lady Greyson murdered Augustus Rutt."

The ballroom erupted with whispers. Frederick staggered backward, and Lord Collingwood clamped his hand over his mouth, his hazel eyes wide. As for Madeleine, she sat on her throne, completely still except for the quivering of her bottom lip.

"Captain Laurel, would you explain the evidence against Lady Greyson, please?" Lionel stepped back to stand next to Aya, who squeezed his hand.

Theo pulled the palace guard forward, and Mrs. Butler and the palace potter followed. Once positioned before Lord Collingwood and the council, Theo cleared his throat. "Your Grace, the scenario I am about to present combines the evidence from my investigation into Augustus Rutt's death with the evidence Lionel and Her Grace uncovered last night."

Lord Collingwood nodded to show his understanding, but he didn't remove his hand from his mouth.

"Mr. Yuri Guard was on duty the night Augustus Rutt died. Early in the investigation, he admitted to falling asleep during his shift but maintained that he had not let anyone through the locked door to the dungeon." Theo shoved the guard forward. "Tell His Grace what you confessed last night."

Mr. Guard's wheezing breath made Lionel wince. He had told Theo to do whatever it took to gain a truthful confession, and it sounded as though it required more pain than Lionel had hoped.

"On the night Mr. Rutt died, I let Lady Greyson into the dungeon." Mr. Guard hung his head. "I didn't think her a threat, so I allowed her to enter and speak with me. She offered me a cup of tea. I get thirsty, being on duty for so many hours, and I accepted."

Theo nudged the guard. "And then?"

"The next thing I remember, I woke up on the ground, near the door." Mr. Guard rubbed the back of his head. "A bag of coin had been left on my chest."

Lord Collingwood's eyes narrowed, and his hand fell to his lap. "Why didn't you say anything before now?"

"Wouldn't you have been embarrassed, being outwitted and overpowered by a woman?" Mr. Guard swallowed. "I knew I would lose my job. I have a family to feed, and I don't have any other skills. Besides, when I saw how she left that whore, I wasn't about to risk her coming after me."

"Well, you have a lot more to worry about now." Theo pulled Mr. Guard a few steps back. "Had you come forward immediately, His Majesty might have shown you mercy."

Madeleine pointed at the guard. "Look at the way he's breathing. They beat a false confession out of him, Father."

Lord Collingwood pushed Madeleine's hand down. "Do you have any other evidence, Captain Laurel?"

"Yes, Your Grace." Theo reached into his pocket and held up the bloodstained porcelain shard.

The warmth of conviction spread through Lionel's chest as his eyes traced the line of amethyst smoke across the white pottery. It was identical to the cups at the bishop's chambers. Out of the corner of his vision, he watched Madeleine's reaction, only to see her wild eyes flit toward the bishop.

"My men and I found this teacup shard next to Augustus Rutt. His wrists had been sliced open with it, and he bled to death." Theo turned in a circle, allowing the rest of the crowd to gaze upon the murder weapon. "Initially, we consulted the palace potter about the shard. Please tell His Grace what you told me."

The potter clasped her hands in front of her and directed her eyes to the floor. "Neither I nor my predecessor made this tea set. It's crafted from porcelain, making it an artifact from long ago. Only a noble would be able to afford it."

"Thank you, Miss Potter." Theo closed his fist around the

shard. "After my interrogation last night, Mr. Guard confirms that the piece matches the cup that Lady Greyson gave him."

"He's lying! That's not mine." Madeleine held up her gloved hands, as if to show she didn't own the teacup. "It belongs to the bishop. Search his chambers! You'll find the rest of the tea set."

"We know." Lionel crossed his arms. "Her Grace and I visited the bishop yesterday for premarital counseling. He told us that you gave it to him as a belated gift for your own counseling."

Aya scoffed. "And that you begged him not to tell anyone where he got the tea set."

Madeleine shrieked. "That's preposter—"

"It's true." The bishop's voice boomed throughout the ballroom. He stepped forward, and his white robes fluttered around him. "Everything His Majesty and Her Grace have said—it's all true."

"Could it…" Frederick ran his fingers through his hair. "Could there be multiple sets with that pattern? Maybe Madeleine and the bishop are both innocent. Maybe there's… there's a third party…"

Lord Collingwood held out his hand. "May I see the shard, Captain Laurel?"

Theo walked up to the throne and handed the weapon over to Lord Collingwood.

As the shard landed in his palm, Lord Collingwood's hand dropped as if it weighed a great deal. His fingers closed around the piece, and his eyes shut. He remained silent for a few moments, then his body shook with a sob. "This tea set is unique, Frederick. It's been in our family for generations. Madeleine…"

"Father, you can't believe them." Madeleine jumped up from the throne and knelt at Lord Collingwood's feet. "Why would I kill Mr. Rutt? What could I possibly stand to gain from the death of a whore?"

Lord Collingwood tore his eyes from his daughter's and

looked down at Lionel. "I suppose you have an answer for that, too."

Lionel nodded and inclined his head toward Mrs. Butler.

The maid came forward with timid steps. "Your Grace, I am responsible for cleaning the royal library. For weeks after King Archon's execution, I noticed someone kept reading *Monarchical Power and Succession*. I thought it was His Majesty... wrongly, it seems." She pointed at Aya. "The book on botany had been read many times, as well, though only in the last month. In addition to the flower used to poison Lord Greyson, it describes several herbs that induce sleep and forgetfulness."

"As Mrs. Butler's testimony implies, Lady Greyson has been planning her ascent to the throne for a long time." Lionel's jaw clenched. "Before King Archon's execution, she showed a desire to marry me and a strong support for him at the trial. After my father died and I committed my heart to Her Grace, Lady Greyson married as high up the noble line as she could— a duke."

Lionel shot an apologetic glance to Frederick, who looked as though he would fall over if someone breathed on him. "When Lord Varick's trial was announced, Lady Greyson saw an opportunity for an open spot on the council. Knowing the evidence against him in connection to Madam Huxley's murder was weak, she chose to frame him for a more severe crime, ensuring he would be removed from the council. Then, once he was, Lady Greyson actively campaigned for Lord Greyson to take his place."

Frederick's hands gripped his stomach again. "Then you moved me out of the way, too."

Madeleine whimpered. "Father, Father, please—"

"Shh." Lord Collingwood stroked Madeline's hair. "Finish, Lionel."

"Once on the council, Lady Greyson had the power to influence major decisions." Lionel's hands balled into fists. "She framed me for the fire and used her vote to strip me of my power, knowing that Your Grace would take my throne and make her the only heir."

The bishop huffed. "And since she had read *Monarchical Power and Succession*, Lady Greyson knew about the two generations clause. With Your Majesty and King Archon both being judged as unfit kings, Lord Collingwood and I would receive equal claim over the throne if you were permanently removed from power." He pointed a ringed finger at Lady Greyson. "That's why you tried to frame me, too!"

Madeleine shuddered and broke into tears. Though Lionel couldn't hear her words, he saw her lips move as she clutched Lord Collingwood's leg.

Placing his top hat back on his head, Lionel stared up at Lord Collingwood. "That's all. I'm so dreadfully sorry, Uncle."

Lord Collingwood nodded. His eyes were blank, and his hand still rested atop Madeleine's head. The air in the ballroom hung thick and silent, and Lionel felt his chest deflate. He had done everything he could to clear his own name and bring justice to the kingdom, to Augustus Rutt, and to the victims of the fire. All he could do was wait for the council's decision.

Zedara stepped onto the platform and lowered herself onto the queen's throne. Slowly, she reached up and rubbed Lord Collingwood's shoulder. "Your Grace, the council needs to discuss what we've heard. We need to take a vote, determine what should be done."

When Lord Collingwood didn't move, Lionel turned to Theo. "Get the citizens out of here. Someone will hold court again in a few days."

Theo motioned to his guards, and they ushered the subjects away. Most of the people left without a fight, though a few attempted to sneak out of the guards' grasps, obviously engrossed in the conflict. Other than the guards' orders, the ballroom remained silent. After a few moments, the doors creaked shut, and only the council, Aya, and the guards remained.

"Your Grace?" Zedara gently shook Lord Collingwood's shoulder. "We have to deal with this."

"Please, Father." Madeleine stared up at Lord Collingwood's blank eyes then wrapped her arms even tighter around his leg. "Look at me, please."

As if awoken from a deep sleep, Lord Collingwood slowly lowered his gaze to his daughter. "Is it true, Madeleine?"

With held breath, Lionel felt for Aya's hand. As her fingers laced through his, he squeezed onto her for dear life.

"Father, how can you ask me that?" Madeleine hiccupped. "Would you betray me, too?"

"That's not an answer." Lord Collingwood's voice turned gravelly. "Are you guilty, sweetheart?"

Madeleine leaned her cheek against Lord Collingwood's knee. "I swear, Father, my hands are clean."

A spark shot through Lionel. "Take off your gloves, Lady Greyson."

"No!" Madeleine spat. "You're not my king. I don't have to do what you say."

With the most tenderness Lionel had ever seen, Lord Collingwood reached down to Madeleine's hands. She tried to pull away, but after a hard look from her father, Madeleine allowed him to tug off one glove then the other. Though Lionel couldn't see from the ballroom floor, he knew Lord Collingwood would find Madeleine's healed pink scar as he turned over her palms.

Sure enough, Lord Collingwood held Madeleine's right hand in his then held the shard to her palm. "Captain Laurel, did Mr. Rutt's body have defensive wounds?"

Theo nodded.

Lord Collingwood sighed. "It takes a lot of pressure to pierce a man's flesh. Murder might maim the victim, but it always leaves a mark on its bringer, too."

"Stop it!" Madeleine batted the shard away, and it shattered against the ballroom floor. "I love you, Father. Please, you can save me. You're the king."

"No, I'm not." Lord Collingwood pried himself from Madeleine's grasp and stepped down from the throne platform. As he approached Lionel, the king's heart beat so hard, he thought it would break his ribs.

"Your Majesty, I've believed in your innocence from the beginning." Lord Collingwood's eyes filled with tears, but they didn't spill over. "Does any other representative object to restoring King Lionel's place on the council and his full powers as king?"

Lionel waited with bated breath. The representatives remained silent, and some even shook their heads, though Lord Collingwood kept his back to them.

"Very well, then." Lord Collingwood clapped Lionel on his shoulder. "You'll forgive me, Your Majesty, if I excuse myself from this council vote. I trust you to do what's right."

The defeated look in Lord Collingwood's eyes told Lionel that he understood what needed to be done.

Lionel felt his own eyes sting, but his anger kept tears from forming. "I'm sorry, Uncle."

"Me too, Son." Lord Collingwood gave Lionel's shoulder a final pat then walked toward the doors. His footsteps echoed throughout the quiet ballroom, and as the door creaked shut behind him, Lionel shuddered.

"Lord Greyson, Bishop, Lord Varick"—Lionel turned to the three noblemen—"because you were all victims of Lady Greyson's schemes, I must ask you to vacate the ballroom, as well."

The bishop and Lord Varick both bowed to Lionel then exited the ballroom in silence.

Frederick shivered, as if someone had thrown cold water on him, and walked over to Madeleine, who still clung to the throne. With an emotionless voice, he asked, "Did you ever love me?"

"Of course I love you, Freddy." Madeleine grabbed at his shirt, but Frederick jumped back to avoid her touch. "Please don't let them hurt me."

Without further comment, Frederick turned and strode toward the door. He stopped to squeeze Lionel's shoulder, and as he did so, he whispered, "For what it's worth, my vote is guilty."

Lionel's breath hitched, and he nodded. Once Frederick

had left the ballroom, he waved over the remaining council members.

"There's only six of us left, so we cannot have a tie." Lionel rubbed the back of his neck. "Lady Greyson's crimes include trespassing, reckless endangerment, manslaughter, murder, and treason. Given that they are all interconnected, I think we should vote on them all as one. So if you doubt her guilt in any one crime, vote innocent."

The representatives nodded to show their understanding.

Lionel motioned to Theo. "Captain Laurel, if the council finds Lady Greyson guilty of these crimes, what is the legal punishment?"

Theo swallowed. "Execution, Your Majesty."

Madeleine groaned, and her sobbing escalated.

"Thank you." Lionel winced at Madeleine's commotion, raising his voice slightly. "Mrs. Farmer, since you are at my left, please cast the first vote."

Mrs. Farmer glared at Madeleine. "Guilty, Your Majesty."

Miss Baker came next, her jaw set with determination. "Guilty."

Mr. Wellman made a noise as if he would spit. "Guilty."

Mr. Chef looked down at the floor and shook his head. "It pains me, but the evidence seems overwhelming. Guilty."

Zedara gave Lionel a sad smile. "Guilty."

"I agree." Lionel sighed. "Guilty."

Madeleine wailed again, and Lionel shook his head.

"Lady Madeleine Greyson, the council has found you guilty of the crimes previously stated." Lionel paused to swallow down his emotion. "By the laws of Desertera and my power as king, I sentence you to execution."

Turning away from his cousin, Lionel nodded at Theo. With a flick of his wrist, the captain ordered two of his guards to detain Madeleine. They approached her with wide, steady steps, as if she were a wild horse.

The guards' approach seemed to stir something in Madeleine, and she rose on shaky legs. As they drew nearer, she leapt between the thrones and ran toward the hidden back exit of the ballroom. Halfway to the back wall, one of the guards tackled her, and their bodies collided against the floor with a deafening smack. The other guard ran up to assist, and though Madeleine hollered and kicked, they managed to drag her back toward the council.

Pain shot through Lionel's heart as he watched Madeleine's struggle. He had only ordered two executions during his time as king—far fewer than his father and even his grandfather before him—but the fact that they were both family members made his stomach churn. The thick heat of bile bubbled up his throat, but he swallowed it down. He couldn't show weakness in front of the council—or anyone else in the kingdom—ever again.

As the guards and Madeleine passed Lionel, she glared at him, and for the first time, her eyes stared straight into his. She opened her mouth as if to speak, but all that came out was a wet, guttural scream. The king flinched and backed away, but Madeleine kept screaming, all the way to the doors. They shut behind her, and her cries pierced through the walls as the guards dragged her toward the dungeon.

Lionel had experienced much horror in his life—watching his mother throw herself over the palace railing, hearing the executioner's ax slice through his father's neck, smelling the young farmer's burning flesh—and each of these experiences haunted him. They emerged in his dreams, rang out in moments of silence, and surfaced when he caught his first whiff of a meal. But already, Madeleine's scream had begun to fade. Unlike so much he'd suffered through, it would slip into that dark part of his mind, locked away with all the other things he'd chosen to forget.

28

*L*ionel and Aya walked back to his chambers in silence. As Lionel unlocked the door, he turned back to Aya and raised an eyebrow. With a deep breath, she nodded, and he opened it. Lionel entered first, and Aya followed, more curiosity than fear in her gaze. Seeing her in the king's quarters sent a calmness through Lionel, and he gazed around the space, trying to view it through her eyes.

Eldric's right. I need to redecorate. I will *redecorate.*

Lacing his hand through Aya's, Lionel led her toward the bedroom. As the bed came into view, her lips tugged up into a tender smile, but it faded just as quickly. Lionel crossed the room, sat down at the vanity, and removed his top hat. Aya stood behind him, helping him shrug his jacket off his shoulders, then his vest and shirt.

Reaching into the water basin beside the vanity, Aya wrung out the washcloth and gently wiped off Lionel's face. He closed his eyes, relishing the cool water and imagining the ordeal in the ballroom wash away with the sweat and dirt. Aya dipped the cloth in the water again and this time placed it across the nape of Lionel's neck. As the water dripped down his back, Lionel shivered. He hadn't realized how overheated he'd become in the ballroom.

As Aya replaced the washcloth in the basin, Lionel turned

the chair around to face her. Then he pulled Aya onto his lap, and she nestled her head in the crook of his shoulder.

Her hot breath tickled his bare chest. "Did you make the arrangements with Theo?"

Lionel nodded, his cheek brushing the top of Aya's head. "Barring any objections from Lord Collingwood and Lord Greyson, the execution will take place in three days. It will give them, and anyone else, the time to say their goodbyes, as well as for Madeleine to make peace with the Benevolent Queen."

"Poor Lady Collingwood." Aya fiddled with the fabric of her skirt. "What a shock that will be. She'll be devastated."

"She will be upset." Lionel sighed. "But my aunt hasn't been very interested in our family for a long time. I'm sure she'll recover, as we all will eventually."

Aya shuddered. "I can't even imagine what you must be feeling. I'm so sorry, Lionel."

"I'm not."

Aya pulled away and straightened. As she stared into Lionel's eyes, he wondered what she saw. *Do I look like my father?*

The cogsmith reached up and brushed his cheek with her thumb. "You can't mean that."

Lionel covered her hand with his, leaning his cheek into her palm. "I'm sorry that Madeleine is my cousin, but I'm not sorry for how the council ruled. After all the horrible things she did—when I think about what might have happened to me had she gotten away with her plans—I can't feel guilty. Everyone knows the price for murder, for treason. If she wasn't willing to pay it, then she shouldn't have committed the crimes."

"I suppose you're right." Aya looked away, and a single tear slipped down her face. "Still, I can't help but feel sad."

"You can feel however you need to." Lionel rubbed Aya's back. "Any loss of life, however cruel, deserves sorrow."

"But this isn't *any* person. She shares your blood." Aya bit her lip. "I was suspicious when she acted so kind to me the other day, but a part of me hoped that we could reconcile. I thought... well, it would have been nice to have a family again."

"I know, love." Lionel tucked a curl behind Aya's ear. "I wanted that for us, too. And now I don't know if things will ever be the same between me and my uncle again."

Aya leaned back into Lionel's chest, and her warmth spread through his body. "They can't ever be the same, but they might be okay. You'll have to be patient while he grieves."

"I will." Lionel ran his fingers through his hair. "And I trust that he'll grow to accept Madeleine's fate. He resigned her to it."

Aya raised an eyebrow. "How so?"

"Uncle Stanton could have spared Madeleine's life when he still held the power of king." Lionel shrugged. "Instead, he reinstated me and left the council vote to my supervision. He knew what Madeleine deserved, but he couldn't bear to sentence his own child to death."

"I see." Aya shook her head. "That doesn't seem fair to you, though."

"Of course it is." Lionel knitted his eyebrows together and looked Aya square in the eye. "If these last few weeks have taught me anything, it's that being king means making the hard choices. It's about putting the needs of the many before the few, about sacrificing your personal feelings in favor of what's right for the kingdom."

Aya frowned. "That's such a lonely way to rule."

"Which is why I have you." Lionel pressed his forehead to hers. "No one could shoulder the burden of the crown alone. We must carry it together, the two of us. No matter how many people surround us out there, how many friends offer support and encouragement, at the end of the day, we are the only ones who can understand the responsibility we've received."

"And you trust me?" Aya twisted her engagement ring around her finger. "Because I don't know if I'm strong enough to do what you did today."

"You don't have to be." Lionel tilted his head up and kissed her forehead. "You have to be strong enough to love me, even after I've done things like that."

Aya took a deep breath. "As long as you follow the law, stay committed to justice, and have as much compassion for those you punish as those you reprieve, I can do that."

"Good." Lionel rubbed her arm. "I will do my best, but I never want you to be afraid to question my judgment. We both know you're smarter than me, anyway."

"In one or two respects, maybe." Aya smirked, and Lionel gently kissed her lips. When they parted, she straightened and wrapped her arm around his neck. "So, now that you've been restored as king, what do we do with ourselves?"

"Well, first things first. I think wedding planning is in order." Lionel touched her ring. "We need to make you the proper queen so that I don't have to do this alone."

Aya arched an eyebrow. "And so poor Zedara is fully free of the burden."

Lionel chuckled. "Indeed."

Aya's smile fell. "I meant what I said about the cogs and the clock, though." She patted her side, where the vortric cog still hid under her corset. "I don't know whether we'll ever find a spare cog, but I won't stop until I figure out a way to make one or otherwise unlock that grandfather clock."

"I agree." Lionel glanced at his discarded jacket, safe in the knowledge that the key rested inside. "We'll figure it out. We must be close now—only one piece left."

Aya nodded, and as her eyes gazed around the room, Lionel could almost feel her mind drifting back to Portside, to her shop, to all the mechanical mysteries she had yet to solve.

"Hey, don't go away yet." Lionel squeezed Aya, and she visibly shook herself out of her trance. "I know today was difficult, and I'm sure we have many more like it ahead, but I want you to know that I wouldn't want anyone else by my side. You're my everything, Aya, and I'm glad we can finally face this world together."

"Me too." Aya cupped his face again and kissed him. They stayed there for a long moment. As Lionel savored each press of her lips against his, a warmth spread throughout his chest, and for the first time he could remember, he felt complete.

A knock sounded at the outside door, and Aya slid off

Lionel's lap. Throwing his shirt back on, he walked through the bedroom and back into the sitting area. He peeked through the peephole and saw Eldric on the other side.

With a sigh, Lionel wrenched the door open. "Is everything all right, Eldric?"

The valet nodded. "I thought you'd like to know, Your Majesty, the little boy who you saved in the fire…"

Lionel's breath hitched. "Yes?"

"He's awake." Eldric grinned. "Dr. Engel says he'll make a full recovery."

Lionel's lips spread into a smile. "Thank you for telling me. I'm glad to end tonight with some good news."

The valet bowed and left.

When Lionel turned around, Aya met him with an equally large grin and wrapped him in a hug. "That's wonderful."

Lionel pulled away. "It is a relief, but I can't let it take away from everything else that's happened during my reign. I can't be that kind of king again."

Aya frowned. "What do you mean?"

"Look what happened to the kingdom when I ruled only from my own sense of morality. First Lord Varick and Augustus at the Rudder, then Rykart in Bowtown, now Madeleine." Tears stung Lionel's eyes, and he held them back. "I can't let anything like those catastrophes happen again. If that poor boy would have died, if anything had happened to you, I'd never forgive myself. I have to be stronger, tougher, more decisive."

"I understand." Aya licked her lips. "Your actions might have to change, but their root will still come from a good place, your Willem place. And I will always love you for that."

"I love you, too." Lionel laced his fingers through Aya's. "I just wanted so badly to be the king that Desertera deserves."

"You were. I think you still are." Aya squeezed Lionel's hand. "But if you say you're not, then what will you be?"

Tears spilled from Lionel's eyes, and he let them fall unashamed. "I'll be the king Desertera needs, and I'll pray to the Benevolent Queen that I don't lose myself along the way."

THANKS FOR READING!

The Desertera series will conclude with *The Queen's Revenge (Desertera #4)*.

If you enjoyed *The Tyrant's Heir*, please leave a review on websites of your choice.

ACKNOWLEDGMENTS

First and foremost, I owe the greatest thanks to everyone who has enjoyed the Desertera series so far. Your comments, emails, reviews, and purchases are the inspiration behind my writing and the reason why I'm able to pursue my dream. I couldn't do any of this without you.

As always, thank you to my family. I know the fire scene was difficult to read. However, I had to write it to grieve and heal. I hope you understand.

A special thank you to my husband Daniel, who has faith in me even when I don't. To Jess, who continues to serve as the best and most enthusiastic alpha reader on the planet. To Jonas, for offering encouragement, listening to my bitching, and improving the cover concept. And, of course, thank you to my Word Count Slayer cabin mates for riding this crazy writing roller coaster with me.

Once again, much gratitude to the wonderful editing team at Red Adept Editing. Every time I work with you, I become a better writer. And thank you to the design team at DamonZa for another perfect cover. You all rock!

ABOUT THE AUTHOR

 Kate M. Colby writes paranormal fantasy novels that feature female anti-heroes, dark magic, seductive monsters, and spooky locales. She has also written a steampunk dystopian series and dabbles in creative nonfiction and poetry.

Kate is pursuing a Master of Liberal Arts in Creative Writing and Literature from Harvard Extension School. She has won local awards for her short fiction, and her first novel, *The Cogsmith's Daughter*, has been taught in college courses.

When not writing or studying, Kate enjoys traveling, wine tasting, playing video games, and giving amateur tarot readings. She lives in the United States with her husband and their feline familiars.

You can learn more about Kate and her books on her website: www.KateMColby.com.

facebook.com/authorKateMColby

instagram.com/katemcolby

goodreads.com/KateMColby